MYSTIQUE

She shifted so she was sitting up on the seat of his thighs, her nose coming level with his as she looked deeply into him. So deep that he felt as though *he* were the one completely naked, rather than she. He felt the warm cascade of her breath against his mouth, flowing over his face and jaw. There was an intimacy to it that made him long to give in to her request. Lord knew he'd wanted her mouth beneath his almost from the very start.

"Then why?" she asked. "Why does being Sánge make a difference? Or why do *you* think it makes a difference?" she corrected herself after a moment.

"Because there is hardly a race on this world that doesn't despise the Sánge, *kébé*. And you may very well belong to one of them."

"I make my own choices," she said, dismissing her unknown people with a shrug of one shoulder.

"You have no idea what your choices are," he growled at her in reserved fury. "You don't know who you are. *What* you are. Who are you wed to? Who are you mother to, *kébé*? Lord and Lady, Mystique, don't you wonder who is missing you? It has to be somebody. A beautiful, powerful, and intriguing woman like you doesn't go ignored, unnoticed, or unloved!"

"Well, you certainly are doing a fine job of it!" she bit back.

Other Books by Jacquelyn Frank

The Nightwalkers
Jacob
Gideon
Elijah
Damien
Noah

The Shadowdwellers
Ecstasy
Rapture
Pleasure

The Gatherers
Hunting Julian
Stealing Kathryn

Published by Kensington Publishing Corporation

Drink of Me

JACQUELYN FRANK

ZEBRA BOOKS
KENSINGTON PUBLISHING CORP.
http://www.kensingtonbooks.com

ZEBRA BOOKS are published by

Kensington Publishing Corp.
119 West 40th Street
New York, NY 10018

All Kensington titles, imprints, and distributed lines are available at special quantity discounts for bulk purchases for sales
promotion, premiums, fund-raising, educational, or institu-
tional use.

Special book excerpts or customized printings can also be
created to fit specific needs. For details, write or phone
the office of the Kensington Special Sales Manager: Attn.:
Special Sales Department. Kensington Publishing Corp., 119
West 40th Street, New York, NY 10018. Phone: 1-800-221-2647.

ISBN-13: 978-1-4201-0985-6
ISBN-10: 1-4201-0985-5

First Printing: November 2010

10 9 8 7 6 5 4 3 2 1

Printed in the United States of America

Chapter 1

Sorrow.

It beat at him like a relentless drum, throbbing through his mind and vibrating into his soul until he felt it burning in his body as though it were his own. Stunned by the intensity of the intrusion, Reule actually hesitated several moments, distracting himself at the worst possible time. He felt the purity of the devastating emotion shuddering through him. Too pure, and too disturbing, Reule realized very quickly as he flung up well-practiced and powerful mental barricades, blotting out most of the wild despair that had strained his concentration.

Careless of him to let something like that intrude on such a crucial moment. Lines of disconcertment etched themselves into his forehead and around his mouth. The source of that unsettling intrusion was a mystery. It tempted him. But that, he realized, might very well be the point. It could be intentional bait.

Reule dismissed the idea straightaway, confident he could tell the difference between deception and honesty. Though he'd never felt such overwhelming sadness in his life, it had been brutally honest. Pushing it all away to focus back on his goal of the moment, he lifted his head and sought the scents of the others, marking their positions in silence as they kept their mental communication minimalized. Their prey would sense their approach if they picked up on the power of their pursuers' thoughts flying back and forth along the telepathic channels between them.

Reule marked the identifications and locations of the other males of the Pack. Rye, to the north along the stone wall in the underbrush. Darcio, to his rear by several yards, low against the trunk of a thick and ancient oak. Delano, of course, on point ahead of them and moving slowly along the perimeter of the hostile territory they sought to enter. Reule focused next on the house hidden deep in the darkness, concentrating until his vision altered to pierce the veil of the brick walls, picking up the greenish white blobs of movement that indicated life in one form or another. It was easy to differentiate their target; seated centrally and surrounded by others like bees buzzing over their precious queen. All of this activity took place on the second floor.

Reule turned his attention to Delano, watching the sleek speed the male used to breach the property line. In concert, the rest of the Pack moved forward, their senses sharply attuned to the rhythm it would take to succeed at their task. He could have closed his eyes and still known that Rye leapt the stone wall with ease and that Darcio kept every step timed to match perfectly with Reule's as he advanced.

Each member of the Pack neared the structure with caution. Reule crouched low on the balls of his feet, sharply alert, and he became as still and invisible as a shadow. His stillness was timed perfectly. His target came through the near door, so close he nearly tripped over Reule. When the unfortunate crossed in front of him, Reule struck with the speed of a cobra. His fangs exploded into full, glorious length as he attacked, but he wouldn't taste of this repugnant creature. He could control the impulse, sparing himself the disgust of such an experience.

Instead, it was his extending claws that struck. Reule grabbed his victim over his mouth, jerking his head back and puncturing his shoulder with needle-sharp nails right through his shirt, the cotton fabric offering no protection. Reule's muscles flexed as his prey struggled and fought, but they both knew it was a futile effort. Once the paralytic tipping his nails broke the skin, it was only a matter of time. Still, Reule held him to keep him quiet until the drug took effect, using his mental power to stifle his victim so he could raise no alarms. When the male finally became deadweight in his hold, he released him. The body of his enemy dropped to the ground like a sack of rocks, thudding sickly as bone impacted earth. Reule kicked him away in contempt. The toxin wouldn't kill him, but if Reule didn't like what he found when he entered the house, he'd be back to finish the job.

Reule straightened and eased toward the door. He was vigilant for other stragglers as he sought telltale heat and motion. They were all upstairs in that central room, and now Reule understood why. He heard shouts of laughter and cajoling, cheering and jeering, and he suddenly realized why there were insufficient guards staged to protect the place. He snarled low in loathing and the sound was echoed by his Shadow, Darcio. The others didn't respond, but they felt Reule's rage and he felt their kindred emotion.

And that opened him up to the sorrow once more.

It slammed into him, stronger than before; a devastating

sadness that stole his breath away and nearly stopped his heart. Chills rushed up under his flesh until it crawled with agonizing emotional response. Never in all his many years had he felt anything like it. He'd shared thoughts and emotions with his Pack for all of his existence, and never had they, *his family*, been able to project such powerful emotion into him. If he couldn't feel such things from his family, who could force it upon him? More, what caused such agony? He was the most powerful, the most sensitive when it came to sensing these things, but surely one of his caste had felt deep, abiding pain before! What made this so incredibly intense to him? How did it invade him so easily in spite of his skill and power to resist such things?

Reule tried to shake off the sensations even as he fell back unsteadily against a near wall. Darcio leapt forward, instantly at his side when he sensed his distress. Reule quickly fended off his friend's concern, recovering and pushing the alien anguish hard away from himself so he could project confidence and strength to the Pack. They were being distracted in dangerous territory, and he'd be responsible if any of them was injured because of it. Reule silently realigned their attention with a powerful emanation and he felt them swiftly draw back into formation. Only Darcio, who had seen him falter physically, hesitated. Reule ignored his concern and reached for the door.

As they entered from three different portals, Reule felt Rye and Delano both engage hostiles, taking them out and discarding them so they could move rapidly to the stairs leading to the next floor. Reule scanned the first floor to be sure they wouldn't leave anyone at their backs and with a silent command sent Darcio after a stray. Then he and the rest of the Pack moved upward.

As soon as they reached the second floor, Reule felt a ripple of awareness go through half of the crowd in the central room. Now they were close enough that emotions, projected or not, gave their presence away. Reule moved like lightning, as did the others, knowing that surprise was key.

Before the Jakals became fully aware of the danger approaching, half of them staggered back from paralyzing puncture wounds and debilitating hand-to-hand combat. Reule moved so fast that he went through three victims before he met with his first resistance. With about a half dozen Jakals on the floor, or slipping numbly toward it, the Pack faced the remaining enemy, which was now fully on guard. It wouldn't be so easy to incapacitate them. Six Jakals were standing alert and in perfect fighting form. Reule only took a moment to survey the room with quick, accurate eyes, and what he saw seared his brain with wrath.

Besides the Jakals, in the center of the room was a chair, bolted to the floor and made of gleaming steel that had to feel as cold as it looked. The sight of it chilled Reule's spine. However, it was nothing compared to what he felt when he saw the figure slumped forward in it as far as his bound wrists and feet would allow; the former manacled to the flat metal arms and the latter to the legs. Blood drained in a steady stream from his mouth and nose, both of which had been battered to a pulpy mess. Steel spikes had been driven through his forearms and calves, as if the manacles wouldn't be enough to hold him. The Jakals were right. Manacles alone would never have held their prisoner. Although now, with the pool of blood growing in an ever-widening circle beneath that sterile metal chair, the prisoner within was not even strong enough to lift his head, never mind escape. The Jakals had been taking their pleasure torturing him, and they'd made a spectator sport of it.

This time the snarl that vibrated out of Reule was violent enough to reverberate against the walls of the room. His eyes turned from their normal hazel to a reflective green as he lowered into a crouch and bared his fangs. His Pack, including Darcio, who had caught up to them, imitated both the sound and the predatory motion in perfect synchronicity. Reule almost smiled when he heard a fifth growl join weakly with them from the chair in the center of the room.

Jakals on the defensive, however, were no easy targets. The Jakals' slender forms were made for speed, their skin smooth to the point of slickness. They were impossible to grapple with. The wily creatures could twist and strike before you even saw them. Discordant hisses and taunting laughter radiated from their midst as venom dripped from their fangs. They were prepared to strike or spit the acidic compound at their attackers, and unlike Reule's people's paralytic, Jakal poison was fatal if the skin was punctured; and a more brutal death had yet to be invented.

Reule wasn't overly concerned about that. What concerned him was that the Jakals were between his Packmates and the prisoner in the chair. If he hadn't already been poisoned, the enemy might take the opportunity to do so before they could be stopped. Since there was no known cure, this was Reule's primary worry. He could tell by the look in the eyes of the Jakal facing him that his enemy was well aware of it.

As a rule, Jakals were the most powerful empaths of all the known species of the wilderness; only Reule's breed was strong enough to block them. However, as a man of significant ability, he had learned that with strong powers of the mind came strong sensitivities. That had been proven just that evening as he himself had been bombarded by a stranger's overwhelming grief and been caught unawares by it. Surely these empaths before him had heard those cries of anguish too? He knew it was no Jakal feeling those emotions, for though they could sense every feeling any creature was capable of, they didn't have the ability to generate such deep feeling themselves. They certainly didn't understand its true value. It was a terrible irony, and it was what made them such vicious little monsters; monsters who found glee in glutting themselves on the intense emotions of others. Like the emotions generated by torture, rape, or any number of things Reule refused to imagine lest he give way to a rage that would blot his focus and potentially feed his avaricious enemies.

This information did allow Reule an advantage. He was the most powerful sensor of his kind, one without measure in the history of his people. He was willing to bet these lowly gypsy Jakals had never seen his type before and would never be expecting him. That would be his advantage, and that would save the Packmate who had fallen prey to these depraved beasts.

And to think, others considered *his* people the lowest of breeds.

Reule sent an emanation to his Packmates, steadying them and preparing them silently, including a reassurance to the barely conscious one in the center of the room. Then he slowly unfolded the layers of protection over his mind so he could release his concealed power.

This time he was better prepared for the anguish that struck him, but still it was bordering on all-consuming. It was just the kind of emotional inundation that a Jakal would take gluttonous pleasure in. He could easily amplify the already overwhelming feeling and overload his enemies with the rawness of it, but Reule dismissed the idea instantly. There was something far too personal and *innocent* about the stark grief. To feed it to the Jakals somehow felt as though it would be a betrayal. Reule didn't understand his reluctance, but he didn't have time to do any soul-searching.

With a mere glance he commanded Rye, who nodded and slid closer to one of the paralyzed Jakals. The enemy lay helpless but conscious, staring up as the hunter contemplated him with a wicked little smile that bared a fine set of fangs. Loosing an intimidating vocalization, Rye reached over to the sheath attached to his biceps on the right and withdrew the blade slowly. The blue metal gleam of the *rubkar*'s blade caught the overhead lighting and made it look even more menacing as Rye lowered himself into a crouch next to the helpless male.

There. That moment. That fear and terror in one of their own, *that* was what Reule caught hold of, magnified, and netted the sensitive enemy with. His fingers curled into fists, his chin dipped down as he focused ferociously on manipulating all of them at once. He couldn't allow a single one the chance to further harm his kinsman.

The effect was more than he would have expected or even hoped for. The Jakals standing in the center of the room suddenly recoiled in horror and began to scream. They clapped bony fingers over their skulls as males and females alike wailed to a pitch high enough to shatter glass. Reule ignored it, pushing and pushing, refusing to let go lest they try to push back and incapacitate him with their sheer force of numbers. As he drilled into them their compatriot's horror of impending death and his helplessness to do anything about it, he felt as though he were stronger than he had ever been before. He was an awesome force to contend with under any circumstances, and there was no mistaking the surge of vitalizing strength sliding into him now.

Reule kept the conduit open, from victim Jakal, to amplification within himself, and back to the small crowd of compatriot Jakals in the center of the room, pouring it out as Rye's knife lowered to a mark. His Packmate closed both his hands around the haft of the blade in a ritualistic manner. Reule prepared for the death strike, knowing that he could put these bastards in a comatose state for the rest of their lives, even though there was a good deal of jeopardy to him as well if he channeled the imminent death throes. But he felt supremely confident that he would remain only the messenger, untouched by what was about to happen.

Rye looked straight into the eyes of the Jakal whose throat lay under the tip of his razor-sharp, dual-edged blade. With the scent of battle and impending bloodletting on him, Rye's eyes were nearly glowing with green-yellow anticipation and his fangs pushed out both his upper and lower lips so they could be seen even without his purposeful sneer.

"Abak tu mefritt," he hissed.

Death to my enemy. Rye spat the battle cry just before plunging deep and with so much rage-filled power that the blade went clean through and was embedded in the wood of the floor. He left it like that and leapt to his feet before the Jakal's blood could touch him. He spat on his victim in obvious contempt.

Reule felt every moment of both the death and the victory, but it was the last minutes of suffering that he passed on. He broke out in a drenching sweat, every last muscle in his taut, powerful body shuddering as he closed himself off from being dragged into the dark of oblivion along with the dying Jakal. Instead he forced himself to magnify the last pulses, the last breaths, and the last horrified thoughts of the Jakals' kin as he drilled it all into the entire group of them. The effect was so potent that Reule was aware of even his mentally guarded Packmates staggering back from his onslaught. But he couldn't gear back the intensity of it. They would be all right, he reassured himself, so long as they weren't his direct targets.

His direct targets, however, were not so fortunate. Reule strove for total incapacitation, but he got much more. All six Jakals tumbled to the floor, some landing on their knees, others flat on their backs or faces. They all began to seize violently, clawing at their throats as though a wicked blue blade had pinned them to the floor. Some coughed up blood, others gasped out strangled breaths.

Then, with a communal, convulsive sigh, each exhaled one last breath.

Reule felt the group of target minds shut down all at once and there was an instant whiplash effect, impacting him physically so that he fell back as if he'd been playing tug-of-war and the other team had suddenly let go. Darcio caught him, but Reule was no lightweight, his build thick with a warrior's muscle and his height stretching to over six feet. Darcio was determined, however, to at least keep his Packleader from landing in an undignified heap, easing him to the floor.

The death was gone, purged from Reule's mind with the break in his concentration, although the metallic ghost of it would cling to him for a long time to come.

Darcio knelt on a single knee beside him, steadying him even though he sat, a disturbed furrow creasing his brow.

Darcio had every right to be concerned. The Pack-mates had seen Reule do some pretty amazing things over time, had even come to expect to be amazed regularly by the sheer potency of their leader's unique power, but never had Darcio seen any one man strike such a devastating blow to an enemy at six-to-one odds. The Jakals weren't just comatose, they were *dead*. Dead by the power of Reule's thoughts. Darcio felt the heavy silence of the Pack, only the captive Chayne making noise as he rasped for breath. Otherwise, the Pack guarded their thoughts from Reule. However, because they were Pack, Reule would be aware of their collective discomfort.

It wasn't his Pack's disturbance that struck Reule's weakened mental defenses, though. His mind was now stripped of the strength to defend itself, and that allowed the desperate sorrow to bombard him again. Reule had also carefully blocked out Chayne's agony and humiliation so it wouldn't interfere with his concentration. Now it washed over him in burning waves, clearly differentiating itself from the sadness that swirled around him. No, it wasn't his suffering Packmate that Reule felt in deep, assailing eddies. There was another, and whoever it was had to be close.

"Reule, don't do it," Darcio warned him, now free to exchange thoughts with him as Reule's mental walls lay crumbled. "It could be a trap. You will end up like them." Darcio flicked a hand at the pile of dead Jakals.

"No," Reule rasped as he struggled to regain his balance and physical coordination. "This is something else. Someone is in pain."

"It's no concern of ours," Darcio said softly, his worry coming through despite his attempts to be cold-hearted. Reule knew Darcio well. His Packmate had one concern in all the world, and that was Reule's safety and well-being.

"Darcio, if it were you, would you appreciate others turning their backs on you and abandoning you to your fate? She is close. In this house, I believe." Reule stopped suddenly, realizing that he was right. What he felt originated from a female. Strange he should know that. Stranger still that he could sense only this tide of one particular feeling, but no others. No thoughts, nothing to identify her, just . . . sadness.

"You see?" his companion persisted. "Even your own mind tells you that something is wrong about this."

Reule frowned irritably, disliking the defenselessness of his mind, which allowed Darcio to read his every thought. He struggled to erect even the slightest of barriers against the intrusion, a filter at the very least. To his surprise he got a monumental wall of protection. It was so strong and abrupt that he felt Darcio stiffen with shock as he was booted out of Reule's mind with perfunctory force. Reule quickly reached up to grasp his friend's shoulder, giving it an apologetic squeeze.

"Your advice is always valued, Darcio. Remember that. But I will act in accord with my instincts on this." The gesture of camaraderie seemed to ease the other male's bruised feelings, and Darcio reached to help haul Reule to his feet. No easy task that, Reule weighing several stones more than the leaner man. Within moments, though, he felt Rye under his other arm helping to steady him.

"Chayne?" he asked.

"We won't know until we get him back home. The apothecary will tell us the whole of it," Rye said softly.

"Go, help Delano with Chayne. I'm well enough," he instructed Rye. To prove the point, he took his weight onto his own two feet and pushed Rye away with a guiding hand. Rye hesitated only a moment before nodding and moving away to do as his Packleader commanded.

Feeling increasingly steady, Reule directed his focus away from the fearful, paralyzed Jakals that yet remained alive, and the noisy thoughts of his Packmates. It wasn't hard to home in on the sorrow. Adjusting his vision once more to detect heated shapes, he scanned the house more slowly. He was in the center of the structure, one floor above him and one below. Wherever she was, she was close. He might have mistaken her for a Jakal in his first scan, but it was clear from the depth of her emotion that she couldn't be.

Yet nothing stood upright in the house save his Pack. He looked up once more and realized there was another floor above the third. And there, up in the farthest corner, he spied a small ball of the dimmest heat.

"Darcio, did you encounter anyone upstairs?"

"No, My Prime. I only sought the one stray you noted."

"Then this is the female I'm sensing. Lord and Lady, but she has strong emotions," he marveled as he stepped over an incapacitated Jakal.

"One emotion, My Prime. One bound to attract a man of good conscience," Darcio said suspiciously. "It's magnified just as you magnified death to the Jakals. What manner of creature can do that besides yourself?" *And even Reule shouldn't be able to do such a thing*, he thought. *No man should hold death in the power of his thoughts.* Reule had always been fair and just with his power, but things like this had a way of changing a man. Even a Prime.

"You're mistaken," Reule said as he moved with increasing sureness out of the room. "There is no magnification. It's . . . pure." The word kept springing to his mind. He decided it suited and left it at that. Darcio didn't say anything, but Reule could feel him repressing arguments because he didn't want to contradict his Prime again. Darcio was a good man, ever his voice of caution and conscience, always advising him to consider carefully. Reule valued him beyond measure, and he made certain the thought made it through to Darcio before they took off up the stairs together.

They made it to the third floor of the ramshackle building, clearly abandoned long ago. The roof had leaked and the ceiling was rotted through, as was the wooden floor they now negotiated. Reule and Darcio took care with every step as they edged toward another stairwell, this one narrow and stinking of must and mildew. Gypsy Jakals were always roaming the lands, scavenging and causing trouble, squatting wherever they could. This band had been around long enough to make this hovel a home. Homey enough to bolt a chair in a central parlor for the purpose of torture. It meant they'd been there for some time. Reule would never have known it if Chayne hadn't accidentally stumbled into capture during their hunting trip.

Reule tested the narrow little attic stairs and wondered how anyone could be up in the garret. Getting there seemed a dangerous task. Then again, it was its own sort of prison.

He made his way to the head of the small stairs, Darcio his ever-present Shadow as he pushed open a heavy, stubborn door. He was instantly confronted with a chasm of missing flooring. A wide section had rotted out. Reule and Darcio could see straight down to the story they'd just left.

"You're lucky these stairs even held," Darcio muttered as Reule entered the room one careful sidestep after another. His Packmate was right. The hole in the floor came to within a mere foot of the door and stairwell.

And of course his target was all the way on the opposite side. Even though it was all one large room, he still couldn't see her. There was a crowd of crates blocking his view of her, though he could still sense her dim heat.

"I'd really like to know how she got over there," Reule said in honest curiosity. Darcio nodded his agreement as they tried to plot the best course of action.

"I should go. I'm lighter. Less chance of the floor giving way."

Good point, but Reule didn't want to relinquish the task, for some reason. Her pain was so bittersweet, beautiful merely by virtue of its purity and depth. Logic reasoned that anyone who could feel pain so deeply was used to accommodating its antithesis. Reule only hoped that pain wasn't all she *could* feel after this.

"No," he responded after a moment. "There's a strip along the wall that looks sturdy enough even for me. Since this is my folly, I might as well be the one to risk breaking my neck."

"My Prime," Darcio protested.

"It's a joke, Shadow. Take ease."

"I will once we're out of this dangerous hellhole," Darcio countered sullenly.

Reule turned away to hide a smile. Leave it to Darcio to take all the fun out of an adventure. Still, he wasn't swayed so easily. His blood rushed with adrenaline as he negotiated wet, creaking boards that were maybe days or even minutes from rotting away completely. He tried not to touch the dank, mildewed wall running next to him as he went. Some molds in the damplands were poisonous or ate flesh. An ominous crack sounded through the room, and Reule abruptly realized exactly how unstable the entire building was. The Jakals were insane to risk staying in such a place. If the floor inside was rotted, he could just imagine the state of the roof above them. He glanced back at Darcio and they exchanged a mutual understanding that they needed to get out as soon as possible. If nothing else, they were agreed on that.

Reule exhaled carefully when he reached the other side of the gaping hole, unwilling to relax so long as he stood on water-stained boards. He gingerly made his way over to the boxed crates and peered into the dark corner behind them.

The only thing he could see was the palest little hand. His heart skipped a beat as he realized that this was probably a child. A renewed sense of rage flooded him and he began to think of the Jakals left alive on the lower floors. When he left this property not a one of them would be left breathing, he vowed to himself fiercely. They had feasted on their very last victims.

Very carefully, Reule grabbed one of the crates and slid it aside a little. The frightening creak of the protesting floor halted him instantly.

"To hell," he muttered, planting both hands on another crate and effortlessly leaping over its four-foot height as if it were nothing. His feet hit the only clear piece of flooring available without landing on the girl. He heard Darcio curse baldly when his weight met protesting floorboards.

Reule ignored him and squatted down to better see her through the darkness. He reached for her hand as he bent forward. Her pain had become like a repetitive tune singing through him, no longer reaching extreme highs or lows. It wasn't that it weakened, only that he was adapting to the force of it.

Reule had no idea what he would find, but he certainly didn't expect to feel a second hand spearing into his hair from the darkness to grip him with surprising strength and drag him down until his face was pressed against a baby-soft cheek that should have been warm, but was instead icy cold. A pair of lips, both rough and supple at once, rubbed over his ear as finally something warm, her breath, washed over him. The contrast gave him an involuntary chill, aided by the hoarseness of her voice when she whispered to him.

"Sánge, bautor mo."

Chapter 2

She went so suddenly limp that Reule almost didn't catch her. Luckily, his supreme reflexes didn't fail him and he quickly gathered her up against his warmth. Her entire body was like ice. Who knew how long she had lain there, shivering in the moldering cold? She was slightly bigger and heavier than he'd expected, but still as light as could be. She wasn't a girl child, but perhaps a youngling on the cusp of womanhood. She was small and fragile in his arms, but there was no mistaking the press of soft breasts against his chest and the rounded curve of her hip as he slid his hand over her to catch up her legs. She wore some sort of nightgown or thin shift, but it was soaked with moisture and reeked of mildew.

Even in this total darkness, she had known what he was.

Sánge.

He'd shown no fangs, no claws, and other than his dusky skin, there was little to identify him. The Sánge weren't the only ones with dark skin in this world, or even this region. There were the Opia, though they tended more toward a beautiful ebony, if they were purebred, that hid them in the night. Or the Gemin, who tanned so richly in the sultry summers. Besides, she couldn't possibly see his skin in this darkness, he reasoned. How had she known he was Sánge and not any other?

She had known. There was no mistaking it. She had said it clearly.

What she had said afterward was too disturbing for him to contemplate while so precariously positioned with a vulnerable female to protect. He would examine the remark at a later time, for he was almost certain he'd misunderstood her.

Sánge, bautor mo.

Reule stood up, lifting her high against his chest, contemplating how to get her out of the crate enclosure without sending their joint weight crashing to the third floor.

"Hand her to me, My Prime."

Reule looked out of the darkness and met the steady gray of his Shadow's eyes. He should have known Darcio wouldn't leave him for long. He was aptly titled Prime Shadow, and he was as dependable as the rising sun and the rotating moons. He was lighter and leaner than Reule, making him the better choice for carrying the girl. The combination of her weight and Darcio's would just about equal Reule's.

Despite Darcio's verbal protests of earlier, and his equally doubtful thoughts, Reule trusted him to take the very best care of the girl. Darcio was loyal to him in such ways. Reule didn't think twice about handing her over the crate to him. He saw Darcio wrinkle his nose at the smell of her, then catch a chill from the dreadful cold of her body. If there was one thing Sánge despised almost as much as Jakals, it was the cold.

"You go first; I'll follow at a distance to keep our weight distributed far enough apart," Reule instructed him.

Neither man breathed easily until they were safely on the second floor, though no spot under that rotting roof could really be considered safe. Reule quickly unburdened Darcio of the girl.

"Quickly, fetch the others out of here. Make fast work of the remaining Jakals. I want none to live. Had they left us alone, I might have felt differently, but this lot will pay for what they did to Chayne. The Lord and Lady only know what they have done to this girl as well. Go. Now. Before this monstrosity falls down around our ears. We will meet at the horses."

Darcio didn't even acknowledge his orders; he merely turned to carry them out. As he exited the abandoned building, Reule decided he would have it burned to the ground once the snows fell and no spark could harm the dry fields of autumn. Although the house was located in the damplands, surrounded by bogs and marshes, a freak wind could carry sparks for miles until they reached the drier plains. But the house must burn. It was a danger to anyone who entered it, and he wouldn't rest easy until he knew the useless structure was safely laid to waste.

The blue moon was turning, the pale gold already gone for the night. Dawn wasn't too far off. He wanted to get the Pack home before the next nightfall, safe behind huge walls of cement and a portcullis of steel. Home. Home to Jeth, the Sánge city, and the provincial lands under his protection.

Chayne had been under his protection, too, one of his Pack, and he'd allowed him to be lost for two days. Reule would have to face the dire consequences of that when they returned to Jeth. He fervently prayed it wouldn't end in Chayne's death. Chayne was a valuable hunter. As Tracker, he was the best they had. The storehouses and bellies of Jeth Keep much required his skills. His mother and sister depended on him greatly as well, since both were widowed. They were now his to care for, including his sister's children. Those young ones revered Chayne. He was Packmate. Prime Tracker. A well-earned honor that placed him at the right hand of their Packleader. Every Jeth child should have such a man to look up to as he or she grew.

Though he could see Chayne's family fed and sheltered should the worst occur, Reule couldn't provide the other attention they would need. He wasn't certain he could give anyone that. What Sánge Prime could? With a burgeoning province to rule, lawmaking, settling disputes, and routing out Jakals, who had the time to think about managing a household, never mind actually do it?

Darkly suffocating thoughts surrounding that topic carried him as he bore the chill of the autumn night and carried his charge to safety. At least, relative safety. By the time he reached the horses, she was even colder than when he'd first found her. She didn't shiver, though, either because she was unconscious or because she was already too weak. He didn't know. He didn't like not knowing.

The horses nickered restlessly at his approach, stomping their thick hooves to express their unhappiness at standing so long in the cold. He approached Fit, his large dappled gray gelding, releasing the girl's legs and supporting her along the length of his body as he reached for his saddlebags. Before he got the chance, though, he felt the hard butt of an equine head dead center in his back. He staggered and recovered his balance by leaning against the animal. He remained after a moment's thought in order to use Fit's heat to help warm the girl. Meanwhile, he turned to glare at the big brown eyes blinking at him in a way that was almost haughty.

"Behave yourself," he commanded the beast. Fit's response was a snort and a shake of his head that rattled his tack and clearly told Reule what he could go do with himself. Strange as it was in light of the past hour, the humor touched him and he chuckled softly against the girl's head of tangled hair as he patted the animal's shoulder hard, just the way he liked it.

Reule ignored another snort of disgust and was able to liberate a blanket from the saddlebags. He wrapped up his bundle in yet another attempt to warm her, keeping her close to his body and gritting his teeth against the chill of her as he buried her face against his neck beneath his hair. She was so light that he was able to swing up into his saddle while holding her; a swift, powerful movement. The gelding didn't even take so much as a step in protest and Reule patted his shoulder again. He balanced his charge over the saddle in front of him, bracing her in position between his thighs and leaning on one arm. He reined Fit with one hand, turning the horse experimentally, testing the security of her position.

"All right, my friend," he said to the animal, "now I need you to take us home."

Reule finished the request with just the smallest influential mental push. Fit nodded before shaking out his reins and harness, his way of acknowledging the command and his willingness to perform . . . this time.

When the others finally appeared, Chayne was grunting animalistic sounds of repressed torment even though his Packmates carried him as gently as they were able. They'd bandaged him as best they could, but Reule could see that Delano and Rye were already covered in blood. They'd have to travel fast for the sake of both victims, but it would make the trip agonizing for Chayne.

Reule turned hard eyes onto Rye, who jerked up his head when his Prime's message reached him and him alone. Rye braced himself as Reule turned his attention onto Chayne. He was gentler this time as he invaded Chayne's weakened defenses and whispered the soft suggestion of sleep into his mind. He reinforced it just as gently, and the wounded man was ninety percent there when Reule brutally slammed his will down over the other Sánge's and forced obliterating unconsciousness on him. He knew Chayne would despise having his choices taken from him, especially after he had struggled so long and hard to withstand the Jakals' torture. However, a mere sleep suggestion would never have lasted. Chayne would have been jarred awake at the first rough pass.

Having the others believe he'd succumbed to exhaustion would be more acceptable in Chayne's eyes than the knowledge that he'd been mentally manipulated by a stronger male, even if that male was his Prime. Reule had chosen Rye as the only other to be aware of what he was about to do because as the second strongest male in the Sánge people, he was the only one guaranteed to be able to keep his thoughts protected from all the others, including Chayne.

They were under way shortly, soft discussions between riders and their horses filling the predawn darkness as the golden moon faded. It was Delano who rode tandem with Chayne. Delano had by far the most powerful horse as well as the physical strength it would demand of him.

Luckily, the house had been at the leading edge of the damplands, so they slogged through mud and mire for only a short time before hitting the harder-packed ground of the plains. They rode quickly for the distant mountains.

All of this land was Reule's province—the inhospitable damplands, the fertile flatlands, and the dense and dangerous forests that stretched endlessly behind the riders' backs. It was all a wilderness, hostile and hazardous, but it belonged to him. Him and his Sánge people. Possessive and protective of it as he was, Reule still turned an impartial eye on any who risked traveling the perilous country. So long as they didn't harm the land or the Sánge, travelers could pass or even hunt in peace. But the Jakals had abused his hospitality. Reule made a note to himself to check with Saber, his Prime Defender, about the patrols in the outer province. Once the snow fell, there would be no need, but until then . . . he wouldn't tolerate his people being endangered by two-legged enemies if they could be controlled by vigilance. There were enough natural dangers in these lands without adding invaders.

Dawn drifted past, as did early and mid-morning, and their pace across the flatlands remained quick and steady. Neither patient stirred during the entire passage. It was just before noon when they entered the Jeth Valley and saw the walled Sánge city of Jeth rising up from its snug position against the Hattera Mountains. The mountain range was infamously impassable, though not so much so to those who dwelt in this valley. Nevertheless, the mountains discouraged marauders and those who weren't easily cowed by the reputation of the Sánge. Only the Jakals regularly thought themselves superior warriors to the Sánge, and only the Jakals had ever tried to threaten Jeth or its outlying farmlands.

The Pack had been passing farms for the past hour, small wood and brick houses settled warm and snug in the midst of the bare fields, prepared for the coming cold of winter. Stubble from the harvested crops stuck up around them. Steel silos and granaries had been bursting from the excellent harvests, and now the last of the fall shipments were headed out for trade in other lands. The city's coffers would burst afterward. Other breeds might loathe associating with the Sánge, but they'd always gladly trade gold for the precious grain the Jeth Sánge risked their lives to cultivate. So long as their money was good, the Sánge couldn't care less what outlanders thought of them. The prejudice was the same all over, and there would never be anything they could do about it.

Reule watched the walls of his small city grow in majestic height as they drew nearer, feeling the familiar explosion of pride and satisfaction at what they'd made of this wild land. It was a home. A grand and productive home with contented people he was able to keep safe. *For the most part*, he thought grimly as he glanced at Chayne.

Perverted Jakal bastards. Their need to gorge on emotion made the Sánge ripe targets because of their emotional complexity as telepaths and empaths themselves. Reule's people were almost universally reviled in the world outside of Sánge-controlled lands, but at least most breeds tolerated or were too afraid to make threats against them. They were also reluctant to go without the crucial grains that fed them. The Sánge had proved themselves to be the only ones hardy enough to survive in the wildernesses where the most valuable crops grew best. The canyons of the Gemin and the rainforests of the Opia had their own resources, of course, but neither was conducive to growing grain.

The Sánge had dangers to contend with as well. Hard winters, the beasts of the dark and fertile woodlands, and those of the damplands that they hunted, which hunted them in return if they weren't careful. There were poisonous molds, blights that threatened crops, and dozens of other risks.

There were the gypsy Jakals and nomadic Pripans as well. The Pripans stayed in the deserts mostly, but occasionally the tribal leaders staged raids on the nearby flatlands to steal grain or women. Pripan males weren't as picky as those of other breeds and considered the quelling of a powerful and deadly Sánge woman to be a conquest that advertised their supremacy and sexual prowess. Grain Reule could forgive, but kidnapping wasn't to be tolerated. Unfortunately, the Pripan tribes were large and numerous, and he had to be careful not to commit an act of aggression that would cause them to combine resources and go to war against him. So, often it was a matter of kidnapping their women back, like boys playing war games of stealth. Luckily, the Pripans had a sense of humor about being outsmarted, as long as Reule stuck firmly to only reclaiming what had been stolen in the first place. His success varied, so he found it best to protect his people from such dangers to begin with.

Their key protection, the monstrous walls rising up from the bedrock of the mountainsides on the north and south slopes, soared above them as they neared. The city sprawled behind the cement, a fair three miles of farms, homes, and merchants before it butted up against Jeth Keep, which in turn butted up against a mountain to the west. There was a northwest wall as well, and a gate, far smaller in width than the one they approached, that led into a treacherous pass with no obvious exits after the first few miles. It was the perfect getaway route in case of seige, and only Reule and his Packmates knew the secret of the escape.

"Hallo!"

The cry echoed over their heads from the guards atop the wall and in the central lookout positions about halfway up the sheer surface. Reule smiled when they set up a cheer for the hunters without even knowing if they'd been successful. Those with the sharpest eyes and minds were the first to fall quiet, however, as they noticed Chayne's empty horse, two of the returning Pack riding in tandem, and an extra body amongst them. Not to mention a decided lack of game hanging from their saddles. It was to have been the final hunt before winter set in, meant to provide meat for the hard months to come. The horses ought to have been laden down with game. Instead, there was no sign of success and all the signs of trouble. Reule felt the buzz of thoughts extending from friends on the walls to those of the party, curious and questioning. Reule put a sharp end to the questions by quickly emanating a warning to silence the Pack. Gossip would abound, but he'd save fact sharing until he could address the province himself. He didn't need rumors exacerbating fears in the city.

There was a hum as the electricity powering the steel portcullis gears was turned on, producing the energy needed to raise the heavy gate. The refined fuels used for the generators came from trade with the Pripans, even more reason not to incite wars with them. The precious convenience of electricity was highly coveted by the Sánge, especially in the winter when the idea of the cold was intolerable. It was the only characteristic of the wilderness that they found nearly impossible to bear. Fuel for electricity was worth every piece of gold or sack of grain they traded for it. Only the wealthiest in the city could afford fully electrified homes all through the days and nights of winter. Many had electric heat and light in a single room. Otherwise it was wood, peat, and coal fires that warmed them, especially in the farms outside the city walls, where there was no access to electricity as yet. It was one of Reule's goals to provide the necessary generators as soon as he could.

He was strongly hoping that Amando, his Prime Envoy, would have great success in his trading this season. He would soon find out, as he expected Amando any day. The final transactions across their trading route must be completed before the first snows flew. Reule couldn't rest until the autumn trades were complete and the winter coffers were full.

For the moment, there were other concerns drawing his attention. The riders broke into a canter once the gate was raised enough for them to pass. They thundered along the main thoroughfare of the city, calling ahead so that pedestrians scattered out of the street. Jeth Keep, stone and steel built to withstand a hostile world, loomed taller even than the city walls. A second portcullis guarded its bailey, but it was raised for the day's business. Reule led the Pack in. Stablehands rushed out for the weary horses, and Reule saw Amando and Saber hurrying from the training yards to see what commotion had arisen.

The Pack dismounted, none of them bothering with

explanations. They pushed their way into the castle, Reule shouting out as he entered.

"Drago! Pariedes!"

Reule's manservant and the principal housekeeper appeared instantly.

"Pariedes, send a lass to fetch the apothecary. We'll need medical supplies, blankets, fresh clothing for Chayne and for a petite girl, and hot food. Make certain some of it is soft. Drago?"

"At your service, My Prime," the elder Sánge said quickly, hustling after Reule, who never once broke his step.

"Wait for the apothecary yourself. When he arrives, bring him to the baths and assist him with Chayne. I only want you and Rye in the bath with him besides the apothecary. You know how Chayne can be. The less exposure, the better."

"Understandable and quite wise, My Prime," Drago agreed gravely.

"See to it, Pariedes, that you attend me and the girl in the Prime's bath yourself. No other."

"My Prime!"

Pariedes's exclamation of shock finally drew him to a halt. The entire hall grew quiet as Reule turned to face the flushing housekeeper, who squared her shoulders in a familiar sign of stubbornness that made him sigh loudly.

"What is it, Para?"

"Surely you don't intend to bring an insensate woman into your bath," she whispered, even though whispering was ridiculous in a hall full of men with sharp hearing and sharper telepathic ability. "There is propriety to be considered."

Reule's burst of laughter heightened her blush, but she only stood straighter.

"Para, my fierce lioness, she's but a cub. I've no interest in a child. Besides, you will be with me. I would also limit her exposure to just you and myself. She is not Sánge."

"Not . . . ?"

That seemed to paralyze Pariedes for a moment, though her mouth continued to try speaking for a good twenty seconds. Finally, she covered her womb with both hands, a longtime habit she had picked up, and inclined her head. Then she was off with a flounce of skirts and a stream of russet hair. The Pack entered the royal receiving room, the sound of boots on the gleaming marble floor thundering off the high ceiling. The marble had been mined from the surrounding mountains, a beautiful metallic red. The royal chamber had been paved with it, except for a border of golden stones that edged the entire room, and the dais where Reule sat in state.

They didn't pause but headed straight out the rear of the room, where a large stairwell was situated. They all marched in resounding accord down into the bowels of the castle. They were well underground by the time they struck the basement's ceramic tiled floors. The Hall of Baths was just around the corner. There were over a dozen doors, big and small, down the long hallway. These were the private baths. There was a set of double doors at the end that led to the communal baths. Opposite the public hall was a private entrance leading to the Prime's Bath.

Here the Pack divided. Rye and Delano took Chayne into one of the larger private chambers. Darcio headed for the communal bath after only the briefest look at Reule to see whether he might change his mind about needing any assistance with the outlander girl. Reule turned to the Prime's bath, kicking the door shut quickly in his wake. He was greeted by a wall of hot steam that he inhaled deeply. He smiled. The baths were naturally self-replenishing hot springs and the best way Reule could think of to warm a girl suffering from exposure. He walked over to a bench close to the edge of the gently bubbling water in the large pool.

He laid the girl out on the bench, intending to warm her with the steam first before introducing her to the water. He didn't want to shock her systems. He figured he was going to be on his own for some time before the apothecary arrived, and Para would have her hands full for a little while before she could come to play well-meaning chaperone. Reule chuckled at the idea. Para was still a reasonably young woman, but she was ferociously protective of anyone she deemed in need of mothering, which tended to be just about everyone. She was perfect in her role of head housekeeper, guarding the undermaids from the roaming hands of the under-butlers and soldiers constantly roaming the halls. She ran the household impeccably and Reule had never had a complaint, except perhaps when she tried to mother him as well. He'd never been comfortable with a woman's concern.

Reule shrugged off the distracting thoughts and concentrated on unwrapping the bundle in the blanket. He pulled back the wool horse blanket, and the stench of mildew struck him again with its pungent odor. The room was lighted by electricity, so Reule got his first real look at the young female. Her small body was curled up tight in a fetal position, and her tangled brown hair was plastered across her face just like her stained shift adhered to her body. Reule lowered himself onto his haunches so he could study the knots and webbing of the hair wrapped around her head and face. He sighed, realizing there wasn't much he could do until after he had her in the water and they'd begun to wash away the dirt encrusted on her. He hoped they wouldn't be forced to cut off her hair. There were Sánge superstitions about cutting a woman's hair. Bad enough to be an outlander in Sánge territory with winter about to trap her inside the city for several cycles, but with the bad luck of shorn hair besides?

Not for the first time Reule wondered how long the girl had been confined in that attic. Had she been a prisoner? Had they thrown her away up there after they'd finished using her?

The thought ripped a furrow of rage in his gut, and his teeth locked tightly together as he fought back the rushing fury. Often, his most potent emotions would spill over, emanating without his intention to those surrounding him. Though normally no one could read his thoughts without his permission, his unique power of emanation took some effort to control. With emanation, Reule could make those around him know and feel his needs. Just as, without a single spoken word, the slamming of a door could leave a perfect impression of the departer's displeasure, he could create the same effect with the flexing of his mind. The trick was preventing it when it wasn't desired.

The Sánge leader reached out to touch the exposed skin of the girl's hands and arms. She was still chilled, but nowhere near as cold as she had been. The blanket and vigorous ride had done their part, and now the heat of the steam seeped into her as well. Reule stood up and ran a hand through his dampened hair, the steam curling the black locks into the natural waves that he usually brushed out or braided back. He grasped his short, brown fleece-lined jacket and his tan hunter's vest, shedding them both into a careless pile at his feet. His coffee-brown leather knee boots were the next to go, their perfect cobbling allowing him to slide them free without Drago's usual assistance. He stripped off his beige linen shirt, the fabric already soaked with moisture from the steam and his sweat. He was three days out from his last bath and he was looking forward to shedding the grime of riding, stalking, and death.

Just then he heard the click of the door opening and shutting, and though it wasn't far from where he stood, he couldn't see who entered through the dense wall of white mist. But he could feel her well enough.

"Come here, Para."

Pariedes moved unerringly through the fog of moisture to find him. When she caught sight of him half naked and standing over the girl, he could feel her disapproval even without seeing the prim press of her lips.

"Now, now, Para," he teased her, "I still have my breeches on. Isn't that what covers all the important parts?" When Para blushed from neck to hairline, Reule threw back his head and laughed. The housekeeper recovered quickly enough to wave him back with a threatening swing of her hand.

"You're a scoundrel, My Prime!" she accused after almost smacking him in the nose with that dangerously flailing hand.

"Aye, and you're not the first woman to tell me so," he countered as he watched her bend over the small girl.

"She's badly neglected," Para said, tsking in disgust. "Bloody bastard Jakals. The lot of them should burn to death staked in the desert sun."

Reule folded his arms across the breadth of his chest

and peered down at her. "Who said Jakals had anything to do with it?"

Her head snapped up and her dark eyes flashed with indignant pride. "I've eyes in my head and a brain as well, haven't I?" She scoffed at him. "What else would keep you a day overdue and have you bringing home two victims as your only game? Really, My Prime!"

"My apologies, Pariedes," he said with graciousness and a conceding bow. "You are right. What of my hunting trophy, Para? Do you think she'll survive?"

"I cannot tell you that. She's an outlander, Prime Reule. I know not what she is. She's too fair to be Gemin or Opia, and while she's got the build of a Jakal, she's—"

"This girl is no Jakal," Reule said sharply, the impulsive urge to defend her riding him hard. "I located her by sheer feeling alone," he said more gently when Para looked at him with surprise. "No Jakal could ever feel the depth of pain and sorrow this girl was feeling when I found her. They only siphon it off others. The utter power of what she felt could have fed a troop of Jakals for a week. I've never—"

Reule broke off when he realized Para was staring at him with open curiosity. When he frowned darkly, she cleared her throat, quickly turning back to fuss over the young woman she now knelt near.

"Poor thing. We can hardly see you." She tsked again and turned to Reule. "Your blade, My Prime?" She held out the flat of her palm expectantly.

Reule wasn't in the habit of handing his dagger over to anyone, not even a Packmate. It was an unspoken tenet amongst warriors never to surrender one's blade. Natural weaponry like nails and fangs worked well enough, but a knife, sword, or throwing star were essentials in battle and self-defense.

Reule reached for the dagger sheathed at his waist, the blue metal blade singing sweetly as it passed over the cusp of its scabbard. "With what may I assist you?" he asked with just enough formality to make her feel, without emanation, that his service was the only way she would see use of the knife.

"Cut away her garment. It's disgusting and riddled with who knows what diseases and parasites. I'll have it burned. Then we'll bathe her and see if we can't make something out of this nest of hair."

Reule bent to his task and carefully pulled the edge of the fabric away from the girl's throat. He could see her pulse beating in her neck and he hesitated.

Sánge, bautor mo.

The words suddenly echoed in his mind in a whisper-soft voice that seemed too innocent to know of such things. He suppressed a shudder of indefinable feeling and pressed the blade to the tattered gown. Slowly, carefully, he cut a good six inches down her breastbone before withdrawing the cutting edge. Then he sheathed the blade and grasped the fabric firmly in his fists. He yanked sharply and the weak linen shredded easily. For a moment, Reule thought the act strangely erotic. He'd never been the sort to tear off a lover's clothes, and this child was certainly no lover, but something about the strength in his large hands destroying something so fragile to expose something even more fragile—it brought a wash of unexpected heat over his skin. He swallowed hard against the ridiculous sensation and pushed it away as he tore through more fabric and exposed a pale length of buttock and thigh.

The perfect whiteness of her skin was completely unblemished in the area revealed. Reule had never seen skin so white in all his life, and he'd been a great many places and seen a great many people. It had to be the only spot on her body that wasn't dirty, and he found it oddly intriguing. The contrast to his own dark skin fascinated him.

Reule realized Para was watching him expectantly and he made quick work of the rest of the tear. Then he withdrew his knife again and cut away her sleeves. He was glad she didn't move, because the blade was sharp and even an accidental brush would slice her. Another reason he'd never share his blade, especially with someone inexperienced. He tossed away the remnants of fabric and unbuckled his sheath and belt, laying the scabbard purposely near the edge of the bathing pool. When he was stripped down to nothing but his breeches, he scooped up the girl and walked with her into the pool, using the wide steps that led down into it. He didn't immerse her all at once, though the hot water pooling around his hips made him want to dive under to soak in the heat.

He wasn't the priority here.

He carefully began to introduce her tightly coiled body into the water. Para watched anxiously for the first minutes until she was satisfied he wasn't going to foul up his responsibility to treat her gently. It wasn't that she didn't trust her lord and master, it was just impossible for Para to believe anyone could care as much as she did. Reule easily forgave her that because she was right more often than not.

Reule worked his way back to the stairs, seating himself on the second-to-last step with his charge resting in his lap. Para took the opportunity to hurry from the room to do whatever it was she needed to do. He couldn't remember what instructions he'd given her. He realized then that he hadn't eaten or slept properly in three days. He was feeling that lack now that he was cocooned in the relaxing heat of the water. Even his patient was relaxing, her small body unfurling in increments. He held her as she unwound, the water rushing over her entire body held in the cradle of his lap and arms. Her head finally lolled back, her hair tumbling into the water as he allowed all but her face to soak.

At last, her arms fell away from their protective cross over her chest. Finally, he could see her entire body. He started to skim assessing eyes over her for damage done to her by the Jakals, but they soon widened in surprise. Small she might be, small she definitely *was*, but while she was smooth-skinned, as the young ought to be, there was nothing childlike or even adolescent about the curves of her unfurled body. Reule blinked, trying to reconcile the woman he now held with the girl he'd thought he'd been holding until just moments ago.

Hair still obscured her face in a net of webbed strands. The heated water had soaked away much of the dirt soiling her skin. Reule brushed his fingers against her to assist the process, hoping to determine the extent of the abuse she had suffered. It quickly became clear that his mild efforts weren't enough, and he reached for a cloth that was soaking in a bowl of soap solution at the edge of the bath. It was a man's scent, the one he preferred because it reminded him of the mountain valley in which he lived: crisp, clean, and natural. It would do for his purposes. The solution was viscous and clung to the cloth even when submerged in water, so he was soon able to produce lathering swipes against her arms and shoulders. He was rewarded with clean skin . . .

And livid bruises. Ugly discolorations hiding under the dirt and grime. As he worked over her neck and throat and upper chest, cuts, scrapes, and abrasions joined the list of injuries. An awful idea began to form in his head and he sat her up so her chest was flush with his, her face tucked against his neck as her head nestled on his shoulder, while he dipped the cleaning cloth in fresh solution. He balanced her now-heated body against himself to free both hands, sliding away her straggling mop of hair to expose her back to the approaching cloth. Her skin was nearly black with grime, but it was soon clean as he coasted over her shoulders, down her ribs, and along the path of her spine.

Reule's gaze was steady and watchful as soap and soil fizzed away in the current of the water and left a clear picture of the damage to her back. His fist tightened reflexively in her wet hair. More bruises, more cuts, but there were also wide swaths of abrasions at her shoulder points and the prominence of every vertebra. Burns, as though she'd been dragged over a surface . . . or repetitively scoured against one.

By the Lord, he thought fiercely as he squeezed his eyes shut and touched his forehead to her collarbone in gentle sympathy. Had she been gang-raped by those monsters? It had to have been unimaginably violent to have left such awful damage behind. If that was the truth of it, then the bastards had died pitifully easy. Reule's fury boiled his blood and he swore softly as he tried to vent it with deep, controlled breaths. 'Twas no use letting it rip him up; what was done was done. They were dead and she was alive and safe now. That was all that mattered.

Reule lowered her away from his body to continue the chore of assessing as he gently cleansed her, forcing himself to clear the persistent red haze of emotion that dwelled in his vision. He once again found himself faced with the curves of a fully fledged woman. Of most prominent note, and next in his path, were her sweetly rounded breasts. He ran a cloth-covered hand over the swell of her right breast, feeling the partial peak of her nipple rippling under his passing fingers. Partial altered to full rigidity by the time he was done, the reaction so quick that he found himself needing to clear tightness from his throat. Confusion soon followed when he realized unblemished, perfectly pale skin, as well as those taut pink buds, was becoming visible through the water. If she had been sexually abused, her breasts would have suffered badly from mauling and manhandling, wouldn't they? What male bent on degradation and sexual gratification wouldn't take advantage of the opportunity to molest such lush, enticing breasts?

Reule was slowly circling soap around the buoyant globe on the opposite side, his eyes fixing on the way the pink of her areola gathered up into a tight ring. It sent the tip of the attractive nipple pointing outward in tempting invitation. He felt her flesh brushing against his bare chest, luxuriant and slippery with soap. The resulting quickening of his body ought to have been predicted, but it took him by complete surprise. All he knew, as a man of honor and conscience, was that he shouldn't be feeling the discomforting rush of blood to his groin for an unconscious and defenseless woman. Last he checked, he wasn't into such callous perversions.

His gaze and hand sought more neutral territory, traveling on to the gaunt curves of her ribs, which hinted at the duration of her neglect. In his lap, her hips and bottom were well rounded and soft, proving her not too far gone to starvation. Though her legs were slim and long for her build, they were a little too thin at the knees and calves. Her ankles were pronounced even through the water, just like the wrists at the ends of her skinny forearms.

Reule rubbed away dirt on her gently hollowed belly, finding more bruises, these already healing. Then, very carefully, he washed over her pale thighs. Her hips were a mess of cuts and contusions. Had she been pinned down? Her flesh was scoured over both hips, but there was hardly even a bruise on the top sides of her thighs. Her knees were only a little dusky with damage. Yet he could see angry red and mottled blue in livid circles coiling around her ankles to nearly a third of the way up her calves.

Bound by her feet, but not her wrists? Reule was more perplexed than ever. His eyes drifted to the triangle of protective curls at the juncture of her thighs, the indeterminable color dark while wet. He found himself swallowing hard against a swell of struggling emotions. Rage. Worry. Empathy. *Fear.*

It was because of the fear and his inability to bear the keenness of it that he turned to a safer emotion. Or so he thought. Curiosity. They were the lightest dusting of little curls he'd ever seen on a woman. Without thinking, he reached to touch the pale inside of one thigh, fingertips sliding against wet, silk-soft skin. Reule didn't even realize he'd dropped the cloth. Those sparse curls, were they as soft as they looked, or more coarse like a Sánge woman's? Did the friction of mating make her more sensitive? Would it be easier for his fingers to slide between her folds in order to seek out the moisture of—

Reule shocked himself with his own thoughts and he jerked his hand out of the water as if he'd been burned. He was stunned to realize he was breathing hard and that his cock was ferociously rigid with arousal. Reule was mortified. *What in hell is wrong with me?* He'd been sitting there, furious at the prospect that she'd been torn up inside by those miserable Jakal bastards, and here he was thinking about touching her himself! He might be Sánge, but contrary to popular outlander belief, *he was no beast!*

In the heat of his upset, Reule forgot that there was a huge difference between thinking and acting. For a telepath, it was the hardest and most important lesson to learn. A mind could concoct great fantasies, majestic schemes of both sinister evil and beauteous good. However, actually acting on those fantasies was another thing entirely. It was unfair to hold someone responsible for every stray thought. Reule neglected to forgive himself for basic inclinations of the mind.

Reule also forgot how hard his emotions could strike out at others when they emanated out of his control. He was harshly reminded of it when the woman in his arms awoke with a traumatized gasp and a forceful jerking of her body. It sent him off balance as he tried to hold her slippery body and keep her head above water simultaneously. Her bottom settled in his lap again, giving him some leverage as he verbally and mentally tried to calm her frantic flailing.

"Shh. Be easy, *kébé*. You're safe," he assured her, emanating a feeling of security to her, hoping to replace his hostile emotional disturbance of a minute ago. The rush of sorrow he'd come to associate with her assailed him once again, but he found it was fueled with fear as well this time. "Hush, *kébé*," he soothed. "Hush, I will keep you safe."

Then, all at once, she seemed to hear him. To comprehend. She went abruptly still, reached up, and shoved the wet mass of hair off her face so roughly that he heard strands tear and snap. Then she looked directly at him, allowing him to see her face for the very first time. For a long minute, during which every muscle in his body seemed locked in a mystical paralysis, all Reule could do was stare at her.

It was her eyes that had the greatest impact. They were so unreal, so brilliantly unusual, that he couldn't quite take them in for a moment. He doubted he'd ever see anything like them ever again in his lifetime, and that was quite a monumental concept considering how long-lived his breed tended to be.

How to begin to even describe them? he wondered.

They were colorless.

No. That was inaccurate. They were far too enthralling to be a null. They were clear as crystal, yet white and silver all at once. They looked exactly like, and *sparkled* like, diamonds. Faceted, beautifully cut, clear and precious gemstones, with a platinum setting behind them to enhance every movement they caught in the light. She blinked thick, black, curved lashes over them, and that's when he broke away from her eyes and saw the rest of her face. It was shaped in the delicate curves of a heart; soft bow lips chapped from thirst and neglect were tucked into a permanent but enticing little pout, and she had a slim nose that ended in the slightest uptilt. She had bruises across both cheeks, some old and yellowed, others fresher, but they did nothing to hide the sweet structure of her bones, and her skin promised to be flawless when free of battering. She was youthful, but clearly a woman; unbelievably pretty, but sorely misused. Those diamond eyes looked at him in utter confusion for several heartbeats.

Then, like electricity flooding a dark room, recognition of some kind lit up her features and she smiled so wide her delicate lips split and began to bleed a little. Wet hands lifted out of the water and framed his face and he started in surprise as her palms rubbed over his three-day beard and her fingers curled over his ears.

"Sánge," she breathed, the single word full of excitement such as he'd never heard before from anyone who knew he was Sánge. Not unless they were also Sánge. It stole his breath even as he tried to convince himself it was a mistake, that she was just in some sort of shock.

"Yes, Sánge," he agreed, pausing to clear the hoarseness from his throat. "What, and more importantly, *who* are you, little *kébé?*" he asked as gently as he could, afraid a rough male as big as he was could be frightening for her in spite of her strangely enthusiastic greeting. After all, there was no telling who had done what to her. To suddenly wake naked in the arms of a stranger . . .

She didn't answer his query. She only studied his face with an expression of utter fascination. She reached up to map his visage with her fingers in slow, gentle strokes that sent electric pulses straight to his spine. Reule wouldn't allow himself another opportunity to disrespect her, so he reached to cover one of her hands with his own, gripping it lightly. He had to steady her with his other arm, so that left her with a hand free, which she promptly threaded deeply into his thick hair. He could've grabbed hold and locked both her wrists in a single hand, but he feared upsetting her with such a maneuver. She didn't know he wouldn't hurt her, although her behavior indicated otherwise at the moment. He was incredibly curious. The sorrowfulness that had drawn him to her was subdued as she smiled.

She shifted in his lap, sitting up straighter and closer until he felt both of her pointed nipples rubbing through the hair on his chest. The explosion of awareness and sexual heat was like being doused in gasoline and lit with a flame. He sucked in a hard breath as his hand slid unintentionally down the line of her back. She leaned so close that her nose nudged up against his. She touched him with quick, delighted strokes of her fingers all over his face, hair, neck, and throat; she behaved like a child after opening a splendid gift. Her eyes devoured and examined him as though he were a prized confection she coveted for her tongue.

The imagery made him groan as sweat rolled down the back of his neck and his snug pants became brutally uncomfortable. Not to mention the fact that she was sitting right on him and couldn't possibly be ignorant of the state of his body. Any minute she would see him for the pervert he'd never known he was, and the touching fingers and eager smile would disappear forever. The idea of it had a devastating effect on his emotional calm.

"Shh . . ." This time it was she soothing him, her soft voice and fingertips stroking against his face. "Your mind struggles so, Sánge. Where is your peace?"

Reule jerked back in shock. He looked at her with hard, mistrustful eyes and even had to fight the urge to shove her off his lap. Perhaps he was disturbed and a little off guard, but she'd spoken as if she were intimate with his mind. *No one* crossed his mental boundaries without his permission.

Just as abruptly, Reule tried to rein in his temper. There was no way she could accomplish it. Perhaps . . . yes, perhaps he'd unwittingly emanated his emotional upheaval. It wouldn't be the first time and unfortunately wouldn't be the last. Still, the way she'd worded the phrase . . . it was something a telepath or empath might say. Reule reached out and gripped both her shoulders, giving her a little shake as he stared hard into her peculiar eyes.

"Who are you?" he demanded.

"No one who will harm you," she responded, wincing.

A sharp cut of remorse and self-disgust lanced through him, and he abruptly released her from his abusive hands. With a startled cry, she tumbled back over his knees and fell into the water. Reule grabbed past her flailing legs and had his hands around her waist in an instant, dragging her above water and back against his chest. She gasped and sputtered, her hands clutching his shoulders. Her thighs, now on either side of him, clenched his sides in a death grip. She shook in fright, her nails biting into his skin as water streamed down her disgruntled expression, which lay beneath straggles of thick hair once again. He apologetically pushed aside the tangled mess.

"Are you all right? I'm so very sorry," he apologized.

Apparently, she forgave him. Reule drew that conclusion when she wrapped both her arms in a strangling hug around his neck and plastered her chest against his. There was desperation in the hold, though, and Reule cursed himself. She didn't need *him* adding to her fear.

"Easy now. I won't let it happen again," he promised her softly, wincing when he felt the thundering of her small heart against his own. "I take it you don't know how to swim?" he asked.

She snorted against his neck, a scoffing laugh that made him smile against her hair. The situation was so surreal, it didn't even surprise him when she giggled.

"Listen," he said softly near her ear. "You need to bathe, eat, and rest. I'll save my questions for later, fair enough?"

"Yes," she whispered against his pulse.

"But then you'll satisfy my curiosity?" he asked her.

"Yes."

"Good. Are you injured? Were you . . . ? Did they . . . ? Do you need an apothecary?"

She lifted her head, sniffling from the water that had rushed up her nose when she'd been dunked. "No," she said. "I only need you."

He was so startled by the remark that his hand tensed against her bare back. It was as though everything that came out of her mouth was dragged from a dusty old place in his brain where he'd thrown away all the things he'd never expected to hear someone not of his people say to him. Questions surged through his mind, but he'd promised to save his grilling for later, and he'd adhere to that promise. However, how did one transition away from a remark like that?

"My Prime!"

Reule closed his eyes and sighed, remembering to be careful what he asked for in the future. He looked up at Pariedes with his best innocent smile. "Yes, Para?"

"Release that child this instant!" she commanded imperiously, pointing at the female as if he wouldn't know which one she meant. The "child" reacted by tightening her hold on his neck to the point of throttling him.

"I would, Para, only *she* doesn't seem intent on releasing *me*." The "she" in question vigorously shook her head to confirm that fact. Knowing Para's sense of propriety would have cast him as the villain, he could have kissed the outlander right on her bruised little cheek for it.

"Prime Reule, this is terribly improper," Para fussed, twisting her hands together.

Before Reule could respond, he felt the woman in his lap react, jerking back and even releasing him slightly as she sought his eyes. He felt her fingers blending into his hair as her expression turned into pleasured wonder. She smiled and he swiftly realized he'd never seen a woman look so ethereal before. She hardly seemed real, with that expression on her face and the ever-present undercurrent of sadness still washing against him in a placid tide.

"Reule," she said softly, her voice musical. Reule looked into those crystal eyes and felt his chest constricting in response. "Reule," she said again, her hand coming to stroke his face from forehead, to cheek, to jaw, and then to the tip of his chin. Her touch was tender and almost . . . treasuring. Reule's heartbeat doubled in cadence, hurting in the closed confines of a chest tightened with unnamed emotion.

She was like a bolt of lightning, searing him head to toe before he even knew what had hit him. Now he was left dazed, his mind blank to anything that didn't involve the two of them, the hot soothing water, or the warmth of their clasped bodies. It wasn't exactly sexual, as his earlier reactions to her had been, but it wasn't exactly not, either. He realized then that she'd neglected to give him her name, just as he'd forgotten to give his.

"What's your name?" he asked softly, reaching up to sweep back an errant strip of hair with his thumb.

"I don't know," she whispered.

The diamonds gleamed with increasing brilliance as her eyes filled with tears.

Chapter 3

Strangely enough, that confession was the first thing that made sense about her. It explained why, when he'd been seeking for her, he'd felt nothing but sorrow and pain. It turned out that she knew nothing of who she was or how she'd come to be in that attic. In truth, the only thing they were both certain of was that she knew he was Sánge, and that she seemed to trust him with outrageous simplicity and totality even though she apparently knew little else of the world around her.

Reule supposed she didn't have much of a choice. He also figured that might be why she felt no revulsion or trepidation concerning his breed. Yet he wasn't certain. If he was confused, he could only imagine how she must feel.

"My Prime, I'm certain she is warm enough now. You ought to leave her to me and one of the girls to tend her bath and work through that hair of hers," Pariedes said with a cluck of disapproval at his lingering behavior. "You can save these endless questions for after she has a full belly and a decent dress on!"

The remark reminded Reule of his own intentions, and he gave the naked woman in his arms a sheepish grin.

"I did promise that, didn't I? I didn't mean to break my word." He hadn't been able to help himself. Her confession that she did not know her name elicited a barrage of questions that he absolutely had to ask. Did she know where she was? What she was? How she'd gotten there? What had brought her to the point at which he'd found her? As he asked each question, she gave a decided no or shake of her head after she gave it a moment's thought. Determined to do the right thing now, Reule tried to stand, gently explaining to her when she tightened her hold around his neck in refusal.

"These steps are shallow, as is all this side of the pool. You could stand and it would never go above your . . . chest." He cleared his throat hastily as he skipped saying "breasts," as if it would help him deny the feel of them against his chest. "Or you can just sit here and Para will help you to bathe. If—"

"No!" she cried, clinging to him as he gained his feet so that her legs were clamped like a vise around his waist and her arms were back to choking him about the neck. He didn't have to hear Para's gasp to be aware of her shocked sensibilities. The poor thing was so flustered, Reule could feel it buzzing all up and down his mind. However, her emotion was nothing compared to the terror coming from the woman wrapped around him. "No, don't go! I don't want you to. Reule, please. You can bathe me, can't you? Why do you want to leave me?"

Reule ignored Para's horrified squawk and looked into frightened, faceted irises. His hands curved around her waist, her silky skin wonderfully warm now.

"I'm not leaving you," he said gently, keenly realizing the reasons why she might react in such a way. She was either so disturbed by the idea of being abandoned that she was willing to throw away all propriety, or she came from a culture in which women behaved vastly differently than in theirs. "I wouldn't abandon you," he tried to reassure her. "I'm only going across the hall for my own bath. Para will—"

"But you can stay and bathe with me. There's plenty of room. I won't bother you. Or I can help you bathe!" she tacked on, clearly delighted to have come up with the inspiration.

Lord and Lady. The images she provoked appeared too quickly and far too vividly before he could head them off. Those small hands . . . the slippery slide of soap . . . his body.

Reule sat back down quickly as tight, wet fabric stretched to accommodate his blazing erection and the rush left him light-headed. Reule sucked in a deep breath because he felt as though he wasn't breathing. He watched her blink at him with innocent candor. She wasn't bargaining her soul away to keep him there; she simply didn't see any reason why he should leave. She didn't understand why they couldn't share this large bath and bathe one another with practicality, and because she didn't understand, she wouldn't believe he wasn't trying to discard her.

"Okay," he murmured as he raised a hand to stroke gently along her collarbone. He wasn't agreeing to anything. Rather, he was merely preparing to be firm as he tried to find the logic that would help her to understand or trust. "*Kébé*," he began carefully, "it's considered improper for men and women in this society to bathe together."

"But aren't you bathing with me now?"

"I was only warming you from a bad chill." That, he realized with an inner wince, was a bit of a lie.

Whatever his reasoning, he had indeed been bathing her. "And, as you see, I'm clothed . . . mostly."

She sat back, her bottom rocking provocatively against his thighs as she obediently looked down at him. The pulse of heated blood that rushed through him would've made a weaker man swoon. He was very nearly that weaker man, Reule thought as his heart thumped with a fury against his breastbone.

"And in your society men and women never bathe one another? Never at all?"

Reule was about to agree, but realized it would be inaccurate. "Well, sometimes if a man and woman are lovers they will share a bath or shower."

"And that's not improper?"

"Um . . . no. What lovers do in private between themselves is acceptable if both desire it."

"Then send her away"—she jerked her head toward Para—"and we'll become lovers. Then you'll have no need to leave." She gave him a satisfied smile at her own logic. Reule, meanwhile, almost choked up a lung. He'd never heard such outrageous reasoning in all of his life.

"*Kébé*," he choked out, "people don't become lovers just so they can bathe together!"

"Well, why not? They become lovers for far less practical reasons, only to regret it later." She paused to nod after a moment's consideration. "I wouldn't regret it. You're very handsome and I can tell you desire me very much." She punctuated the observation by sliding her hand quickly down the front of his body and over the bulge in his breeches. She boldly cupped his balls and cock, outlining her evidence with palm and fingers. "I suspect you'd be an excellent mate. You're strong and powerful, and quite well-endowed for a male."

There was a resounding thud as Pariedes hit the floor in a dead faint behind them. Reule hardly had the presence of mind to care. He was strangling, in clothes, in reactions, and in raw heat that far outshined that of the pool. He could feel the difference between that small, small hand and his large, engorged body, and it was devastatingly arousing. He hated himself for feeling that, for wanting that, when he knew this was all so wrong. Even so, he saw her eyes widen as she got a true idea of his measure and he throbbed against her seeking touch in response. She licked her neglected lips slowly and he knew her thoughts, no telepathy necessary.

She was killing him, he thought with a groan.

He was hungry, tired, and *honorable*, and yet she made him ferocious with the desire to throw it all away and accept her taunting invitation.

"*Kébé*," he rasped as he reached for her wrist, "you've been through too much to make such choices right now. Especially when you can't remember if . . ."

If she already has a lover? If she's been raped? If . . . ?

"Besides," he forced out in cruel reminder for them both as he placed her hand safely at his neck, "you wouldn't want to be my lover. I am Sánge. Outlanders don't take Sánge for their lovers. Though I know not which kind, you are most obviously an outlander."

"Why not?" she asked softly, her frown deeply troubled by the revelation. "What's wrong with taking Sánge for lovers?"

Tension coiled through Reule instantly, clenching at every muscle in his body. *She doesn't know.* This was why she'd been so warm and accepting. Of course she didn't know. If she'd known, she'd have reacted with disgust just as all the others did. He'd been foolish to expect or think otherwise. But how to explain what she'd said the moment he'd found her? A remnant of memory? Of nightmares? A fevered snatch of recall from a horror story about the Sánge?

"You don't want to know," he said sharply, his tone extremely harsh as he got up and stepped out of the water.

"Yes, I do! Tell me, please," she begged him as she clung as tightly to him as she could.

Tell her? Could he tell her? Impossible. At the moment, he was the only anchor she had in a world torn apart by terror. If he took that trust away, replaced it with fear, who would she have?

And how could he ever explain it so she'd truly understand that the drinking of a lover's blood wasn't the horrifying, blasphemous act other cultures thought it was? How to describe that moment, just before climax, when a man sank his teeth into a woman? That instant when the essence of her very life pulsed onto his tongue, slid down his throat, and then spilled through him in the most intensely erotic sensation, so that it made his entire body clench and shudder with pleasure until he came in endless, drenching pulsations of ecstasy? There was no delicate way to explain an act that was so intensely wonderful when he knew none but Sánge could ever really understand; could ever really accept. If he couldn't explain that, then he couldn't explain the rest. Acts of body and mind beyond outlander sensibilities. The possessiveness, the ferocity, the sheer intensity of mating with a telepathic Sánge. Especially a telepathic Sánge like *him*.

In a sudden fit of anger, Reule overpowered her physically to pry her off him and she landed on the bench with a thump and a small sound of pain. Regret twanged through him, but he couldn't pause to apologize or he'd never leave the room. He had to leave. Now.

Reule reached down to Para and lightly smacked his fingers against her cheek until she opened her eyes with a flutter. "Wake, lioness," he called to her gently. "Your cub needs you. Are you well?" She blushed and nodded vigorously and he felt her embarrassment over her display.

Reule surged up to his full imposing height, unable to find it within himself to reassure her just then. His tone was clipped as he instructed the servant. "Bathe her, dress her, and feed her. Install her in the north wing." In his current temper, he wanted to forbid her from staying on the same floor as he. But her innocence didn't deserve punishment. He was the only one she trusted, whether she should or not, and it would be wrong to exile her to a lonely place in a strange world. "Across the hall from my suite will do. No one is to approach her save yourself and another girl to help you. She's frightened enough."

It was all the instruction he could give. He turned on his heel and marched out of the bath. He didn't have to look back to see the beseeching hand that tried to grab for him or to hear the panicked gasp of fear as he completed the act that terrified her from sense to soul.

He abandoned her.

But he felt it all quite plainly as that tidal wave of sorrow burst forth in full majesty once more.

As promised, Reule didn't go far. Apparently he was something of a masochist, he thought grimly as he sat in a private bath across the hall and washed away the grime from his body, if not the spreading stain on his soul. He could feel her like a sharply rising and falling aria, painfully honest as her emotional expression expanded from mere sorrow to fear and a raw sense of betrayal and rejection.

Lord. Reule rubbed his fingers against his temple as his head began to throb painfully. He despised knowing that he'd provided those newer emotions to her mostly blank canvas of feelings and thoughts. But what was he to do? It was the only choice. If she knew the depth and truth of what was seen as Sánge savagery . . .

Sánge, bautor mo.

The phrase she had spoken rushed into his mind like a flatland wind scour, an infamous windstorm that scrubbed away everything along its path. People, animals, every blade of grass, all would be swept away.

Sánge, bautor mo.

Sánge, drink of me.

Reule shuddered at the erotic rush that remembering the words sent through him. If she didn't know, why would she say that? It kept coming back to that single, crucial command. It wasn't an accident she'd said it that way. It couldn't be. It was ritualistic, that phrase. It was what a Sánge bride said to her husband on the night of her marriage, the first time she stepped into his arms and prepared to make love.

Reule reached below the water and wrapped a fist around his savagely aroused penis, closing his eyes as another shudder rocked through him. He shouldn't be feeling this. He shouldn't be reacting like an untried boy getting hard at every thought of a woman. It wasn't who he was. It never really had been, even as a youth. He'd been born in war and the desolation of starvation and persecution. He'd learned to flee before he'd learned to walk. He'd been heir to devastating responsibility, taking on the mantle of it when he was only sixteen years old. Too young to become responsible for the lives of a tribe numbering in the thousands; old enough to understand his parents had been murdered simply for being what they were.

Sánge.

With a curse, Reule released himself and ran wet hands through his hair in furious frustration. He hadn't thought about these things in so very long. Why now? Why were these memories invading his peace and the safety he had found in the stone walls of his valley fortress?

Reule couldn't say he was surprised when a sharp knock sounded on the door a short time later. With a long sigh, he relaxed back in the wide, sunken tub and spread his arms along the ceramic-tiled edges before bidding his visitor come in.

Darcio entered, shutting the door quickly to keep the warmth in. Reule watched warily as his companion turned to face him. His hair was wet from his own bath and his clothing neat and fresh. Reule's Shadow was even freshly shaved, which was more than he could say for himself. Then again, Darcio hadn't been tending to . . .

Reule shoved the thought aside. He'd probably been emanating far too much emotion as it was already. Darcio's presence was proof of that. He didn't need to rehash his conflicts while his friend was staring at him so intently.

"What is it?" Reule asked, unable to keep the irritable bite from his voice.

"Now, that's strange," Darcio mused. "I was going to ask you the same thing."

Darcio ignored the steam and the wetness coating everything in the room and moved to sit back casually on a bench as he regarded his Prime. The smaller private baths like this one were plumbed and tiled, rather than naturally replenishing like the Prime's Bath. In comparison, the oval tub was rather small . . . if a tub big enough to hold four people could be called small. Still, it gave Reule little room to escape Darcio's scrutiny.

"Now, I know I'm not as easygoing as Rye, nor as powerful, for that matter, but I imagine I'm as good to talk to as anyone else," Darcio speculated.

"Of course you are," Reule snapped, hating it when Darcio denigrated himself like that. It was as if Darcio, whom Reule couldn't imagine living without, didn't feel himself worthy of his role as advisor and protector. Reule believed it was his inhibition about his low-level telepathy that made him so, but Darcio had skill and ability that made him powerful in other ways. Reule just wished he'd acknowledge that to himself from time to time. "I just don't want to talk," Reule mumbled irritably.

"Well, I'm not so sure that's a good idea."

"Why?" Reule barked, his darkened hazel eyes flashing furiously.

Darcio shrugged, a slight lifting of a single shoulder that belied the intense focus of his carefully assessing gray eyes. "Because I know how fastidious you are, and how determined to shield others from your emotional emanations. You rarely lose control. However, every upper-level 'path in the castle has been getting a slideshow of their Prime's moods ever since you crossed beneath the portcullis. My suggestion to you is to vent this emotional pollution you're swimming in and gain your privacy back."

Reule had little to say in argument, so he didn't bother. He turned his head aside for several minutes as he struggled to draw his tattered thoughts together.

"I have to ask you something first," he said carefully, knowing Darcio's reaction could be potentially volatile. "It's a favor to me, but one you won't like."

"I rarely like doing favors for anyone *but* you, Reule," he said, dropping all formality in light of the request. "Ask your favor."

"I need to know if she was raped," Reule said quickly, meeting his friend's eyes in time to see them widen.

"Shit," Darcio hissed, leaning forward to place elbows against knees and running thick fingers through dark blond hair. Reule wasn't fooled. He saw the shudder that his Shadow tried to hide with the gesture. "Can't the apothecary tell you that?"

"She won't let him near her, I promise you that. She regards even Para with nothing but suspicion and fear. Pariedes, who everyone makes fast friends with."

"You should wait for her to tell you in her own time."

"I would, but she can't even remember her name, never mind how she got mapped with bruises and half the skin on her back scoured off. Friction burned off," Reule added, menace creeping thickly into his tone.

"Shit." Darcio's voice shook as he uttered the curse.

"I wouldn't ask you—"

"I know," Darcio cut him off hastily. "Why do you need to know so badly, Reule? If she can't remember, shouldn't you leave it at that? What will you say if you know the truth and she doesn't? Don't put yourself in that position."

"You don't need to know my reasons," Reule said carefully. "The task won't be any less difficult for you if you do. Let me worry about my motivations and the results. But if it helps you, I'll at least be able to tell the apothecary, and he'll be able to act accordingly without putting her through the trauma of an examination."

Reule could tell by the weight of his sigh that Darcio would agree. He didn't need to be a telepath, only a longtime friend, to know it. The method was simple, even if it was unique and potentially traumatic for Darcio. The Prime Shadow had been born with a gift as exclusive and powerful as Reule's ability to emanate. But like that gift, it was hard to control and not always a pleasant thing to have at one's disposal. Reule's mother and his granddame had both had the gift of emanation, so it had come with a name and a measure of training. Darcio was the first of his kind to exhibit his particular power and so he'd named it himself, calling it "the Curse."

Darcio had the ability to sort through the physical trauma of the living and the deceased, the conscious and the comatose, in order to find out what had happened to them. Since it was a mapping of the body and not of the psyche, the victim could be brain-dead or just plain dead and Darcio could still gather history. It wasn't a pleasant gift, and Reule didn't blame his Shadow for his reluctance to use it. Especially when Darcio had once explained it to him as "traumatic empathy." He didn't merely read the memory, he was overcome by it, reliving the disturbance in his mind as if he were in the actual moment, suffering the abuse, or the death. It took him days, sometimes months to shake the experiences. There were even those that never let go. Perhaps if he'd practiced the power more, he'd learn how to release them. Understandably, he refused to use it unless necessary. To his mind, practice was utterly out of the question.

Reule had only asked this favor twice before. Once to discover who'd murdered his parents. Darcio was seven years his senior, and at the time he had never once told a soul about his ability, which he considered horrifying. Upon learning of the terrible deaths of the Prime and Prima of their Sánge tribe, Shadow had had a knee-jerk thought impulse and the already powerful Reule had caught it like a brass ring. That time, he'd forced Darcio's compliance, and it had taken three years for him to earn his forgiveness. The second time was the day they'd come upon a wagon train torn asunder by Jakals, where men had been tortured, women and children raped for the pleasure of their emotions. Reule had hardly needed to ask. Darcio had been black with fury, whipping his power out with a ready vengeance.

Shadow didn't do that now as he sat up straight and closed his eyes. He would tread more carefully, protecting himself and as much of the privacy of his target as could be preserved under the circumstances. Reule quietly watched him. It was a testament to how Darcio's power had grown that he didn't have to be in the same room as his subject in order to read her. Last Reule had known, Shadow needed physical contact with his target.

Darcio sought for basics first, body memories of the most recent hours, which would orient him and then allow him to backtrack in a steady, chronological fashion, keeping him from getting confused once he lost familiar reference points. He would know enough of her past hours to catch the rhythm of her body cycle.

The first memory was always forcefully intense. It flashed into Darcio's consciousness like a percussive explosion, abruptly striking up a discordant symphony. Lights flashed, noise blared, sensations were magnified . . . and this time was no different.

Oddly enough, it was a memory of Reule that came to Darcio. Shadow hadn't considered that Reule's recent upset might be rooted squarely in the outlander girl. She hadn't even been conscious when Reule had brought her down. Darcio had thought this request to use his Curse had been Reule's way of dodging his inquisition about his emotional well-being. In truth, Shadow realized, this was Reule's way of answering without answering. Reule knew Darcio's ability would allow the Prime Shadow to have a front-row seat to the memory of his disturbance.

Five seconds later, Darcio became intimate with what had disturbed Reule so deeply. He recalled everything the nameless girl had experienced in that pool; every wave of heat and every touch of Reule's ministrations. She hadn't been awake, but her body remembered, and therefore Darcio remembered.

Shadow knew that his Prime was sharing the experience, using his telepathy to observe as he read the outlander. Had it been any of the rest of the Pack, Darcio might have been embarrassed, witnessing acts that were by turns tender and seductive. However, Reule and he had walked as Prime and Prime's Shadow together for eighty-five years now. They'd trained and warred, aged and whored, and seen many things, both good and evil, in the world. At ninety-one and ninety-eight years old, they were in the prime of a Sánge's life cycle. Darcio anticipated that, though they were no longer wild with youth, he and Reule would experience much more of life together before all was done.

While learning of Reule's sexual interest didn't make him blush, it did worry him. He'd withhold judgment until after he completed his scan, but even so, outlanders didn't welcome Sánge, and Sánge didn't welcome outlanders. Reule would be a fool to think otherwise, no matter how unusual her attachment to him was. It seemed to Darcio that she was merely clinging to her rescuer in the wake of a great trauma and . . .

. . . and then the trauma itself began to burn into life, searing across his mind and body until he felt as though he were on fire. He threw back his head and gasped in a harsh breath as agony pummeled him from head to toe. He swallowed, gritting his teeth at the confusing and brutal abuse, tears pricking behind his lids as he tried to hold on. *If she can endure this, so can I*, he commanded himself.

Within his mind, he was far from the bath and Reule, yet he knew his Prime was now physically by his side, watching him steadily, ready to end the pain he'd asked his friend to suffer if necessary.

Mildew, must, and terrible cold. Every inch of his skin was throbbing and burning with open, fresh, and barely healed wounds. There was something strange about what he felt, even as sadness overwhelmed him again and again, a despair that tightened his lungs, forcing tears to fall even when he was too thirsty, too hungry, and too tired to weep. There was sleep in short, taunting snatches, but always the cold. Then that strange vibration again, humming the length and breadth of his—her—body. Weak, but growing stronger as time continued to reverse her condition.

Jakals. He sensed them, was aware of them, but she could hide herself from the Jakals dancing gleefully right beneath her. Then he (she) felt her arms and legs exploding in horrible agony.

Darcio leaped forward, roaring in pain as he fell before the bench onto his knees, Reule's hands guiding him and now holding him as he yelled and shook. Alone, but not? Alone, but being tortured? No marks, only the pain of it. Driving, driving deep. And still they didn't know of her, even though she wept and shuddered with the emotions the Jakals so desired to devour. Days rotated further into the past, hunger easing so it was sharp but not agonizing, as did thirst, the presence of the Jakals fading within forty-eight hours until she was alone in truth.

Splinters rammed under skin disappeared, mildew and mold rashes faded, cold gave way to warmth as her body slid to the third floor, the second . . . the first. Slow, the trip taking most of a day to make because she'd crawled up while in ferocious agony. There was the burn, the raw scorching along her hips, spine, and shoulders. Hair tangled, scalp torn and bloodied. Every inch bruised, bones even broken. Some twice over.

Since the scenario was running backward, Darcio was confused. Three days ago she'd had broken bones, today she didn't. How was that possible? He wasn't required to seek the answer. Reule had only wanted to know if the Jakals had raped her. They hadn't. They hadn't even realized she was there, though he knew not how. Still, what trauma had left her alone in such a state? A fight? Had she been attacked after all, only by a different assailant?

Confusion swept through him as his body ached and throbbed in sympathy with the plight and pain of a small woman who turned out to have the stamina and fortitude of the most seasoned warrior. Experiencing the trauma she'd undergone secondhand, Darcio wasn't so sure he would've been so persistent or resourceful. Then again, she wasn't Sánge, and his natural defenses would've made this a much altered experience for him.

"Darc, stay focused," he heard Reule encourage him gently, his Prime's voice concerned but firm.

So it continued. Dampness and the stench of the

swamps and bogs of the damplands. Earth. Grass. Beneath his hands and knees. Crawling inch by inch over changing terrain, every movement exquisite agony, yet the only thing keeping him warm in the pre-winter chill. A fall, brutal, snapped his arm in two. Then soreness between his legs, hard aches in his thighs.

Shadow felt Reule tense next to him, but his Prime mistook the cause of the discomfort. Darcio had been an accomplished horseman for far too long not to recognize a saddle-sore backside. The fall had been from a horse. She'd broken her arm falling from a high-set saddle. She'd fallen from pure exhaustion.

Then there was riding, the speed breakneck. He could tell by the windburn on his face, the whipping of hair that pulled at a scalp already beaten raw. How? How had it come to be, the battering that caused pain to worsen as time drew nearer to the origination? He was close to the cause. Darcio could feel it, and he dreaded it. He dreaded it because he knew it would be worse than all the other pain he felt through her body's memory.

He had braced for it, yet still was blindsided. There was screaming oblivion and then vicious nausea. Blood from his mouth, his nose . . . everywhere. Shadow lurched forward and vomited violently.

"Enough! Darcio, it's enough!"

Reule's command was followed by the feel of his Prime's hands gripping his shoulders. Shadow was sick again, caught up in the cycle of body memory and suddenly unable to let go.

But as always, Reule was there for him. He felt the instant his ruler unleashed his own power. Reule used it to seize control of Darcio's thoughts and emotions, jerking him into the present, into the steam and heat of the private bath.

Forgive me, old friend. I asked too much. Reule's regret weighed heavily in the telepathic sentence, but Darcio waved it off as he focused on his Packleader. Reule had pulled on a robe after leaving the tub, he realized, and the small detail centered him, pulling him even further away from the horrifying memories of what a small female body had endured these past few days.

"I didn't find out how she was originally injured," he said apologetically. "I fear that was only half the hell she's been through."

"You did enough." Reule frowned darkly, lines of disturbed emotion etching into his forehead. "I'm sorry I even asked. Now I'm left with still more questions."

Darcio nodded, his body aching with the ghosts of pain and brutalization.

Reule had one answer that he'd not had at the start of this, however.

He now knew why she felt such sorrow.

Chapter 4

After he'd bathed, dressed, and taken some supper, Reule entered Chayne's quarters. To his surprise, the room was in a total uproar. Chayne was the center of a ruckus that looked like a mass wrestling competition, he realized a moment before an arc of blood spattered in droplets against him.

"What in the name of all that is holy are you doing?"

Reule's bellow sounded like the hard crack of a whip, and everyone, including the heavily panting Chayne, froze in mid-tableau. Delano, Saber, and the smaller man Reule recognized as the apothecary all turned their heads to look at their thunderous Prime's visage. Rye, who was standing back as though supervising, was closest to Reule and also turned. Delano and Saber, it appeared, were attempting to secure Chayne to the bed by physical force so the apothecary could tend him. How Chayne was even moving after so much blood loss was beyond Reule.

The Prime was infuriated and he made it very clear with an emanation that sent his Packmates staggering.

"Damn!" Rye yelped, jumping back from his Pack-leader in shock.

"Uh!" Delano concurred, bolting away from the bed. Saber staggered back as well, the Prime Defender swinging around hard to stare at his leader. The apothecary cringed and shook.

"Back off!" Reule commanded even though they were backed away already. "Would someone care to tell me why you're wrestling with an injured man?" But they all knew that Reule was really asking how they dared try to strong-arm Chayne when they knew— absolutely *knew*—it was the worst way to go about getting his compliance. Chayne loathed being held down. In light of his recent captivity, it would be even less tolerable to him.

Chayne, the last one he'd demand an answer from, ground out in response, "That demented son of a bitch was going to clamp that contraption on me!" Chayne swung a shuddering arm toward the apothecary. An arm, Reule noted, that had been broken when it had been skewered by a steel spike.

"By the Lord," Reule swore as his Packmate's agony beat at him. Yet he forced himself to move closer. Chayne's other arm and his legs were no better off.

The contraption in question made Reule's blood curdle as he laid eyes on it. The steel vises were meant to hold realigned bones together, screwed tightly in place against the skin to form support. But this was often at the cost of utter agony and flesh that would break down over the weeks of healing. Most men opted for splints, taking their chances with lameness rather than facing a vise. Reule himself had done so once when a sword strike to his upper arm had broken the long bone. Bearing four splints on four broken or very likely shattered bones would be sheer hell, but vises as well? It was unthinkable, and he didn't blame Chayne for finding the power despite his suffering to resist those who thought to force him.

"Since when," Reule asked through gritted teeth, "do we force a sane, independent friend to go against his wishes?"

"The bones are sh-shattered, M-my Prime," the apothecary stammered, though Reule had been addressing him not at all.

Reule swung a black glare at him, and a percolating growl of fury elicited a gasp of fear from the physician. Then he glowered in turn at the three others in the room. "I await an answer," he spat, dismissing the apothecary's response.

"We weren't. W-we would never!" Delano said, cursing when he realized he was stammering as well. "We were trying to calm him after the apothecary tried to put on the vise, but he got more upset and started flailing. Reu . . . My Prime," he corrected himself, choosing formality at Reule's black scowl, "we've all been faced with vises at one time or another. We'd never take the choice away from Chayne. It just got out of hand."

"Chayne—" Reule moved Delano back and looked down at his friend as he lay quivering with nauseating agony. "They'll use no vises. You have my word. But you must allow me to put you to sleep. There's no need for you to suffer."

Chayne shook so hard his chestnut brown hair vibrated with motion, but only his tan eyes, dull with suffering, moved to look up and acknowledge him. It was difficult to watch him, to know that the damage to some bones was likely to be irreversible. It was worse than a death sentence, and Reule felt his friend's recognition of it. Chayne also knew that none of his companions would condescend to him or act with pity. What Reule offered was mercy. Mercy for a boyhood playmate, whom he knew as well as he knew himself, who'd rather die than beg for what Reule was offering to him.

Chayne *could* accept a request made by his Pack-leader, however, and still maintain his dignity. "No drugs," he rasped out, blood appearing on his lips as he spoke. He shook so hard, he'd bitten his tongue. "Sleep only, Reule."

Reule nodded. Even in torturous pain, Chayne sought a way to justify accepting the offer to put him under a forced sleep. Drugs weakened a man and, as with the vises, few Sánge males accepted them.

Reule wasted no time. The Pack knew the moment their leader swept into Chayne and seized his mind. The shaking of his body halted and Chayne went still, his breath holding . . . holding . . . and then the release of a rushing exhale, and Chayne was in oblivion.

The rest of the Pack should be so lucky. When Reule whirled to face them, it was with another snarl of displeasure. He even flashed fangs, though mostly at the apothecary. "With all the years each of you have known Chayne, what made you believe that *holding him down* was the way to calm him?" It was a rhetorical question because Reule gnashed his fangs when Rye opened his mouth to argue. "Leave!" he snapped at them. "I will tell myself that three days without sleep or food have impaired your judgment!" Reule's contemptuous look at Saber spoke volumes for the fact that the Prime Defender had no such excuse, as he'd not been out on excursion with them. "And as for these . . ."

Reule marched over to the apothecary and snatched the offensive metal vise from his hand. The contraption, with its cuffs and screws, looked like the instrument of torture it was. "These," he hissed, "are banned from this keep. You will never bring them onto these grounds again, is that very clear?" The vise crashed down on the table with a clang.

"B-But . . ." the physic sputtered.

"If you do, I will have your balls cut off. Can I make it any clearer?" There was no need. The apothecary swallowed and nodded. "Now, you will care for him as you would me," Reule commanded the physician.

Disgusted and furious still, Reule gave them all a sharp nod before he drew his temper up around himself and attempted to take it with him when he left. It was apparent by the chills that washed through the room that he wasn't entirely successful in his endeavor.

Pariedes found him a few hours later sitting before the fire in his study. She moved in near silence, thinking he was probably asleep after the ordeal of the past few days, but as she came up on him, she saw him turn his head and incline his chin to acknowledge her.

"How is our guest, Para?"

"Fast asleep, My Prime," she responded promptly, although he probably could have taken the information from her mind.

Prime Reule had manners and used courtesies, unlike others who thought-read whenever the impulse struck because they believed it was a birthright to nose around in everyone's business. Prime Reule preferred to cultivate spoken conversation and disdained the discourtesy of strip-mining his people for information just because he was the most powerful telepath in the city. He also expected the same of those within his circle.

The exception was, of course, the Packmates. Packmates were the sworn companions of the Prime Packleader.

As such, the group was in constant mental conversation with one another. They did not use words, but a harmony of connectivity that made them always aware of one another. A Packmate had to consciously work to break away from the collective awareness of the Pack if he sought privacy. They were welcome to do so, but the Pack had existed in this connective state for so long that it became uncomfortable for a Packmate to remain closed off for very long. It also became discomforting for the Pack to be missing the input of a member.

Para had cared for Prime Reule's household for five decades now, and she had learned a great deal about the workings of the Pack. She knew that none of them would rest easy as long as Chayne suffered pain. With the added distractions of sleeplessness, worry, and the volatile mystery of an unexpected guest in the house, it didn't surprise her to find her master staring dumbly into a fire.

"She was out on her feet. Tetra and I barely had her nightgown on before she was in dreams." Para fussed around the room as she spoke to him, tidying up things he'd set carelessly aside, including a wineglass that sat empty nearby. "She asked for you many times," she ventured.

"You cared for her far better than I would have," he murmured in reply.

"Shall I inform you when she wakes so you may visit with her? That apothecary wanted access to her," Para added with a scowl, "but I believe sleep is the only medicine she needs. And plenty of good hot food. She ate like a starving animal. I was forced to moderate her lest she make herself ill."

"So you sent the apothecary away, I take it?" he asked, turning inquisitive hazel eyes on her, the expression making his handsome visage seem boyish. Since his looks were quite dark and fierce, it was a surprising turn of countenance. It made Para smile at him warmly.

"I did," she pronounced, straightening her shoulders in silent challenge. "He's a quack, plain and simple. She's better off with herbal wraps for the wounds on her body and, as I said, food and sleep."

"Para," he said, her name a warning, "I don't enjoy having my orders countermanded without being consulted. I would have heard your arguments. You shouldn't have gone behind my back."

"'Twas not going behind your back, nor a defiance of orders, My Prime," she argued firmly. "You never specifically said she had to see the physic. She was asleep, resting, and calm at last. That fool would have upset her all over again. Especially if he thought to touch her. She would barely let Tetra and me touch her."

Reule lifted a brow and exited his chair in a smooth movement so he could face Pariedes and digest her curious remark. "She struggled with you?" he asked.

"She pitched a regular fit, My Prime," Para informed him with a snort. "And if I might say so, that girl is battered and starved within an inch of her life, and I dread to see how strong she is when she's perfectly healthy!"

Para had a point, Reule thought as he folded his arms across his chest and regarded the servant. He recalled the strength his foundling had used when she'd been trying to keep hold of him. It was another piece in the puzzle of her identity.

"Very well. I want you checking on her as though she were a baby, Para. Be frequent and attentive. Tetra was a good choice. See to it she helps you so you're not overwhelmed."

"Yes, My Prime," she said, offering him a dipping bow of respect before hustling out of the room.

Once she was gone, Reule turned back to the fire, standing with feet braced apart as he stared hard into the flames once again. His mind was abuzz with questions and concerns. He knew he should let everything go for now and take to his bed, that he'd solve nothing without sleep to clear his roiling mind, but he was too disturbed to find rest. Most of the Pack was abed, save himself and Darcio. Darcio too was sitting and brooding, and it left Reule with the bad taste of guilt in his mouth. He knew Darcio feared his dreams after experiencing the agony of their unexpected guest's body memories. There was no way of helping him. He knew his Shadow well enough to know that he preferred his own company and introspection in times like this.

The mystery of the outlander woman wasn't even worth thinking about any longer. He could make no more sense of it than he already had. But Reule couldn't make himself dismiss the memory of his volatile physical reaction to her. It wasn't just because he couldn't shake the lingering feel of her body wrapped around him, the warmth of her, the feel of her fingers in his hair . . . No. It was all about his lack of control. It disturbed him until his gut was taut with tension.

When a Sánge male reached Reule's age, he'd been in his sexual prime for a good twenty years. Oh, he had known the true craft of lovemaking since his twenties, but males like the majority of his Pack hit a powerful sexual stride around their seventies, lasting fifty years before calming into a steadier pace. Females went through something similar, but it tended to occur a little later in their lives. Sánge were a strongly sexual breed, but these periods, known as *mnise*, intensified their natural desires in triplicate in order to ensure perpetuation of the species. Most of his Pack reveled in this increase in sexual appetite. Reule didn't have the luxury of joining them as they sniffed after courtesans, women considered acceptable for dalliances. He had to be far more careful in his choices.

Not one of the Pack was mated, and none were interested in changing their bachelor status, a fact that frustrated court ladies who sought ambitious connections. There was only one way to secure a male against his will, and that was by bearing a child that was irrefutably his. So a great deal of care was needed when choosing partners if one didn't wish to find oneself precipitously wed.

Courtesans were sterile females, of which there were, unfortunately, plenty. Since males rarely wished to wed a woman who couldn't provide heirs, these women either lived as spinsters who never knew the touch of a man, or they became courtesans and mistresses to those men seeking the comforts of a woman without the risk of marriage. Until recently, Reule had kept such a mistress—Wenda, a juicy little redhead whom he'd taken delight in for nearly a year before dismissing her. She'd become complacent and dangerously attached, so he'd ended the association. She'd been hurt and angry, ruining what had been a good friendship.

It was a heady thing to be mistress to a king. Especially a bachelor king who had no wife to protect from a courtesan's presence. It meant she could openly attend him in court and exhibit her powerful position. It could bring out the best in a woman. It could also bring out the worst. Unfortunately, Wenda had forgotten to take care in how she treated others during her installation as royal mistress. Her favor with him had protected her from the retaliation of the women she'd insulted, but the minute she'd been released from her shining spot, it had all come back to haunt her. She had forgotten that her power was temporary.

Wenda had since found another sponsor and was living in comfort and contentment. Reule had checked up on her discreetly to make certain she was happy.

The point was, he'd learned a measure of control. One that had even earned him the reputation of being rigid. Some accused him of being cold and passionless, these "some" usually being women who tried to sway him sexually only to find he wasn't easily swayed. Other men looked at him in bafflement, trying to figure out how he could bear the *mnise* without a woman. Some courtiers and commoners worried about the future of their throne when it looked as though he wouldn't be taking a mate any time soon. Only his Pack understood fully why he held himself in such perfect reserve when it came to sex and women.

It was because he was so deeply in control of this single aspect of his body, he thought with frustration, that he ought never to have reacted to the female stranger the way he had. And yet, even now, just remembering how hotly she had affected him, remembering how she had touched him so boldly . . .

Reule cursed himself and his hardening body. He cursed the memory of the scent of his soap on her, the sparkle of tearing diamond eyes, and the desperation of need as she'd begged him not to leave her. In all good conscience, he ought to check in on her, visit her and let her know he wasn't far from her side. But he told himself it wouldn't matter because she was asleep and she wouldn't know the difference.

He refused to believe the little voice in the back of his brain telling him that he was a coward.

* * *

"Reule! Hand me up that line!"

"My Prime!"

Reule was throwing rope up to Amando when Pariedes came running at full steam, puffing for breath and holding up her skirts in both fists in a way that showed far more ankle and calf than he'd ever seen on her in all her time with him. It was such a shocking display for one as conservative as she was that the courtyard immediately erupted in wolfish whistles from the teasing Pack and the workers standing around.

Reule was forced to reach for her in order to stop her momentum from crashing her into him. She was clearly flustered because she was drawing male amusement. Her elfin face was flushed bright red, and he didn't think it was all from the exertion of her mad dash into the courtyard.

Reule steadied the housekeeper on her feet, throwing an admonishing growl over his shoulder at the raucous men still making a fuss over her. They silenced instantly except for some chuckles of laughter, but all watched them with full attention while Para caught her breath to speak.

"Very well, Para," Reule said, "what is it?"

"The girl . . ." she gasped.

It was all she needed to say. Her concern struck out at him like a fist slamming into his belly. Cursing himself for not feeling it sooner, Reule abandoned Para and bolted for the keep. He hadn't seen his guest for three days; she'd done nothing but sleep, Para forcing her awake only long enough to eat before she fell back into her exhaustion. He'd known every time she'd come awake, however. That wall of sorrow had struck him whenever she was conscious.

He didn't feel it now, so he didn't understand what was happening. He hadn't bothered to scan Para's thoughts; he was too focused ahead of himself as he tore up the stairs. He was barely up the first few when he heard the screams. They caught his spine, chilling him as he started leaping three and four stairs at a time. Reule ripped into the bedroom across from his and saw Tetra wringing her hands helplessly by the bedside, watching the woman thrashing and screaming in the bed.

"Out!" he commanded roughly, probably frightening the young maid half to death with the savagery in his voice. He couldn't help it. His heart was pumping out an awful cadence in his chest as he grabbed for the bedding and tore it away. He reached for the tortured woman, his large hands circling her upper arms as she threw back her head and screamed again, tears streaming from her closed eyes.

Three days of good intentions went to hell in that instant between grasping her arms and the decision to pull her up against his chest. Ignoring her blood-chilling screams in his sensitive ear, he pressed her face against his neck with a hand at the back of her head and held her to the warmth of his body with another against her spine.

"Hush, *kébé*," he soothed softly against her ear. "You're safe now. Safe with me. Hush, sweetheart."

Straight telepaths and empaths had no access to the thoughts or emotions of a dreamer. Only Sánge Dream-weavers could enter the subconscious of another via dreams, and that was a talent almost as rare as his ability to emanate. This was why whenever she fell asleep or unconscious, it was like shutting off a switch, which was only turned on again when she woke. So even though she was clearly suffering and in terror, he could feel none of it but what he could glean from her physiology. Her racing heart. Her tears. The hoarse horror in her voice. And now the clawing clutch of her hands as they came up to grasp the back of his shirt so strongly, he could hear it tearing in tiny increments.

"Wake up," he begged her in a soft whisper. "Please wake up. Come be safe with me," he urged her, his rapid heartbeat nothing compared to the speed of hers crashing against their joined chests.

Reule closed his eyes and focused on his power of emanation. He gathered up all the strength and safety he felt in his home, surrounded by his Pack, and adored by his people. He fashioned it into an arrow of intention, which he then sent singing into her heart and her mind, hoping somehow it would touch her. He pushed it into her relentlessly and with all the force of his impressive will. He would give her his emotions to fortify her. At least he hoped so. He'd never tried emanating to a sleeping person before.

She'd screamed herself hoarse, but he knew instantly that wasn't the reason why she suddenly stopped. The sound halted as if it were choked off. Then, like the burst of the sun coming over the horizon, sorrow and anguish flooded through Reule until he laughed in relief; he'd never thought he'd be so happy to feel such things. In this case, it meant she was awake at last.

She was gasping for breath, still clinging to him, but her body had otherwise gone very, very still. He heard her sniff, thinking it was to clear her tears, until she did it again. This time, slowly, deliberately, her nose twitching in a series of nuzzling rubs against his neck as she took in his scent. Reule gritted his teeth together fiercely as a wild thrill rippled over his skin, making the fine hairs of his body stand at attention. *It is nothing!* He told himself this as he fiercely tried to get the rampant reaction under his control. Sánge greeted each other by smell as frequently as not, he argued to himself, and there was absolutely no reason why he should feel such an erotic rush with no other provocation. This was no different from any other—

"Reule," she sighed, her voice rough from her abuse of it, her satisfaction so damned obvious it made every nerve in his body draw taut in response.

By the Lord, she recognized me by scent. That meant she had a keen olfactory sensitivity and had taken note of his particular scent. He forced himself not to read anything more into it than that, locking off any idea of attraction or flirtation on her part. That was Sánge cultural behavior, and she wasn't Sánge. Hell, she was barely awake! Her relief, he told himself, was what anyone would feel after waking from what had obviously been a horrible dream. He was all she knew anymore. It was as simple as that.

Still, it was a heady thing to be the sole focus of her appreciation and contentment. Strange that being the central focus of an entire people had never made him feel what being her hero of the moment did.

"You're safe," he murmured to her softly and he closed his eyes and turned his nose against her hair. He breathed in her scent as he spoke, finding it marked in his memory as well, the sweet musk that was unique to her beneath the light scent of vanilla flowers that Para had bathed her in recently.

"You left me," she sobbed out achingly. "You left me and there was no one for me."

"No, *kébé*, that's not true," he said hoarsely, her pain stirring up his guilt. "I was close all along. Para was here. And Tetra. I would never leave you alone."

"No! No . . ." She shook her head slightly as her clutch on him tightened, and he had the distinct feeling that they were talking from two separate worlds.

Reule just held her tightly and let her cry herself out, let her wake further into the real world. "I'm close to you now. I will protect you for as long as you need protecting. You have my vow, sweetheart," he whispered into her small ear. "The vow of a king, amongst the Sánge, is a powerful thing, *kébé*."

"I know," she breathed against his neck.

Reule closed his eyes again and tried to supress the shudder that the awareness of her words sent through him. Again she spoke as though she knew Sánge culture, and the warmth of her breath on his skin seemed to drive it into him like an exhilarating force of nature. What did she really know? *Who is she?*

"Do you dream of what happened to you, sweetheart? Is that what makes you scream?" he asked as gently as he could. He felt the reflexive dig of her fingers into his back.

"I don't remember what happened to me," she rasped.

Reule wasn't so sure about that. She remembered something of it. Whether it was disjointed flashes of horror in consciousness, or full clarity in her dreams, she did remember something. It'd take time, but one day she'd come to understand what she had been through. Right now, her mind was protecting itself from the trauma. Waiting for the rest of her body to heal, perhaps, before forcing her to mentally deal with what she had suffered.

"Please don't leave me again," she begged him softly, her voice breaking with fear.

"I never did, *kébé*. I swear. I was close all along."

"But I couldn't touch you. I couldn't hold you or speak to you. I couldn't see you!"

Reule swallowed hard, clenching his teeth as guilt flushed through him again. He'd purposely distanced himself from her because he'd not been able to control his reactions to her bold, strange ways. He'd punished her for his failings. Disgusted with himself, Reule swore restitution.

"What could I have done for you?" he said, inserting the lilt of a tease in his voice as he gathered her into the cradle of his arms and lap. He turned to settle back against the headboard. "You've been snoring away quite peacefully for days. You barely woke to eat, and I believe you slept through your most recent bath."

She snorted softly against his throat, a halfhearted sound of sarcasm that told him she saw that as no excuse for his absence.

"If you plan to join the waking world, *kébé*, I'll be glad to attend you."

She hesitated a moment, then lifted her head at last and looked into his eyes. That was when Reule noticed her hair for the first time. To his absolute and utter astonishment, it was a deep, dark red unlike anything he'd ever seen before on a woman. It was even more unexpected on this woman because he'd held her and bathed her and never once had an inkling that this astounding color had lain beneath all that filth. He'd expected black, or even brown . . . but not this deep crimson color. As red as blood, and there was no denying the comparison. Though not the bright flash of a smear, it was rather that nearly black darkness of a single fat drop as it solidified.

Nor had he realized her hair was so long. In fact, it touched her elbows, and it was lightly curled enough to form casual, wide spirals that took several inches to make a complete revolution. Unable to stop the impulse, and perhaps unwilling as well, Reule reached out and picked up one of the clean locks between two fingers so he could run the length of it through them. It was soft as silk, a little lank from being slept on, and damp from the sweat of her dreams. It was also quite beautiful, dark as it was, and Reule found it an enchanting complement to her diamond eyes.

"You like my hair." It was a statement, albeit a slightly shy one.

"Yes. Is this a bad thing, that I like your hair? It's very lovely."

She blinked those sparkling eyes up at him. "I like your hair as well." She reached to touch his hair and Reule stiffened reactively. She felt it with all of her body and she stopped just before touching his hairline. "Do you dislike my touch so much?" she asked softly, a combination of curiosity and hurt showing in the tilt of her head and brows.

"No," he said on a rough exhale. "Your touch . . ." He cleared his throat. "Your touch is an astounding pleasure, *kébé*. Sánge hair . . . our scalps are one of our most sensitive erogenous zones." Best to be blunt with her, he thought. She seemed to understand things better that way. To prefer them that way. Frankly, so did he.

"Oh," she said softly, slightly lowering her hand. "I remember things about the Sánge so clearly sometimes, but I didn't remember that."

She had no way of knowing how that statement tore at him. So, she remembered the Sánge in bits and pieces, did she? Granted, she seemed better informed than most, but it explained why she had disjointed ideas about the Sánge.

"We're a complex people," Reule said to her kindly, making certain to banish any hint of disappointment and frustration from his voice. "But we're not the beasts we're accused of being."

"Beasts!" She jerked into a sitting position, her hands coming to wrap around his biceps. "That's ridiculous! You, Para, and Tetra are angels! Kindness personified! Taking in a stranger rank with dirt and troubles when you could've easily left me to wither and die!"

"Never!" His sudden, savage growl seemed to take them both by surprise. Reule's hands had fallen to her narrow waist where they now circled her lower rib cage. He held her so tightly that she was afraid to draw a breath for fear she wouldn't be able to. "I'd never leave even the lowest animal on this planet to suffer as you were suffering," he explained awkwardly. "Y-you were crying out to me. I could never ignore so sad a plea."

She felt desperation in his hands as he held her, a tremor riding through his muscles as he suppressed a tangle of emotion. This man who seemed so gruff and powerful struggled to tamp down his emotions so no one would see them. Or see them as a weakness, she added to herself as she cocked her head. How must that feel? To experience emotion so deeply, yet never feel comfortable sharing it because there was an image to be maintained? It would be confining and lonely, she realized in an instant. Far lonelier than being in a strange world without even a name to ground you. She at least was free to feel and say and think whatever she wished. More so than anyone else, because she had no society or rules to follow at the moment. Although, as she began to examine her mind and instincts, she suspected that those things remained ingrained within her, whatever they were.

"Reule," she said gently, running both hands over the hard contours of his muscular arms, up to his broad shoulders, "you are no beast. I know it with all of my instincts and with all of my spirit. And I have a feeling I'm the sort of woman who is always right."

A startled laugh barked out of him and she smiled brightly. His hands left her waist and she soon found her head enveloped between them, his callused thumbs sliding over the crests of her cheekbones as he stared hard at her with his eyes of multicolored greens and golds. She knew she was small, but trapped between his hands like this, she felt incredibly fragile. The calluses told her that this was a man used to hard physical work, the muscles beneath her fingers giving more evidence of that. He could probably crush her to dust if he wanted to.

"You have a beautiful smile, *kébé*," he murmured in a tone so low it rumbled a vibration through his hands and into her facial bones. It tickled. His thumbs dropped to her mouth where they brushed lightly against the smooth surface of her bottom lip. "You've healed remarkably well," he noted.

She had no mirror to look into, save his eyes and the expression on his face. She knew just by looking at his appreciation and steady regard that the bruises were probably gone and her chapped lips healed. She smiled and reached to brush her fingertips against the warm skin of his neck.

"May I ask a favor of you?" she asked him, enjoying the feel of her lips moving against his thumbs as she spoke.

"Ask," he commanded simply.

"You cannot keep calling me 'foundling.' Or at least not solely. Perhaps we should choose a name for me until I can recall . . . Why, whatever is wrong?" She widened her eyes when she saw the tautness that came over his expression and radiated down into the tensing of his fingertips. There was a sudden shuttering of his hazel eyes.

"How did you know *kébé* means 'foundling'?" he asked quietly, a sickening feeling of doubt and suspicion once again crawling through his belly.

"Reule . . . I don't know. I just do. I can't explain these things. I swear to you, I—"

"Your pardon," he said quickly, pausing to try to clear the rough rumble from his tone that made him sound like the predator he was. "I meant no accusation." It was part lie, part truth. Reule didn't know what he meant anymore. All he knew was that she baffled his senses and his thoughts like no other could. "Have you already given thought to a name? Do you have a preference?"

"I . . . I thought you might suggest something." Her tone was subdued and Reule could feel her confusion and her uneasiness.

His moody behavior made no sense to her, and wouldn't to someone completely free of ulterior motive. He believed that she had no nefarious purpose. At least at present. He reminded himself there was no possible way for anyone to spy on the Sánge, considering the power of their telepathy. A deceiver would be discovered easily, would they not? Especially under Reule's nose. The castle was all but overrun with his Packmates, the most powerful men of their breed.

But if someone was going to be a successful spy, wouldn't they know the native language and appear in just the sort of way that would cause them to be brought into the very midst of the workings of Sánge government? How much better if the spy's mind could be altered so that even *they* were ignorant of their purpose and the value of the things they were seeing? That would allow her to move without suspicion among them, her thoughts free of duplicity, free from detection. Then later she could be somehow recovered and . . .

Reule sighed, reaching up to rub at an ache in his temples. He was beginning to sound paranoid. But didn't he have cause to be? Growing up as he had? Watching a third of his people die of starvation, exposure to the elements of the lands they'd trudged over, and victims to beasts both two- and four-legged. All in two decades. It had more than taken its toll on him. He'd vowed to never allow such a horror to befall his people again. He'd kept that promise, and he'd done it by being sharp, shrewd, and even paranoid through the years.

He was lost in these grim thoughts when he felt the skim of warm, rough fingers sliding around his. His attention swung to the hand holding his, comforting him when he was so obviously distressed. However, the gesture inadvertently upset him even more because he could see the tattered state of her nails and the healing wounds on her palms and knew the damage had been inflicted as she had crawled across a wilderness. What right did he have to persecute her without even the slightest shred of proof? Even Darcio's very personal and taxing invasion into the history of her body had revealed nothing to prove she meant any of the Sánge harm, and it wasn't like Reule to bear prejudice against anyone, not even Jakals, until they gave him cause.

However, he rather suspected that part of the problem was the uncanny way she had of disrupting his steady, long-familiar calm. She had barely been in the keep for three days. What would he suffer throughout a long winter, should she remain here with them?

What did it matter? To treat her poorly because of his own inadequacies was reprehensible. Reule determined to get himself under control. No matter what she had been before this, right now she was innocent and she was frighteningly lost and alone. Given time, the mystery surrounding his foundling would begin to unfold.

"Mystique," he said abruptly, the name snapping out of him unexpectedly. The moment he said it, he knew it was perfect. If he went by the smile spreading with pleasure over her face and in her glittering eyes, she agreed.

"Reule, it's beautiful. Thank you."

Reule decided he liked the name very much himself. "But," he said with a playful grin overcoming him, "I think perhaps I will still call you *kébé* from time to time."

"You, My Prime, may call me whatever you wish," she said with a soft uptilt of her lips and her eyes smiling with delight. "So long as it is complimentary and full of praise," she stipulated with a sly glance from under her lashes.

Reule had to laugh. It wasn't until just that moment that he realized women didn't usually tease him like that. Oh, his Packmates mocked him incessantly, the practical jokes between Packmates the stuff of legend. Lately, though, Reule had withdrawn a great deal from their antics as his position as Prime pressed him into the responsibility of running a successful city. "I will make a bargain with you," he said as he eased her from his lap and went to stand up away from her. She held on to him, but he smiled as he grasped her reluctant hands. "I will make every effort to be a fount of praise and compliments, so long as you promise to let me step away before Para comes in the room. She is coming up the stairs as we speak and I have no desire to be scolded for my improprieties with you. I think she sees you as a chick she needs to protect."

Mystique hardly thought a Sánge Prime had any

reason to be swayed by the views of a servant, but she realized with pleasure that Reule was making the effort simply to please Pariedes, whom he clearly felt respect and affection for. She released him as he'd requested and settled back in the bed just as Para came bustling breathlessly through the door.

"Oh! Well! Lady bless you, child, you're awake at last!" Pariedes gasped as she shut the door and shifted her eyes between her lord and her charge very slowly and with some apparent thought. "I knew the Prime would quickly set you to rights. Are you roused enough to get dressed today? We can draw a bath or go downstairs to the springs. If you're up to it you can have a meal at table. Well"—Para fluttered her hands before tucking them under her apron to contain their nervous gestures—"you decide, of course. I must say you look very well."

Reule followed Pariedes's assessing gaze as she evaluated the compact and beautiful girl a dank attic had given birth to. Reule's eyes slid over Mystique's waist, hips, and legs, the soft curves he realized he knew very well even after so short a time. Once she began to eat well, he imagined she would fill out more in those places, transforming simple curves into delicious lushness that would make her even more of a temptation than she already was.

"We have chosen a name for me," she said with delight, eager to share with her first companion. "Mystique!"

"My, that is very lovely. And apropos. I approve," Para said with a firm nod.

"Reule chose it."

"Our Prime is a clever and surprising man," Para said with a lilting sort of smile that earned her a scowl from him as he tried to figure out what that was supposed to mean. "My Prime, I believe Amando was hoping you would return to the caravan as soon as you were able?"

Reule lifted a thick black brow at Pariedes. He was being summarily dismissed, and there was no doubt about it. The smothered giggle from the bed didn't please him and he tried to figure out who deserved his darkest look of warning more. They were both gazing at him so innocently and so completely expectant that he'd meekly accept the directive . . . that he did exactly that.

"Mystique, if you're well enough and would enjoy it, I'd like your company at my table for dinner. The entire Pack will dine together tonight because Amando is about to make his way along the final trade route of the season and we like to send him off with luck, a full belly, and memories of his companions waiting for his return. They would be honored by your attendance and would be pleased to see you looking so well. I will also understand if you feel it is too soon . . ."

"I would love to!" she said with a burst of excitement he felt sparkling all over his skin. "I feel just fine, and I wish very much to see my new home and to meet those who attend the leader who has rescued me so gallantly."

Reule didn't respond to being called her hero, afraid it might go to his head. Instead he gave her a partial bow, wanting to exit the room before Pariedes decided to eject him.

Chapter 5

Mystique watched him bow from his great height as he towered above her bed, and she felt her breath catch in her chest. She released it in a sudden sigh of approval as she let her eyes move from the top of his black-haired head to the shiny tips of his polished leather boots. The sound of her breath drew the sharp attention of hazel eyes that she suspected never missed a thing. He watched her steadily from beneath sooty lashes and waves of pitch-colored hair that had settled in a shaggy mane around his forehead and cheekbones, covering the entire back of his neck in differing gradations of length.

He gave her a half-smile, a flash of two or three white teeth that had a sort of wolfishness to it. It was his way of letting her know that everything she was thinking was open to exploration and, whether he took advantage of the opportunity or not, he was very aware of being the subject of her contemplation.

She dipped her chin and narrowed her eyes right back at him, the silent message of a woman who didn't care if he knew she was appraising him. She hadn't meant for it to be a secret anyway. She boldly carried on.

When it came to his overall stature, the Sánge male

before her was positively breathtaking. He was extremely broad in the shoulders and chest, thick with muscle from top to bottom, and his dark hair and changeable eyes were the perfect accent to pronounced, rugged features deeply tanned from a season spent working outdoors. She could as easily imagine him in the fields as she could envision him sitting in state. The versatility of the man was fascinating to her. He was a complete stranger, yet Mystique felt that every moment, every breath in his company was telling deeper stories about him. It was subtle, something she was learning without even knowing she was absorbing the lesson, but she was certain it was happening. She liked it. She liked knowing she was observant in such ways. It made her feel that she knew herself better.

She smiled slyly, a feeling of confidence surging through her as she watched him turn toward the door to take his leave. She knew she was being obvious, but she didn't care. She sat up straighter, tucking her legs beneath herself and tilting her head so she could watch him as he moved.

Sánge males wore snug pants in clinging, comfortable fabrics tucked into boots that reached just to their knees. On Reule, both boots and breeches were tailored tightly in universal black. His fit legs were sculpted by material that stretched and stretched to accommodate the thighs of an accomplished horseman, lean hips, a heavenly backside, and . . .

Well, Mystique had more than a fair idea of the rest. She had felt it, close and hot, when she had been sitting in his lap in the bath that first night. She'd also felt his firm, ridged belly and the hot, smooth skin of his sculpted chest, both of which were now hidden beneath a rather plain white linen shirt with sleeves that he'd rolled back over his forearms and a beautifully tooled leather vest that buttoned with handsome turquoise catches. The strong leather weapons belt and its wickedly prominent dagger rode diagonally across his hips, adding a dash of swagger to an otherwise simple fashion.

His long, thick fingers closed around the knob of the door to draw it open. As she watched, sureness and care radiated from every gesture he made. She remembered roughened calluses and a smooth, long caress along the bare line of her back. She knew little about herself, but she was positive she'd never felt anything as stimulating as this Sánge's touch against her skin.

Frustration sketched through her as she realized how much she was missing from herself. Fortunately, the longer she was conscious and the better she felt, the more she remembered about basic things. There were no memories of a personal nature, no recollections of people or places of origin, but she had strong impressions of a lot of little tidbits about herself. For instance, while she knew how to speak with the gentle mannerisms of a lady, she realized she also knew tricks to surviving in wild places. She knew, she'd realized, how to fight both physically in order to defend her body and verbally in order to defend her wit. Actually, it was really quite strange the things she remembered . . . or rather . . . *felt* she knew.

She was glad of it. This time when Reule left her presence, she wasn't so frightened and she didn't feel so alone. Initially, he'd been the very air she breathed, and when he'd walked away from her it'd been suffocating and terrible. *They must remain together*, the voice of the spirit within her cried even now. *Why?* She just felt it. And slowly, as different lights flicked on in her faulty brain, it was the one thing that became steadily more certain.

So when the door closed behind him, she had to take several moments in order to wrestle down the urgent sense of panic that overcame her. When she could breathe again, Mystique realized she could feel him still. She could even *smell* him. That blend of his woodsy soap, the musk of his vital body, and the earthy tang of leather. Sensing him beyond the door like that was the first hint she had of possessing heightened senses. She hadn't noticed it before, but something just told her . . .

She was oblivious to Para's chitchat as the attendant worked to prepare Mystique to face the impending meal with the Pack. Her focus was completely on the male just beyond her chamber.

He was simply standing against the door. She could even picture his hand still on the brass knob. Curious, she found herself straining to listen. The low, rhythmic whoosh that reached her made her heartbeat stutter, then join the pulse of his life perfectly. She heard his heart-beat suffer a mistimed interruption in its smooth cadence. She listened to the rush of his pulse, the rasp of his breath against his throat, so rough and sexy to her hungry ears. She shuddered as she remembered how the cascade of his breath against her neck had felt, her breasts growing taut with the sensual memory, her nipples tightening into expectant peaks as she . . .

"Mystique." He whispered her new name on a low, intense breath. "Never forget that I can read your mind, *kébé*," he said softly, his words the barest murmur.

Mystique gasped in a small breath. She'd forgotten. Confusion reigned a long moment and her heart pounded while she tried to recall what she'd been thinking about him all this time. It was a foolish thing to do because if he'd missed her thoughts the first time, reviewing them would certainly finish the job.

She heard him chuckle softly under his breath. She could picture his grin easily. She could picture everything about him easily. Mystique hastily swept that thought away before she ended up somewhere more personal than she was prepared to be at the moment. She was certain it was already too late, knew he'd probably seen her every covetous thought, and realized she really didn't mind.

She slipped out of bed, gathering the material of her sleeping gown because the skirt was too long for her height. She walked almost as if she were entranced until she came to a dressing table and a large mirror. She looked into her own eyes in the mirror, a smile lifting the corners of her lips. Her heart picked up in rhythm as she looked at herself, knowing very well that Reule still hadn't moved from the other side of the door. His breaths rose and fell with an increasing intensity. She tilted her chin down slightly, the slant casting sleek angles over her face, a couple of ringlets of hair brushing over her throat and chest. Mystique slowly lowered her eyes along her reflection. The thin fabric she wore was low against her bosom, damp from the sweat of dreams that lingered. She let her eyes fall to her own breasts, the dark pink of her nipples actually visible through the pale silk, as were the shadows and curves that made it abundantly clear she was a lush sort of female, for all her petite frame and underfed form.

She was paying very close attention to the sharpness of her senses. She wasn't disappointed. Reule's breath vacated his lungs with a hissing rush and she heard the clench of his fingers on the brass of the knob. She took in a slow breath and her sly smile grew in ratio to the heat and scent of a decidedly aroused male. She thrilled in the racing of his heart and luxuriated in the pheromonal changes oozing off his heated skin.

And they weren't even in the same room.

Mystique wished she was alone. She might have taken hold of the slim straps of the gown and . . .

"Enough!" he whispered sharply for her mind alone, the command ferocious enough to make her start. *"Lord and Lady, you fiendish little minx,"* he accused her hotly, *"you try my restraint on purpose!"*

"So you think I'm playing games, then?" she murmured through her thoughts. *"I'm not entirely sure I know how, or if I'm any good at them."*

"What do you call this, if not a game?" he demanded. *"You're making calculated moves toward an end goal, the very definition of a game. I don't think you'll expect what you will win if you continue to push me."*

The sudden sureness of her feminine power sang through her. *"What I expect, My Prime, is to draw you to me. What I know is that I like what happens to you when you think of me. And I enjoy my response to that. Don't think to frighten me with what I can expect from you."*

Leaning nearly all of his weight against the sturdy door, Reule shuddered in response. There were few things more stimulating than a confident woman who knew what she wanted. She was like a bolt of lightning out of a clear sky. Unexpected, shocking, and able to make him sizzle from head to toe in a single strike.

Damn. It was as if his little foundling had been conjured just for the torture of his senses. Senses that were reacting wildly to her. Reule glanced down the front of his body at the positive proof of his reaction, which was fiercely testing the seams wrought by his tailor.

This was wrong, he thought with an internal groan. It had to be wrong. His Packmates were the ones who loved to sniff around women, flirting and bedding whoever suited their ravenous appetites.

Not he. He was in control of his needs and his desires at all times. And yet, this painful state of body, this low, taunting pulse, seemed to fiercely whisper his need for the outlander woman. A woman who might not even know what she was getting herself into. A woman who had been in his existence for all of a few days!

Curses spewed through Reule's mind as he finally pushed away from the door. Once he was in motion, his stride began to eat up yards of wood, stone, and carpeted floors, the step of his boots striking out a tattoo he found satisfying to his temperament. He at last began to master his body as he distanced himself from the too-near temptation of a compact beauty with hair of deep, breathtaking crimson.

Darcio was sitting before the fireplace in the Pack's common room, located just outside the dining hall. He was in his favorite chair, relaxed into a slump with his booted ankles crossed and propped on the large ottoman in front of him. His slim fingers were threaded together and both hands rested palms down over his flat stomach. His eyes were closed beneath the spiky fall of his straw-gold hair, which gleamed and caught the colors of the flames.

Finally he opened an eye and, tilting his head so the fall of his hair shifted out of his line of sight, he narrowed eyes the color of a coming storm on his Pack-mate, who had moved soundlessly up beside him.

"Something I can do for you, Rye?"

"I'm worried about this girl."

Darcio smiled. He could always count on Rye to get straight to his point. In the position of Prime Blade, Rye was captain of the Jeth armies as well as heir to Reule's throne should he die without issue. Their Prime's family had been destroyed in the persecutions and the aftermath of the wanderings before they'd finally found a home in the Jeth Valley. With no blood heirs, Prime Reule had long ago selected Rye from his Pack to succeed him. It was a well-deserved honor. Rye was the second strongest 'pathic in the city of Jeth, as well as having a head for matters of state and the even temper Reule himself strove for, even if their Prime didn't always succeed at it.

"Why would a half-starved and wholly abused girl disturb you, Rye?"

"Because she's just too damn convenient," he muttered, throwing himself into a nearby chair when it looked as though he wasn't going to be able to stir Darcio from his relaxation. "And I'm not the only one who thinks so. Delano is—"

"Delano is Prime Assassin, it's his job to suspect everything that breathes of foul play."

"Well, I'd never discount his opinion," Rye said with a dark scowl lining his already dark features. Rye's sky-blue eyes fixed on Darcio. "Did you see how Reule reacted today when Para came running into the courtyard? Did you *feel* it?"

"Of course I did. I'm neither blind nor as 'pathically challenged as some think I am," Darcio scoffed.

"That isn't what I meant to imply and you know it," Rye snapped. He caught his own tone and exhaled his frustration with Darcio, running both hands through his mane of black hair as he leaned back in his chair. "Why are you being purposely obtuse?"

"Because I don't see anything to worry about. Yes, Reule reacted strongly. I would have, too, after the way Para came running up on us. Reule sees things that we don't, and that's a fact. He feels things that we don't. I wouldn't presume to question so simple an incident as him running off to help someone in trouble."

Rye snorted. "I hardly call a nightmare being in trouble."

Darcio studied Rye through lowered lashes. He knew Rye well, and he could safely assume that this wasn't necessarily the Blade's own opinion he was hearing. Rye wasn't the sort to be easily swayed, unless it was by Reule's desire. Or unless someone was trying to convince him that Reule was in danger. Delano and Saber, Assassin and Defender respectively, were the only ones capable of doing so.

"This is more than Delano's usual paranoia, isn't it?" Darcio guessed. "Saber must be in a twist as well to compel you to seek me out." The Prime Shadow tried not to smile at the flash of surprise and sheepishness that struck the heir's features. "So, one very small girl has an entire Pack of brutes shaking with fear and worry?"

"Darc!" Rye protested loudly, sitting up straight in his affront.

Darcio sat up as well, letting go of his teasing as he gave Rye a soothing smile. "There are some mysteries about this girl, it's true. And there is definitely something attaching our Prime to her that even he can't seem to figure out." Rye's brows shot up at that. "However, it's purely an emotional reaction. Reule is sensitive, despite his hard exterior, and we all know this."

"Not that we'd bring it up to his face too often," Rye joked.

"Not that we would. But even I have felt the sorrow and pain this female carries with her like a heavy cloak. Reule can't abide suffering. And I assure you, this woman has suffered."

"So you believe Reule is fixated on her out of compassion?"

"Fixated?" Darcio laughed. "He's spent time with her twice since she got here, and you call this a fixation?"

Rye hesitated. It wasn't like the heir to do that, so Darcio was extremely curious as he waited for him to gather his thoughts.

"You can't tell me you haven't noticed he's in heat for her," he said at last, opting for his usual bluntness.

Darcio had more than noticed. He'd experienced it pretty much firsthand when he'd relived the petite woman's body memory. The Shadow dismissed telling Rye about that, figuring it wasn't his place to share any information Reule had privately requested him to seek out.

"Rye," he said at last with a little sigh, "she's an outlander, not a criminal. I thought you above all would be more tolerant of that. You usually follow Reule's example in these things. If anyone has cause to be prejudiced against non-Sánge, it would be Reule. The persecution of this tribe could have scarred him in that way. Instead, it marked him the opposite. It made him despise intolerance and strive to set an example of acceptance. You'd best be careful around him if her outlander status is all that compels you to be suspicious of her. If you hadn't noticed, Reule has taken a bit of a shine to her."

"Oh, very funny," Rye said, not sounding at all amused. "You're telling me you aren't at all worried that our Prime is forming an attachment to an outlander woman whom we know nothing about?"

"We know more than you think," Darcio hinted cryptically, "and no, I'm not worried. Reule isn't the sort to lose his head or his heart easily. And even if he did, Rye, I'm not entirely certain it would be any of our business."

"Everything is Pack business," Rye contradicted.

"Oh? Does that mean I can demand details about that

pretty Janna you've been sniffing after all month?" Rye flushed a deep red at the mention of his rather serious flirtation with a young lady of the court. "After all, you are heir. If you're seeking to attach yourself to a woman who might one day be our Prima, perhaps we ought to be more involved in this."

"All right! Do you have to be such a cocky shit all the time?" Rye demanded. "You're right, as usual, and Delano, Saber, and I are assholes. Satisfied?"

"Immensely." Darcio chuckled. "But I'd never say you're entirely wrong, Rye. We all have cause to keep our attention on our Prime. Love and duty demand that we do. I just want you to measure your reaction. I think we're all on edge after this incident with the Jakals. We're all worried for Chayne . . ." Darcio trailed off and frowned as they both looked up to the ceiling above and to the left, to the place where they could feel agony, waking nightmare memories and the knowledge of impending horror.

"I stopped asking the apothecary if there was any change," Rye said gruffly. "Every report was worse than the last. Have you heard anything?"

"His fever is life-threatening. The infections are rampant. There are definite signs of putrefaction and nothing the physic can do about it."

"So you're saying it's hopeless," Rye snapped off. Darcio knew the anger wasn't directed at him, so he took no offense.

"The apothecary wants to amputate."

"His legs?" Rye was aghast.

"And his arms," Darcio added quietly.

"Lord and Lady damn me," Rye hissed. "Better to put a dagger in his heart! Better he hadn't survived at all! What man could live like that?" Rye was so upset that he surged out of his seat and began to pace furiously back and forth before the fire. "Chayne would rather die."

"So would we all," Darcio agreed gravely. "Chayne will refuse. If he can't, Reule will refuse on his behalf. The odds of his surviving so radical a surgery—"

"At the hands of that quack," Rye interjected.

"—are nonexistent to begin with," Darcio finished. "Better he die, intact, from the fever. The Pack can keep his pain to nearly nothing. Even so, it will be a long and terrible death, not the kind a Packmate deserves."

"Why is he awake now?" Rye asked, swallowing convulsively as he glanced back up at the ceiling.

"Reule is with him. I don't think even our Prime will be able to put him to sleep this time, though. The fever alters the mind so much, it's impossible to soothe and guide it. I think he's trying to talk Chayne into allowing drugs."

"He won't do it."

"He will," Darcio contradicted softly. Knowingly. "Even Chayne's principles fade under this kind of torture."

Reule's thoughts were heavy with Chayne's plight when he strode into the Pack dining hall a short time later. All but two chairs were filled with his subdued Packmates. Chayne's period of consciousness had taken its toll on all of them, each having to experience a part of their Packmate's agony even though they'd no doubt tried to block off their empathy with him. But to be Pack meant that there was always some connection when emotion and pain ran that high, just as it would be if they were actual blood brothers.

As Reule approached the table, he paused to lay a hand on the back of Chayne's chair. The Pack fell silent and they all bent their heads in a prayer for their suffering friend. After a moment, Reule continued on to his own seat at the head of the long table.

"It doesn't appear . . ."

Reule broke off when a sound near the entryway caught his attention. The Pack watched as he surged suddenly to his feet; then five sets of eyes tracked the path of his. The entire Pack stood when they saw Mystique standing in the doorway, the surge of movement and the sound of scraping chairs on marble flooring appearing to startle her slightly.

She deserved to be startled, Reule thought with a mental laugh of astonishment. Turnabout was only fair, because the sight of her was a shocking pleasure, for all that he'd been expecting it. She stole his very breath, his every thought, and he suspected his men were equally astounded.

Para had dressed her in silver.

Para was a blessed genius.

The gown was the height of the court's most recent fashion. A simple design: an empire waist gathered beneath her breasts, a neckline that scooped just shy of being indecent, and elbow-length sleeves edged in a fall of lace to match the brief train sweeping over the marble floor. She wore wristlet gloves, probably more to hide the damage to her hands than for fashion, and a lady's fan swung from her wrist.

But her hair . . .

Para had dressed the bloodred locks in a high twist, but had left a single thick coil to bleed down over her pale throat before springing to a stop against her corseted bosom. It revealed delicate ears and accented the frailty of her small neck. She wore a simple silver medallion around her neck, the chain thin and the charm itself no bigger than a thumbprint. Her silver crepe overdress and the cloth-of-silver gown beneath it glittered brilliantly around her body, offsetting her bold hair color as well as the sparkle of diamond drop eyes that were smiling at him.

Reule could smell the divine scent of her first thing, sweet and clean, smelling of vanilla flowers and that compelling fragrance that was purely hers. He felt his entire body react to it instantaneously. Every nerve awoke and drew to attention; every muscle pulled to tense readiness to anything she might need.

He stepped toward her, extending his hand palm up in welcome. She was smiling at him, but he felt her hesitation prickling along his skin as she let her prismatic eyes drift over the Packmates standing at respectful attention. Reule followed her gaze to his men and found them unabashedly gaping at her. She didn't realize that their stares and speechless lapse in manners was to be taken as a divine compliment.

"My lady Mystique," Reule said strongly as he stepped up to take her hand in his, gently drawing her into the room once her tiny palm had settled within his. "We are thrilled you could join us."

He brought her to the table in just a few steps and she bumped her body into his as she sought the protective shelter of his build. Reule looked down into sparkling irises as her smile trembled on pretty pink lips.

"Pariedes said this was what Sánge women wear," she whispered to him, touching her hand to her dress self-consciously as she peeked at the males staring at her once more. "I don't think it's what I'm used to wearing. Have I done something wrong?"

"No, *kébé*. You look beautiful. I believe my Pack is merely surprised to see how much you've changed since they last saw you," Reule explained, raising his voice to a firmness designed to snap their attention to him. "Gentlemen," he said, turning her toward them, "I introduce Mystique. Mystique, these are my Packmates. Amando, Prime Envoy," he began, going around the table from left to right. "Saber, Prime Defender. Delano, Prime Assassin. Rye, Prime Blade. Darcio, Prime Shadow."

Each inclined his head in turn as he was introduced, some murmuring her new name in greeting. Mystique looked at each carefully as she was introduced, trying to guess at what some of the titles they bore implied, attempting to match each one's duty with his stature and demeanor. In the end, it was the empty chair that drew her full attention.

"One of your friends is missing?" she asked Reule curiously, even as Amando shifted away from the chair he'd been seated in, in order to take the empty chair she spoke of just to his left. It left a place for her at Reule's left hand.

"Yes. Chayne is ill," Reule explained.

Mystique might still be new to this Sánge world, but she knew a ripple of emotional reaction when she felt one. It whipped strongly through every last man at the table. This led her to believe that Reule's simplistic explanation didn't quite reveal the truth of the matter. It wasn't her business, though, and she could tell a discussion would be painfully unwelcome. She wisely kept quiet as she was seated.

"We trust that you're feeling much better," Rye said as the men got comfortable once again. "You certainly look well."

"Thank you," she said. "I feel very much better. And I'm starving!"

The remark earned her warm masculine chuckles and she clasped her nervous hands together in her lap. How was it, she wondered, that she could so easily face Reule and his imposing ways, but suddenly she felt overwhelmed and out of balance around these other men? It didn't feel like a natural state for her. Somehow, she suspected that facing up to men had never been difficult for her. It must be something else putting her on edge.

As the servants entered the room with large trays piled high with hot food, Mystique took the opportunity to peek at Reule from beneath her lashes. The instant surge of excitement that rushed over her gave her goose bumps. She shivered deliciously. He was freshly bathed and dressed for dinner. She could smell it on him, that wonderful soap he used, the dampness still in his hair, and the crisp, clean scent of his clothes. Sitting just at his elbow, she was close enough to feel the heat his big body generated. He was by far the best-looking man at a table full of beautiful male specimens.

He sent her entire body into a fury of sensual activity. Her pulse soared, her temperature spiked, and her breath grew scarce. She wondered what he was thinking. Was he thinking about her? Was he angry with her for her earlier flirtations? Did he think she looked pretty? She hoped so. She liked the dress well enough; Para had gone through a lot of effort to see she had clothes that fit her properly, but she'd already decided that she hated this corset more than she hated not knowing her real name. Why on earth did Sánge women wear such ridiculous things? Para said it was to keep one's figure in shape, but when she had tried to point out that starvation had robbed her of any figure, Para had ignored her and stuffed her into thé silly contraption anyway.

However, as Mystique watched Reule's eyes drift her way quite a few times while they were being served, she quickly realized that the rigidity of her posture and the

resulting thrust of her breasts was actually far more
flattering than she'd realized. She sat up even straighter,
giggling inside when the movement instantly attracted
Reule's attention. Maybe, she relented, there was something to be said for corsets after all!

Feeling much better and far more confident all of a
sudden, Mystique turned on a brilliant smile and began
to chat with the others at the table. It only took her the
span of a single soup course to figure out who was suspicious of her and who wasn't. Saber and Delano were
reserved but polite, and they never looked away from
her once. Both sets of eyes studied her as though she
were a puzzle to be figured out. Darcio and Amando
were congenial and open, and bandied brilliant humor
about with ease. They took great pleasure in making her
laugh until she was little more than a fit of giggles
during the appetizer. Rye, she realized, was on the
fence. He wasn't sure what he thought of her, but at
least he was giving her the benefit of the doubt through
dinner so they could have pleasant conversation.

There was only one man's opinion that truly mattered
to her, in any event, she thought as she pushed at her
food with a fork and spent a few more minutes sneaking peeks at him. She sighed, trying to tell herself that
she really ought to be worrying about other things. She
ought to worry about who she was and where she was
from and what had happened to her.

But she wasn't.

No. What she felt, and she felt it soul deep, was that
she was right where she was supposed to be. Right
where she *needed* to be. So long as that didn't change,
she was content. Besides, forcing herself wouldn't be
likely to help her remember anyway. So she focused in
the present.

And a little to her right.

Mystique flushed when she found herself colliding with Reule's direct hazel eyes. There was something in the way he looked at her that set more than just her skin on fire. His eyes were full of hunger. Far too much hunger for a man nearing the end of his meal. She tried to steady her abruptly quickened breathing, but her heart was pounding so hard that she needed the added oxygen to keep from passing out in the snug corset. Mystique was a little outgunned at a table full of telepaths and empaths. She was afraid everyone knew what she was feeling and what she was thinking. Mostly, she couldn't care less. One of the pluses of living the life of a blank slate was that she had no obligation to perform for anyone's pleasure. As a guest in a foreign place, she supposed she ought to use care not to alienate those who sheltered her, but she'd already made a champion of the strongest voice in this Sánge keep.

However, these men were important to Reule because of their political positions alone. Only there was something else. They were closer than that to him. These were friends.

No. These were brothers, she realized. It was as though the same blood flowed in the veins of every man there. There was a harmony between them that buzzed just beyond her normal perceptions. A connection beyond position and duty. It was so powerful that she felt rather breathless all over again. This time when she looked at Reule, it was with the knowledge that he was the sort of man who had earned the complete loyalty and devotion of these other potent males. It was a heady realization and, without even thinking of curbing the impulse, Mystique reached out to cover his hand with her own, her small fingers slipping against his palm.

She saw his pupils expand suddenly with the contact,

felt the kinetic energy of his surprise and delighted in the smile touching gently at the corners of his lips.

Reule looked down at the small hand covering his own and let his bemusement come out in a smile. No one outside of the Pack would ever think to touch him, but she did it all the time. He had to remind himself that it was because she didn't know the finer points of Sánge etiquette, but he couldn't help thinking that it wouldn't matter to her anyway. There was something about her that said she did what she wanted without much concern what others thought.

Reule closed his fingers around hers in a gentle squeeze and felt her delight over the gesture. In fact, the entire table felt it, which was how intense an emotion it was. Reule felt the Pack react with startled silence for several beats before Amando, sitting to her left in Chayne's chair, leaned forward to grab another breadcake from the diminished pile.

"This trip will only be for two weeks because we're just going to Harth Outpost in the Pripan Desert, the last on our circuit before winter," he said to Mystique as if they'd been in mid-conversation about it. "Unfortunately, the Pripans haven't a clue about decent cooking. I sorely miss breadcakes when I'm traveling."

"Cook always packs his saddlebags full of the stuff and sets out a huge plate whenever she knows he will be at table." Rye snorted out a laugh. "He has her charmed, you know. Most of these"—he gestured to the food—"are *his* favorites."

"If he weren't charming, he wouldn't do me much good as an ambassador, now would he?" Reule said dryly.

"That's all well and good, but you will begin complaining yourself when he comes home for winter and we get served nothing but breadcakes for dinner each night."

"I sense a great amount of jealousy at this table,"

Amando rejoined, leaning back with an unconcerned air as he popped bits of breadcake into his mouth. "Mmm. Mmm."

Mystique spoke up. "Since this meal is a send-off in your honor, I think it only natural your favorites be served." Reule watched her lean closer to Amando, and a hasty, unruly instinct made him tighten his hold on her hand, reminding her that he was there. As if he were being . . .

Territorial.

Damn. Reule knew well enough what trouble territorial impulses amongst the Pack could be. Amongst Sánge males in general it was bad enough, but in the Pack it was a disaster waiting to occur. Reule forced himself to relax his grip and made very certain he made no emanations to Amando or any of the others. He did so by keeping his attention fully on Mystique, easily allowing himself to become lost in the delicate prettiness of her features and the sinful beckoning of her figure. He watched the movement of pale pink lips as she spoke, the flash of white, even teeth as she laughed at something Rye said. She bent her head to Amando as he murmured a confidence into her ear and Reule's vision was filled with the ivory line of her bared throat, his keen eyes automatically picking out her pulse as it fluttered quickly beneath her skin.

In that instant Reule's entire body lit up like a bonfire, the rush of heat sinking to the base of his spine and flooding low in his groin until he was hard and aching with want. He couldn't remember ever feeling so overwhelmed with arousal before that he would react without control in a public venue. Oh, he'd reacted in public before, but it'd been something he'd allowed himself or used purposely in flirtation with a woman. But never had it controlled him. He went to draw his hand away from Mystique, not wanting to alert her to his untoward desires, but she held him with strength that prevented a subtle removal. In that delaying moment, he remembered she wasn't 'pathic in any way, and it allowed him to relax his effort to withdraw. As long as he kept control and didn't emanate, she might remain ignorant of his boorish baseness.

"What does that mean?" he heard her ask, drawing him out of his fixation with his reactions to her.

"When we say 'pathic, it refers to any of the 'pathic powers. All Sánge are 'pathic. All Sánge are, to some degree, both empathic and telepathic. Some of the more powerful Sánge have a third 'pathic ability as well," Darcio explained. "Each member of the Pack has a third 'pathic power, for instance."

"I see. How do you filter through all of that information?" she asked. "How is it you keep from going mad? Forgive me, but this place is filled with people who are filled with thoughts and emotions . . ."

"There are two kinds of 'pathic abilities," Reule answered her. "Autopathic and interpathic. Empathy is autopathic. That means that for all of us, it's always switched on. The only control we have over it is to build walls within our own minds against the information it's trying to feed us. Not all empaths can do this. Jakals, for example, cannot block out the emotion they sense."

"Not that they would even want to," Delano said, his contempt coming out in a grunt of displeasure.

"We believe the Sánge can create walls because of our telepathic ability. Now, telepathic ability for us is interpathic. That means that, for the most part, we have to work at being able to use the ability. We don't automatically know everyone's thoughts. We have to consciously scan for them."

"Unless—" Darcio prompted needlessly.

"Unless," Reule agreed, "someone is intentionally projecting their thoughts or the thought is being 'screamed.' Meaning, being experienced so loudly within the mind that it can't be ignored by any telepath in a certain radius or with a personal connection to the projector. Also, telepathy is usually limited by proximity, though for some it is only possible with eye-to-eye contact. There are many gradations of 'pathic power amongst the Sánge."

"I understand," she said thoughtfully. "Thank you for that explanation. However, it's good to know one doesn't need to be 'pathic in any way to know how furious Delano is with you all at the moment for telling me such details."

She didn't even look at Delano as she said this. She simply reached for the spice shaker on the table and began to pepper her meat lightly, as if Delano's reaction didn't bother her in the least. And to Reule's delight, it *didn't* bother her in the least. He could easily feel her amusement at Delano's suspicious nature, and the shock the Assassin was now experiencing that she had not only noticed, but had boldly brought it out into the open. Reule had to admit, it was a pretty audacious thing to do considering the company she was keeping.

Reule pulled her hand up to his lips for a firm kiss just before he burst out in deep, rich laughter. Mystique almost dropped the spice shaker as the warmth and pressure of his mouth went through the sheer lace of her gloves. She could even feel his hot breath penetrating to her skin as he laughed against the back of her hand. Like steam under pressure, that heat burst up the entire length of her arm and instantly spread across her chest until her breasts tingled with reactive sensation.

"By the Lady, you have a sharp wit, Mystique," Reule

chuckled. "Delano is Assassin, you must remember. It's his duty to be suspicious of everyone and to seek out ulterior motives. I wouldn't mind him."

"Did I say I minded him?" she countered quickly. "It was an observation, not a complaint."

"So it was," Reule agreed, his hazel eyes aglow with his humor. Mystique felt a warm flush spreading over her face and arms as she realized his smile transformed his features from his usual seriousness to a striking vital male beauty that would make any woman glow with warmth.

"Would you please stop talking about me as if I weren't sitting right here?" Delano demanded petulantly, a disgruntled expression on his face.

Delano got his wish as he became the brunt of merciless male humor for the remainder of the meal. It reached a point where Mystique was wishing she'd kept her remarks to herself. She felt sorry for the beleaguered Assassin by the time she laid aside her dessert spoon, but she did give him credit for taking it all so good-naturedly. She worried that this would permanently spoil his opinion of her, though. She had no desire to alienate any of Reule's Pack.

Reule had given her back her hand some time ago, but he instantly felt the disturbance of her anxiety against his empathic senses, even though she tried hard to contain it. It was strange, but he only just then realized how muted her sorrow had become. She had, he noted, an incredible control over her emotional projection that he'd not really appreciated before. He'd credited himself, he realized, with blocking out or having grown used to the stimulus she projected, when in fact, he now comprehended that it was Mystique who had managed to tamp her feelings down into submission.

He was still mulling over this anomalous discovery as Amando stood to help her from her chair, drawing it back for her. As she rose, she stepped on the train of her dress, stumbling. As fast as everyone's reflexes were, even Amando could only grab her arm as she sat down hard in the chair he'd just vacated beside her. She laughed, a burst of self-deprecation that bubbled around the men until they were all grinning at her. She lifted her feet from the floor and rocked back slightly as she gave in to her mirth. By the time she was forced to stop for breath, they were all chuckling.

"I'm afraid I'm not used to women's finery such as this," she admitted, tugging on her skirts and lifting her hands helplessly as she looked at her gloves. Then she shrugged and pulled off the lace quickly, giving a sigh of relief as she exposed her injured fingers to the room. Reule felt the humor flood out of his Pack, as if a drain had swiftly been thrown open. They were all looking at her bruised and torn fingernails as she wriggled the fan off her wrist and laid the collection of feminine items on the table.

It wasn't until she was done that she realized the subdued attention she was getting from the serious faces all around her. She looked up, feeling surrounded by men, all of whom were looking at her hands. Reule felt the sharp clutch of tension birthing itself in her chest, and he moved to rescue her from his Pack's unintentional scrutiny. Amando was closer, however. The Envoy reached for her hand gently.

"We usually retire to the library after our meal," he said. "I'd be happy to lead the way."

"Oh. Thank you," she said, her breathless voice disturbing Reule deeply. He didn't like seeing her confidence shaken like that and, though they hadn't meant to, his men were responsible. Still, he could hardly blame them. They'd forgotten that three days ago she'd been little more than a filthy waif curled up in a terrified ball after clawing her way across the wilderness.

As she stood, Mystique reached to grasp the back of the chair to steady herself so she wouldn't stumble again. He was watching her carefully, hovering just beyond Amando's back, but he needn't have bothered.

There was no missing the psychic whiplash that shot through each and every Packmate.

It was like an electrical conduction, jumping from one to the other until all were held in the shock of it. The startling sensation was punctuated by the long, horrified gasp that was uttered by their female guest. Reule watched as she, then Amando, turned pale to the point of bloodlessness. He was already forcing himself into action by the time they both started to fall.

"To hell!" Reule spat as he caught Amando behind the shoulders, watching helplessly as Mystique fell back. Luckily, the chair was right behind her and, by the time her bottom struck the cushion, Saber had come around to steady her in place with a firm hand.

It was a mistake.

The entire Pack jolted when Saber came into contact with her, this time nausea flooding through them all. Reule saw Saber's mouth open in shock, speechless horror widening in his black eyes. Mystique's hands were now both clutched around the back of the chair so tightly that her knuckles were white and her healing nails began to split open afresh. By now, Reule had thrown up every mental block he could manage and guarded himself from the connectivity of the Pack. Although, because of the nature of their connection, it couldn't be done completely, he'd at least cut away the excess psychic information. He'd eased Amando to the floor and, stepping over him, he struck Saber's arm, knocking his hand out of contact with the source of his agony. The minute he did that, the Pack released a collective breath, each man reaching to brace himself when his suddenly weak knees and body wouldn't support him.

Rye was the first to pull himself together, and he watched as Reule reached out for Mystique.

"No! Don't touch her!"

Reule ignored the command, trusting his own power. He reached out and grasped her fey face between his large fingers, tilting her head back until she was looking blankly up at him. He felt emotion and pain crashing against his mental wards, but they held as he looked down into those glazed glass eyes.

"Mystique? *Kébé*, sweetheart, talk to me," he encouraged softly as the Pack regrouped around him. As each recovered himself, it added strength to Reule. He emanated warnings to them not to touch her or to interfere, so they concentrated instead on tending Saber and Amando and simply being there for him. He lowered himself slowly to a crouch, drawing her still glassy gaze along with him. "Tell me what's wrong." Then, after a moment's thought, "Tell me what you're feeling."

He would have used his power to probe her and find out for himself if it were only himself at risk, but it was apparent that the entire Pack would be threatened if he did that. True, they'd been taken totally by surprise and by now were very much on their guard, but he could hardly take the chance until he understood a little better what he was dealing with.

"So much—" She gasped, cutting herself off, but she'd spoken, and that was a start. She was also focusing slightly on him.

Just enough so he could see the agony in her eyes along with the welling of crystal tears. "So much what, *kébé*? Talk, baby, just talk," he encouraged her, his voice churning out roughly as her pain twisted his insides into tight knots.

"It's endless," she ground out between her teeth, closing her eyes as her entire body shuddered and sent tears spitting down her pale cheeks. "There will be nothing for me. How can you leave me like this? Will you even know? Reule . . ." Her eyes snapped open and Reule had to hold his breath to keep from cursing aloud, the way Darcio behind him was softly doing. Her eyes had changed color, becoming an even tan with the lightest speckling of black around the outside edges. Reule would have known those eyes anywhere, if they hadn't presently been on a woman.

"Chayne . . ."

He and Darcio spoke in tandem, confirming to one another what it was they thought they were seeing. Her gaze pinpointed on Reule when he spoke Chayne's name.

"Reule, don't make me cry for what I need," she said, her low voice registering even lower.

"Lord and Lady," Rye whispered in horror as he and the others understood at last what they were seeing.

"I won't beg to be a man," she rasped. "Don't make me beg for my Packmates to do right by me."

"Stop her!" Delano cried out, his hurt ricocheting through them. "Lord damn me, Reule, *stop her*!"

Reule swept his gaze away from Delano and fastened it on Mystique's position in the chair. Blood oozed from her fingertips as she dug nonexistent nails into the ornate wood of . . .

"It's Chayne's chair," he whispered, the fact registering on him like a shout in his face.

"She's telemetric!" Darcio exclaimed, following his Prime's thinking instantly.

Reule was inclined to agree. It was the only explanation that made sense. Coming into contact with an object Chayne had touched so often must have set the ability off and Mystique, who had no idea who she was or what she was capable of, had been left wide open to the psychic influx of Chayne's suffering. Telemetrics could make contact with the location and thoughts of another by touching the belongings of the target.

Reule stood up straight and glanced at Rye. "I'm going to pry off her hands. You have to pull the chair away. Until we're sure you can block her, try not to touch her. Not until she breaks the connection with Chayne. Ready?" Rye simply nodded and Reule reached out to work his fingers beneath her palms.

"Reule, you know what to do," she whispered in his ear. "Don't leave me this way. Don't let them butcher me. Don't . . ."

Reule overpowered her grasp and her hands came free with a pop. The minute her hands released, she crumpled against him and he scooped her up off the offending piece of furniture. She fell limply against his chest, reminding him of the first time he'd ever held her. She was conscious, though. She was mumbling something incoherently against his throat as he held her tightly and strode out to the common room with her. The Pack trailed after him, all recovered from the ordeal to one degree or another, only Amando needing Delano's hand for support.

"What—?"

"Hush!" Reule commanded, cutting Delano off. "We can question what she said later. Right now, we tend to her." Reule did, however, double-check on Chayne to see if he was conscious. Finding him deep in the latest induced sleep he himself had guided him to, Reule was content to concentrate on Mystique's well-being.

He hesitated on the threshold of the Pack's common room, sweeping his eyes over the furniture and suddenly seeing a minefield for her.

"Reule," Darcio said quietly, "place her by the fire in my seat. She was sitting in Chayne's chair a good minute or two before she placed her bare hands against it. I think if you keep her hands in her lap, she'll be all right."

Reule nodded in agreement. He made his way to the fire and settled her down, kneeling between her feet as he took hold of her wrists in a single hand and held them against her skirt in her lap. Blood smeared over the pretty fabric, as well as beading against his palm, but he ignored all of that and reached to touch her too-pale cheek.

"*Kébé*," he beckoned, turning up her eyes to his, relieved to see them back to their usual diamond beauty.

"What . . ." she said hoarsely, struggling to speak.

"Mystique, look at me," he urged her, trying to get her to focus.

"What . . ." she tried again, swaying forward slightly into his hand.

"She must have experienced everything Chayne has been feeling, as if she were Chayne himself," Rye noted. "It must have been like a raw psychic dump. She is overloaded."

"I can see that," Reule snapped. He was agitated enough without Rye pointing out the obvious. He should have suspected something like this could happen. He'd known something was off with her. The power of her sorrow, the way she seemed to intuit things so easily, and the control she used to guard her emotions were all reflexive abilities a 'pathic being developed.

Losing his temper made Mystique cringe and she jerked on her hands, trying to free them, but he held her tight. She then leaned forward until she could touch her cheek to his, to his surprise snuggling up against him as best she could in the awkward leaning position. He aided her effort instinctively by drawing closer to her.

"What," she whispered against his ear, "happened?"

"It's okay, sweetheart. You'll be okay in a little while. You just need a minute to adjust."

"No!" She gasped the word against his skin, the flutter of her lashes stroking his cheek. "What happened to *him*?"

Reule pulled back from her so he could see her face as understanding dawned on him. His chest tightened as he tried to decide what he should say to her. She'd been through enough of her own tortures; did she really need to relive those of another?

"Please," she begged him softly, her head turning until he felt the gentle press of soft lips against his palm, "please don't try to protect me. I must know."

For a moment, Reule's pulse roared in his ears in deafening crashes. Once again, it was as though she had read his thoughts, and now he could no longer dismiss the possibility she might be capable of it. He wasn't omnipotent. It stood to reason that somewhere in their world, there was someone more powerful than he. Was that someone sitting across from him right now?

It didn't matter at that particular moment. He couldn't make himself draw up caution against her. Not when she had been so clear a conduit for the pleas of an old and valued friend, and not when he was looking deep into her eyes while her kiss still burned into his palm.

"Jakals tortured him," he told her quickly. "His name is Chayne, and they took their pleasure in his pain."

"They fed from him," she breathed. "They fed from his fear that they would learn of you. He worried you were vulnerable as he'd been because . . ." She hesitated as she searched herself for the part Chayne had left stamped within her. "You insisted on hunting without Shadow."

"To hell," Darcio swore softly, knowing exactly what she was speaking of, even if she didn't precisely understand.

"They invaded his body," she whispered, "four times. Twisting and shattering and . . ." She began to gasp for breath as the memory overwhelmed her, spilling tears from her eyes.

"Enough, *kébé*, please . . . We know."

"No! I was . . . I was there. I . . . felt it. I felt it all. I was there." Reule felt her beginning to shake violently within the clasp of his hand.

"I thought telemetrics could only sense the present status of the person associated with the object?" Delano said, sounding highly agitated as he began to pace behind Reule's back. "She's talking as if she was there when it was all happening!"

"She was."

Reule's head snapped around to confront Darcio, his hazel eyes narrowing on his Shadow. "What?"

"She was. She was there. Right upstairs. Maybe she isn't talking about the telemetric episode, Reule. Maybe she's remembering the house. She was there. Upstairs. While it was happening."

"Yes," she breathed. "I was. I felt it. I felt the sharpness and the shattering. The twisting and the pleading. He wouldn't give up. Not ever would he give up."

"She was in contact with the house itself. Her hands on the floor. She didn't need to be in the room to know everything Chayne was feeling and suffering. It was like having a front-row seat for someone of her power. Lord damn me, no wonder she was out of her mind when we found her." *It also could explain how she knows so much about the Sánge*, Reule mused. She had probably absorbed it from Chayne, or even the Jakals. Even her feelings toward him. She might have absorbed Chayne's sense of loyalty and devotion to him and not even realized she was responding to it.

"Take me!" Mystique unexpectedly tried to surge to her feet, the abruptness of the movement nearly sending Reule onto his backside. Instead he stood up with her and absorbed the thrust of her small body as she tried to push her way out of his keeping. "Take me to him! Reule! I beg you to take me."

"To Chayne?"

"No. Absolutely not!" Delano barked. "Reule, I forbid it!"

The directive was met with absolute silence and stillness, even Mystique freezing in place as the Assassin's words made their impact. Rye was the first to move, and the step was well timed to intercept Reule, who swung around to face Delano with a snarl and a flash of fangs that made Mystique gasp and throw her hand up to her astonished mouth.

"My Prime!" Rye had thrown himself into the path of fury, but when Delano growled with a gleam of fangs as well, he found himself in the dead center of a challenge. "Wait! Both of you! My Prime, remember that Chayne is Delano's natural brother. He has a right to his emotions getting away from him. I don't think he meant to challenge you." He turned to Delano while keeping a hand against Reule's chest, even though the power of the muscles bunching beneath his palm told him his efforts only succeeded for as long as Reule allowed them to. "Delano, you know even you will never survive a Prime challenge, just as we all know that you didn't mean to issue it. Brother or no, as a Packmate, Chayne is Reule's responsibility until he has breathed his last. We all made that choice the day we took our oaths. You have no right to make demands on his behalf, but you know Reule will always listen to your wishes."

"Will he? Will he listen to my words when he has been bewitched by this . . . this . . ."

"Think carefully about what you say, Assassin," came the threatening hiss from behind Rye.

And Reule.

The entire Pack was snapped out of the tension between the two men when the small woman at Reule's back issued the threat to the Assassin as though she had never known an instant of fear in all of her life.

"Mystique?" Darcio lifted a brow at her and tried to repress a wave of delighted humor.

"Do you doubt me, Shadow?"

Darcio threw up his hands in submission when her eyes flashed furious platinum sparks of outrage. "Not in the least, good lady," he said quickly. "Frankly, I would be a fool to underestimate you at this point. But I think we all would like to know why you want to see Chayne. He suffers badly and is very proud. He wouldn't wish for strangers to see him so."

"No doubt," she agreed, pausing to take a calming breath. She turned to Délano. "And no doubt you have great cause to suffer hurt, as well as think me a grave danger. Especially after these past minutes. But I promise you . . ." She looked at Reule to include him in her statement. "I promise you both that you can take a blade to my throat the very instant I do him a harm. Although, by now, there is little anyone could do to harm him more than was already done. Reule," she coaxed, reaching out her hand, "take me to him. Please." Her eyes flicked to Delano. "Ready your blade, Assassin. Even your Prime cannot outmaneuver your speed."

"Let's go, then," Delano said grimly as he slid his dagger from its sheath.

Chapter 6

Reule was wary as they entered the parlor just outside of Chayne's private room. Mystique was right. Though he'd yet to figure out how she'd known, Delano was faster than he was. The Assassin was far lighter on his feet, for starters, and he'd achieved a mastery with the dagger that even Reule couldn't match. Regardless, he wouldn't let Delano come close enough to Mystique to put her throat or any other part of her in jeopardy. He knew his Prime Assassin far too well, and he knew that Delano would never let go of an opportunity to rid Reule's realm of a perceived threat. Since he'd seen Mystique as a threat even before this business with Chayne, Delano would risk his life and his Prime's wrath if he believed he was protecting Reule and Jeth in the long run.

Mystique was bold and fearless as she strode ahead of them and grasped the door handles to Chayne's private chamber. She hesitated, and he understood why. Any sensitive who approached that room would have. Beyond those doors was a maw of raw emotion and agony. Even in sleep Chayne fought, striving for some kind of survival. Or release. Reule couldn't forget the words she'd spoken on the Prime Tracker's behalf. He watched her push open the doors as he moved in behind her protectively, placing himself squarely between her and Delano.

The stench was the first thing to hit the entire gathering, making them all stop in shock. Mystique was the first to recover, however, pushing on into the room as the men struggled to overcome the innate dread they felt at seeing a friend suffer this kind of death.

The room was nearly pitch-black and Mystique paused to allow her eyes time to adjust. There was a single tallow candle sputtering on the nightstand beside the bed. The air in the room was stagnant and reeking of rotting flesh. Mystique realized immediately that it was a smell she was familiar with, to the point that it almost didn't bother her. She didn't question the understanding. She was already on automatic pilot and was allowing her body and instincts to do whatever they wanted to do. Apparently they both had a memory that had outlasted that of her conscious mind.

Next she focused on the bed and the man not within it, but sitting beside it. It was clear by the start he gave and the way he struggled to his feet that he'd been dozing. She knew what his purpose was instantly, just as she knew that sleeping wasn't a part of that purpose. A rush of fury injected itself into her when she thought of how the injured man in the bed was suffering day in and day out, yet this healthy creature couldn't find the strength and concern to watch over his patient with more attentiveness.

"Charlatan!" she spat out, pointing a nasty, accusatory finger at the apothecary. "How dare you call yourself Healer! Where are your herbs? Where is your common sense? I see no disinfectants, no sponges freshly made to soothe his fever. Or do you have magic that will heal this sufferer while you sleep beside him?"

She felt the stunned eyes of the Pack on her as she stormed to the nearest window and threw it open. Cold, fresh air swirled in, sweeping up the smell of gangrene.

"W-who . . . ? How dare you!" spluttered the apothecary. "The cold will kill him in his fever! My Prime! You bring another apothecary? You usurp me because I cannot help a hopeless situation?"

"Speak to *me*!" Mystique's command might have come from a small body, but it reverberated with astounding power around the rafters of the room. "Answer *my* charges and seek no solace from those you know are ignorant of the ways of medicine! Answer my questions, charlatan. Herbs? Sponges? Clean air? Lighting? Disinfectants?"

One of the Pack, she knew not which, hit a switch and light flooded the room, blinding everyone. Mystique recovered quickly and finally looked at the man in the bed.

"By the Lord and the Lady," she breathed.

"To hell," Delano gasped when he saw his brother.

Chayne was lying in sheets drenched with putrefaction, yellow and brown fluid-soaked bandages at all four points of injury. The mattress was ruined. Chayne was wet and flushed with fever, blessedly insensate from Reule's sleep command of earlier.

"It was always dark. The room was always dark," Reule heard himself saying, shocked to understand that Chayne's condition had been deteriorating right under his eyes all this time. Mystique also knew that even if he'd read the physic's thoughts, he'd have found no hint of deception because the apothecary no doubt believed he was doing what any medic would do. Dark sickrooms, closing in the ill, waiting out fevers or death, these were common practices in many cultures. But he could have done more, even in his ignorance. He could have changed dressings and bedding. He could have soothed the fever. Herbs might have fought off the putrefaction in its early stages.

"Dismiss him, Reule. He is useless to you," Mystique said bitterly. "I'm surprised he didn't insist on those barbaric vises in order to set the bones . . . as if that would help anything so shattered."

Reule faced the apothecary even as Mystique turned her back on them, no longer interested in the useless medic. By the time Reule's snarl curled back his lip to give the physic a glimpse of fang, his eyes were gleaming the green-yellow glass of threat. The apothecary didn't need to be told twice. He didn't even make any attempt at apology, protest, or even explanation. He still had a gauntlet of severely riled Packmates to run before he could consider himself safe, so he concentrated on that until he was out of the door.

"What do you need?"

The question was punctuated by the sound of a sheathing dagger. Mystique looked up at Delano and cocked a brow, but she didn't crow or gloat. She merely answered. "A fresh bed. Fresh sheets. Bandages. Gather dried herbs from the kitchen. I'll need desert spice, Jakal root, gloaming goat, white singer, and kettle greed. He will need a good hot broth when we are done changing this mess. I need disinfectants. Barley fluid and . . . what do you use for your soap base?"

"I can find out," Darcio promised as he headed out with Delano to split the tasks she'd set.

"Reule, Rye, you are the strongest here. I'll need you to lift him. Anyone who doesn't have the stomach for this should leave now. When we remove these bandages it'll be an unbearable stench."

"Eh, if I lose my dinner I'll have cook whip me up some more breadcakes," Amando quipped, giving her a grin that reflected the determination of the entire Pack.

"Moving him might wake him, Reule," she said, biting her lip apprehensively.

"Believe me, *kébé*, nothing will wake him."

"Good," she whispered. "Then let's clean him up."

In a half an hour Chayne's broken body was lying on a sheet in the middle of the floor of his private parlor while the men worked on switching a fresh mattress onto his bed. Reule and Delano stuck close to her side while she finished washing his broken body clean of every touch of infection. Both legs were rotted nearly to the bone already, the arms only slightly better. The clean bandages awaited, but Reule and Delano exchanged a look over her head.

"I don't know what she thinks she can do. We've both seen this before. There's no cure for such extensive rot."

Reule nodded shortly in agreement. *"But she can hardly do worse than an idiot willing to hack him apart or just let him die."*

"Can either of you dress a wound?" Mystique asked quietly, drawing their attention from the thought exchange.

"We've both field dressed wounds before," Reule informed her.

"Very well. But this will be more complex. Listen carefully. Crush the desert spice and Jakal root in the mortar and pestle until it makes a paste. It will smell nasty and be yellow, but that is normal. Cut up the gloaming goat, white singer, and kettle greed into very thin slices no bigger than a coin, and drop them in the broth you will feed to him when we're done. It isn't important he eat the herbs, only that they are in the broth he does eat. The heated liquid will absorb the medicinals. Once I've done what I can, drench each wound on both sides with the barley fluid, spread the salve on afterward, again on both sides, and then dress the bandages snug but not too tight."

"I don't understand . . ."

"Shh." She hushed Reule before he could ask something she wasn't sure she had the answer to. Nor did she think he'd like the answer even if she did have it. There was something inside her, in her mind and in her body, that was guiding her to something she knew was critical to the survival of this man. He was too important to Reule and his Pack for her to listen to anything that would discourage her or make her think it was acceptable to be afraid.

Her last instructions given, she knew there was nothing left to do but give herself over to intuition. Her heart was pounding out a terrible rhythm, and she hoped Reule wouldn't take note of her fear until afterward. She took a deep breath and laid a hand on Chayne's pale, sweating face. She looked down on him for a moment, then closed her eyes and pictured his face in her mind. They'd been closed, but she knew his eyes were a pretty light tan with little specks of black around the edges. She saw them and the startling contrast that they made to his rich chestnut-colored hair. His complexion, she realized, was supposed to be tan. The paleness of his fever was a death pallor. This Sánge Packmate was on the cusp of death.

"Not if I have any say about it, Sánge," she whispered over him.

She slid her hand down his throat and on to his breastbone. She pictured his shoulders, the mangled arms connected to them, and the breadth of his chest with all its whorls of curls resisting the draw of her fingers.

"Shh," she exhaled softly, cutting off the building protest crawling up Reule's larynx as his glittering eyes watched her small hand trail almost sensuously over the body of another male. It was an insane and ridiculous impulse to feel threatened by an unconscious male, especially over the touch of a woman he had no claim on whatsoever! But the logic failed to settle the territorial raising of his hackles as her fingertips ran down the center of Chayne's bare belly.

"What's she doing?" Delano asked in confusion.

"I don't know!" Reule thought back in a growl of intensity.

One hand became two and Reule had to grit his teeth to keep from growling aloud this time as he watched her stroke her fingertips across to Chayne's hips and begin moving down his legs. She didn't stop until she reached his knees. Then she grasped his shins just beneath those joints and just above the terrible damage done by spikes and neglect. The smell was still overpowering in spite of the cleanup job she'd done, and Reule wondered how she could bear being so close to it for so long. She was a surprising woman, his *kébé* was. He could hardly look at her without feeling a sense of wonder.

He still didn't understand what she was trying to accomplish. She wasn't even watching what she was doing. Reule relaxed though, feeling better now that she'd settled her hands in a safe, nonsexual place. He sought briefly for Chayne, making sure he was still well asleep.

He only looked back at Mystique when Delano suddenly reached out to grab him by his biceps and shook him hard. He followed his Assassin's speechless gesture to the small hands of his *kébé*.

There, right before their astounded eyes, Chayne's

rotting sinew slowly changed from putrid black, brown, and green to the fresh colors of pink, healthy flesh. Reule looked up at the small, pale face of the stranger he'd brought into his city, into his home, and wondered what star had shined on him that he should find such an extraordinary gift in so incongruous a place as a rotting attic.

"Lord and Lady," Delano whispered, unable to help himself.

Reule didn't even look at his Packmate. He could feel Delano's astounding gratitude. This toward a female Chayne's brother had wanted to kill under an hour ago. Instead, Reule remained focused purely on Mystique's face. There was one rule every 'pathically inclined being knew as well as they knew their names: When it came to the use of great psychic power, there was always a great price to be paid. For himself, it wasn't so much the telepathy and empathy that demanded a price. Those were actually very natural, only as taxing as running in short bursts might be. Eventually it would wear him down if he didn't rest, but it'd take the equivalent of miles and miles of telepathy before he reached that point.

His emanation power was another story entirely. It taxed him twice, sometimes thrice as quickly as his other abilities and took as much energy not to use as it did to use. It burned his candle at both ends, so to speak, and anything outside of the normal daily use he was accustomed to became an exercise in fortitude.

After the unexpected telemetric episode that had taken her over, Mystique was already worn. It was still too soon after her ordeal in the wilderness for this healing to be safe, but he couldn't call a halt to what was likely the only way to save Chayne's life.

"A true naturopathic ability," Delano telepathed in

awe. *"Reule, there hasn't been a naturopath in this tribe since before your parents were born. Where in hell did she come from? This is no Sánge woman."*

"No. She has no telepathic ability and no real empathy outside of the usual sensitivity. All Sánge have both. No, she is something else . . . something I've never known in my experience nor heard of in our history."

Then again, their history had been lost in war. All he had of it was what little remained of their tribal library and the oral stories his parents had handed down to him before their deaths. This was the experience of his Packmates as well.

Reule heard a soft squeak and he quickly looked back at Mystique. Had she grown paler in the past few minutes? He took in the lines of white suddenly etched into the corners of her mouth. It was pain. She was in pain.

"Kébé . . ." He spoke gently, not wishing to startle her. When she didn't respond, he carefully reached out to take hold of her shoulder. Before he touched her, though, he made very certain he'd blocked himself from all of her psychic feedback. The last thing the Pack needed was to be caught up again in the backlash of her unexpected power. He grasped her, shook her minutely. To his astonishment, she violently threw him off and shifted her hands up to Chayne's shoulders without ever once opening her eyes.

It was when she leaned forward that he saw the stain spreading through her skirt. The silver had darkened with saturation from a fluid he couldn't identify. He could only assume Chayne had shed body fluids onto her. He glanced down at the wounds on the Prime Tracker, which were still open and raw, but completely free of any sign of decay. And, unless he was hallucinating, the pulverized bones that had left his legs bent and deformed were now lying straight as if they weren't broken at all.

Reule looked up from the floor when he sensed the rest of his Packmates coming to stand over the unbelievable tableau. It was a picture of hope, of a future for a fallen comrade they'd all but given up on. Her telemetric ability had proven that Chayne had given up on himself as well. They stood and blinked back emotion as the diminutive outlander woman handed them a miracle.

For Mystique, the next few minutes were little more than a haze of red swirling around in her brain. It swept into her nose every time she breathed in, turning her brain redder and redder. Her body had long since gone numb and disappeared. All there was now was Chayne's body. It had been through five days of utter hell, but other than that it was a good body, a strong one fortified with healthy muscle and unbelievable determination.

He'd fought her at first, demanding release and comfort instead of help. She'd spent precious time and energy explaining something to him she barely understood herself. He made her swear he wouldn't be left half a man. She had sworn. Now he called her an angel, sent by the Lord and Lady, and at last lent his spirit to his own healing instead of fighting her.

"Angel?"

"Yes, Chayne?"

"Who sent you?"

"Your Prime sent me. He loves you very much. He refused to fail you."

"Angel, what did I do to deserve this miracle?"

"You survived, Chayne, when others wouldn't have."

"Reule would have survived."

"Yes. He is extraordinary, your Prime."

"You have feelings for him. How does a man earn the fondness of an angel?"

"Hush, Chayne. Focus on your healing. Your loved ones anxiously await your recovery."

Mystique concentrated on the connection of her hands to his skin. She'd learned while healing his legs that it was best to envision a pair of tubes, one in the seat of each palm, and each was used to draw the putrescence and fever into herself and away from the raw wounds. She took it all, as best she could, drawing it off and away. She knew it worked by instinct alone, and knew when she couldn't push herself an inch further before she had to switch tasks. Mending came next. His bones were ground to splintered shards, and she was amazed none had found a way into his blood system to shoot like a knife into his heart or brain. He'd been luckier than he might ever know. She shook her head as the redness within began to burn, as though she was looking too long at the brightness of the sun. Her face, arms, and legs were burning. But she'd sworn to Chayne he'd be whole again, and she'd at least see him mended to a point that he could carry on for himself. Nothing would be perfect. His bones wouldn't be fully healed and his wounds wouldn't be closed, but she'd leave his skeleton positioned for healing and she'd instructed Reule and Delano on dressing the wounds. It would be enough until she could find the strength to return to him.

As for right now, her strength was . . .

Gone.

Reule had already gotten up and moved to the opposite side of Chayne, so he was on his knees braced behind

Mystique with his hands hovering close in case she should need him. This time he opened himself to her in increments and very carefully tried to feel his way into the strange confusion of her thoughts. It was as though she'd put herself into a dream state, and to his frustration all he could see and feel of her was a bright red haze of interference.

"Reule!"

Reule jerked free of his search in order to attend the alert of his Prime Blade. He glanced at Rye and then followed his eyes down to Mystique. Reule watched for a moment of incomprehension as that sickly fluid began to drip onto the floor near his knee. Puzzled, he traced it back to the sleeve of her dress. To her elbow. To her forearm. She began to sway just as he realized the fluid was being generated by *her* body, not Chayne's. In fact, right before his eyes, he saw two wounds spiral open in her flesh, spitting out more of the evil sickness until they were weeping freely. Understanding struck him like lightning, and he grabbed her seconds before she fell back.

All he could take in at that moment was the image of her saturated skirt. He cradled her limp body in a single arm and grabbed her skirts, jerking them back until he could see the horror of his suspicions realized on her shins. Two ugly sores almost as wide and as long as the bones themselves had appeared. These oozed as well, and Reule felt a moment of horror unlike anything he'd known since the moment he'd discovered the bodies of his beloved parents.

She'd been kneeling all this time, his mind cried out. She'd made that sound of pain, he'd heard it, and so she felt every single moment spent kneeling on the terrible wounds. She'd done it so she could move on and take even more pain into herself. Now she was like a lifeless doll in his arms, her breath rasping in and out heavily and her skin pale and clammy. Her beautifully dressed hair was a touch of perfection on a body now riddled with sickness.

Reule gathered her close, lending her his warmth just as he'd done when they'd first met. Why had he allowed this? Would she die now, having taken the poison of Chayne's body into her own? Had he sat by and willingly allowed her to trade the value of her life away . . . because he'd valued the life of another above her?

"By the Lady, I pray not," he whispered against her wan cheek.

"My Prime," Amando said very quietly, reaching to lay a hand of support carefully on Reule's shoulder. "Don't despair. If she is a naturopath, she will heal very quickly. She needs only to rest. My grandmother was one of the last naturopaths in Sánge history. I grew up on stories about her ability. They heal, but their bodies and minds have a safety valve that shuts them down if they try to do too much. Naturopaths cannot hurt themselves healing. It would be a contradiction in nature's intentions."

"You call this not hurting?" Reule hissed, indicating her punctured arms and legs and the filth of poison they were shedding.

"It's called mimicking, Reule," Amando said carefully. "The healer's body mimics the patient's wounds to provide an exit point or points through which all the absorbed toxins are released. It's a good thing. If it didn't happen, the toxins would stay inside her and kill her."

"Enough!" Reule surged to his feet, his small burden cradled in his arms. "I'm taking her to my bath. The rest of you can see to Chayne."

"Shall I send Para to you?" Rye asked as Reule strode

toward the exit. His Prime stopped and shot a glare over his shoulder.

"What in hell for?" he demanded.

"Oh . . . uh . . . nothing. My mistake," Rye said quickly, holding up his palms submissively.

Reule grunted and stormed out of the door.

Chapter 7

His life seemed to be repeating itself a lot lately.

That was Reule's main thought as he laid Mystique out on the bench beside his steaming bath. At least, he tried to make it his main thought. If he allowed himself to think for any amount of time on the harsh realities of the moment, he was afraid his temper might get the best of him. That would do him little good because there was nowhere to direct his anger. So, unless he wanted to storm about ranting and raving at the walls and an unconscious woman, he was best served to keep himself preoccupied.

Reule sighed heftily, running a hand through his hair before perching on the edge of the bench beside her, his hip in contact with hers through layers of soiled skirts. He reached to touch Mystique's face, an impulse he was beginning to realize came upon him with great frequency. He couldn't curb it, though. Her skin had healed to a softness that seemed to beckon his touch. He was lost to any semblance of control. He let his fingertips slide over the rise of her cheek, feeling the warmth of her skin and the brush of her long lashes against his nails as he moved past them.

"I knew there was something," he said to her closed eyes and deceptively peaceful expression. "I felt it in my soul that there was something more to you than what we were seeing on the surface." Reule shook his head, his disbelief easily shed now that he had proof to the contrary. Telemetric and naturopathic. Two rare and powerful talents, and she bore them both.

Reule harshly shrugged off his awe. He had more important issues to deal with. He could marvel over these latest developments later. He reached for the ruined dress and began to work it off her limp body.

Mystique began to stir the moment her bare skin touched the water. He didn't use soap to cleanse her this time, letting the water itself do all of the work. He couldn't bear the idea of stinging her or harming her by doing the wrong thing. Not that he was certain he was doing the right thing.

Her first soft moan was quickly followed by a second, and then her arm came up to snake around his neck. She found her familiar niche for her face against his neck and he settled onto the step with a sigh. *Every time.* Always, the moment she settled against him like that, he felt the same sense of . . . he couldn't even put a name to it. All he knew was that it felt good. Damn good.

"Mystique," he murmured against her forehead. He drew her closer, until her soft breasts snuggled against his chest and her back was covered by his palms.

"Reule," she said, his name rolling out of her like a contented purr as she hugged him tightly.

"By the Lady, *kébé*, you test my sanity," he swore softly, pressing a grateful kiss between her brows. He reached up for the arm around his neck and pulled it down so he could see her forearm. He let it drift through the water, washing away debris from her newest wounds.

Mystique winced with her entire body, sucking in a sharp little breath.

"*Kébé*, look at me," he said firmly, encouraging her by tone of voice to obey. She did, her lashes fluttering upward instantly. Even her eyes were pale and luster-less, he recognized. "What can I do for you, sweetheart? Tell me how to help."

She gazed up at him for a long minute, leaving him with nothing to do but count her breaths while she for-mulated her response.

"Will you kiss me?"

Reule blinked, positive he was hearing her wrong or he'd slipped off into a daydream for a moment. How-ever, when she reflexively licked her delicate pink lips, wetting them in preparation or expectation, he knew he'd heard her perfectly well. He also knew he wanted to oblige her with every bit of his soul.

"Mystique, I meant to ease your pain," he hedged even as his gaze fell on her mouth and fixed on the tiny curves and details of her gleaming lips. From the sharp little dip at the apex of her upper lip to the way they pouted out sweetly at his poorly concealed dodge.

It was a protective instinct that made him hesitate. He was afraid he wanted her too much for his own peace of mind. She was already starting to remember things. Whether by accident, instinct, or actual memory, it was clear her mind was recovering itself. She'd had a life before coming to his province. For all either of them knew, she was mated. Or . . . by the Lady, she could be a mother.

The very idea of her belonging to another man, of having some faceless, nameless male's children, sent a haze of black outrage over his mind like the casting of a net over water. His entire being rebelled at the thought of her belonging to another. Why? Lord and Lady help him, he barely knew anything of her. Why was this happening to him? Why did he feel so strongly about this, as though his entire world would come crashing down around him if she was taken from his grasp?

Reule's hand tightened reflexively against her, as if someone were already trying to pry her away from him.

"Reule, don't make me beg you for this."

The request froze his breath in his lungs. He stared down at her soft eyes as he tried to make himself breathe. "I'm not trying to make you beg," he choked out after a moment. "I'd never demean you like that. I just don't think—"

"You don't wish to kiss me?"

"To hell! *Kébé*, that's not the issue!"

"Is it because you're Sánge?"

"Among other things, yes. That's as good a reason as any," he said sharply. He shifted his hold on her so he could dip her opposite arm in the hot waters of the bath. He used the activity as a reason to pull his eyes from hers. She was so bold, so straightforward. He never felt compelled to read her 'pathically when they were face-to-face. It was admirable. Something he took too much pleasure in.

"You seem to disapprove of your Sánge heritage," she observed quietly.

"I don't disapprove of my heritage," he barked, his attention snapping back to her inquisitive eyes. "I'm very proud to be Sánge. I would never defile my parents' memory by being ungrateful for the life and culture they birthed me into. I'm content with who I am and I'm extraordinarily proud of my tribe."

Mystique shifted so she was sitting up on the seat of his thighs, her nose coming level with his as she looked deeply into him. So deep that he felt as though *he* were the one completely naked, rather than she. He felt the warm cascade of her breath against his mouth, flowing over his face and jaw. There was an intimacy to it that made him long to give in to her request. Lord knew he'd wanted her mouth beneath his almost from the very start.

"Then why?" she asked. "Why does being Sánge make a difference? Or why do *you* think it makes a difference?" she corrected herself after a moment.

"Because there is hardly a race on this world that doesn't despise the Sánge, *kébé*. And you may very well belong to one of them."

"I make my own choices," she said, dismissing her unknown people with a shrug of one shoulder.

"You have no idea what your choices are," he growled at her in reserved fury. "You don't know who you are. *What* you are. Who are you wed to? Who are you mother to, *kébé*? Lord and Lady, Mystique, don't you wonder who is missing you? It has to be somebody. A beautiful, powerful, and intriguing woman like you doesn't go ignored, unnoticed, or unloved!"

"Well, you certainly are doing a fine job of it!" she bit back.

"Mystique," he warned gruffly.

"Let me ask you something, My Prime," she hissed, the sibilant spear of her words scouring his mouth as she nudged up to within a half inch of his lips. "When you picture my former life, the one you're so adamant about preserving me for, what part of it do you find so worthy of my return? Would that be the people who allowed me to fall into danger in the first place? Would you entrust my safety to them again?" She lowered her lashes, casting a slumberous sensuality across her features as she slid her arms around his neck. "Perhaps I made love with a man who beat me and left me for dead? If he is my mate—"

"Enough!"

The roar radiated from every inch of his body. Mystique could feel it building at first in a fine tremor, then exploding into a shudder of pent-up wrath that was released with the command. The psychic emanation of his fury struck her like a physical blow, making her gasp and jerk back in his hold. His hands tightened automatically to stop her from moving any farther away from him than he desired.

She'd pushed him purposely, setting off his strong sense of honor to get her way. It was selfish, she knew, but she needed him. She always needed him. How could he be so powerful a 'pathic force and yet be so ignorant of the craving within her that demanded him over and over?

Now, exhausted as she was, she had no control over the urges and the impulses that pleaded and cried for him. The ache of her need was so much more intense than the wounds on her arms and legs. So, when he'd asked if he could provide relief for her in some way, she'd answered him honestly. And relief was only the first rushing emotion she felt when he dragged her beneath his mouth at last.

His anger at the images she'd stirred within his mind had stolen any possibility of tenderness. The command of his lips said he knew he'd been played, and he wasn't happy about it. It didn't matter. All that mattered was the press of his strength and heat against her lips, the push of his tongue past her teeth so he could steal her taste while leaving his behind. That wet touch of flavor set dynamite off in her body, wreaking havoc everywhere until she groaned her delight and her eyes teared with relief. Both of his hands came up to trap her head, his fingers fanning over her cheeks and his thumbs framing her jaw. When her tears came, they dribbled over his fingers.

The evidence of her intensity of emotion collapsed Reule's anger in on itself. He softened his kiss as he ended it and withdrew from her mouth just far enough to look down into her eyes. She lifted her lashes as though she knew exactly what he wanted from her, letting him see the need in her soul. There wasn't even a hint of doubt. It was as though she believed she had been born to be with him.

This time when Reule took up her mouth, there was nothing but raw desire between them. Everything was banished except the lust that sprang open within him the instant he permitted it, and the force of it was heady and rich. Her taste flooded his tongue, a sweetness without compare, a confection he devoured. His tongue dipped deeper and deeper, and he groaned as she first accepted his aggression and then, grasping thick fistfuls of his hair in her hands, she dragged his head to the side and returned a fever of her own. A fever that caught his body like a spark in the dry flatlands, a vortex of fire that roared furiously through him and consumed everything in its path.

Mystique broke away from his mouth and threw back her head, gasping for breath as she guided him to the length of her throat. He obliged her easily and without thought, his lips stroking skin that tasted of sweetness and spice. He felt the excited vibration of her breathing in her throat and became aware of the wild cadence of her pulse beneath his tongue. He reached up to cup the back of her head, tilting her favorably. His fingers disturbed her styled hair, releasing a cascade of bloodred curls. He felt them all around his face, neck, and hands, their perfume intoxicating as she shifted her body impatiently against him. Reule tongued the pulse at the base of her neck, near the elegant crest of her shoulder. She gasped and shuddered when his hand plunged beneath the water to possess the small of her back and drag her up tighter against him.

There was no controlling the sudden stretching appearance of his fangs. Just as there was no hope, nor any desire, of controlling the violent hardening of his sex. With this woman, the two reactions were instantly part of one another. Sex and savagery. The need to claim both body and blood. This wasn't always a Sánge norm, despite what outsiders thought. Oh, the need for a lover's blood was real enough, but that usually didn't come into play until just before climax. What Mystique did to him was a breathtaking anomaly.

"You destroy my calm, shred my command of myself," he accused her roughly, groaning from his own depths when her small hands slid from his hair and over the too-hot skin along his shoulders and arms. Did she know what she risked? Did she understand what would happen if this was pushed to the limit? Reule pressed his lips tightly together against her skin, hiding the sharp edges of his teeth before she could feel them. He closed his eyes as he tried to steady the tilting careen of his senses. "You make me forget that you're injured," he rasped, hoping she didn't notice the way a mouth full of fang altered his speech. He needed time. Time to explain, to help her understand and adjust. To learn if she truly understood what it was she was demanding. And there was truth in what he'd said. He wouldn't allow her to tough out pain and injury for the sake of passion with him.

She had suffered too much already, and he wouldn't be one who added to that pile of abuse.

"*Kébé*," he whispered warmly against her skin as he kept his telltale teeth buried against her neck and hair, "take your hands away from me, sweetheart. Your touch drives me to distraction."

She smiled. He could feel it even though he couldn't see it. "You're being noble again. You frustrate me, for all I admire your principles, My Prime," she murmured in a sexy tease against his ear. But she let her hands fall away into the water without any argument.

Reule finally lifted his head when she let hers drop back and she allowed her body to bend back over his hand and into the water, where she let herself float on the surface, eyes closed and a very smug grin teasing her gorgeous lips. She was pleased with herself for breaking his resolve and getting her way, the little vixen. But he let her enjoy her simple victory. It was a battle he wouldn't mind losing, provided . . .

He'd never been faced with this situation before. He wondered if any Sánge ever had. The one good thing about having a reputation was everyone already knew about the Sánge "depravities." Since this isolated them from outsiders, what were the odds of having to explain the needs of sexual culmination to a partner?

But Mystique had no preparation, no rumors, and no prejudices. Though he couldn't decide if she had more information than he suspected, he knew he could make no assumptions. It would be wrong to let her face the intensity of Sánge lovemaking without making very certain there was a clear understanding of the details between them.

Reule watched her as she arched her back and swung her hair through the water, her beautiful breasts thrusting up in exaggeration, the tempting tips drawn into taut crests that had him curling his free hand into a brutal fist as he tried to maintain control of himself. By the Lord, he wanted to taste her there, to suck her between the fangs pricking at the inside of his lips, pulling her nipple against his craving tongue.

"To hell," he breathed, turning his head aside and closing his eyes as he tried to control his fevered blood and breathing. It certainly didn't help that her swaying body caused her bottom to wriggle against his already raging erection. Reule had half a mind to read the little tease's thoughts to see if she was doing it on purpose. She was too sophisticated about her sexuality not to know better.

"Reule? How is Chayne?"

The question snapped his head around and he looked at her with a numb sense of surprise. He hadn't thought of Chayne once since he'd walked in the door. It wasn't like him to ignore his sense of an injured Packmate. He absently reached out and swept her straggling hair off of her forehead, his fingers threading into the floating sea of red.

"I think you saved his life, *kébé*. No. I *know* you saved his life." He cupped the back of her head and drew her torso up out of the water, holding her against himself once again as he gazed into her eyes. "For that, I will be forever grateful to you. My Packmates are pieces of me. Pieces of my spirit, if you will. I've never lost one, but I expected to lose Chayne. I even expected to hurry him on his way. When you channeled him, you felt what it feels like to be Pack. When you saved him, you spared the Pack a pain beyond outside understanding. Even Sánge don't always understand what it feels like to be Pack."

"I know what it feels like to be Chayne," she corrected him, giving a delicate shudder.

"Chayne at his most desperate, *kébé*," he reminded her, touching his lips to her cheek.

"I know. Trust that." She slid forward and rested her cheek against his shoulder. He felt the reflexive twinge of sympathy radiating out of her as she recalled the experience of unexpectedly becoming Chayne's voice. "Why did you ignore him, Reule? He will want to know that."

Reule stiffened even though he heard no accusation in her voice. "I'm not sure I understand your question, Mystique," he hedged warily.

"He understands why you all couldn't enter the room once the decay began. You trusted the apothecary to care for him and you couldn't bear to watch him suffer. But you were the one in his mind, Reule. You were the one he was asking for release. He knew Delano wouldn't be able to do it, but he believed you wouldn't refuse him. How did it go so far without your intervention?"

The uncanny understanding in her observations told him that she wasn't speaking from a half-realized concept. For those few minutes in the dining hall, she'd known Chayne's heart, and certainly his mind. But in all fairness, it was the first time Chayne's wishes for euthanasia had been clearly voiced. Up until that moment, all any of them had known was what instinct told them he'd want. Instinct and ages of friendship. But it was true that it would have come down to Reule in the end. As a Packmate, Chayne's life was Reule's to give or take as he saw fit. It was part of the oath all of his Pack had taken when each had committed himself wholly to their Packleader.

"In truth, I have no answer to that. Certainly no excuses. It is difficult to know the mind of a suffering man, *kébé*.

You aren't a telepath or empath, so you don't understand how hard it is to filter out what's truly desired from what the mind cries when it's being tortured by things like pain and fever. In time I'd have come to understand Chayne's needs. In a very short amount of time," he added. "I knew it was coming time to make a stand for him. Chayne will know that as well. I wouldn't have let him down. But neither would I have let him go too soon if there was the slightest hope in his favor. As it turns out, hope existed after all." Reule flicked a thumb across the rise of her cheek. "Perhaps on some level I knew there was a reason for waiting. Maybe I was—"

Reule broke off and Mystique cocked her head in curiosity as his warm eyes grew distant for a moment, as though he'd left her alone. She reached up to cradle his face against one of her small hands as she leaned closer to him, her flushed lips brushing his gently.

"Maybe you were what?" she coaxed, watching his eyes carefully as he slowly returned to awareness of the moment.

Reule didn't answer her. He was too lost in the tenderness glittering in her faceted eyes. He was speechless at the realization flooding through him that something integral had changed in his sphere the day she'd entered it. He always maneuvered within his life with a sense of waiting. Waiting to declare life and commerce in Jeth a success. Waiting to find a proper time to take a mate and produce heirs. Waiting for the next adversity to challenge them. Waiting for Sánge acceptance in the outer world. These were milestones that he held in high priority, and so it was important for him to time everything accordingly.

Anyone who had ever walked up a steep hill would have known the feeling well. An endless pushing of oneself, a slowing of one's natural speed and agility to conquer the steepness and combat one's own weight. This was what the Prime of Jeth felt every single day of his life as he traveled a precipitous road for his people. It was honor. It was necessity. It was even love. All motivators that drove a man of his essence.

But suddenly, in this very instant, it was as though the angle of his path had tilted to a smoother and more manageable degree. He hadn't been aware of it at first because so much was happening simultaneously.

But, oh, he felt it now. Like the ring of a crystal bell around his head, he felt the resonance of it. Something had changed. Something had exhaled, relaxed, and now lay with palms spread wide in gentle welcome. It wasn't a guarantee, nor was it a submission. It was something he was very aware he had to earn and, once earned, value highly. A gift. Priceless and beautiful.

Sitting literally in his lap.

Reule knew in that very instant that she had no mate. No children. The clarity was irrefutable in his mind, though he had no proof to support it one way or another. He simply knew she would belong to no one.

No one but him.

Mystique's breath caught when Reule's curiously thoughtful expression was replaced suddenly by the look of a proprietary predator. He smiled at her, the quick gleam of even white teeth flashing in such a way that she shivered in spite of being mostly submerged in very hot water.

"I think," he said, his tone pitched low and intent, "that I ought to carry you to bed. I'm told that rest will best help you heal."

"Reule, I'm nude. You can't very well carry me through the keep like this," she laughed.

"I think I'd enjoy the trip very much. Especially if it sparked a bashful streak in you at last." His hazel gaze swept down her torso in a way that finally, after all this time with him, made her feel as naked as she actually was. Her breath caught in a soundless gasp as he reached out to run his spread fingertips down her chest and slowly along the slope of her breast. "I want to see this perfect paleness flush rosy pink with blushing. Or perhaps . . . yes, better yet . . ."

Before she could even draw breath, his hands were against the ribs of her back and he was dragging her up out of the water until her nipple brushed against his lips. She clutched his rock-hard biceps in startled hands as his lips parted to allow the flick of his tongue. Mystique gasped, the delicate sound strangling off halfway through when the tongue was quickly followed by his entire mouth closing over her. Fire rushed over her skin, stabbed deep inside her chest and belly until her body writhed with flame as he very gently suckled her.

With nothing to brace against, her legs floated around until her knees hugged his ribs just under his powerful arms. It was obvious he thought nothing of her weight as he supported it in the palms of his hands without so much as a sign of effort. Just that potent flex of muscle sent excitement rushing through her, colliding with the sunburst of sensation his mouth caused as he toyed with her nipple. There was the soft flick of his tongue, the gentle rub of his teeth, and the tease of his lips. She squirmed helplessly, unable to maneuver, trapped where she was, stimulated and frustrated all at once. She wanted . . .

"What, kébé? *What do you want?"* His voice was arrogant as it ran through her mind and she flushed when she realized he'd been purposely monitoring her thoughts. *"Of course I have, sweetheart. I want to know*

*what you want. What excites you. Telepaths make the best
lovers because they can follow the thoughts of pleasure
of their partners. Now tell me what you want, sweet."*

He already knew what she wanted, damn him. Mystique knew it without any doubt. He was teasing her senses on purpose, holding back, just to gauge her. Stubbornly, she lifted her hands to his hair, sinking her fingers into the black, shaggy softness of it until she had hold enough to pull his head back from her breast. Her wet nipple slipped free and his brows arched to match the superior little grin twitching at half of his mouth as he lifted amused eyes to her.

Stroking a hard hand through his hair for a moment, she studied him. Then, very decisively, she turned off her thoughts and turned herself over to impulse. Closing her eyes, she drew him forward just as she locked her legs tight against his ribs. She dragged him against her and rubbed his face over her, from breast to breast, covering him with her softness and surrounding him with the scent she knew rocked his senses. Her nipples prodded his lips, but slipped away just as they parted to taste her again. She settled him briefly in the valley between them, his nose against her breastbone and his face surrounded by her warm flesh. Her lips stroked his forehead in sensual little kisses.

His fingers around her back tightened so savagely that she had to work to take in a breath, but she smiled at the reaction. She added to the allure by drawing herself up against his chest with her legs, rubbing her heat against him shamelessly. She knew the scent of her aroused sex rose up to surround him, teased him mercilessly with his own sharp senses. She had learned one thing with clarity in her time with the Sánge, and that was that they had the potent nature of predators in the wild, and that they gave themselves over to that side of themselves with pride and frequency. In a sense, she knew very well that she was a form of prey to him. In fact, she was counting on it.

"Reule . . ." she whispered in a sensual hum. "What do *you* want?"

His response was rough and dizzying. Everything spun, water splashed, and suddenly she was on her back on slippery tiles that, though they were warmed, were still astonishingly cold in comparison to her body. She gasped with the shock, her back arching sharply as Reule settled possessively over her. He lay along the center of her body, his hips caught intimately against hers and her breasts flattened beneath the weight of his chest. His hand hit the tiles near her head, the startling slap purposeful as he ground himself forward against her, fitting himself tight between her thighs and letting her feel the effect she had on his body. He was hard and hot through the wet fabric of his pants, the tight garment once again having been left on for propriety's sake. Propriety definitely wouldn't be satisfied if it could feel the state he was in.

Mystique caught her breath at the magnificent heat and solidity of him, as hard as marble but oh, nowhere near as cold. His hand reached down to grip one of her thighs as she grasped at his hips with them, moaned from her soul, and arched her pelvis to meet his blatant thrust.

Reule hissed out a fevered curse as he buried his face against her neck.

"I want to taste every part of you. Touch every part of you. Lord damn me, I want to be inside you," he growled. "I want to feel you surrounding me so tightly that I feel strangled by you. I want to make you come until I'm drenched with you and you're screaming my name. *That* is what I want!"

"Oh!" she gasped as she felt him rock and tease her body with his. "I want that, too." She sighed gustily against his hair. "I want to feel you all over. Your hands, your mouth, but not always like you are afraid I will break. I'm small but I'm strong. I want to know your body," she breathed. "I want to feel you pushing inside me until I can't bear to be filled any more."

"Lord, help me," Reule ground out almost savagely as his entire body tensed into a taut mountain of muscle above her. He shook with the effort he was using and she tried to see his face but he had purposely turned away from her.

"Reule? Did I say something wrong?" she asked anxiously.

"Shh," he said softly, turning to press a tender kiss against the skin of her shoulder before lifting most of his weight off her and onto his hands and knees. She felt the loss of the warmth and pressure of him as though half her body had been stolen away. She shivered at the terrible deficit, and he noticed when she withdrew her arms and crossed them protectively over her breasts. He studied her only briefly with hazel irises that were nearly invisible around passion-dilated pupils. Then he lowered himself to kiss her cheek before pressing lips just beneath her ear.

"Listen to me, *kébé*. Firstly, I won't do what we both desire when you're injured. And I pray you know how hard it is for me to withdraw from you, sweetheart. All you need do is look at my body to see how badly I want to give us both all of those things we want. But not while you are hurt. I can barely stomach myself as it is for ignoring your care this much."

"Stop," she whispered. "I'm fine. It almost doesn't even hurt anymore."

"That's not the point. And it's also not the only reason. There are things . . ." He hesitated, drawing in a deep, shaky breath. "There are things I need to tell you first. You need to know everything before . . . There are things about Sánge mating that you'll need to know. I'm afraid if I don't prepare you, you'll be terrified. To hell, you may be terrified anyway."

The shocking dawn of comprehension splashed over her like frigid water, awakening her to what she hadn't been seeing. What she hadn't been hearing. She suddenly sank powerful fingers into his hair and forced his head up, making him face her. She studied him sharply, then touched his sealed lips with a tentative fingertip.

"Show me," she said in a whisper. Then she leaned forward and dragged her lips over his, coaxing and warm. "Show me, Reule."

Reule parted his lips just enough to cover hers and then kissed her. He let the passion of it grow gently, listened to her exhale with the relief the contact gave them both. Then he opened his mouth and dipped for her tongue, finally exposing himself to her.

Mystique felt the brush of deadly fangs against her lips and tongue, and it made her shiver. Her tongue touched the exaggerated canines in a curiously sensual stroke and Reule shuddered against her briefly. It made her smile and draw his mouth tighter against hers so they could enjoy the discovery of a kiss of passion with him in that state. It really wasn't all that different, although the small pricks of sharpness were actually a little too stimulating. It sparked off her imagination about feeling the sensation elsewhere on her body. But before that happened, she would need him to tell her why he'd been so reluctant to tell her that arousal caused this to happen.

She pulled back from his kiss, just as reluctant as he was to do so, but knowing it was needed. He met her eyes, refusing to shy away from her reaction. It was a bravery that made her heart clench hard in her chest, a sense of pride overwhelming her though she hardly understood all the reasons why it mattered so much to her. She smoothed her fingers through his wild hair, knowing she was mostly responsible for its state of disarray. She smiled, a feeling of possession taking root inside her. She allowed it to stay.

"Did you think that these would frighten me away?" she asked, her fingertip stroking his lips again and the pronounced fang beneath.

"They may still," he said, his tone a mixture of apprehension and hope. "*Kébé*, do you know about Sánge mating rituals?"

"I told you that I did," she said with a shrug of one elegant little shoulder. "You didn't believe me?"

"I'm . . . not certain. There was mixed information. Mystique, I want to be very clear about this, so I'm going to be very frank. Sánge cannot climax without taking the blood of their partner. It means a bite, usually in the throes of ultimate pleasure. There are places on our bodies where these bites, when received, can cause overwhelming gratification. We're designed for this. You aren't Sánge. I can't predict how you'd respond if I . . . if we . . ." *To hell*, Reule thought with frustration. Even the thought of it was sending surges of hard heat into his already aching arousal. He thought of his teeth breaking past that parchment-pale skin and it was enough to nearly make a lie of his claim about Sánge release.

"Sánge take blood in moments of extremity," she said, her voice whisper soft as her fingertips soothed over the contours of his face and blended into his hair until he was reeling with the pleasure and sensuality of it. "In agony, passion, rage, climax, starvation, exhaustion, and the heat of battle. I know this," she assured him, "and it's never disturbed me. In fact, I believe there's a part of me that craves your extreme passion, Sánge." She lifted her head to kiss his lips and capture his soulful groan.

"I cannot bear the idea of hurting you, *kébé*," he cried against her mouth. "Mystique, what if I—"

"You won't," she said, silencing him with fingers, lips, and tongue.

Reule gave in to her confidence with a sigh, resigning himself to the knowledge that in spite of his attempts to argue, a part of him had already decided to claim her, in every way. He'd have to hope that her fearlessness was well-founded. If there were problems, they could be dealt with at the time, but he was determined that it wasn't now. He knew she was intent on convincing him otherwise, but he wouldn't allow himself to be swayed by his body or hers.

"Reule!" Mystique cried out when he suddenly surged away from her and rose to his feet. He left her grasping hands empty and her small body entirely chilled. But then he was there scooping her up, hauling her against his chest. He moved with confidence through the thick steam until he'd set her on a bench and was wrapping her up in the dry, full warmth of clean cloths. He took special care with each of her wounds, his head bent silently to his task. That was when she understood with absolute certainty that she wouldn't be learning what it meant to be loved by a Sánge male that night.

Chapter 8

Darcio was many things, but a fool had never been one of them. He was respectfully cautious as he watched his Prime prowl the common room in a deep, moody pacing that would've set up the hackles of any Sánge who happened to stumble on their predatory king. Darcio was Shadow. Always there, but silent and unobtrusive. His ability to be so had earned him his exalted position as the Prime of Jeth's personal bodyguard, so he wasn't about to change his habits now. Not that Reule looked like he was much in the mood for conversing, in any event.

A servant entered the vicinity and Darcio quickly came to attention, waving the unsuspecting man back to a safe distance from their agitated Prime.

"What is it?" Darcio asked.

"There is . . . That is, a farmer has come to request assistance, and he is waiting . . ."

"Why do you disturb me with this?" Reule's barked demand made the Sánge attendant leap in his own skin and he went pale beneath his normal swarthiness. Keep attendants were aware of Reule being a gruff and even sometimes impatient man, but he was never mean or cruel. The servant's reaction was a testament to the rawness of Reule's tone. "Rye is Prime Blade, and he's in his offices today. It's his duty to award assistances. Why do you come to me?"

"M-my Prime," the attendant stammered hastily, "it's not the type of assistance you think. The farmer doesn't wish to see any of the Packmates."

"Well, then who?" Reule asked sharply.

But Darcio instinctively already knew and, fearing Reule's volatility, he dug for truth and clarity in the attendant's mind. Thought flooded him and instantly confirmed his suspicions about what was happening.

"Tell the farmer that he cannot be helped today. He can return in a day or two. She'll be ready to receive visitors then."

Reule's head snapped to attention before the attendant had even begun to reply and Darcio realized his mistake a moment too late. He shouldn't have said "she."

"A farmer has come to see Mystique? How does a commoner know of Mystique? For that matter, what assistance would he ask of her?"

"My Prime," the attendant said with surprising aplomb, "there is hardly anyone in Jeth who hasn't heard of the foundling woman. The apothecary alone was—"

"The apothecary?" Reule roared.

"Apparently, our apothecary has taken his leave," Darcio answered for the servant. "On his way out of the city, he had a great deal to say, to any and all who would listen, about your 'outlander whore,' My Prime. As the apothecary told it, she dismissed him after she insulted him and all Sánge. The physic then informed his listeners that she was single-handedly going to be responsible for the death of the Prime Tracker because she's using her outlander ways on him."

"By the Lord and Lady, the bastard will pay for that! He knew full well Chayne was near dead at his hands already!"

"Of course," Darcio agreed, his manner still casual and unconcerned. "That was the point, I'm certain. No matter what we said, if Chayne were to die, the 'outlander whore' would be responsible and we'd just be covering the truth of it."

"If anyone calls her that again, Darcio, I will personally gut them," Reule spat roughly.

"Your pardon, My Prime," Darcio said sincerely, following it up with a charming sort of grin meant to ease his leader's temper. "But let's not forget the farmer, Reule."

"The farmer," Reule repeated, his brows drawing down in thought. "Why has a farmer come to seek Mystique after the apothecary's lies?"

"Firstly, My Prime," the attendant said quickly, "there's no longer an apothecary for the people to go to. He even took his two apprentices with him. Therefore, the only healer that remains is the one who challenged and usurped the former physic's position."

"Mystique," Reule breathed. "But he warned them she was going to kill a Packmate. That's as bad as accusing her of trying to assassinate me."

"Secondly, My Prime," the attendant continued methodically, "I believe the farmer's son is considered terminally ill, and that he would try anything, even the ways of an outlander . . . uh . . . woman." The attendant flushed when Darcio snickered. "He has nothing left to lose."

"I don't care what the father's motivation is, only that the boy is in need."

All three males turned to see Mystique walking rapidly

past the common area, skirts swishing around her determined steps. She was twisting her hair up quickly, looking for all the world like a woman about to take care of serious business. Darcio watched as Reule all but ran to catch her by the arm and stop her progress.

"*Kébé*, you're supposed to be resting."

"Yes, I know," she said, trying to gently extract her arm. She might as well have been trying to escape a prison. Her glare at his hand also did little good. Darcio had to bite his lip to keep from making any sounds of amusement. He leaned back in his chair as if watching a sporting event. The Shadow was amused by Reule's behavior. He was protective by nature, but this was downright proprietary. "Reule," Mystique said with obvious exasperation, "I feel fine. Look at my arms. See?" She held out her free forearm, which was left bare by the elbow-length sleeve of her dove gray velvet gown.

Mystique's gesture showed off the nearly healed expanse of her arm, only bruises remaining of what had been ugly and painful wounds the previous evening. Amando had been correct. A single night's rest had done wonders for her. However, Darcio could see she was still unusually pale and there were shadows beneath her eyes. Healing Chayne and then herself had taken its toll. Mystique's straight spine and no-nonsense bravado was more than an act, though. Darcio didn't doubt for a moment that she'd find whatever resources it took if she needed to.

"Mystique, you look exhausted. One night of rest after what you did for Chayne isn't enough. You're barely recovered from your own wounds, *kébé*. You can't keep pushing like this."

"I feel fine," she insisted. "Better than I have in a while."

This time, she did not pull away. Darcio watched as

she leaned closer to Reule, her small body fitting to his bigger one and somehow matching perfectly against him. The Shadow's eyes widened at her bold public familiarity, and the whiplash of response from his Prime that snapped like lightning through the Pack connection. He glanced at the attendant, who looked like he needed to sit down very badly. Darcio hardly blamed him. Outlander or no, it'd been a long time since anyone had seen Reule welcome the affections of a fertile female. Not since he was an adolescent, Darcio recalled more specifically. But even with his mistresses, Reule had never been one for public affection.

Her tactic was obvious and almost devious in its up-front nature, if that contradiction were possible. It was certainly powerful, if the look on Reule's face was anything to go by. And that was totally discounting what he was inadvertently emanating to his sensitive Pack-mates. Not that the Pack wasn't already completely aware of the way Reule was responding to the pretty stranger. Every time the two of them touched, it had a tidal effect that crashed through all seven men. The Prime was the epicenter, and the shock wave would radiate out to the others.

Darcio had never felt anything like it. Not from Reule, not from anyone. The result was breathtaking and arousing. Even now his heart was racing madly, echoing the leap his Prime's had taken. The entire Pack was unable to wholly protect themselves from so powerful a psychic feedback. The mistresses of the Pack were getting a fair dose of feedback themselves as a result. It was the first time Reule had ever given himself over to the full power of the *mnise*, and with an entire Pack within the age of *mnise* it was bound to have volatile repercussions. Especially given Reule's emanation ability and the difficulty of controlling it when he was feeling emotional extremes. This was what had set Delano and Saber to worrying. However, after what she'd done for Chayne last night, Darcio doubted there would be another sound of protest from the Pack where Mystique was concerned.

"Considering the length of your memory and the physical state you've been in for your five days of awareness, that isn't truly saying much," Reule said wryly to her, although his fingers had come up to sweep over the arch of her left brow in a gesture of tenderness.

Mystique lowered her arm and gave him a patient smile. "Reule, there's no apothecary in your city." Her nose wrinkled when she thought of the odious physic who had failed at his duties and maligned her as well. Darcio suspected she wasn't concerned with the latter much at all. "Despite his questionable competency, he served a purpose. There will be fear, even among brave Sánge, if they feel there's nowhere to turn when illness and injury strike."

She used Reule's reaction to her logic as an opportunity to slip out of his lax hands, stepping around him in order to confront Darcio, who quickly rose to his feet. "I'll need Pariedes and Drago to help me. I need rooms, somewhere on the ground floor. One room with good light, and the other a dark, cool room close by the first with no natural light whatsoever so I can store herbs and medicinals. A hearth in each. I'll need many sturdy shelves, a few cots."

"You wish to create an infirmary in the keep?" Darcio asked.

"Where better? Unless you prefer to move me to my own lodgings in the city proper where—"

"No! You'll stay here where it's safe and where I

can keep an eye on your insane behavior," Reule
commanded. "City proper," he grumbled irritably, "as
though I'd set an outlander woman who has just been
accused of threatening a Packmate out alone among
Sánge? Not to mention being touted as the reason for
the city losing its apothecary in the first place. You
wouldn't survive the day."

Mystique seemed to take affront to that and Darcio
had to cover a laugh with a cough as she glared at his
Prime from her diminutive height as though she wanted
to bash him over the head.

"I'm quite capable of taking care of myself," she
argued indignantly. "Don't think just because I needed
rescuing that I'm some sort of fragile thing in need of
care all the time."

Darcio certainly hoped not. If she thought to run with
Reule and his Pack, she'd have to be made of stern stuff.
However, she had proved herself to have endurance and
a tolerance for hardship already. It was Reule's remark
that was in the wrong, and the Prime of Jeth knew it on
a logical level. Darcio just didn't think Reule was thinking very logically at the moment.

"I hardly think you could face down an angry mob of
Sánge, Mystique," Reule countered sharply.

"You'd be surprised at what I've had to face down!"
she snapped furiously.

There was a beat as the remark made an impact on
everyone in the room, including Mystique herself. Her
anger rushed away and so did all of the blood in her
upper body. Darcio and Reule both leapt for her, each
catching her under an arm and holding her steady as
she gasped for breath. She recovered and tried to break
away, but she certainly wasn't strong enough to shake
them off. The temptation to read her thoughts was

fierce, but Darcio respected her privacy even though her horror and fear were already overwhelming his senses.

"I'm all right. Please," she said tightly, trying to loosen herself again from the hands circling her upper arms.

"To hell you are," Reule said bluntly, using his grip to draw her away from Darcio and into his full captivity. "What is it? What did you remember?"

Darcio turned to the forgotten attendant, who was trying not to look interested in what was happening. With a sharp mental command, the Shadow sent him on his way with instructions to feed the farmer while allowing him to wait in the kitchens. He turned back in time to see Mystique glancing at him with discomfort.

"If you'll excuse me," Darcio said graciously, not wishing to hinder what was clearly a need for her to talk about her trauma. But Reule halted him before he could move an inch.

"No. Stay, Shadow. *Kébé*, Darcio is trusted every day with my life and has been since I was born," he coaxed her gently. "I'll only have to repeat this to him later. I need the help of all my Pack in order to assist you in remembering what happened to you. To bring to justice those who hurt you."

"It's nothing," she said, shaking her head and burying her face against Reule's broad chest. She was hiding from the truth now, rather than hiding it from them. Darcio couldn't imagine what could possibly encourage her to want to relive what she'd been through. He'd relived much of it for her, and he was still having nightmares days later.

"Talk to us, *kébé*. Don't trap it inside you. It will cause you to live in fear."

Darcio had to hand it to his Prime. He seemed to

know exactly what to say. She jerked her head up and wriggled away with sharp twists of her shoulders.

"I'm not afraid!" It was an untruth. Her heart was racing hard enough to give it a fit. "I won't be afraid," she corrected herself in a meeker voice. She wrapped her arms around herself and lifted her chin bravely in spite of the trembling of her body. "I just remember people. A lot of people. Shouts. Laughter." She shivered so hard, Darcio heard her teeth clicking together. "Jeering," she corrected again. "It was hostile and all around me."

The Shadow felt his Prime's eyes on him, but he didn't need to look up to know his expression. This was nothing they'd discovered together through Darcio's ability. She'd been alone during his tracing of her body memory. Even when the Jakals had been in the same house with her. They'd never once known she was there. Darcio theorized that she'd somehow managed to block them off from sensing her. The strange thing was, none of the Pack had directly felt her sorrow that day either. What they'd felt had traveled through the Prime first before reaching them. It was yet another mystery.

"A group?" Reule encouraged gently.

"A crowd. A . . . large crowd. That's all I know," she said abruptly, turning her back on them and pacing away. "I should see this farmer and his boy," she said, her fingers sweeping both of her cheeks quickly, a useless attempt to hide tears from them. But they both understood she needed time to digest these memories and the feelings they evoked. She would talk to Reule when she was ready.

"How did you know someone was here to see you?" Darcio asked casually, trying to change the subject.

"Well, I . . ." She turned around, surprise on her face as she looked from Darcio to Reule and back again. "I just . . .

I felt their need. I feel the son's sickness. I just knew they were here and that they needed me to heal them."

"Them? I thought the son was the only one ill," Reule said.

"Reule," she chided softly. "What good father's spirit wouldn't be sick when his son is so ill?"

She turned and walked briskly away, as if that would explain everything.

Oddly enough, Darcio believed it did.

It took another argument and a great deal of coaxing to convince Reule and Darcio not to accompany her into the kitchen. She tried to get them to go about their normal business, but that was apparently asking too much of either of them. She suspected she was gaining the mercurial Shadow's championship, though she knew not what she'd done to deserve it. But it was his relaxed attitude and remarks that eventually kept Reule away from the kitchens.

Mystique was grateful for that. She wanted to face this on her own, without Reule's handholding. He was so imposing, and as the ruler of Jeth, he'd command awe, respect, and obedience. She wanted none of that by proxy. She'd inadvertently made herself responsible for the health of this Sánge nation by chasing away their apothecaries. Considering the way he'd cared for Chayne, it was no wonder he and his apprentices were all that had been needed to care for thousands of Sánge. It must have been effortless to hand out his lackluster instructions. She even suspected the monopoly was by design. Why train others who might outpace him and one day come to realize his shortcomings?

Mystique was grateful she'd been able to heal Chayne,

and she was even glad she'd called attention to the untrustworthy medicine the apothecary of Jeth had been practicing. What she wasn't so certain of was whether she could help the rest of the Sánge. She didn't even know how she knew what she knew, or even how far that knowledge truly went. She was afraid of making a mistake that could cause harm to someone. Just because she was one of those so-called naturopathics, that didn't make her infallible.

However, she wouldn't walk into the situation letting anyone else know her self-doubts. She swept into the hot kitchen, feeling its great bustle of activity in clouds of steam and the noisy clatter of pots and cutlery. There was an absence of talking, though, and the way the small hairs on her arms stirred to life, she realized that the entire staff was communicating telepathically rather than shouting over the din of their work. As a result, there was an almost musical rhythm to the way they were doing everything. Even when they wove around one another it was like a perfectly timed dance. It made her smile.

Mystique turned her attention to the man in rough clothing sitting at a table set out of the way. She felt the boy instantly, or perhaps she'd never stopped feeling him and only became more aware when she laid eyes on him. He was as roughly dressed as his father, and though he seemed lean and small, she suspected he was much older than he looked. His clothes hung on his frame too loosely and it was clear that though they weren't of fine material, they were clean and well-kept enough. The garments had no doubt once fit him quite well, probably too well, with a mother racing to keep her growing boy properly clothed.

He was dying. Mystique blinked as she realized she

could see a shade of gray all around him that had nothing to do with what anyone else would see if they were to look at him. Just like no one else would have felt the boy's illness with such clarity without even seeing him or knowing he was there. Pain, yes. The father and son's obvious sadness, of course. The keep was full of strong empaths who would sense all of that. But all she could feel was sickness. A pestilent virus that seemed to be everywhere within him.

Less intensely, she also felt the sick spirit of the father. But this was purely a mental instability. This man, she realized, might never recover from the loss of his son if something wasn't done to help him. She didn't know what she could do for him, other than try to save his child. They looked up at her with a combination of suspicion and hope. She would have laughed at the contradiction if she hadn't known how serious the situation was.

Outlander or not, she was dressed like a lady and she was the guest of their Prime, and it showed in the way they clutched their hats as they rose to greet her.

"Please, stay seated," she said gently, raising her hands palms down. They seemed unsure for a moment, but she took a seat herself and they followed her example. She didn't think they were used to sitting at a table with a lady of station, and they seemed uncomfortable and awkward. It was a different experience for her. Reule seemed to value every Sánge under his rule, right down to this type of farmer, making no real distinction of class when it came to personal interaction. The reverse, it seemed, wasn't as easy for the commoners.

"Please tell me why you have come," she encouraged them gently.

Both males were staring at her with wide, shocked expressions.

Staring at her eyes.

"I cannot be of any assistance unless I know what's wrong," she prompted again, refusing to lower her gaze in any way that would allow them to think there was a good reason for them to be wary of her strange eye color.

"It be a blood fever," the farmer said shortly. "Starving my boy from the inside out. I figured, you being an outlander physic and all, maybe you know more than what a Sánge physic knows."

Mystique didn't correct him about being a physic. She supposed that was exactly what she was, considering the knowledge she had swimming in her head at the mention of a blood fever. She didn't think it was a big jump to assume that was what she'd been in her former life. She turned to the young man and gave him a gentle smile, this time lowering her lashes so her eyes weren't so intimidating.

"What's your name?"

"Stebban, my lady," he said with a sniff, raising a pointed chin to prove to anyone who cared that he wasn't afraid of a woman, even if she was an outlander. It made the woman in question grin. She took in his lank brown hair and the dullness of eyes that ought have sparkled with blue the color of the sky. He was squeaky clean, well cared for in spite of his illness. His skin had grown sallow under his natural russet coloring.

"My name is Mystique," she said warmly, holding her hand out palm up. "May I see your fingernails, Stebban?"

The boy hesitated only long enough to glance at his father. The elder man nodded grimly, as though giving him permission to take poison. Mystique merely concentrated on the hand that, deprived of health, was almost as small as her own. Stebban laid his palm on hers and she could feel the cold in him. She could see the yellowish tinge to his nails indicating the duration of his illness, and the bluish hints beneath that meant something more dangerous. She closed his hand in her warm one, making him shiver at what was no doubt a welcome warmth. Sánge disliked the cold. She had learned that from . . .

She didn't recall, so she firmly kept herself on task. "You lose your breath easily, Stebban? Do you have an appetite? When you move, is it like walking uphill even when the ground is even?"

He answered all of the questions she came up with, even though she amazed herself with her own efficiency and how naturally it all came. She drew him closer, inch by inch, question by question, until he stood between her toes and she could reach to touch him. She asked more questions to keep him distracted as she ran her fingers over his throat, under his arms, and down to his wrists. She'd remained seated so she'd be less threatening. It kept him from hesitating in any way when she asked him to shed his shirt. She worked hard not to react when she saw the protrusions of his ribs and the hips that were barely keeping his pants on. Every bone in his body stood out in stark relief.

"Thank you, Stebban. Please put on your shirt and go sit closer to the ovens for a little while. There's a chair close by right over there that will be out of the way." Once he'd gratefully gone to the warmest part of the kitchen, she turned to the father. "Your name, sir?"

"Uh, Kell, your ladyship. But I'm no sir."

"You are to me," she said dismissively. "Now about Stebban. How long has he been this way?"

"The apothecary said he had the fever four months

past. He got sick just before planting. He was able to help us plant some, but come harvest he could only sleep and eat. He's a good boy and a hard worker. Not like him to be so lack like. My wife, she be feeding him constant. Good food too, like the physic said to. No expense too much for my son, and that's the truth."

"Of course it is. What good foods did the physic recommend, sir?"

Kell twitched a smile when she called him sir again.

"You know. Thick foods, to make him fat like. Though they didn't work at all. Meats in stew. Lard and good fats. Fresh breads. Cakes and mash. Gave us this tonic, too. Seems to make him terrible sick though when he takes it."

He handed her the bottle with its cork stopper and she smiled through clenched teeth. Medicines ought to be sealed tighter than that to preserve potency. She pulled the cork and sniffed delicately. She coughed when the unexpected odor of greenroot struck her. Greenroot was an emetic! Of course the boy was sick when he took it! Her gaze swung to the boy in horror as an unthinkable possibility ran through her. Had the physic made a boy purposely ill? The emetic would cause weight loss if taken over enough time, no matter what he was fed. Not to mention the foods suggested were poor recommendations to start with. What would he have done next? Withdrawn the medication and presented another, pretending to cure a boy on the brink of death?

Mystique forced herself to take a deep breath. No. The emetic and bad advice were only part of the problem. The boy was genuinely ill, even if the physic hadn't recognized the actual problem. His cures had only made Stebban weaker more quickly and with a more dramatic effect.

"Can you help my boy, my lady?" the farmer asked, looking so terribly hopeful in spite of tired, disillusioned eyes.

"I might just at that, sir," she said, the response so thoughtful that the farmer felt a real surge of hope this time. She had strange eyes and peculiar hair, but he sensed the truth in her even though he couldn't read her thoughts or emotions. He wasn't at all a strong 'pathic, but instinct served him well. "Can you leave him here at the keep, Kell? Would you trust me to care for him? You can visit anytime, his mother as well. We'll make a place for him and take good care of him. I'll need three or four days before I'll know for certain what path he's on."

Reule leaned back against a corridor wall as, just across from him, he watched a storeroom with three long windows and an unused larder being transformed into an infirmary. They were summarily stripped of their contents, cleaned within an inch of needing to replace the mortar, and restocked according to the wishes of the little whirlwind of feminine energy at the center of the ruckus.

He wouldn't care if she took over the keep in its entirety, if it would make her happy. It'd be worth handing it over just to be able to watch her flush with color and laughter, as she was now. The Pack, a flock of attendants, and the lower servants fell all over themselves to amuse her, responding to her every wish and basically keeping just shy of falling at her feet in devotion. Rumors of what she'd done for Chayne had spread like springtime throughout the keep's residents, winning their affection overnight.

On the downside, she now had four other eligible,

potent males in her path at every turn. Rye oozed his courtly charm. Darcio was constantly teasing her. Even dark, broody Delano was making a spectacle of himself trying to see to her needs and win her smiles. Saber was a flat-out dead man, Reule thought darkly. The Defender had put his hands on her twice already. Once to swing her out of the way by lifting her by her little waist, and again by catching her when she'd toppled off a ladder. If his hand had come any closer to her bottom, Reule thought with heat, he'd have pulled back a bloody stump.

Every last member of the Pack, exempting the traveling Amando, knew he wasn't pleased with their antics, so of course they pushed him. They wanted to see just how far they could go before provoking him into making an ass of himself. Something he refused to do. So Reule stood against the wall, clenched his teeth, and held his arms folded tightly against his chest. He focused on Mystique, poured all of his concentration into her, drinking in her effervescent spirit and energy.

She fascinated him as she used incredible logic and a streaming fount of knowledge to set up her infirmary. There were cots, separated by brocaded curtains in dark colors, lined up head first around the walls nearest the windows. Sunlight spilled on each bed, a direct contradiction to the way they'd found Chayne and to the way Reule had always known sickrooms to be. The curtains provided privacy when needed, but could be drawn back completely.

Across the room she'd placed a steel table in a large, low copper tub, curtaining it off in a corner. When Rye had asked her about it, she'd explained that steel was easiest to clean, and that the tub would save the floor from blood and other soiling. That was when Reule realized how seriously she'd considered this responsibility. She knew what to expect. Jeth was a large city with a strong and hearty people, but they could experience very serious injuries while managing life alongside the wilderness.

The darker, cooler larder was shelved and filled with all manner of herbs and disinfectants, jars and bottles, and a variety of supplies and equipment that they had to send servants to the shops of the city for. It didn't surprise him when two more people arrived at the keep searching for satisfaction not found at the hands of the former apothecary.

Not one to tolerate slights, Reule had already seen to it the physic wouldn't get far. Maybe, if he'd left quietly, the Prime would have overlooked the disrespect to Jeth caused by his desertion, since Mystique was able to fill the need left by his departure. However, he *hadn't* left quietly. He'd dared to call a woman in Reule's favor a whore. There was no forgiving that or the lies spread against her. It wasn't all a matter of insult, either. The apothecary's intent was to turn opinion against an innocent stranger. She was also the only medical aid left to Jeth now, and those words would make people leery of coming to her even when in dire need.

Such a dangerous affront was unforgivable. Because of this insolence, the apothecary would lose his life.

Reule hadn't sent Delano, although as Prime Assassin this was very much in the realm of his office. He'd resisted sending Delano away while Chayne was still ill. His Assassin would be peeved when he found out, but it was Reule's choice to make and that would be the end of it.

For now, he contented himself by watching as Mystique turned her full attention on the newest of her patients. She spoke in an easy tone, her movements slow

and careful as she asked questions. Her eyes moved in
steady sweeps to observe what wasn't being said. She
was, he thought, brilliant and beautiful, and she set his
whole world off its axis.

It was instinct that sent his gaze to the left, finding
Darcio's inquisitive gray eyes watching him. His Shadow
kept himself a blank in thought and emotion, depriving
Reule of any insight into why he was being observed so
closely. So he turned back to the more satisfying task of
watching Mystique tend his people. She was able to send
her two new patients away with herbs, instructions, and
a request that they return in a few days. They both left
and she brushed back damp, straggling hair from her
forehead. While his Pack was in ideal health and had the
vigor to drive themselves accordingly, Reule could see
that this wasn't the case for his little *kébé*. She was tired,
and it was getting hard for her to hide it.

"*Kébé*," he said as he pushed away from his spot
against the wall to approach her. She looked up and her
smile became tentative. Damn, he hated that. He supposed he deserved it, though, after acting the overbear-
ing ass that morning. To be fair, though, he'd been
motivated by a need to protect her. He wanted her well.
He wanted her healthy.

In all selfish, male honesty, he wanted her. Period. So
badly that he felt as though he were pacing in the trap of
a too-small cage. He'd set the limitation on himself to
wait until she was well, and it had been the right thing to
do, but that didn't mean he wasn't screaming inside for
her. By the Lord, when she'd come striding into the
common room bustling with healthy energy and purpose,
it had been the equivalent of what a striptease would do
for other men. And because he'd been thinking with other
things besides his brain, he'd acted like an ass and upset

her. Then that upset had triggered a memory from who knew what type of horror, and now she didn't want to trust him with it for fear he'd see her as delicate and weak. Which, in all fairness, she was. At the moment.

But he'd never meant to imply that he thought her frail. She didn't know he and Darcio had traveled through her body memory. They knew what she'd endured in the wilderness. It was enough to prove she was a survivor. She was also quite powerful, 'pathically speaking. It'd be ridiculous to accuse her of frailty.

Reule had kept the information gleaned via Darcio to himself, unsure what to do with it. He couldn't escape the notion that the longer he held on to it, the less honorable an act it became. He should tell her what he knew. It would mean explaining Darcio's gifts, something no one outside of the Pack really knew of, but he could sense Darcio trusted her well enough. The downside was what her reaction might be. Mystique might resent him for keeping the information secret. Or, if he told her all he knew, it could trigger a chain of memories like this morning's, and he dreaded being the source of more pain and fear.

With all this weighing on his mind, he stepped up to her and held out a palm.

"*Kébé*, the evening meal is in thirty minutes, and you'll want to clean up and change. As will your companions," he added as the Pack stood watching him with poorly repressed amusement. All he cared about was that she didn't hesitate to put her hand in his, and he closed his fingers around hers gratefully.

"Rye, please see that Stebban is made comfortable in here for the night, with a servant to tend the fire so he catches no chill."

"Don't worry, Mystique. If there's one thing no

Sánge will ever allow in this keep, it's the catching of a
chill. Tomorrow we'll see about putting electric heat in
your infirmary."

"Truly?" She looked delighted and breathlessly ap-
preciative. "That would be wonderful."

"It's an easily accomplished task," Reule said shortly.
"Come, *kébé*, before Para pitches an apoplexy. She's
pacing your rooms as we speak."

She laughed and Reule drew her tight to his side as
they moved into the hall. He felt the warm length of her
body moving sinuously against his, and it just about
drove him mad. He made it as far as the stairs, then
seized her and dragged her into the dark alcove beneath
them. She squeaked out a sound of shock when she
abruptly found herself up against the wall, his body
trapping hers against the stone and mortar.

"Reule!" she gasped, her chest heaving against the
crush of his as he swooped in to seize her mouth. She
opened instantly to him, sighing as he tasted her as
deeply as he could manage and still give pleasure. She
was sweet as ever, the slight tang of a wine she'd enjoyed adding a pleasant surprise to her flavor.

Reule was lost in the wet enthusiasm of her hot mouth
in a flash. She never hesitated, never pulled away, never
demurred. She took what he gave and gave the whole of
her response in return. It was so honest it had the power
to bring him to his knees.

Her hands were curling into his hair, holding him
tight to her lips. Her feet didn't even touch the floor any
longer because he had dragged her up to meet him. Did
she even notice, or was she too consumed by the fire
they made together?

His hands, framing her head and face, slid down the
slim column of her throat until her breasts and the

velvet of her bodice filled his palms. Reule groaned when her nipples responded instantly, hard points seeking the play of his fingers and the feel of his mouth. He buried his hips against her, making very certain she knew that all it took was her kiss and the feel of her to make him thick and ready.

"I want to touch you everywhere," he growled against her open lips. "I want every inch of your skin to know me. Would you like that, *kébé*?" He took the shudder rippling through her body as an answer. "I want you on my tongue," he groaned into her mouth, making her moan so sensuously he lost all sense of where he was. He scooped up her skirts in a single sweep of his hand, baring her leg to the upward stroke of his palm. Her skin was smooth and hot, growing hotter with every inch upward he traveled. Behind her knee, the back of her slim thigh, up to the curve of her pretty little bottom.

"Reule," she moaned.

"Ah, the sound of my name on your lips has the most incredible effect on me," he said with pleasure as he kissed her down her throat. He felt her wriggle with surprise when his hand cupped one bare cheek of her lush little backside, his fingertips skimming the sensitive crease. He hummed against her pulse in speculation. "You aren't wearing underclothes?" And just as quickly the wolfish grin faded from his tone. "All this time? *Around my men?*"

"I don't like . . . they're . . . I didn't mean . . ." She couldn't form a complete sentence as he slid his industrious hand up over the curve of her hip, fingers trailing low along her pelvis until they touched sparse curls.

"You don't like them?" he supplied for her helpfully, lifting his head so he could burn her with the fierce green-gold heat of his eyes. She nodded mutely, and then gasped breathlessly when she felt the flutter and flick of his teasing fingertips. Reule could smell her heat now, the dampness seeping from her body that was laden with musk and pheromones. It made his head spin and his cock harden into steel. She was excited, hot, wetting herself in preparation for him. He'd only meant to kiss her, to claim his place in her attentions after feeling so slighted by his own friends. In an unexpected instant he'd gone far beyond that.

Reule lifted his mouth back to hers, kissing her even though he had to dodge his own fangs to do so. Then he slid his seeking fingers through feminine folds drenched in liquid heat. He caught her cry of surprised pleasure against a groan of his own.

"*Kébé*, you're so hot," he rasped as he glided through soft flesh and sought her center. He found her entrance, circling the sensitive borders silkily before retreating to find the small nub of her clitoris. If he'd doubted his accuracy, he was reassured by her cry and shudder of response. Leaving his thumb resting against that sensitive spot, he once again sought her core. He easily slid a thick finger into her, the way made simple as her body welcomed him with a liquid greeting.

Mystique canted her hips forward, riding his hand with pure instinct and a passionate reaction that dragged Reule down into her uninhibited intensity. He tugged aside her bodice, freeing a breast to his mouth, using a ferocious suction that made her squeal against the prepared seal of his palm against her lips. One hand suppressed her pleasure while the other evoked it. His thumb toyed with her while his finger slid rhythmically deeper. With teeth scraping and sucking her nipple, he slid a second finger into her incredibly snug channel. He reveled in the jerk of her body as she was overwhelmed with sensation. Her hands held him to her desperately and she cried out again from his teasing fingers.

Reule moved his stifling hand and replaced it with his mouth, wanting his lips and tongue against hers as he stroked her responsive body to climax.

"Shall I make you come, sweet?" he asked her roughly. "Can I make you come? What if your people are like the Sánge? Do you need my blood on your tongue to make you climax? Hmm?"

"Please," she gasped, her diamond eyes heated with a need as bad as his own. He didn't think she was aware of anything but the response of her wild little body, but then she was looking at him with those hot eyes and he knew she saw him. "Please . . ." she repeated on a moan before drawing his mouth to hers. She kissed him hard, brutally, causing his fangs to puncture the inside of his bottom lip. He knew she had done it on purpose the moment her tongue swept inside to stroke his blood into her mouth.

She threw her head back in a silent scream as her body closed tight around his torturous fingers. She orgasmed with blinding intensity, her body squeezing around his hand as her hips jerked with violent release. Had he been inside her, she would have milked him dry, and he smothered a frustrated growl against her breasts at that knowledge. The taste of his own blood in his mouth made it all the worse. It should be hers. Her flavor on his tongue as he spilled himself inside her and made her his.

Reule heard her dragging in wild breaths, her entire body falling limp against him. His touch made her jolt in sensitivity and he carefully released her from it. He let her skirts fall back in place, but he kept her pinned hard by the force of his hips and the throbbing erection nestled tight against her. He kissed her gasping mouth as he repaired her bodice, making everything just as it was before he'd pulled her into the alcove.

Except for the wild flush on her skin, the swollen, well-kissed look of her lips, and the topple of red hair that had come down from its constraints. She looked for all the world like she'd just been tumbled, and the idea pleased him ridiculously even if it wasn't precisely true. His smiling lips drifted to her ear.

"Para is coming to look for you," he informed her.

"I don't care," she sighed sincerely.

"I mean right now. She's at the head of these very stairs. And while I can keep her from sensing me, you won't be so lucky."

With that information and a perverse sense of humor, Reule thrust her out of the alcove with a single sudden shove. She stumbled and corrected herself, whirling in an instant to glare at him and give him a piece of her suddenly violent mind.

"My lady!"

Mystique froze when Pariedes bellowed from the stairs. She quickly smoothed hands over her wild hair and her crooked dress while Reule folded his arms over his chest and leaned back perfectly concealed in the dark alcove. He was grinning when she shot him a deadly look. He simply shrugged a shoulder. As far as he was concerned, it was perfect payback after she had spent the day flirting with his men. Besides, it wasn't as though she were the one left unsatisfied.

"I'm coming, Para," she called as she picked up her skirts and started to run, clearly hoping that it would help account for her flush and disheveled state.

"Liar, you already came," he thought to her with a smug chuckle.

"I swear you will come to regret this one day," she thought back with a feminine growl of frustration.

"You were the one who didn't want to be treated as fragile and weak," he countered.

That made her hesitate in her mind, although she was still running up the stairs straight past Para, who was lecturing her on the need for a lady to be more concerned with her appearance and not to rush. One day soon Pariedes would realize her lady was full of independence and quirks that would never fit the perfect mold of a Sánge lady. And that, Reule decided, was a very good thing. Mystique was bold, honest, and refreshing.

"Reule?"

"Yes, kébé, I'm still here."

"Did you do that to punish me?"

"Did I do what to punish you?" he demanded, stepping out of the alcove and looking up the stairs though she and Para were already long gone.

"You said it served me right . . ."

"I meant exposing you to Para's censure, sweetheart," he thought gently to her, though his first reaction was fiercer. *"I made love to you because I can't keep my hands off you. Don't ever think I'd use that as either punishment or reward. Lovemaking is independent of those things."*

"I'm sorry. I didn't mean to insult you. I just didn't understand."

"And now you do. Don't worry, kébé," he thought with pure heat, *"you're going to learn everything you need to know about me. I promise you that."*

There was no thought response, but Reule felt the sexual excitement that surged through her right down to his toes. He groaned softly, streaking both hands through his hair.

He began to plot how to keep Para far, far away from Mystique for the rest of the night.

Chapter 9

"By the Lord, Reule had better bed that wench soon," Rye growled as he restlessly paced the dining hall. "Mara is going to start thinking her pussy is made of gold if I keep frequenting her bed like this."

"You mean it's not?" Saber joked, chuckling softly. Rye was the most sensitive of the Pack and he was suffering the worst of it, but they were all feeling the backlash of Reule's unfulfilled needs.

"I don't get it," Delano grumbled. "Reule has chased women before. Wanted women before. And yeah, it's made us all a little edgy because of our connection, but this is unreal! It's practically savage! What to hell is it about her that's so different? Isn't anyone else worried about her being this close to Reule?"

"That's your frustration talking," Darcio countered, by far the calmest of the Packmates. "The fact is, Reule is in *mnise*, and it's been a long time since he gave himself over to it. Mystique is provoking him whether he wants it or not. Stop obsessing over your erections and pay attention. Look at them. Feel them. Feel Reule when he stands back and watches her."

Darcio leaned forward toward them. "We were all

giving him a hard time today by flirting with her, and it was a kick, but did any of you really feel that jealousy? *Jealousy.* From Reule, who cares about only two things: Jeth and the well-being of this Pack. He displayed hostility toward us because we were buzzing around a woman he has marked as one hundred percent Prime territory. Kidding aside, if any of us dared to touch her, we'd find ourselves in the middle of a challenge more savage than we could even imagine. Pack oaths would mean nothing. It would be as if one of us challenged his rule."

"Darcio, you have a point?" Rye said shortly.

Darcio knew all their tempers were a little taut because of the hormones flowing so strongly through them. "The point is, my friends, that you need to start looking at Mystique and wondering how you will feel when she becomes Prima."

"To hell!" Delano barked.

Saber snorted. "Reule would never wed an outlander."

"I can't imagine Reule wed at all, and neither should you, Darcio. You know him best of all of us. He's not going to get tied down until he has no other choice," Rye said.

"Rye, that remark would be true if Reule had been forced to choose from the flock of marriageable noblewomen he considers to be uptight, grasping, and spoiled. He would have done his duty eventually, but now there's an opportunity for him to do his duty, but to do it with someone he actually likes a great deal.

"Saber, while marrying an outlander would be risky and something he'd never have considered doing before this, I believe Mystique has changed his mind about what an outlander is capable of learning and appreciating about the Sánge." Darcio took a deep breath and leaned back with a contented half-smile on his lips.

"Then there's the fact that he's in heat for her, she's a powerful 'pathic, and, oh yeah, she's a sweetheart."

"To hell," Delano repeated, though it was more thoughtful than a curse.

"She's coming. With Reule," Saber said suddenly, making all of them stand up straight behind their chairs. There was a conscious shedding of frustrations and emotional reactions to what Darcio had just said, and for those who couldn't shed, protective walls rose in defense of any leaks that might disturb their Prime.

It was one thing to consider and discuss the Prime's love life, but it was quite something else for him to *know* it was being considered and discussed.

Reule knew something was wrong the instant he stepped into the room and found things unusually calm and quiet on the 'pathic front. His Pack had a bad habit of blanking him out like that when they didn't want him to know something was bothering them. He glanced at Darcio, who was by far the most relaxed of the group, while he guided Mystique into the room with a gentle hand at her back. This time she wore gloves all the way up to her elbows, and he felt sympathy for her fear. She had a fully fledged set of powers, but no true sense of how to control them. However, he had faith that she'd either remember or relearn.

Mystique felt highly self-conscious as she took her seat at Reule's left hand. The last time she'd been in this room, she'd unearthed terrible feelings and secrets. Tonight, everyone was acting strangely, different from their lighthearted play of earlier. She worried her bottom lip with her teeth as she wondered if they were remembering the previous night's meal.

Then there was Reule, and that was an entirely different landscape of emotions and wild thoughts. She could hardly peek at him without her heart racing into overdrive and her skin bursting out in a moist flush. He'd been so gentle with her, so careful and respectful, that she'd never once expected that sudden rupture of savage passion from him. Not that she hadn't known he was capable of it. She had known that he was holding himself under a very tight leash of control. But to have it sprung on her so suddenly had left her with only half a brain and knees that were decidedly weak.

One thing about having no memory was that she had nothing to compare the experience to. She was rather glad. She expected everything she'd known beforehand would pale in comparison, and he hadn't had to work very hard at it. She thought of his hands on her, inside her, and her face flushed while her body went taut and damp all over again. She had to struggle to control her thoughts, to keep her gaze averted from him so she wouldn't begin to crave what she hadn't yet had. The room was full of telepaths and empaths, and it was the last thing she wanted to be thinking around them.

She felt as though all eyes were on her and examining her from all quarters. It made her very uncomfortable. Even Reule was staring at her, but she suspected she knew what he was thinking. He had definite plans for her tonight, and it was about time. She needed him. Badly. Her entire body cried for him. The intensity of it left her with a fine tremor of excitement shivering constantly through her. She'd been given a wild taste of Reule's passion, and she wanted more. She wanted endless time wrapped up in it. She wanted Reule.

She watched him as he ate and spoke to his friends, thinking of all she had learned about him. His kindness, fairness, and tenderness were wondrous. He was gruff and even cold when it was imperative that he be that way, and always quiet and observant before he acted or reacted. He had a temper, but it was usually set off over matters of honor. It was hard to see that as a bad thing. Honor, truth, and friendship enriched his rule. He laughed when he wanted to, wasted no energy on the frivolous, and cared about his city first and foremost.

All these disparate qualities came together to make up an extraordinary man. One she was quickly coming to care about. If nothing else, his choice in trusted companions would have told her all she needed to know about him. Each man was unique in his own way, and their personalities were as different as the seasons. The binding fiber was the honor and loyalty they all had for the man they loved above all others. The fact that these powerful men loved Reule, enough to hand him power over whether they lived or died, made an impressive impact.

Reule was wishing he'd arranged a private supper for just himself and Mystique. He was getting a little tired of the distracting presence of his Pack. But then he'd have Para hovering over them, and that would be just as bad. What he wanted, what he needed, was Mystique in his bed, beneath him and surrounding him. He'd been in a state of arousal ever since their encounter in the alcove and he ached with the sheer potency of his desire for her. He hardly ate anything as the meal progressed, and he knew he was staring at her more often than not because a permanent blush had taken up residence on her fey features.

Needing contact with her, he reached out and covered her near hand with his own, closing her into his palm possessively and watching as she rode out a shimmer of excitement before she sneaked a peek at him from below her lashes. He longed for her mind in that moment, but he resisted provoking her when there were other strong 'pathics nearby.

He wasn't stupid. He was well aware of the backlash his Pack was picking up from him as he struggled with his desire for Mystique. He knew he'd never felt the *mnise* so strongly before, and he was convinced it was Mystique who caused the intensity. The result was a powerful urge to throw her over his shoulder this very minute and drag her behind closed doors where—

"Damn!"

Rye lurched up out of his chair, drawing the attention of the entire table. The Prime Blade swung his gaze to Reule and his dark expression turned to one of pure surprise. A tangible ripple began to flow through the Pack until Reule finally withdrew from his fog of preoccupation enough to realize why Rye was looking at him so strangely.

"Jakals." Reule heaved to his feet as he spat the cursed word, turning to the door just as one of Rye's lieutenants came rushing in, one of Saber's sergeants hot behind him.

"My Prime! Jakals. A horde of them. There's fire beyond the walls!"

The Pack mobilizing all at once was a daunting thing. Gone were the courtly manners and good-natured smiles of earlier, and in their place rose stone-cold warriors. 'Pathic power surged throughout the room instantly as every man opened himself to the others, a chain of communication so familiar to them it was like breathing. Mystique could feel the feedback of it buzzing all around her, even though she wasn't sensitive in the same way that they were.

Reule stepped up to her briefly, folding his large hands around her small shoulders and squeezing them in tight reassurance. "Don't worry. This happens a lot out here. Without the snows, the field stubble and winds will spread the fire unless we fight it back quickly. I'll return later. Don't wait for me." He gently brushed an affectionate finger down the slope of her nose before releasing her and rushing out with his Packmates.

She stood staring at the abandoned room for all of a minute before she closed her gaping mouth with a snap and shook indignation into herself with a sharp shudder.

"To hell!"

She scooped up her skirts and ran for the stairs. Cursing her corsets and high-handed males, she burst into her rooms and gave Pariedes the fright of her life. She reached for her laces and began to whip them apart.

"I need trousers. A boy's should fit," she panted as she wriggled out of her overdress, leaving the plum creation in a pool as she stepped out of it.

"But . . ." Para began.

"Para, don't give me any arguments! Fetch me breeches and a shirt or I swear I'll walk naked through this keep searching for them myself!" Para closed her gaping mouth quickly when she realized how perfectly serious her mistress was. "And send that blasted girl in here to help me with this damnable corset in the meantime. Now hurry!"

Pariedes had gotten to know her charge quite well over the past few days, and she found her to be an intelligent and even-tempered woman for the most part. This was the first time she'd ever heard her address anyone with the authoritative tone of a woman used to giving a command and having it obeyed. It resulted in Para helping Mystique into a set of boy's snug pants, shirt, and vest within minutes. It was indecent, but the sigh her foundling released and the expertise she used to bind the clothing onto her body said that this wasn't the first time she'd dressed herself in such a fashion. It was scandalous, but Para had to admit she wore the disguise terribly well.

"Para, dearest, I need you to listen carefully," Mystique said breathlessly as she rapidly twisted her dark hair into a plait. "There's fire on the flatlands. One of the soldiers mentioned farms. That will mean injuries, burns, smoke cough. They'll need a healer there, rather than waiting here. I need supplies. I haven't had a chance to make salves or creams yet, but we can find disinfectants, clean cloths, and fresh jars of water for the cough. Men. Good strong men and litters to carry out the injured. We cannot have them in the way of a shifting fire. I need someone who can keep her head and stay beside me. A girl with nerve and a head for listening to instructions. You know everyone in the keep." Mystique looked at her with expectancy and waited while Pariedes digested all of what she was saying and its implications. She waited to see if Para's instincts would be to help or to hinder.

"I know just the girl," Para breathed at last.

Reule hadn't bothered to saddle Fit, time being precious and the smoke having been visible even as they'd exited the bailey of the keep. Now, rounding the fire burning ferociously in the field grasses, his legs gripped Fit's bare sides and they tore over the land as a perfectly blended creature of speed. He rode the off side of the fire, the winds pushing smoke and heat away from him and making it just barely bearable for him to approach so close to the line. It was a dangerous thing to do, flatland winds being extremely shifty and unpredictable. The wind could turn suddenly and he would be ash before he even realized it.

But the speed and dangerous shortcut were very necessary.

The fire was extremely close to the walls of Jeth,

only a few farms standing in the mile between fire and civilization. The height of the walls would prevent most damage, but sparks could travel forever on the wind, and all it would take was one spark on a thatch roof within the walls to light hell around them.

They must keep the fire from advancing toward Jeth even so much as a foot. The wind was partially in their favor; there was even a river of good size to act as a fire-break. What Reule didn't trust was the Jakals.

They wouldn't be far. They'd want to watch and devour the fear and anxiety of the Sánge as they struggled to save their homes. They'd never pass up the opportunity to gobble up such powerful emotions. And if they were close, then they were capable of making the situation much worse. Reule wanted armed guards and soldiers riding the flatlands in tight circuits while their compatriots fought the hellish fire itself. He was too far from Saber at the moment to make the orders clear telepathically, so he was racing back around the fire and toward the walls of Jeth.

Reule drew within sight of the main road and saw a dust trail coming from Jeth that was quickly growing nearer to him. At first he thought it was reinforcements from the city, but it took only a moment for him to realize the riders were too few. He recognized the livery of the city guards even from a distance because of the red in the design, but the leader of the group was wearing common clothing.

He'd already turned to intercept them when it struck him who he was watching approach the danger of the fire. *Struck* was the perfect word, because it was like a psychic wall of kinetic energy that slapped him back. Fit felt the tensing of his rider and jerked into a turn and canter by instinct. By the time Fit came full around to the road again, Reule had a full visual of the redheaded beauty riding to hell on a big russet stallion named Riot that Reule had added to his stables only a year earlier. The young horse was all speed, youth, and attitude, and Reule was furious to see Mystique riding a creature that was dangerous for a telepath to ride, never mind a tiny female who had no means of communicating with it.

He was going to kill the stable hand who had given her the beast.

Several times.

With this thought of venom hazing his brain, Reule rode Fit to cut off her and her little entourage. At least she'd had the sense to bring an armed escort. With Jakals nearby? Had she come out alone he'd have likely burst a blood vessel in rage by now. As he neared her and got a good look at the outfit she was wearing, he almost did exactly that.

Mystique was riding short-stirrup, which brought her feet high to the saddle and allowed her to ride above the leather. Her knees were bent close to the animal and her backside was lifted in the air as she leaned into the animal's neck for speed. This position, while fast and graceful for horse and rider, was giving the others a fine display of her tightly clothed bottom as she jockeyed high above the saddle.

He knew when she saw him because she slowed and stood against her stirrups. She turned to meet him, loose strands of her hair flying across her face as she now rode partway into the wind. As furious as he was, as terrified for her safety as he found himself, Reule could hardly breathe for how beautiful she looked to him right then. The remaining riders stayed on the road and drew to a halt as she came up to him alone, dust and now traces of smoke drifting around her, the braid of her hair bouncing against her breast. She was small, but she was vital and alive. He could see her eyes shining bright with determination. This, he realized, was no lark to her. She was here for a purpose, whether he agreed with it or not, and it was written grimly in her pretty features and the emotion he felt washing off her.

By the time they reached one another, blind fury fueled by fear had ground back to a more controlled anger. He reached for the horse's leather and jerked them both to a halt. Without a word, he stripped her out of her saddle and sat her in his lap before she could so much as think to protest.

Yet even when she was seated against the hard flex of his thighs, she still made no protest of his treatment of her. All she did was tilt up her chin and gaze at him with expectant eyes, her hands resting resolutely against his chest. He was covered in soot, dirt, and sweat, but she didn't complain. He wondered why he kept expecting her to act like the high-born women he was used to.

He reached out and seized the side of her face and head in a proprietary palm, the grip of his fingers in her hair drawing her to within inches of his emotionally stormy eyes.

"You come out into danger riding a treacherous animal and dressed indecently. Tell me, *kébé*, why I shouldn't be strangling on outrage at the moment."

He spoke softly and purposefully, so Mystique knew very well just how much he was controlling his temper just then. She reached up and curled her fingers into the collar of his shirt, her skin touching his warmly as she grasped hold.

"I'm a healer. Danger always begs the presence of a healer. I didn't choose the horse, he chose me. Rather insistently, I might add. He's fast, beautiful, and spirited,

but only dangerous to an inexperienced rider. I'm
delighted to realize that I'm a greatly experienced rider.
As for the clothes, I hardly think skirts would have sufficed. They slow me down. I'd rather not be slow while
near a fire, thank you."

"By the Lord and Lady," he swore softly, giving her
a sharp shake that drew her to his chest. He despised her
logic and matter-of-fact tone, especially when she made
it so hard to argue against her. "Have a care, Mystique!
I don't want you near this fire and out on the roads
when a horde of Jakals is running wild! You don't have
the power you need to protect yourself if—"

He broke off to crush his mouth against hers. He felt
her determination and stubbornness and that she
wouldn't let him sway her no matter how hard he tried.
She'd just as soon force him to physically restrain her,
something he would have no right to do. Besides, it
would hurt her deeply if he did.

He smelled and tasted of smoke, but she opened herself to his assault, taking his attack the way she did
everything from him. With acceptance. Always such acceptance. And he knew it was only for him that she
would ever exhibit such patience even when she didn't
agree with his opinions or behaviors. His heart squeezed
into a knot. It was this acceptance that was teaching him
to be more tolerant himself. He loved to preach about
how open-minded he was, railing against those who
turned away from the Sánge, yet he barely tolerated the
independent ways of a single woman.

He gentled his kiss, and she accepted that as well.
Reule broke off, holding her face in his huge palms and
rubbing her wet lips against his. "The wind changes too
fast, *kébé*, for you to set up a permanent place. Find
your injured and take them away from here. Keep

moving and keep telepaths with you. Two guards, at all times. Put them to work if you like, but keep them near. They'll be responsible for your life and safety, and I will kill them if you're harmed in any way. Are you willing to take that responsibility? Do you understand this is a truth and not an idle threat?" he demanded.

"Yes, my Sánge lord, I understand quite well. I've brought two guards and five other attendants to assist me, as you see." She lifted a hand in the direction of her escort. "I'm not eager to die, Reule, but I won't wait around while others risk their lives for what is now my home. Not when I can be useful to them. You would never be able to do that, and neither can I."

"I fear losing you," he said, suddenly fierce against her lips again. "Do you understand that? I fear nothing so much as I fear losing you!"

Mystique took his kiss, blinking as tears welled above her lashes. She felt his words throughout her soul, and they sang delight deep into her bones. She wrapped her arms around his neck and kissed him with the boomerang intensity of the emotion he'd created within her. His hands wrapped around her ribs, thumbs brushing beneath her breasts and fingertips grasping her back. He crushed the breath from her in his intensity.

"Now," he said gruffly, his voice hoarse from emotion and need, "get to a safe distance and follow my orders. If I see one thing . . ."

"You'll send me to bed without dessert. Yes, I know." She sighed in a put-upon manner, but she was smiling.

"Oh no, kébé," he corrected her, those thumbs sneaking up over the undersides of her breasts to rub over her accessible nipples through the very thin material of her shirt. They hardened rapidly beneath his skilled taunt. "I won't be denying you your sweets tonight."

The implication was clear, and Mystique shivered as she looked up into the hot promise of his eyes. She nearly protested when he removed his touch and hoisted her back onto her saddle. He shot her a final warning look before reeling Fit around and leaping off in his original direction. She watched him go for a minute. He was so beautiful, hair streaming behind him and muscled legs clutching muscled horseflesh as though they were part of each other. She felt the imprint of his hands on her body. One day she was going to have to let him know exactly how frustrating that could be. But first they had to take care of the Jakals' latest deadly mischief. Shielding her eyes, she looked toward the fire and the wall of black and brown smoke. She prayed there wouldn't be too many homes lost and that the conflagration could be stopped quickly.

Grabbing her reins, she turned and headed back to the group waiting on the road, determined to be what help she could.

"What do you think?"

"I think this is Chayne's area of expertise," Darcio said with a sigh as he rose from studying the ground. "Where's Delano? He's far better equipped to track the bastards."

"He's fetching Saber from the city. Now that the fire is out, the Jakals will want to find a nice cozy camp to enjoy their glut of emotion." Reule spat onto the ground, then looked up at the bright moon. "I won't wait until morning for this. I know we're all tired, but I won't let them get away. We lost three innocent people tonight. Not to mention a hundred acres of farmland that won't be able to grow anything until the char has been gone at least a year."

"Think this is retaliation for our killing the Jakals in the damplands?" Rye asked.

"I don't really care. If the Jakals are wanting an outright war, they'd best be prepared. We have shelter, food, supplies, and electricity. The winter can be very long in the wilderness if I start kicking them off my lands. Ungrateful animals."

"Reule, before Delano and Saber get here, I want to ask you something," Rye said suddenly.

"Mmm?"

"It's not like you to be the last to sense trouble. What the hell was that at dinner tonight?"

Reule looked up at him, understanding instantly that Rye knew perfectly well why he'd been slow to identify trouble. "Well, Blade, I could be wrong," he mused scornfully, "but I'd guess it was because I was preoccupied by the idea of making love to the redhead to my left. Since you damn well already know that, stop playing games and get to your point."

"It's just that you've been really distracted over this, My Prime," Rye said, bowing his head in respectful apology. "The entire Pack feels it. It's been a little—"

"Rye!" Darcio cut him off sharply.

Rye's amputated point suddenly became clear and Reule couldn't help the fit of laughter that came up unexpectedly. It made lungs and a throat rough with smoke rebel into coughs. It took him a while to recover, and when he did he saw Darcio and Rye looking at him in bemusement.

"Let me get this clear," he chuckled, coughing again. "Are you trying to tell me I need to get laid? That the Pack is inconveniently horny and restless because for once I'm not obsessed with the workings of Jeth, and you don't know what the hell to do with yourselves? I gather if I take Mystique to bed all of *your* problems would be solved?"

Reule snickered when Rye winced at the painful accuracy of his observations.

"That about sums it up," Darcio said with a self-deprecating grin. "But it's just a suggestion, mind you."

"Darcio, you're an ass," Rye grumbled. "Just because I said aloud what we were all complaining about doesn't mean I'm the designated idiot."

Reule looked from one man to the other, aware of approaching hoofbeats in the distance. "Doesn't it bother any of you that Mystique is an outlander? That she's a fertile woman? What if I bed her and she conceives? I would be honor-bound to make her my Prima. You would have an outlander for a queen."

"Does it matter if it bothers us, Reule?" Darcio countered. "We know you care for Jeth and the Pack above all else, but there are some choices a man makes solely for himself. Prime or no," he insisted when he saw Reule building a response, "there are things that make being king worthwhile, and one of those things is the power to choose whomever you wish for your queen. Don't worry about us.

"I saw you born, Reule. In all the time since, I've never seen you take to a woman the way you've taken to Mystique. That says something to me. To us all. We're all aware of how extraordinary she is."

"We know so little about her," Reule said absently as he tried to absorb Darcio's surprising words.

"We know she has a good heart, more guts than most men, and the grace and beauty needed to guide and represent your realm," Rye interjected. "She's also a powerful 'pathic, which means introducing fresh power into Sánge royal bloodlines. And," Rye paused a beat to grin, "I think she's sweet on you."

Darcio burst into laughter as the approaching riders finally drew to a dusty halt. Three of them dismounted, another ten remaining on horseback. The smell of smoke and soot was heavy on the newcomers and Reule turned to greet them.

He looked straight into diamond eyes that glittered in the moonlight.

"What the . . . ?"

Before he could work up the appropriate protest, Mystique stepped up against him and slid her arms around his waist. She tilted her head back and smiled at him as she infused his tired, soiled body with her pleasant warmth.

"Delano and I had an idea. One that could end this hunt far more quickly than a routine tracking. Since we're all tired," she added, "and would enjoy a bath and our beds . . ." Reule felt her fingers stroking him along his spine as she said *bed*, making sure the word received appropriate emphasis in his mind. "I thought a faster solution would be welcome."

Delano stepped forward and held up one of the canisters of fuel they'd found emptied near the field where the initial fire had been started. The metal was melted and charred and bent, but there was no mistaking it. Mystique stepped away, swiping at her already dirtied face with a small soot-covered hand. Then she held out both hands, nearly black as they were, palms up to show him just how bare they were all of a sudden. No gloves. Nothing to protect her from connecting to whoever had held that can before it had been maliciously emptied.

"Your telemetrics," Rye whispered. "An excellent idea!"

"To hell it is! I don't want her anywhere near a Jakal camp!" Reule roared. He rounded on Mystique, pointing a finger in her calm face. "And don't you *ever* try playing me like that again, *kébé*!"

"I wasn't playing you. I was communicating silently." She shrugged. "I thought a subtle hint would be more acceptable than bluntly saying I wanted to help so we can finally get around to becoming lovers. Since I prefer the frank and honest approach better anyway—"

She broke off and grinned, a flash of white teeth in a soot-streaked face, when the entire Pack all but fell on the ground laughing. Reule was just grateful he was filthy because he had a feeling he was blushing. He'd forgotten that nothing embarrassed her and she was never afraid to be forthright in company.

Reule found himself grinning when the snickers and snorts of laughter surrounding him were lowered in an attempt at respect. She was waiting expectantly, her big eyes blinking with a pretty moonstruck effect she was completely unaware of. He folded his arms over his chest and, very slowly, allowed his gaze to travel from the top of her head to the tips of her toes, with some strategic and lascivious pauses along the way. The cough-covered laughs began again, but his grin grew because he felt the quick response of her sensually attuned body leaping across the distance between them.

"Gentlemen," he said without looking away from her. "You heard the lady. Let's get this over with. I have some . . . business . . . awaiting my attention." To his pleasure, Mystique laughed at his taunt. She was a treasure, and he vowed never to let himself forget that.

Delano waited until everyone was quiet and focused completely on Mystique before handing her the canister. Since she was unfamiliar with the terrain, Reule would read her thoughts and pick out landmarks and other notations that she resurrected. He moved to stand behind her, holding her around the waist.

The canister wasn't a personal item like Chayne's

chair, used with regularity so that a bond had been formed, but with focus she was still able to pinpoint the most recent owner of the object. Reule felt her jerk in his grasp, watched her hands tighten fiercely on the container, the already fatigued metal buckling under the pressure. She threw her head back and stared upward with blank, changing eyes. Their color turned a muddy sort of brownish black, and Reule's mind was suddenly filled with what she was seeing. The moon. In a different position. The Jakals were outdoors. Or at least this one was. She drew down her head and looked around, and he saw the camp, cold and dark, large rocks, trees.

"The forest," he murmured.

"Sánge," she said in a guttural version of her own voice. "Stupid Sánge. Beasts. Feel so much, spewing emotions like offal, wasting it." Reule cringed to hear her say those things. It was blasphemy to hear them on her lips because he knew she would never think or feel such poison. "Sánge murderers. We will hurt Sánge prince as he hurt us. He will pay."

Mystique jerked sharply and Reule held her close, following her eyes around the Jakal camp, counting sleeping forms, watching for a unique formation or tree.

"I will enjoy the day I can pluck the skin off the Sánge prince," the Jakal thought, unaware of how close he actually was at that moment to the Sánge prince. "He will come and we will trap him. Trap him here. Him and his Pack."

"By the Lord, they're waiting for us," Rye hissed.

"Thirty, maybe more," Reule murmured quietly. "Camped in the open forest. I don't see how they expect to trap us."

He assumed the Jakal was a guard because he kept moving and looking around until finally, Reule saw a recognizable landmark. A cave. The Jakal went to enter it.

"Winter safe place here," Mystique rasped, "after Sánge king is dead. Food is plenty. Cave is warm."

"That's no guard," Delano murmured, "that's a leader making plans."

"Sacks of supplies line the walls," Reule said, his confusion evident. "This is different. I've never seen Jakals travel with so much weight before. The cave is lined almost . . ."

And that was when Reule noted the red stamp on the sacking nearest the Jakal as he passed it. It was the merchant stamp of the City of Jeth.

"By the Lord," Rye whispered as he realized what it meant. "The grain convoy. *Amando.*"

Reule reached around and jerked the can from Mystique's hands, turning on his men furiously. "I want to know what the hell is going on here!" he roared. "This is the second time a member of my Pack has been threatened by these bastards! Defender! Blade!" He turned to Rye and Saber, his multicolored eyes snapping into the yellow glow of threat. "You sent outriders with Amando?"

"Of course we did! It was a large shipment. We know full well the Pripans would rather take it than trade for it if it was not protected properly."

"I sent a good twenty guards with Amando to drive and manage the convoy," Saber said stiffly. "With the merchants and their apprentices, that made a good fifty Sánge for four wagonloads."

"Five," Rye corrected him softly.

"So you're telling me we lost a shipment that well guarded to a band of thirty Jakals? I don't believe it. I won't believe it," Reule spat.

Mystique said gently, "There is a trap, Reule. One

that Jakal is so confident in, I can still feel it. There is something we don't know."

"That isn't the worst of it," Darcio noted in a low voice that shook with repressed outrage. "The worst of it is there were no Sánge prisoners in that cave or the campsite."

Mystique couldn't deny the observation. She'd never once felt the Jakal think about Sánge prisoners. Then again, she hadn't figured out the trap that was set for the Sánge either. When she had channeled Chayne, she'd known his deepest thoughts. Why hadn't she learned of the trap or what had happened to the other Sánge? To Amando?

"Don't worry," Rye said as he reached out to touch her arm in a comforting gesture, "Amando is tougher than he looks. Like Chayne, he'd be more valuable to them kept alive. It's only been a day."

"Which means they're close by," Darcio noted.

"And I think I know where," Reule said. "That cave has to be deep to store that much grain. This was very well planned."

"We're tired from fighting the fire," Mystique said. "That was the purpose in setting it, I think. To wear out the Pack. They know how strong you are. They also know you'll come after them yourselves. So they weaken you first, then lie in wait with a trick that they no doubt tested out on the convoy first. Yes. This is very well planned, Reule."

She reached back to touch him and he slid his arms tightly around her in a hug of comfort. She took it gratefully, closing her eyes as she used his warmth to shed the chill of being in the mind of their enemy.

"You have to let me channel him again," she said softly. "I can find out more . . ."

"No. You're exhausted, *kébé*."

"So are you all," she countered, her tone gentle rather than confrontational.

"There's a time constraint," Rye said abruptly, his eyes snapping up to Reule's with understanding dawning over his handsome features. "That's why they set the fire. They needed our attention and they needed it quickly. Why? What advantage grows weaker with time?"

"Strength? Perhaps Amando's?"

"Right," the Prime Blade mused as he looked at her in surprise. "If they're using him as bait. They know Pack will sense one another. If he's dying, they need to rush us."

"Listen, *kébé*, it's time you went back to the city."

"No. You need me with you if Amando is injured. Or anyone else, for that matter. Don't argue, just agree," she pleaded as she turned in his grasp to face him. "You have no time or men to spare to go with me. Besides, you may need my telemetric abilities. There's still an unseen snare."

"Send her back, Reule. She'll just distract you," Darcio thought to him.

"Darcio's right," Delano agreed.

"I think she could be useful," Rye countered. *"And she's right. We have no time or resources to send her home. You'll be worrying about her whether she's there or not. Better to have her in sight."*

"*Kébé*, keep near me. Ride close to Fit. We'd better go before it gets any later and any colder."

Reule was right. The Jakal camp wasn't that far away. They had to traverse the rest of the flatlands, which, being even ground, went rather quickly. It was when they reached the leading edge of the forest that things got rough for the horses. There was a road at first, which then became a trail and eventually disappeared altogether. The second moon was up before Reule finally called a halt. Everyone dismounted, tying up the animals in the best shelter that could be managed in such rough country.

"It's still a good mile, but we can't risk their hearing the horses. Sound travels in this forest in strange ways."

Reule pulled Mystique to his side, gripping her hand in his, his fingers lacing tightly with hers. She shivered when, with an eerie synchronization, all of the men withdrew weapons. There was a vibration among them, one that Mystique had never felt before. Their movements became increasingly quiet, even though the terrain grew denser with every step. Before long it was like walking with ghosts, men who were there, yet not. Their thoughts and bodies were focused amongst themselves, communication passing in silence between them, until she was left with the eerie feeling of walking alone through the wilderness, in spite of the strong fingers wrapped securely around hers.

That loneliness chilled her to her bones, nibbling at the edges of her memory until she shivered and forced herself up against Reule's side. He sensed her disquiet and wrapped his arm around her waist, guiding her over rocks and fallen trees. It helped her feel once again a part of the group's movements and she was able to keep herself calm.

Reule was fully focused on the Pack, determined not to have any more casualties among them. He would see to it he made no mistakes. This shouldn't even be happening. Had he been too lax? Too tolerant of the contemptible Jakals? There were Sánge who thought he ought to slaughter the gypsies without discrimination. And he could do so if he wished it. These were Sánge lands, and he was the law.

He glanced at Mystique and in an instant he knew he could never slaughter any species so indiscriminately. It had been done to the Sánge, and he knew what that sort of persecution felt like. Whether or not they were deserving of it, if only one Jakal was different, like his *kébé* was different, it would be unforgivable. He recalled too easily how close he'd come to losing her. To never knowing her.

Anxiety built within him as they drew closer to the cave. He didn't like her being there, but logically he couldn't refute her usefulness. He'd use any resource he had if it would protect his Packmates and his city, just as he'd use his Pack and his city to protect her.

Reule drew them all to a stop without a word, his arm around Mystique's waist bringing her to a halt. He stepped against her, backing her up into the thick trunk of a nearby tree. Mystique let out a sound of surprise as his huge body herded hers to where he wanted her, trapping her between muscle and bark until she was looking up at him with her hands grasping the sleeves of his shirt. Her breath clouded on the cold night air, the temperature having slowly dropped as they'd traveled.

"Stay here, *kébé*. Don't follow us. I'll come get you when this is over. I mean it," he said when she opened her mouth to argue. "Don't make me tie you to this tree. I'd rather leave you able to defend yourself. There are nasty things in these woods." Reule flipped his dagger against his palm and handed it to her hilt first. There wasn't a sound from any of the other men, but Mystique could feel the shock that rippled through them at the gesture.

Not really understanding the significance, she

reached out and grasped the handle of the weapon. She automatically imitated the nimble flip Reule had used, reaching down and tucking the blade into her left boot. When she lifted her head, Reule was staring at her hard.

"You're always surprising me," he said softly as he reached to rub his thumb over her cheek. "I might regret the day I figure you out."

He leaned in to kiss her, a firm, territorial gesture. It left her dizzy, breathless, and tasting of char and Reule. He tore himself away from her as if he had to do it quickly or he would never succeed. He instructed a guard to stay with her, and then she watched them disappear into the dark underbrush in perfect silence.

"I might as well have stayed with the horses," Mystique grumbled through her chattering teeth some time later. "At least they're warm."

And better conversationalists, she thought petulantly as the guard continued to ignore her. He didn't look happy to have been left behind either. Especially guarding an outlander female he probably thought shouldn't have come along in the first place. She had an unreasonable urge to walk up to him and kick him in his shins. It seemed like the sort of thing a woman would do. Certainly tamer than her earlier urges to draw pretty pictures on his chest with her dagger. Those didn't seem very ladylike at all, so she'd worked very hard at pushing the impulses aside. Para's lectures on proper behavior had echoed in her head the whole time.

When the guard was suddenly thrown back off his feet, it was as if her venomous thoughts had struck him. It took a moment for Mystique to realize it was a whiplash of psychic feedback that had hit him. Then it was on her, prickling and screaming all around her, trapping her in invisible terror. She threw her hands up over her head to protect herself, but the lashing mental screams whipped around her and through her again and again. She fell to her knees in the brambles, the cold dampness soaking through her clothes. Her head pounded with pain as she began to hear shouts and screams made by real voices that echoed through the forest. She whimpered softly as the thrash of psychic abuse snapped harder against her, and she tried to force up some kind of protection. There must be some way to shield herself, if only she could grasp hold of it.

She was so overwhelmed that she couldn't even tell who she was hearing in the melee of noise. Did any of those masculine cries belong to Reule? His Pack? Instinctively, she drew the blade Reule had given her, grasping the weapon in a sturdy grip. Arming herself seemed to help. The feeling of guarding herself somehow countered the psychic dump of pain and death. She sobbed, partly in relief and partly because an incredible feeling of sorrow overcame her. She'd been so complacent lately that she'd almost forgotten the overwhelming sadness that stalked her everywhere. It was more intense than ever.

Able to stand now, Mystique made her way over to the guard still lying prone on the ground. She bent over him, blinking back the swell of tears in her eyes. All she wanted was Reule. Safe. His living warmth beside her.

"Are you well?" she asked the guard hoarsely, carefully touching his shoulder lest he grow hostile at the contact.

"Yes. Lord and Lady," he gasped.

"We need to go to Reule."

"No. My Prime would have my head if I took his . . .

you . . ." he stammered and Mystique understood his
dilemma. No true lady would behave as she had, saying
things that made no secret of her lust for Reule. It hadn't
bothered her to be so free. Not until this man had come
just shy of calling her a whore.

"I'm sorry," he said quickly as he sat up, his tone desperate now. "I meant no offense. Please, my lady, I'm
just an uncouth guard and I . . ."

"It's all right," she assured him quietly. "What's your
name?"

"Sath."

"Sath. Well, Sath, you're only speaking the truth as
you've seen it. I admire that in anyone. Now, please, can
we go? I feel strongly that I'm needed."

"Don't ask me to go against the Prime's orders, my
lady. As fair as he is, he and all of the Pack would take
a turn at me. If anything were to happen to you . . ."

"I see." Mystique sighed. "I'm sorry."

"There's no need to apologize."

"Yes. I'm afraid there is."

She wasn't even sure how she knew she could do it,
but she reached out quickly and slapped a hand over
Sath's forehead. In an instant the map of his brain flared
into her awareness with all its many tiny pathways and
functions, just as Chayne's bones and muscles had done
when she'd healed him. Except this time, she didn't
heal. She manipulated a natural, healthy function and
Sath fell back into the moist rot of leaves on the forest
floor, fast asleep.

He'd never had a chance.

Mystique tried to regroup, her head pounding with
exhaustion and exertion. Knife at the ready, she stood
up to make her way toward the place where she heard
the forest churning with activity. She'd barely gone a

step when the entire forest spun away from under her, pitching her forward until she landed flat on her face. She fought for control as her stomach churned.

"Stay where you are."

There was no mistaking the owner of that imperious command in her head. She was so relieved to hear him that she didn't even take exception to his high-handedness. Instead, she just rolled over with a sigh and reminded herself that domineering and commanding behaviors were requirements for a ruler. Besides, staying right where she was suddenly seemed like an excellent notion.

It was only minutes before she felt him standing over her. He knelt down as she opened her untrustworthy eyes. "What happened?" he asked gently, reaching to gather her to him. She grasped his arms to steady herself but was shocked to feel warmth and wetness beneath her fingers.

She forced herself to focus on the dark fluid soaking his shirt. "You're hurt!" she exclaimed as the anatomy of the injury instantly flared into her psychic awareness. He'd been stabbed in his left biceps and clawed across the right.

"No. Don't," he said firmly when he sensed her power. He drew her up into his arms and stood easily. She blinked away the diagnostic images of his injured body when he refused her help. "Save your strength for those who need it more."

"Amando," she whispered, knowing by the tension of his body and the lines around his mouth that it was bad.

"Amando is dead. It's Rye. He took the brunt of the trap."

"What was it?"

"Electricity. Rye was right. There was a time constraint. They were running out of the fuel they were using to power an electrical trap around the camp."

The screams of agony she had felt and heard. Reule and his men walking into that painful death trap. "Amando is dead?" She felt fresh tears and sorrow burn across her soul.

Reule set her on her feet, but held her up against his body. "There's nothing you can do, *kébé*."

"What does that mean?" Her gaze snapped up to his at the oddly worded reply.

"He was bitten by a Jakal." Delano spoke up from behind her, making her twist in Reule's proprietary hold. "Jakal venom is fatal."

Reule growled threateningly at Delano, and she knew the Pack had been warned against involving her.

"But he isn't dead yet?" she demanded.

"As good as. It's a matter of minutes, Mystique."

"Take me to him. Let me help him!"

"No!" Reule held her in a grip of iron when she tried to wrest herself away. "Amando made me swear not to let you try. *Kébé*, the suffering from Jakal venom is horrific. He saw how you took on Chayne's wounds. We can't know if you'd survive. He made me promise . . ."

"Then break your promise! He's in pain and doesn't know what he's saying! Let go!" She lunged hard against his grip, sending her braid whipping against her face. "Please!" She didn't want to throw a tantrum, but couldn't seem to help herself. Sobs wrenched out of her chest in hard rasps as tears fell wildly.

"Mystique, stop it!"

Anger overwhelmed Mystique. She gripped Reule with infuriated strength, and the workings of his body flared into her mind's eye. Reule was the most powerful telepath and empath she'd probably ever know. This would be no easy task.

She was right.

Mystique felt the sudden seal of an enormous hand around her throat and she was jerked completely around until her back was flush to his chest and her breath was being slightly restricted by his powerful grip. He wasn't hurting her, but he was making himself perfectly clear.

"Don't you dare try to strong-arm me, little girl," he gritted out in a savage warning into her ear.

"Then let me go to him! I can save him! Please! I'm begging you."

"Don't you think I want that?" he demanded, giving her a sharp tug. "Amando is Pack. My blood flows in his veins and his in mine. My mind is within his this very moment. I'm feeling him die. Don't you think I want to let you go to him?"

"*No!* I think you're choosing me over him! Please! Darcio, Delano, please!"

"Stop! I'm begging you, baby, please stop." His voice broke and she abruptly stopped struggling when she heard the pain in him. He lost control over his emanation and suddenly she could feel it. All of it, driving into her. His grief and the agony of watching Amando die from the inside out. The wretchedness of the entire Pack. The knowing and the helpless fury. "You could never save them both, you know. Rye needs you too, and at least he has hope. You can't possibly save him *and* Amando. Who will you choose? Can you choose?" He dragged in a hard, stuttering breath. "I'm making the choice for you. Don't you see? That's what I am meant to do in this world. Let me protect you."

Reule scooped her up, her totally passive body telling him that she'd finally absorbed the terrible truth of the

situation. He swallowed back his own torment and
carried her over to where Saber and some others had
laid Rye's savagely burned body. The cosmetic wounds
weren't the problem. He'd taken a terrible hit, the pulse
wracking his body for a while before Reule and Delano
had figured out how to free him from the trap. They
couldn't even feel his mind anymore, and they were terrified of losing two Packmates in such a painfully short
timespan. The psychic effect alone would be devastating. Reule wasn't in a position to dwell on the personal
ramifications, though. It was a luxury that, as Packleader, he might never truly have.

Reule dropped her down beside Rye. She curled up
onto her knees and reached out for Rye. She stopped just
before she touched him, hesitating as her eyes flowed
over his big body. Reule didn't need to be a telepath to
know her thoughts. She was reconciling herself to the
idea that if she committed herself to healing Rye, she
would eliminate any hope for Amando. Reule already
knew there was no hope. In another minute Amando
would truly be gone. The backlash of his death would
tremble through the Pack, including Rye, who might not
be able to survive the devastation of it in his present state.
Reule wanted to tell her to hurry, but he'd pushed her
too much already. She was tired and feeling ill, and badg-
ering her would be of no help.

She took a deep breath and laid her hands on Rye's
broad chest. She went straight for his heart and lungs,
knowing what electrical shock could do to both. His
heart was beating erratically, his lungs filling with fluid.
His numbed brain couldn't correct the problems. In a
way, the current still lived within him.

But she would change that. She eased his heart into
matching her own slower, steadier beat. She was smaller

but he was generally healthier than she was, so it was a fair approximation. She emptied his lungs, coughing as her already smoke-abused chest absorbed the damage.

Reule stood quietly over her, as did the rest of the Pack. Silence reigned in the dark forest as though they were at worship, rather than fresh from battle. Rye became the center of Mystique's existence. Pictures of his anatomy burst into brilliant color and detail. She marveled at how much she knew about the small structures whose delicate balance was necessary for the miracle of life. Her hands slid over the charred male body as she forced him into a deep sleep, no longer needing another to divert pain for her. She was proud of that. If nothing else, that development was worthwhile.

In the end it was the exterior burns she left uncared for, partly from exhaustion, but mostly because Reule snatched her away, calling an end to the healing. She murmured instructions about how to dress the burns and then fell asleep.

She didn't feel it when, moments later, Amando finally slipped away from the rest of the Pack.

Chapter 10

Mystique stood facing into the winds, drawing her cloak tight as the cold bit at her exposed skin. She was looking down over Jeth City from her position on the highest battlements of Jeth Keep.

Even from her great height above, she could see the plain gray and tan stone of the houses and buildings below, and the speckles of red everywhere that decorated them now as they had not three days ago. The red banners of mourning, hung everywhere the loyal citizens of Jeth could possibly reach. The symbol of the city, splashed against a black background, was displayed in respect for the death of one of the cherished Pack.

As usual, the slightest thought of Amando made her chest constrict and sent hot tears searing into already raw eyes. Still, she'd rather watch the distant sadness of the city than remain within the keep where the loss was felt so keenly, so much closer. It was as though every male in the Pack had been stabbed deep in the belly, a wound slowly bleeding, killing them with as much pain as imaginable. They walked, they talked, they drew breath, but their spirit had abandoned them.

Never had she expected the violence.

Not against one another, but against themselves. Every day for three days it had been the same. The training grounds, the chapel, the wilderness—wherever they could lose themselves in a moment of privacy, these men would butcher themselves in devastation and loss. It was something ritualistic, the bearing of one's dagger against one's own skin, cutting arm, chest, or thigh as deep as one dared. Worse, none of them would allow her to heal them afterward. Since she was sensitive to injury now, she was aware of every new wound a Packmate endured. She'd first learned of the practice when she'd felt Reule suddenly wounded soon after they'd returned to the keep with Amando's body. She had run to him, encountering him as he was leaving the keep's chapel. She'd demanded to see his wound, insisted he allow her to heal him, and he'd summarily rejected her. He wouldn't even allow her to heal his injuries from the battle with the Jakals.

She wondered if she would have fled the keep had she known then how truly bad it was going to get over the next few days. How much longer would this continue? She couldn't bear much more. She felt every single wound in a way none of them could comprehend, each a little voice crying out to her for healing. The deeper the injury, the louder the voice.

Reule was the worst, taking Amando's loss even harder than the others. No matter how careful her approach, he wouldn't let her near him. He could hardly bear to look at her, and that hurt more than she would have thought possible.

And Rye . . .

Reule's heir was openly hostile to her. She could feel his outrage and hate, a force he made obvious to her empathically challenged brain. It stung to have lost his

faith in her, but it cut deep to feel his soul-blackened
contempt. Rye had been warm to her, even when he
hadn't been certain of her motives. This bitter man
blamed her, Reule, and most of all himself for
Amando's death.

The revelation had come when she'd been walking
alone and a brutal hand had sealed around her throat
from behind. She was jerked into a dark place and
slammed hard against a stone wall. Seeing stars, she had
barely comprehended it was Rye who held her. His face
raw and red in the wake of her latest healing, he snarled
as he cut off her air.

"Why? *Why?*" he demanded. "I saw what you did for
Chayne. Why couldn't you save *him?* Answer me, you
heartless bitch! Did you waste too much precious
energy panting after my Prime? Running around where
you weren't needed? Saving *me?* What am I, but heir?
Amando was the heart of our commerce, the peace we
keep so precariously. You sat next to him, broke bread
with him, *how could you let him die?*"

He had thrown her to his feet, knowing no real answer
could possibly be forthcoming. She made no defense of
herself, not feeling she deserved to. He'd felt that guilt,
the knowledge evident in the disgust on his face.

Mystique touched her throat where the bruises of his
fingerprints were fading now, two days later. She'd been
avoiding them all ever since. She mourned alone for a
man she'd hardly known and yet knew perfectly through
the intensity of the love of six other males who were
floundering without him. So she stayed in the cold wind
where she knew it was unlikely she would be found or
joined. The sky was overcast, the sharp scent of first
snow growing as the temperature dropped. She had
learned one more thing about herself, she thought with

a humorless laugh. The cold didn't seem to bother her very much. It was almost as though she was used to the extreme temperature. Strangely, this made her feel more of an outlander than anything else in this place where warmth was so highly coveted.

Reule watched Mystique from just around the corner. She leaned into the wind, shedding a single tear that was quickly blown away, chapping her cheek an even brighter red than it already was. It was a novel experience to be able to watch her undetected like this. How much of her obliviousness was caused by her obviously deep thoughts, he didn't know, but he'd been there a good twenty minutes. Long enough to know she hardly moved, didn't sit, merely stared out at the city, thinking and feeling.

Her thoughts he left alone. The empathy of a city of mourners was intense enough; he didn't need to hear painful inner dialogues as well. He felt her sadness reaching deep, but it was the loneliness he found surprising. There was a keep . . . a *city* full of others feeling exactly as she was. The chiming harmony of Sánge grief lent him a kind of comfort, and he didn't understand why it wasn't the same for her. She was confused and angry, and he knew she was having a hard time understanding their mourning rituals. She'd accepted so much so easily, but here she floundered in Sánge differences.

Still, none of them were performing at their best in the wake of this devastation.

He had sought her out to tell her there was a ceremony tonight. Upon his death, the rights to Amando's body had reverted back to his blood family. It became the choice of his mother, father, or siblings what would be done to recognize his life and his death. Amando's family had deeply honored Reule by extending his rights as Packleader in this regard. It meant they wished Amando to be paid homage in state, rather than make it just a familial affair.

Reule wouldn't disappoint them. Tonight they'd begin the seven formal days of light and dark mourning with all the proper pomp and regalia that the Packleader could muster. No one in Jeth would ever forget how deeply he had treasured Amando, or how terribly he felt the loss of him. He knew Mystique would value being present tonight, and he hoped the ceremony would help her understand that amongst the Sánge, no one truly ever mourned alone.

He looked up at the gray skies, felt in his bones the coming storm, and found it almost poetic. The snow always came just as Amando ended his final trade journey of the season. It seemed appropriate that it had come early, marking the occasion as the Prime Envoy came home for the last time.

Reule allowed himself to feel the pain of grief, pressing his hand over his heart where the deepest bite of his ritual dagger lay, provoking hurt in muscle and sinew that echoed the hurt he couldn't touch.

And this, at last, alerted her to his presence. She'd grown extremely sensitive to detecting physical pain, he realized as she turned her head to look at him. The movement threw her hair to the mercy of the wind, sending tendrils whipping wildly across her face and throat before she could reach up and pin it back with her hand. She faced him, silent and unsure in a way that twisted him into knots because she suddenly seemed so fragile. In just a few steps he'd closed the distance between them, his wide palms reaching to frame her small, cold face. It was the first time he'd touched her in three days, and he felt the awareness of it cutting them both to their very souls. It brought him low, the way his entire body seemed to shudder with relief at the long-awaited contact. She reached up with both hands to circle his wrists, holding him fast, as if she feared his escape.

"I came to tell you there will be a ceremony tonight," he said roughly, emotion changing the stroke of his voice.

She blinked and then gave him a peculiar little smile. "No, you didn't," she corrected him. "Reule, anyone can see there's going to be a ceremony tonight. It's hard to miss such extensive preparations. So you came here for other reasons."

He thought about it for a moment, easily seeing the truth. The ceremony had been an excuse to approach her, to breach the distance he'd crafted between them.

"I haven't wanted to feel good," he uttered, her brow wrinkling at the half-explained thought. "I want you to understand that, Mystique. Touching you, even in this small way"—he drew her against his lips, kissing her forehead and then inhaling the cold, clean fragrance of her hair—"for me it's so sweet, so damn glorious a feeling, and I didn't want to feel that." He watched as the ache of her loneliness brought scorching tears into her red-rimmed eyes. He felt an answering sting lance through him. "He was Pack, *kébé*," he said hoarsely. "I can never adequately explain what that means, what it feels like to have him torn away, but I can try to explain mourning rituals."

"Please," she begged, "Para has been too beside herself to even speak and . . . I had no one else to ask. I don't know about this the way I knew other things."

"I'm sorry. I shouldn't have assumed. Can we go somewhere warmer? We can talk and, if it's all right, I'd like very much to hold you close for a while."

Her response was to fling herself forward against

him, wrapping her arms around his body as far and as tight as she could manage, burrowing beneath his cloak for his warmth. She exhaled a heavy sob of relief and he suddenly realized she'd taken his distance as rejection and maybe even reproach. He held her a moment, closing his eyes tightly against the bitter wind. This was the second time she had mistaken his treatment of her for a form of punishment. It spoke loudly to him of her unknown past.

He moved them indoors, letting her cling to him however much she wanted. Did she know how good the closeness felt to him too? He discarded their cloaks and other outerwear, then took her into a small study. A fire burned enthusiastically and they both headed straight for it even though the room was electrically heated and warm. Reule took a seat in a large chair and, hooking her wrist in hand, he pulled her down into his lap. She sighed, making no arguments whatsoever, and snuggled against him.

"There are ten days of mourning for the Sánge," he began quietly. "The first three are called the Depths. This is when we immerse ourselves in our grief. We do this," he took her hand and laid it over the wound near his heart, "so that every time we move or touch the wound, the pain will force a reminder of our loss and grief. The more intense and plentiful the cuts, the more we seek to honor the one who has died. The tradition is very old, but it has evolved to a point that these cuts are usually shallow marks done for symbolism more than anything. But Amando was Pack."

He said it as though his words explained everything, and Mystique supposed they did. Now she understood why it would be an affront to him to be healed. She didn't care for the practice, but she did respect what it represented to him.

"The Depths ends the third night, tonight," he continued, "and the light and dark mourning will be initiated with the ceremony. Tonight we will inter Amando in the royal crypt, honoring his lifetime spent as a Packmate."

"Light and dark mourning?"

"It means we laugh and cry as we remember him together. We celebrate and mourn together. The first days are solitary, but these seven are spent close to family and friends who were all touched by Amando in his lifetime." He placed a finger on her windblown cheek. "The Depths is a very dark and painful period. You understand? It would disrespect others to disturb the grief with improper emotion. This is doubly true of Pack, because our feelings are so interwoven. The Pack feels what I feel, *kébé*, especially now. They expect me to help them cope with their grief."

He drew her closer, his lips to her ear. "I couldn't accept your solace or endure your sympathy, sweetheart, because of how it makes me feel. Comforted. Soothed. These feelings would have disturbed the Depths of the others. Besides, I wouldn't have contented myself with the solace of your words and heart." He slid his fingertips down to the edge of her modest neckline, running its edge as though it were something low and daring against her breasts. "Only all of you would have sufficed, Mystique. The slaking of my voracious lust for you would have been insulting to the Pack. I believe it would have been insulting to you as well. You wouldn't have wanted to learn me as a lover under those circumstances."

"And now is different?"

"Now is different," he agreed. "Dusk is coming and soon we will shed the Depths. It will . . ."

He stopped and, because she was sitting in his lap, she felt the tension that suddenly locked tight in his muscles. His thighs beneath her bottom became so hard that she shifted uncomfortably. His hand clamping onto her shoulder stopped her movement, and he turned her toward him as he lifted his hand from her neckline and tipped her chin back. She glimpsed the green-yellow glare of his eyes before she was forced to look at the ceiling, baring her throat to him.

"Who did this?" he demanded, his voice a threatening rumble that made her heart skip a beat. She felt his fingers close around her throat, fitting over the impressions Rye's hand had left on her. "Answer me, *kébé*, or I will take the answer from you."

"No! Please." She gripped his wrist, pulling at his hand so she could lower her eyes back to his. "It was an accident."

"*An accident?* The grip of a man's hand around a woman's throat?"

"Something you've done yourself in your temper," she argued. "To this very same throat. He was grieving terribly. You cannot . . ."

"This was *Pack*?" Reule surged out of his chair, taking her with him until she was hanging in his grip by her arms. "Someone from the Pack put their hands on you like this?" Reule wanted to shake her as her accusations penetrated his rage-blind brain. "Don't dare talk to me of my temper! I restrained you. I didn't hurt you, bruise you, and I most certainly would never lay a hand on you if I thought I couldn't control my anger! Do you really mean to compare my actions to this . . . this act of brutality against you?"

"No," she whispered, knowing how it would make him feel if she did. "But I'm begging you to understand that the volatile mix of grief and anger, the suffering . . ."

"We're all suffering! Does that give us all the right to

strangle you? What next? Beating? Whipping our frustrations out on you? No, Mystique. There is only one being we may injure in grief, and that is ourselves. With the *jihmak*, the cutting that you are so disturbed by, for honorable remembrance. Don't tell me there is any excuse for a Packmate to hurt you!"

"Isn't there? What if he felt that I had failed him? Or that I was responsible for Amando's death? Or what if," she said quickly when she saw protest about to explode from him, "the rage he feels is really toward himself because he survived while his friend has been ripped away from him? From you?"

"*Rye*," Reule breathed as understanding dawned.

"He blames himself! Cutting himself is never going to allow that feeling to escape. He lashed out at a convenient target—"

"Then let him target me! I made the choice! Lord damn him, I'll kill him with my bare hands for this dishonorable treatment of a woman! Of *my* woman!"

"Reule!" she gasped.

Mystique froze for several long beats, her eyes wide, her lips quivering. She gripped the fabric of his shirt, feeling his chest rapidly rise and fall with his emotion. Then she flung herself at him, clinging to his body with all her strength. She dragged herself up his height, cursing the confinement of skirts that prevented her from using her legs to aid her. It turned out not to be necessary because he helped her with hands at her waist and drew her tightly against himself as he met her questing mouth. The kiss was soft, despite her demand, and brief, but it was still more than enough to heat their blood in anticipation of more.

"Say it again," she begged him against his lips. "Without the anger, Reule, please say it again."

"My woman, Mystique," he said, his breath and lips as hot as the passion behind the phrase. "Did you doubt it? Did you think I'd simply forget how you make me feel? How extraordinary you are? By the Lord, I'd be insane to let you slip away from me."

She laughed tremulously as he kissed her cheek and chin. He made it sound so simple. So logical. When he knew it was positively outrageous. "I'm not Sánge," she breathed as his hands slid up the length of her spine and into her hair. "I'm no one. I have nothing to offer you."

"You have everything to offer me," he said roughly, giving her a warning shake just before he sealed his mouth to hers and burned her to her soul with sentient hunger. She became keenly aware of it with each deep stroke of his seeking tongue. She was gasping for breath when he finally broke away. "Beauty, intelligence, power, courage. These are all I crave in a mate, Mystique."

"A history. A homeland," she argued breathlessly. "A name."

His mouth trailed away, striking out for the length of her throat and scorching her with kisses of need and temptation. "I've given you a name," he coaxed softly. "You will make new history with us here. We will be your homeland. Let us love you, sweetheart."

The phraseology curled a fist of anxiety between her lungs.

"I will let *you* love me," she responded quietly.

He felt the sharp sorrow in her resistance, like a weight tied to her spirit. She might not have actual memories, but she reacted with emotional instinct to things. He suppressed a frown, opting to be accepting rather than confrontational. They'd worry about this later, when their mourning for Amando wasn't so keen.

For now, the exclusivity of her offer thrilled him. There

was a possessive need that was immensely satisfied by the offer. He was all too used to sharing everything, in spite of having the power to shut his thoughts away from others. He craved this exclusivity between them.

"Thank you," he said very softly. "I intend to do exactly that." He ran his fingertips around the marks on her neck and frowned darkly. "*After* I beat Rye to within his last breath for treating you this way. And don't think you can reason with me," he warned her sharply when her grip tightened convulsively. "There are matters on which you will find me intractable, and this is one of them."

"Please, Reule. Please. Let me approach him tonight at the banquet. Give me a chance to resolve this with him before you do something that could turn him against me forever. I will have no future here if your heir despises me. You have to know that."

"Then he'll no longer be my heir!" Reule thundered. "This is about what is and isn't acceptable behavior within my Pack! Rye knows my rules and, by the Lord, he will obey them or he'll suffer consequences!"

"Then devise another penance, My Prime, because I cannot see how an act of violence can rectify another act of violence!"

Her emotional explosion set Reule back a step, his anger mutating into honest puzzlement as he searched her stubborn features. "Why do you do that? Why do you use my title like a castigation?"

"I . . . I don't." She flushed, her slim neck turning red enough to rival her hair.

"You do. You deprive me of my given name when you're angry with me."

"Reule, this isn't about me," she said haltingly, her words flustered.

"This is *all* about you," Reule corrected her. "All of this ties into this past you think you know nothing about. I believe you know more than you realize. Even I know more than you realize just by observation of your behavior. For instance, you won't trust anyone but me."

"That's not—"

"You behave as though abuse is to be expected," he pressed. "The larger the group, the more you're resigned to it." She pressed her lips tightly together, stepping back farther from him, but he wasn't letting her get off that easily this time. "What is it you think to accomplish by speaking to Rye? What do you think will appease me? An apology? The act is unpardonable, *kébé*. No apology will ever be sufficient. Tell me, what would you have me do instead of violence? Give him a stern talking to? What reprimand do you wish?"

"I wish tolerance! I wish understanding! You of all people should grasp that!"

"I understand that when my parents were killed, there was a price due, and I saw it paid. My tolerance has limits, else I will be made a victim, Mystique. And victimization is something *you* should understand. Something chased you into this wilderness, something so bad that you would rather crawl on your hands and knees across the flatlands with broken bones than stay still where it might catch up with you. You dragged yourself up three flights of stairs, through mildew and mold and Lady knows what, just so you could hide behind crates on a floor this close to collapsing under you!"

"I . . . I didn't have . . . broken bones?"

She ended the protest in a confused query, staring at him as she tried to decode what she'd heard. It didn't take long for a frightful sort of understanding to dawn in her faceted eyes. Reule cursed himself for his loose tongue, for not picking his time as he'd told himself he would, and instead allowing his temper to rule him. He just couldn't control himself when he thought of someone causing her harm.

"You did. You fell from a horse," he said. Her eyes went wide as she crossed tight, protective arms over herself. "I guess you healed in your sleep over the next few days while you were in the attic. Darcio," he explained at last with a sigh. "His third 'pathic power is the ability to learn a body's history. Not your memory, but the experience of what your body has been through."

"And how long have you known all of this?" she asked chillingly.

"Since the first night we found you. I asked him to read you so I would learn how to care for you. To protect you."

"Why didn't you tell me? Why haven't you told me any of this? You let me struggle not knowing . . ."

"It isn't about punishment!" he roared furiously, making her jump in her own skin. "Can't you understand that? You aren't being punished! No one wants to see you disciplined, taught a lesson, or anything else! Not here. Not in this place and, by the Lord, not as long as I draw breath!"

He reached out and grabbed hold of her, dragging her against him and forcing her gaze onto his. "Don't you see? This is the whole point, Mystique. You're safe here. I swear it. No one will harm you. I won't allow it. That's why Rye must pay consequences for his actions. Why didn't I tell you about Darcio? Frankly, because I'd be damned happy if you never, ever had to remember what that crowd of laughing, jeering people did to you! Everything I tell you is a potential step backward toward that memory and, since I couldn't protect you from it the first time, I'll damn well do it now if I can!"

"I-I don't . . ." *Understand.* She couldn't seem to make herself understand what he was doing for her; the significance of his efforts to protect her at all costs. Why was that? She wasn't a stupid person. Mystique stared up at him in open-mouthed shock. Yes. It was shock. She was always stunned by his vehemence as he went about championing her. Did that make his point? Did she behave as though she didn't deserve such consideration?

The question was, what did she believe in her heart? Instantly she knew there was a furious streak inside her that refused the notion of her being a victim. Instinctively, she knew she had never been the type to meekly accept punitive retaliation. It wasn't her nature.

"I have this question that keeps going around and around in my head," she said, reaching up to toy with the fabric of his shirt over his chest. "I keep wondering what it was. What could I possibly have done? What terrible, awful thing did I do to deserve being chased out of my homeland?"

Reule sighed and, cupping the back of her head in a large palm, he drew her closer, cuddling her against himself. "Sometimes people don't need legitimate reasons to do what they do. They make up reasons to justify their desires. This Sánge tribe once lived in a beautiful place of sand, of warmth that lasted all year round. I swear," he insisted when she made a sniggering sound of disbelief. "It's very far from here, over some of the most hostile lands and waters you will ever know. It was a treacherous route that made this place instantly look like a haven when we found it. We were chased from our home of tropical beauty because we were Sánge, but also because greedy people coveted the beautiful place we lived in."

"Like Jakals. They take what they want," she said with disgust.

"Yes."

"Why did you never go back? Why not reclaim what was yours? You're certainly powerful enough now."

"And I'm also content. So are my people. We're safe here. A journey like that would cost more than it would be worth. I used to think that way—about vengeance and righteousness—when I was young, but luckily there was too much for me to do while I was maturing for me to act on those impulses. By the time I could actually return, it was no longer important."

"And that's what you wish for me. That I will find my place here, with you, so when I do remember where I'm from, it's no longer important?"

She watched him swallow visibly. "Yes. Is that terribly selfish?"

"Selfish?"

"Yes, damn it. I want you for myself, understand? I want nothing to take you from me. Mystique," he said vehemently, "I would make you my Prima. Don't you understand that?"

"You . . ."

Mystique gasped for breath as everything suddenly seemed to close in around her. The enormity of the offer was too much. It was all too much. Blackness, starting in spots, began to blossom in her vision. Now she couldn't breathe at all. Her mouth was open, she tried to draw breath, but it wouldn't come.

"Mystique!" Reule swung her around and sat her down in a nearby chair, kneeling beside her as she struggled to draw in a breath. "It's all right, baby, just breathe.

Slow. Small breaths." He drew her forward, leaning her against himself. "Stop this." He gripped her head in his hands, forcing her to look at him. "If you don't want me, that's one thing, but by the Lady, *kébé*, stop thinking you don't deserve my regard. If you truly trust me, then believe me when I say there has never been and never will be anyone so suited to me and the Sánge people than you are."

Mystique reached out, her hands clinging to his shirt-sleeves. Her eyes were tearing from her fight for breath, but she was looking at him and he knew she comprehended him.

She breathed.

A single, deep gasp that instantly faded the bright red of her face and chest. She sobbed out the breath she'd taken and drew a second as she threw her arms around his neck. She was sensitive, so he'd seen her struggle for control over tears before, but never had he felt her sob as hard as she did now. Her entire body shook as she was racked over and over with them, the sorrow she'd kept so carefully at bay suddenly everywhere.

He hadn't felt a truly anguished woman up close like this in a long time. One of the disadvantages of a bachelor household and an exclusively male Pack. Still, he knew enough to cradle her close and tight and let her cry herself out. He felt her small hands gripping him convulsively wherever she could catch hold. Her tears soaked his shirt, but he paid it no mind. She felt warm and real, and somehow more whole than mere minutes ago. It was his empathy feeding him that knowledge.

"Hush, baby," he soothed her softly. "Everything will be well. I promise you that."

"I know," she hiccupped. "I know!"

He smiled against her hair at that, amused at her

contradictory responses. It was several more minutes before she calmed enough to let him turn up her ravaged face to his.

"I was lost," she sniffed, her eyes seeming so much bigger now with the flushing sparkle of tears. "I know I was. I had nothing, and I was lost, and now you want to hand me the world. You want to give me a place again. And I feel in my heart that you'd never let me be lost again. You are so beautiful, Reule," she whispered fiercely, leaning into him so their warmth meshed and her mouth stroked over his. "There is poetry to your culture, your honor, and the values you hold dear, and I would be a fool to deny you anything. And whatever I was in my former life, I know I was no fool."

Reule smiled against her seeking lips. "You cry as though the world were ending, *kébé*, but you speak words that breathe exhilaration into my soul. But it's not your gratitude I want. This request is wholly selfish, remember? What I want you for has nothing to do with charity. Knowing this, speak plainly to me, Mystique. Will you be my Prima? Will you be my wife, bear my heirs, and rule me with that sweet wisdom of yours for all the rest of your days?"

"Yes," she breathed into his mouth, her lips nibbling his in hungry little bites that incited unruly needs. She intensified the pressure, connection, and heat with each successive kiss, her small hands cupping his face and holding him to her demands. This was why it took so long for him to truly hear her, the response sinking slowly into his brain.

"Yes?" he repeated, doubting what he wanted so badly to be true. He was afraid he was imagining it.

"Yes."

In his lifetime, Reule had known moments of certainty that were outside explanation. They came as a

clarity beyond all compare. He had known it each time
he'd sworn in a Packmate. He had known it when he'd
stepped into the Jeth Valley for the first time.

He knew it now.

She was his match. His soul mate. A part of him had
been aware of it since the moment he'd first sensed her,
and it had refused to let him leave her behind. Their connection was undeniably unique and powerful. It was the
sort of bond upon which great kingdoms could be made.
She was made to be a queen. To be his queen. He was
made to be her husband. As he drew her soft, welcoming
body forward out of the chair and onto his, he knew he'd
been created to be her lover. No chemistry so potent
could be a mere trick of chance. It was a destined thing.

His heart told him so.

When she had won it, Reule didn't know. He hadn't
even had a chance to balk at the idea of loving a woman.
In his ninety years, he had dealt with enough women to
know the only thing he understood about them was that
they were hard to fathom. Mystique was even more of a
mystery than most. But he wouldn't fear that if it meant
feeling the rush of adrenaline and joy that he was feeling now. He ought to have quelled it, curbed it for the
sake of his mourning Pack, but he couldn't. It was dusk,
the fading light outside the windows telling him that the
Depths had ended. He also knew Amando would never
have forgiven him for letting this moment pass in re-
pression because of grief for him.

So he felt, letting it all wash over him to open his
mind and senses in uncanny ways. The wind-washed
scent of her clothes and hair ebbed over him with the
sweet perfume of woman on its back. Her hands dove
into his hair, fingers skimming his scalp until he invol-
untarily shuddered from the sensation. Her mouth, soft

and luscious, teased against his in long, shallow kisses. Her soft bottom was seated on his thighs now that he had pulled her into his lap, and her warm thighs caged him in at his sides. All he needed to do was grasp her sweet backside and drag her a few more inches forward and he would be fitted perfectly against her.

Not trusting his control, he didn't give in to that desire just yet. Instead, he drew his hands up over her body, riding up her sides until she squirmed and gasped in hot, breathless little sounds that opened her mouth to his swift and thorough assault. Then the kisses became deep and drugging. His hands were suddenly cupping and curving over her breasts through the heavy cardinal red velvet she wore. She wore the color of his city, the mourning color, and the respect it showed swelled his already bursting heart.

"Damn me," he muttered when the fabric impeded his explorations. Longing washed over him in waves that craved one thing from her body and another from her mouth. There was the sound of tearing fabric as he forced the material to give way to him.

He dragged down the tight bodice of her dress, exposing breasts and body free of a corset. Reule groaned when he felt the bare skin so warm beneath his fingers. She panted for breath in tortured little gasps that taunted the hell out of him because they sounded so damn sexy. Blotting out her world with a wildly hot kiss, Reule cuddled a breast in his palm, marveling at how well she fit him, and at her response as her nipple budded like a tight little rose between his seeking fingers.

"Please, I need to put my hands on you," she begged with a desperate whimper as she dragged at his shirt, seeking his heated skin even as he reached to strip off the impeding garment. Her hands were on his belly seconds later, sliding up over him, leaving blankets of flames in her wake until every inch of skin burned with the feel of her small, thorough fingers. Her fingernails scraped like tiny dull blades through the hair on his chest, seeking his nipples just as he'd sought hers, enjoying his vocal response when she stroked over them. Then she was reversing direction and, all of a sudden, the path became ten times as arousing just because she was heading toward his waist rather than away from it.

Reule remembered quite well that she wasn't shy about her likes and curiosities, but he didn't think he could bear her boldness just then. Fangs were already pricking against his mouth, and his aroused body ached right along with them. He drew away from her, abruptly surging to his feet and watching her eyes roam him with blatant appreciation as she took in his height looming over her. Her gaze lowered to the prominent evidence of his need, and when she licked her lips with sultry hunger, it sent his pulse screaming. He reached down and grabbed her hand, jerking her up against his bare chest so he could feel her brazen breasts against him.

"Bed," he said, his voice a low rumble of command. "I want you in a bed."

He swept her up and headed out of the study. He held her tightly to himself so it was only her bare back exposed to others, should they encounter anyone, but Reule knew they were all busy with preparations for that evening. Before long he was striding into his bedroom and all but tossing her onto the huge platform bed. Seeing her there, half naked in his bed, his for the taking, stole his breath away. It sharpened his want so badly that it physically hurt.

He reached out and flipped her over onto her belly, giving himself a fine view of her slim back and adorable fanny. Oh, the position had beautiful possibilities, he thought as he ran blatant hands over her bottom, listening to her squeal softly in delight. His goal, however, was the laces of her dress, which he'd ignored previously. He stripped her out of them with nimble, impatient fingers and shucked her out of the confounding layers of skirts and underskirts. Mystique giggled and squeaked the entire time, twisting alternately toward and away from his roaming hands while he bared her body to his pleasure. When she was completely naked, he groaned with tortured satisfaction and turned her slowly back over. He watched every curve, every line as she rolled to his command.

It was different. It was different to see her nude this time and know he would be taking her. It made his heart kick into double beats, his skin turning so hot that it was moist with perspiration. She was breathing hard, her breasts rising and falling in temptation each and every time until he couldn't stand to look at her a second longer. As if reading his mind, she slid to the edge of the mattress, dangling her legs over the edge until her knees bumped his and her hands came out to frame his hips.

She looked up at him with her flushed face and wanting eyes and Reule knew a brief moment of utter terror. She was his match. Perfect for him in every way imaginable. The need of his body was outstripped only by the needs of his heart. In her hands, she held the power to complete him, and she could potentially cause him pain unlike any he'd ever experienced before.

And just as quickly the fear faded away, because he knew damn well that the risk was worth it if the reward was even half of what he was expecting it to be. He looked down at the top of her red head as she leaned close to his body, her warm mouth kissing his belly just below his navel. His stomach muscles clenched and his groin was seared with heat. To add punch to her gesture, he felt her little tongue flick out to taunt his skin with warm, wet promises.

He didn't realize he was holding his breath until it left him in a great rush when her hand came over him, cupping his erect flesh through his trousers. Then she swiftly went about untying the laces containing him. He clenched his hands into fierce fists as she slid her fingers inside his loosened waistband. Her cheek nestled against his belly and she slid hands and fabric sensuously down his thighs. He kicked his trousers away, but the relief he felt at being free from restriction was short-lived.

She purred.

It was a low, greedy sound of appreciation as she reached out and closed her hand around his jutting length. Her hand was small and he was thick, thicker by the second under her touch, and she couldn't completely encircle him, but that didn't discourage her in the least. She made that ravenous sound again and his knees went weak as she stroked him once, from base to tip, as though she were worshipping his every contour. He throbbed with a violent pulse against her palm, all of his will focused on keeping his hands out of her hair and encouraging her to . . .

Her tongue touched him and he cried out a guttural curse as it slid like warm, drenched velvet right over the head of his cock. His fingers were suddenly deep in her hair and he had no idea how they'd gotten there. He felt blind and deaf, his pulse roaring in his head as her tongue stroked him over and over again, swirling around him. Then, like a clarion call from heaven itself, she drew him into the perfect seal of her mouth. Reule could hardly bear it. He wanted to rip her away; he couldn't possibly stop her and survive. The contradiction was proof of how intense the feelings were. His extended fangs ached. Ached for her flesh, to sink deep, his tongue thirsting for her blood. But first he needed to be inside her. Deep, deep, stretching her until she screamed with bliss.

Reule all but pounced on Mystique, disrupting her pleasurable sampling of his cock as he threw her back on the bed and surged over her with his enormous body. She gasped, suddenly feeling so small in comparison to his bulk and the virile muscle packed tightly onto him. He drove his hips up between her thighs, making a way for himself. It only made her feel smaller as he urged her thighs farther and farther apart to accommodate his approach. Her hands pressed defensively against his chest.

"Shh," he whispered, his mouth leaving soft kisses against her temple. "I won't hurt you. I swear it. Just let me touch you, *kébé*."

Bracing himself on a single hand, he dragged his fingers over her collarbone, down over the peaked slope of her breast, onto her sensitive tummy, which he felt quiver in tense anticipation. He could tell she didn't know whether to be excited or afraid, and he knew that meant everything was going too fast, but for his life he couldn't slow down. It was too much to ask of him in that moment. His hand turned to cup her mound as his fingers dragged gently through russet curls. With a soft stroke, he found her already quite wet. Her exploration of his body had excited her. He groaned soulfully as his fingers slid over her with perfect ease.

Reule wanted more. He lowered his mouth, trailing it down the slope of her breast until a jutting nipple slipped between his lips. She sucked in a breath, her body rising and writhing as he suckled her and stroked her simultaneously. He listened carefully to her mind

and body, waiting for her to tense with just the right
level of frustration before finally slipping a thick finger
inside her. Muscled walls clamped down at his invasion
and he sighed against her, his entire psyche anticipating
that feeling around his throbbing cock. He pushed into
her until she was moaning, canting her hips and grasping blindly at his shoulders. He purposely let her feel
the pricking of fangs against her breast and was rewarded as scorching, dripping heat flooded over his
toying fingers.

When she was close to coming, he drew back, listening with perverse pleasure as she cried out and begged
him in unintelligible whimpers not to stop. It was
enough. It was too much. He swept a hand under her
bottom, tilting her hips toward him. He shuddered as his
engorged penis slid against her, bathing in heat and
liquid welcome, his whole being focused solely on that
sensation. Her response was wild and uninhibited. Perfection. Unable to wait any longer, he set himself against
her entrance, thriving on the ache of her emotions as
every fiber of her body cried out for him.

"Reule!" she groaned, panting as she trembled in
his hands so hard her teeth were chattering. *"I'm begging you!"*

Reule surged forward into her, stopping only when
her tight body resisted him. He was too big to move
into her with haste, he realized, and for all her desperation, he would hurt her if he didn't slow down. She
wriggled up against him, testing his control as he
thwarted her efforts and gave her a moment to adjust.
She began to speak his name, over and over, gasping it,
groaning it, crying it out as he slid deeper into her. She
was so snug that he could barely move, but he withdrew slightly and then inched farther forward until she

exploded in an unexpected orgasm that made him shout out with the unbearable pleasure of her clutching muscles around him. He felt the ecstasy of it all throughout his body, the delight wrapping around the base of his spine as his body begged for release.

He wasn't even fully inside her.

But the instant she went lax with postorgasmic weakness, he sank into her to the very hilt. She was drenched in sweat now, so he slid over her body with all the more ease as he withdrew to the very limits of his length and then thrust back in return. He caught her head in his hands, giving her a little shake to focus her passion-dazed eyes on his. He was rousing her overstimulated body again, making her moan softly.

"Look at me, *kébé*," he gasped, barely able to talk as violent thrills and urges for her blood washed through him. He buried himself deep inside her again, shocking her with the intensity of his thrust, forcing her eyes onto him even as she grasped him with her hands and knees, clearly undecided if she wanted to hold him at bay or encourage him further.

"Reule," she begged.

"Feel me, sweet baby?" he rasped as he locked his gaze to hers and rocked her body with his. "Mercy, Lord, you feel like home. So hot, so beautiful. Paradise."

Reule's body forced a rhythm, the need beyond his control and ignorant of her cries of enjoyment. Her nails bit into his back as she gripped him, her hips rising to meet the downward rush of his. He knew the very instant it would become too much. It thrashed through his mind like a demanding serpent, constricting everything within him until he thought he would implode. He reached for her, his hands gripping her shoulders and jerking her neck up to his mouth as he stretched his fangs wide and, finally, sank deep.

She screamed just as her blood burst into his mouth. For Reule, it was like swallowing pure sunshine, the rays searing down through his body on a straight path to release. He was barely taking his second sweet swallow before he was climaxing in vicious bursts of pleasure. He came so hard it was almost like hurting. He'd had no doubts about her, and now as he poured himself hotly into her, he knew just how blessed he was.

He slowly surfaced from the haze of completion, the tide of rapture receding as he still sucked at the crest of her shoulder. The very essence of a being was in the blood, and Mystique's was a potent combination of her power and her passions. So potent that he had to force himself to disengage, knowing he was being greedy now. He nuzzled her, licking the wounds he'd made with lazy strokes of his tongue until the flow of blood had ceased, not a single drop wasted.

He lifted his head and looked down into her face. His heart all but stopped when he saw the expression of joy on her sleepy features. He knew instantly that she had been given release once again, though he couldn't remember it for himself. He'd been far too seized by his own pleasure. But it was clear that this orgasm had been far more intense an experience for her. The bite of passion, when received, was an intoxicating thing, and she'd had no hope of escaping the gratification even if she had wanted to.

Pleased, Reule rolled her over him, laying her out against himself as he relaxed back into his pillows. He was suddenly exhausted and it made him chuckle. He'd never been the type to curl up and sleep after sex, but he could feel this was different. This was contentment, trust, and the sort of feelings you didn't want to rush away from. This was worth relaxing, taking time, even napping just for the pleasure of sharing his lover's wonderful warmth. Now he understood. He understood what it was his parents had had.

"Reule?"

He smiled. Her voice was hoarse from her passionate outcries. He realized he was feeling very self-satisfied and his smile grew. "Yes, *kébé*?"

"If this is how you treat your Prima, I'd like to be wed as soon as possible. I want you to be legally responsible for doing this to me at every opportunity."

That said, she fell into a contented sleep.

Chapter 11

He'd been a little more selfish than normal, and as he watched the deep breaths of her sleep, Reule theorized that it was because he'd never felt that level of emotion before. Nothing in his experience had prepared him for the fever that had overcome him the instant she'd promised herself to him. The urge had been fiercely territorial, and he'd been unable to focus on anything but taking her and making her his.

She'd been sleeping now for an hour, and he'd watched her every minute. She'd tried to slide away from him a few times, but he'd held her stubbornly close against him. She was no more used to another in her bed than he was, and he had no doubts that her attempts at withdrawal were self-protective. It would take time, he reminded himself, before she'd feel secure. He took heart in the fact that she'd fallen trustingly into sleep. That she was trusting him with her entire future was only slightly more important to him than that.

Reule sighed, glancing at the dark window that warned him their initial time together would have to draw to a close very soon. There were some changes that would need to be made now, and he'd see to them before the banquet began. By now the Pack was well aware of the choice he'd made. He could hide only so much. His joy had been emanated in healthy doses, he had no doubt. He needed to confront his friends before much more time passed.

Reaching down to his affianced bride, Reule ran gentle fingers over the length of her bare arm, from shoulder to fingertips, letting the roughness of his calluses stimulate her. She twitched and tried to roll away again. He held tight with a chuckle, then second guessed himself and let her roll away onto her back, but no farther. Now her gorgeous breasts were thrust into his line of sight like an offering and he exhaled in a rush as his body instantly tightened. He rose up over her on a single elbow and slowly bent his head until his lips brushed her nipple. It was the barest of kisses, but she moaned a tiny sound of pleasure as the dark rose tip tightened into a beckoning peak. He touched his tongue to it, then added the scrape of his teeth when her warm taste filled and stirred him.

When her eyes flew open with a gasp, he was sucking her in earnest, his hand sliding up her thigh in a stimulating path toward damp, delectable places.

"Reule," she breathed.

He released her so he could smile up at her. "I had better be," he observed. "I hear he's developed a bit of a jealous streak where you're concerned."

"Oh?" She raised a single slim brow, amusement glittering in her eyes.

"Insanely so," he assured her gravely, moving over her until her mouth was just beneath his. "You are so very beautiful," he said, his tone becoming all seriousness to match the eyes looking deeply into hers.

That was how she knew he wasn't speaking of her

hysical beauty. The entire compliment was spoken as
e looked inside her, rather than outside. She had the
unniest sensation in her chest, like her heart tumbling
ver, and she swallowed hard as the feeling spread all
hrough her body. She recalled oh so vividly how he ex-
ressed his delight with her exterior beauties. Her entire
ody still hummed with the pleasure he'd served to her
n large portions. She shivered when she anticipated
eing loved by him into the future. And if he expressed
is appreciation for her inner qualities with even half as
nuch intensity as he had her outer, she suspected she
night be very happy indeed.

She reached to ruffle his hair with her fingers, loving
he soft feel of the shaggy mass. Then she slowly
lanced down the connection of their bodies, the con-
rasts of his dark skin against her pale. She smiled, en-
oying the visualization of their differences. The feeling
urprised her. She'd thought she might be disturbed by
o visible a reminder that she wasn't Sánge, but how
ould she be when he looked so sexy lying naked
gainst her, felt so warm and, apparently, already
roused?

She met his eyes, licking her lips in sultry antici-
ation.

"A better than fair idea, my sweet *kébé*, but we're
oon due at Amando's banquet." He chuckled, accu-
ately reading her expression.

"How soon?" she asked hopefully.

"Soon enough. You will want Para to repair the gown
tore if you intend to wear it tonight. I also imagine you
vish to bathe. There are things I must attend to as well."
Clever girl, Reule thought as her eyes narrowed in in-
tant suspicion. He probably shouldn't have woken her
vith the comment about his jealousies.

"Are you going to hurt Rye?"

"No." *Not until after the ceremonies*, he thought, fresh anger radiating through him.

"Then why are you clenching your teeth?"

Reule sighed, the exhale releasing tension. "Because I'll be dealing with him in the morning. I don't look forward to it because I've never had to harshly reprimand Rye before. He's usually warm and congenial, more dangerous as a flirt than anything else."

"Which only goes to prove my point that it was grief that made him violent," she didn't hesitate to point out.

"I know," he said, leaning back onto his side of the bed with a noise of frustration as he threw an arm over his eyes. "I have no idea what to do, Mystique. He must suffer a powerful consequence for his actions, yet I know you'll be devastated if I make it a violent one. How do I please us both?"

"You know him, Reule. Enough to know how to punish him without making it a challenge. You must make the consequence equal to the act, but temper it with the knowledge that he's in a great deal of pain already."

"I'll think on it. For tonight, I have a way of satisfying my need to see him squirm a little."

"Oh?"

He laughed when she tried to sound nonchalant but ended up sounding terribly curious. There was a part of her that wanted to see Rye made to pay for his act against her, even if she would accept no violence.

"That will be my concern. You're . . ."

There was a brief knock on the door that interrupted him and Reule reacted with amazing speed, jerking a coverlet over her bare body. The fabric was still settling even as the door swung open to admit Drago. He carried a small tray and bustled in with his usual brisk efficiency.

"My Prime," he greeted Reule without looking at the
ed, "I hope you've enjoyed your rest. The ceremony
ill be—"

The Sánge attendant turned as he was setting the tray
own and froze midsentence as he took in the tableau of
is master and the woman tucked up tight against him.
Vhen he recognized the bloodred hair, he lost all coor-
ination and the tray banged down onto the table with a
lattering of its contents. Mystique had never seen him
lustered before; his dignity was usually unflappable.
he instantly had the urge to laugh, which she smoth-
red by pressing her face against Reule's bare shoulder.

"My . . ." Drago sucked air, searched for words,
iving himself a fishlike appearance that worsened
Mystique's predicament. She snorted against Reule's
kin, which made him suppress a chuckle of his own.

"I rather recall the idea of knocking is to give an op-
ortunity for someone within to respond," Reule mused.
Ie turned his attention to Mystique. "Isn't that so,
weetheart?" She responded with a smothery snicker he
ok as a yes. "Very well. Mystique agrees with me."

Reule was torturing the poor fellow. Drago had been
rith him for decades, and he'd always had free access
o Reule's chamber. Reule simply didn't bring women
o his own bed. Ever. He didn't like the idea of the mark
f a woman in his private chambers, so he'd always met
is lovers elsewhere. It was quite possible that Drago
ılly understood the significance of what he was seeing:
ıe declaration of an event he'd often complained about
ever seeing in his lifetime.

"My Prime! I beg forgiveness. I . . . of course I ought
o have waited. It was . . . um . . . unforgivably rude. My
ıdy Mystique, I'm most apologetic," the attendant
tammered as he kept his eyes strictly on the tray he was

suddenly very interested in organizing. Drago had flushed an amusing shade of red, no doubt wondering exactly how bad his timing had actually been. Mystique gave him credit. Para would be stretched out on the floor by now. "I'll just go get something I've forgotten," he continued, edging toward the door without looking at the bed, "and I'll return to help ready you for the ceremony in . . . uh . . . about . . ."

"Ten minutes," Reule provided gently.

"Ten minutes. Just so. Excuse me, My Prime."

The attendant dashed out the door, shutting it tightly behind him, and Mystique finally burst into irrepressible giggles.

"You'd think he'd never seen you with a woman before."

"Well, I don't believe he has," Reule mused thoughtfully. "Certainly not in this bed. Probably never at all without at least a little forewarning to prepare his dignity for the affront."

Her laughter ended so abruptly that Reule looked down at her curiously. She was looking at him with an indecipherable expression, and the wave of emotion coming from her had the chill of that fear he was beginning to associate with her past. Instantly disliking whatever she was thinking, he threw himself into her mind and read her thoughts, giving her no opportunity to hide.

"Yes, it's true," he said softly as he reached out to touch a thumb against her temple, brushing her in a tender caress. "No woman before you has been in this bed, and no woman beyond you will ever be. I won't pretend to have never had lovers, *kébé*, nor will I pretend you won't run into a few in my court. This is a closed society, you being the first outsider to ever take up permanent residence here. It makes for a lot of

ossip and few strangers. But I promise you this, there
will never be anyone else for me so long as we draw
breath together, and beyond. Anyone who tells you
otherwise will be a liar and an enemy to you. There-
ore an enemy to me. I've barely begun to love you, but
can already swear to you that it will take me a great
eal of time and energy to satisfy myself with you,
Mystique. I'll be fortunate to find the stamina to rule,
ever mind take a mistress."

He got a smile for his efforts with that remark. Still,
t didn't light her eyes and he knew she wasn't certain,
ust as she wasn't certain where her conviction that all
nen were philanderers came from. It marked her
eeply, but he felt her powerful desire, as always, to
rust him. He'd said all he could on the matter. It would
e up to her to come the rest of the way.

As he'd said earlier, the more she regained snatches
f memory, the less he liked it, for her sake. She'd been
ar more bold and confident before this. Then again,
he'd also not felt her heart was at risk before. He could
nderstand her caution. He'd felt it keenly himself, that
ear of potential hurt.

That thought was followed by the realization that if
he felt her heart was at risk, it meant her heart was ac-
ually involved. She'd said nothing to him of her feel-
ngs for him. Not even a hint. Just that she was willing
o allow him to love her. But her fear hinted at so much
nore, and it made his pulse dance with joy. He hadn't
sked for her love. He'd hoped to win it slowly through
ime, trust, and contentment. This was a promising first
tep, and he felt happier than anyone probably had a
ight to feel.

"Come!" He leapt out of bed and grabbed her, swing-
ng her onto her feet in a rush that sent the blanket

flying off her body. He held her naked figure against his for a long moment, reveling in the sensual warmth of her and her amused chuckles. "Get dressed so Drago can feel at ease about returning. It's time you had Para ready you for the banquet. Wear this red," he encouraged her as he scooped the dress from the floor, frowning briefly at the wrinkles. "If you think she can repair the damage I've caused," he said ruefully.

She smiled at him as he gathered the dress and dropped it over her head and arms. "Must it be this red, or any red, My Prime?"

He grinned at that. "You mean Para has given you more than one?"

"Well, there is a black velvet that is quite beautiful," she said, leaning into him as he frowned slightly, "and it has your crest, My Prime, in a repeating chain of red around the hem. Also, here." She leaned back and ran her palm along her neckline to indicate the path of a second, smaller chain of crests. "Only the neckline is far lower, so it will actually come across here . . ."

Reule watched with a suddenly parched throat as she swept slow, teasing fingers in a dip over her breasts. So slowly, in fact, that she stimulated herself, the perking up of her nipples under red velvet sure proof of that.

His crest, across her incredible breasts.

The idea had the most intensely satisfying erotic effect on both his mind and his body. It almost landed her in bed again, on her back with her skirts tossed up around her ears.

"Wear the black," he commanded her in a growling rumble that made her laugh at him, her light eyes dancing with mirth. He was happy to see her usual spirits returned, even if it was at the expense of his overheated body. There would be plenty of time after the ceremony to make her pay the price for her mischief. "Now, off to Para with you," he said, dragging her to the door by her arm and using a spank on her backside to propel her out into the hall. "Drago! Get in here," he barked to the attendant he'd known would be waiting close by in the hall. He grinned as he listened to Mystique giggle all the way down the corridor.

When Drago closed the door, sealing away the last of the bright, wonderful sound, Reule moved to inspect the contents of the tray brought in earlier. It was all the decorative emblems required when he dressed in state. Two rings, chain of rank, a belt decorated with his seal in front, and several short gold chains, with small hexagonal rubies set within and his seal etched on the surface, to be affixed in his hair, also an indication of his rank. One day, he hoped this regalia would be seen by delegates who came to visit Jeth City with respect, without fear, without prejudice. He knew it was possible it wouldn't happen in his lifetime, but he did wish it.

Drago's silence was notable and he turned to see the attendant brushing out the handsome choice of black trousers, a black shirt, a golden vest with red embroidery, and a ruby red evening jacket that tied low enough to display both the vest and the shirt beneath. He would look all of the Prime Packleader paying his deepest respects to an honored friend and colleague. But usually Drago would be trading bits of information with him about the preparations, the goings-on in the keep that might be of interest to his Prime. Not chatty, not like Para, but informative and discriminating. His quiet was telling, and Reule became aware of his tight displeasure.

He frowned. "Out with it, Drago. What troubles you?"

"It's not my place to say, My Prime," he responded politely.

Reule grabbed up the robe Drago had draped on the end of the bed, tying it on. He faced the attendant once more. "Don't play the demure servant with me, Drago. We both know it's horseshit."

Drago turned, his almost black eyes gleaming with hard repressed emotion. "May I speak freely?"

"As you dare," Reule said, his permission just as tight as the request.

"Or as you do," Drago countered instantly. "How can you possibly take a woman like *that* to your bed? It's shameful and a disgrace! You completely disregard—" Drago broke off with a squeak when his Prime was suddenly nose to nose with him, a low, vicious growl of warning turning over in his throat.

"You watch your tongue regarding Mystique, valet, or you will find yourself feasting on it!"

"I won't, and I beg your pardon, My Prime, but how dare you treat such a fine woman in so low a manner! Tumbling her like a common . . . common . . . well, she's not like the women you're used to! She's good and caring and she has no idea how to handle a male of your experience!"

Reule snorted out a laugh. She'd been handling him better than fine since the instant she'd first looked at him with those diamond eyes of hers. The Packleader had to blink through his surprise as Drago flushed bright red with indignation. The man's dignity had flown out of the window, as had his unswerving loyalty, apparently, as he prepared to furiously defend the honor of . . .

Of a foundling girl who had clearly made her mark. At first he'd thought Drago was insulting her, calling her common or beneath his notice, but in truth, he realized with no little shock, the valet was acting as though the opposite were true.

"Drago," he said sharply, cutting off further retort with a raised hand. "Do you think so ill of your Prime? You've known me for much of my life. When have I ever taken an innocent girl—a fertile innocent, at that—to bed without regard to the consequences?"

"Well, I must say that was why I was so shocked when I saw . . ." Drago blinked. "Well, then, you mean you've considered the consequences?"

"Happily," Reule said dryly. "It's good to know my honor is so easily doubted when it's supposed to be the mainstay of my rule."

"Oh, but I—! That is to say, I didn't mean . . . Well, yes I suppose I did, but I knew you were terribly attracted to her, and she to you, and I thought perhaps it just got out of control . . . perhaps in your grief. The entire Pack has been acting so out of spirits."

"They are grieving," Reule said carefully. "We've never lost Pack blood before."

"It shows," Drago said gravely. "Rye isn't himself at all, contentious and full of rage. Delano ceaselessly stalks and prowls every hall and every chamber open to him. Saber walks the walls and rides sentry without sleep. Chayne won't leave his quarters even though Mystique finished healing him two days ago. And Darcio . . ."

"What of Shadow?" Reule demanded.

"Merely the fact that you don't know should tell you something, My Prime. When has he ever left your side willingly?"

He'd seen none of them for days, only felt their anger and grief as it ran through them all in a ribbon of anguish that flowed in repetitive whips. He'd closed his thoughts to them, and theirs to himself, unable to bear the added intensity it would bring. He was intending to change his isolation now that the Depths had concluded. Being solitary, yet together, was a normal way of grieving. He hadn't even considered Darcio's absence. Or anyone else's, for that matter.

"Damn selfish of me," he muttered. "Seems like a lot has been going on in my keep right under my ignorant nose."

"You're not the only one," Drago said with pointed dryness, glancing at the mussed bed.

Reule chuckled, casting off the pall of worry. He would straighten his house up over the next week, starting tonight. "Relax, old friend. I plan to keep her very close and in just as high esteem as you apparently do. I'm glad to have your reaction, truth be told. I was wondering how others would accept our relationship."

"Do you care?" Drago queried.

"Care? Of course. Worry? Not in the least. It's a subject not open for debate, and adjustment will come in time. I have faith in my people."

"Well, I know you'll have little to no effort to make amongst the commoners," Drago remarked.

"Oh?" he asked as he moved into the adjoining bath and began to wash up and get dressed. He needed to see the Pack before guests arrived.

"Yes. My lady Mystique has been making quite an impression these past few days. She cured the farmer's boy Stebban and he's already gaining weight. She's been working steadily in the infirmary ever since. Word of mouth, I suppose. Like wild flatland fire, My Prime. Though you might want to have a closer care for her if she's going to be . . . um . . ."

"Prima, Drago. You can say it. She will be Prima. Before the end of this month, if I have any say about it, and I think I do. And she will have a Prima Shadow in her Pack first thing, trust me."

"Oh, yes, a wise idea. But I was more concerned with her health."

Drago looked up when there was a soft clatter and his Prime came to the entrance between bedroom and bath, half shaved, and narrowed his hazel eyes on him. "Would you be so kind as to explain that?"

"Of course, My Prime. Our future Prima has no heart for turning people away. She is with her patients from dawn until late at night. When she retires, she's exhausted and can barely stand. Para and I have had to walk her to her bed between us these past three nights."

"Are there so many sickly among my people?" Reule looked flabbergasted at the idea of the powerful Sánge being so afflicted.

"They are when the fires burn them. Then she heals Chayne on top of a long day. Winter comes, the elders have various physical complaints. Many ailments have gone long neglected because of that man she rightly labeled a charlatan."

"And he will pay for that, I promise you," Reule muttered angrily as he returned to his grooming. "She didn't work today. I found her on the battlements."

"She takes an hour twice a day to escape onto the battlements. I think it overwhelms her, all the healing and the mourning. She clears her head and then returns."

"You seem to know a great deal about this."

Drago was no fool. He tried not to smile as he recognized the jealousy lurking in his master's tone. "Para keeps close to her, and I talk to Para. I often visit and try to help."

"And your suggestion? I know you have one, so don't even think of hedging."

"Just that you limit the gate. No callers for healing after dusk or before a decent hour."

It was a fair and simple solution. But Reule would have to discuss it with Mystique first. He had no intention of making decisions that would affect her without consulting her first. Playing Prime over her, however much he had a right by birth to do so, wouldn't be a way of gaining the trust he so craved.

"Thank you for the information. You're right, she wouldn't turn anyone away and would work herself into a coma if she thought it would help someone. I think it might be wise to find her a promising apprentice as well. She knows much that has nothing to do with her naturopathic power. She has a great deal of knowledge, and passing it on would eventually ease the medical burden from her shoulders."

"The fewer her burdens, the better. Being Prima will be burden enough."

"I don't deny that," Reule agreed grimly. "But I'd lay fair odds that she's up to the task."

"I'd rather run like a loon through a Jakal camp than take a bet against that."

After Reule had called Para and Drago together and told them about the significant changes he'd require before guests arrived from the city, he strode down the corridor to the private areas in the keep and entered the Packmate common room. They felt him coming, just as he felt them, so they were all on their feet by the time he came within sight. He stopped on the threshold of the wide room and studied them each in turn. Every member stood before his favored chair. The only empty chairs belonged to him and Amando.

Without any delay, he strode sharply into the room, his high-polished black boots snapping against the stone of the flooring as he grabbed for the golden ceremonial dagger at his waist and pulled it free of its sheath. He walked straight up to the first empty chair, knelt down on a single knee, and with a shout and all of his strength, he stabbed the blade into the seat belonging to their fallen comrade. The wood and cushioning shuddered and cracked under the mighty blow, but in the end the dagger remained embedded deep, jeweled hilt gleaming in the firelight as the Prime of Jeth stood up tall and backed away. He clasped his hands before him, widened his stance, and bowed his head. He heard the Pack do the same, and silence prevailed for a long minute as they each wished Amando on his way to the warmth of the House of the Lord and Lady.

The Sánge Prime had given up his dagger. It was the highest of honors, and one that every Packmate would wish for himself when the time came.

Reule turned then to face them, looking them all over with keen, judging eyes, eyes that refused to miss any of the details, large or small, that he'd overlooked in the Depths of his grief.

"Shadow, I expect you back at my side," he said pointedly to Darcio, cocking a brow until his Packmate nodded. "Chayne, are you well?"

"As can be," he said quietly, his subdued response indicative of his ordeal.

"Very well. As you all may know, my relationship with the outlander woman, Mystique, has taken on a new cast. I have requested that she become Prima and she has accepted."

Everyone, save Darcio, looked and felt as though he'd just walked into another electrical trap. Each was stunned speechless, except Rye, who burst out with, "Lord damn me! Reule, are you mad?"

Rye's response was apparently even more shocking than Reule's announcement because all attention swung to the heir. If they felt as though they'd missed a page in the story, they weren't alone. Reule felt as though he'd risen from a three-day coma. He ignored the outburst, even though his teeth did come tightly together as he fought his temper.

"This isn't open to discussion or debate," Reule said instead, addressing them all in the cold tone of a ruler who would let one insult slide, but wouldn't allow another. "The joining will be announced this night in Amando's memory, and the service will be performed by month's end. Your future Prima is inexperienced and an outlander still familiarizing herself with our culture. I expect you all to assist her just as you have been. To that end, Chayne, I'm temporarily titling you Prima Shadow." Reule drew the chain of office from the inside of his jacket and stood before Chayne, holding it out to him on his fingertips.

Chayne's stunned expression was priceless. It made Reule's lips curve up.

"My Prime—" Chayne paused long enough to clear the startled rasp from his throat. "I am honored, but . . . I am beyond honored," he swore, making certain Reule felt the truth of it, "but I'm not at my peak health yet. You must prefer—"

"What I prefer," Reule interrupted, "is that a man who owes her his life take on the duty of guarding hers. He will be best compelled not to fail her."

"But Rye also—"

"The Prime Blade has already expressed his feelings on the matter enough to satisfy me that he wouldn't be the best choice." The Pack shifted uncomfortably as hostility jolted through them. As polite as the phrasing was, Reule's displeasure was keen. "At half your health, you'd do twice as much to protect her."

The insult wasn't even veiled and, moments after Chayne lifted his new emblem of office from Reule's hands and exchanged it for the one he now wore, Reule turned the full brunt of his icy displeasure on Rye.

"After sunrise you and I will meet. You will recall, I pray, that every peaceful minute earned between now and then is by the grace of my lady's merciful request." He turned to the others. "Seating has been rearranged to accommodate these changes. Now, shall we lay our comrade to peace?"

Chapter 12

Mystique's heart was pounding, her anxiety level peaking as it had earlier that day in Reule's arms, but she maintained control over her breathing by sheer force of will. Para stood with her in the vestibule where she waited, fussing over the way her gown settled and the rubies and gold that dripped from her hair. Mystique could only struggle within herself for calm. She didn't know why meeting with Reule's courtiers should rattle her so. She wasn't cowed in any way by the nobles she would be meeting tonight. Her natural confidence assured her that she would eventually find her footing. Still, she couldn't shake a feeling of inexplicable icy dread.

She shook away the hyperactive apprehension, focusing instead on good things, things that made her feel content and secure, to soothe herself.

Mystique smiled as she shifted position and realized she felt contentment in every tender place on her body, and security in the way Reule's scent lingered on her skin as though indelibly placed there in their passion. If that weren't enough of a claim on her, Reule had sent her a large ruby teardrop pendant etched with his insignia, which she now wore proudly around her throat.

Mystique smiled at his territorialism. It was all about marking her for all his world to see. In his culture, this was a lavish honor, proclaiming her of incomparable value to him.

She blinked back sudden moisture in her eyes as she realized that she knew, even without actual memories, that she'd never been so treasured in her life. Now she would be close by Reule's side as he interred the companion of a lifetime. She would support and strengthen him in any way possible. She only wished she could have done more for Amando.

The vestibule doors opened and she turned. She saw him leading his Pack into the receiving room, and her breath flew from her body. He was so incredibly beautiful. Dressed in full formal regalia, he looked vibrant and stately in the red, black, and gold clothing, but it was all Reule behind the emanation of confidence and power. She was sure she had never witnessed anyone as dazzling and as incredibly sexy as he looked to her just then. Her spirit felt as though it were floating up out of her body when she saw his eyes light with pleasure upon seeing her.

She'd made no false promises when she'd tempted him with how exotic her dress was. On her body it came alive with passion and purpose, as well as secret sensual promises made just between them. His eyes fell quickly to his gift to her, forcing him to swallow back a groan as the pendant's promise was also fulfilled. He'd envisioned it lying in stark relief against her pale skin, nestled at the very top of her cleavage, and he'd been so right. The gem lay in that delectable little spot, twitching almost imperceptibly with every beat as her heart jittered wildly.

He felt her untamed response to him, and it had the power to undo all his staid focus and control. He reached for her, forgoing the chaste propriety of clasping hands. He grasped her upper arms and swiftly hauled her against his aching body. He kissed her, oblivious to their audience, stealing her taste like the eager thief that he was. A red-gloved hand slid around his neck and he felt the flex of her strong fingers as she held him to her. Her sweet tongue swept into his mouth, seeking to be an equal partner, pushing his need to the very limits.

Reule reached up to catch her chin in his hand, and he eased away until they both settled back with sighs and eyes that glowed with unconcluded passion.

"Come," he said loudly, addressing the room though his gaze remained fixed devotedly on her, "let us warm the memory of a Packmate with honor."

"Aye," the rich male voices of the Pack agreed behind him. Then Chayne broke away from the others and moved closer to Mystique while Darcio did the same for Reule.

"*Kébé*, Chayne will be temporarily taking a place at your side as Prima Shadow until you choose your Pack and replace him."

She turned to look at the proud Packmate, his tall, lean form looking capable; seriousness and pride radiating from his tan eyes. He looked so much more vital now, as though the wounded man had been someone else entirely. This man stood fresh with health, his chestnut hair tied back with a gold and ruby clasp.

In fact, all of the men wore gold and rubies in their hair in one fashion or another. It wasn't until they walked out to greet the court that she fully realized that it was a mark of royalty. All of the elegantly dressed people, a sea of red and black clothing, wore jewels in their hair, but rubies and gold were nowhere to be found save on the Packmates.

And on her.

It sent home the understanding of her position unlike anything else, and her spine, already straight within her corset, went even straighter with the swell of delighted pride she felt. Of course, it made her the center of a lot of stares and the subject of many whispers behind hands and fans, but that was to be expected. She was an outlander in royal regalia. That would incite gossip from all corners of the room, even from those who tended not to gossip. Reule made no announcements; apparently the sight of her on his arm was all the announcement that was needed.

"Liandra. Justas." Reule first greeted a pretty young woman and then a man with familiar eyes. "I greet you with warmth, and share my heart." The solemn greeting came with a clasp of hands. Reule brought their linked hands to his chest over his heart, locking eyes with them until the gleam of tears appeared. "Mystique, this is Amando's brother, Justas, and his sister, Liandra. My friends, your future Prima, Mystique."

Reule watched Mystique as she reached out with both hands and clasped the sister's in one and the brother's in the other. "Our loss is profound. Your brother was the sort of man who made enduring impressions. It took only moments for Amando to win the heart of a foundling girl who felt lost among such great men. I will be forever grateful that I knew him, and forever regretful it was too brief an acquaintance."

Reule's feelings of pride and satisfaction emanated into the surrounding crowd, but he was unable and even unwilling to suppress them. He wanted everyone to know the esteem in which he held her. He had great cause to be proud of her. Amando's siblings were quite speechless. Reule felt the jumble of their emotions and surprise. They were no more used to acceptance and warmth from outlanders than he had been. But she'd worked her magic, and Liandra sobbed softly as Justas bowed his head graciously.

"Thank you, my lady. Those are kind and thoughtful words."

"Come, Liandra," Mystique said gently, reaching to draw her close, moving an arm of comfort around her shoulders. "There's much I don't know about Amando, and you are just the one to tell me. Who better than a sister to know her brother best? Let's talk while we find Para. She'll lead us to fresh water for your face."

She had no empathic power to speak of, but she sensed Liandra hadn't wanted to make an emotional spectacle of herself tonight. Their withdrawal gave the woman privacy and a chance to recover her dignity.

Liandra looked up as she patted her face dry in the private vestibule a short time later, her fern green eyes bright with freshly shed tears. Her beautiful blond hair, swept up into a twist that seemed to make dozens of intricate loops, was as gold as the chains she wore in it. It was decorated with onyx to match the smoky black-gray velvet of her mourning gown. A red scarf around her tiny waist was all she wore of the royal colors, a tribute to her dead brother's chosen profession.

"You're like no outlander I've ever seen," she said directly, her startling green eyes direct and honest. "Where are you from?"

"That's a very involved sort of story," Mystique admitted, "and one I'll be glad to share, but I know Reule is waiting for us so we may lay Amando's body to rest in the royal mausoleum."

"Please." Liandra reached out and clasped her hand tightly, clearly looking for support. "Will you stay with me? Justas is so . . . He's my brother and I love him, but he will need time to shake off the Depths before I can depend on his support. What you said took me by surprise and that's why I cried, but I just know your support will be helpful tonight. You're a woman. You understand."

"I do." Mystique squeezed her hand and smiled. "I would be honored. Perhaps if we're seated close to each other at the banquet, I can tell you how I came to be here."

"I would like that."

The Prime and future Prima of Jeth should have sat at the head of the table on the royal dais with Shadow on either side of them. These were the changes Reule had made, giving Mystique the honor due her. The change preserved her comfort as well. Especially since she would have sat next to his heir previously.

However, the future Prima had abandoned him early on, stealing a seat from another in order to sit by Liandra, and the two had been whispering together ever since. Oh, he was eaten up with curiosity, dying to eavesdrop on what had them intermittently so serious and then smothering giggles. But that was the very meaning of light and dark mourning, and he had no right to be nosy. He was merely amazed at how quickly she seemed to make friends of total strangers. She'd had that ability from the outset, he being a prime example.

After the interment, the mood at the banquet had grown increasingly more festive. Conversation buzzed everywhere around him, though no one directly spoke with him. Darcio had given up some time ago when his attention had strayed far too many times to where Mystique sat. Chayne, ever the vigilant one taking his duties seriously, had found a seat in a chair against a nearby wall, just behind his charge.

"Smitten."

Reule turned his head toward Darcio, who was grinning at him.

"Isn't that the word for it, My Prime? Smitten? When a man is completely obsessed with a woman to the point of fawning over her every second of the day?"

"It's possible you're correct and that is the word for it. However, only men who want to lose important limbs would ever use the word with their Prime."

"Come now, My Prime," Darcio chuckled, "be proud of your grand fall from bachelorhood. You wear it well. And so does she." Reule followed his Shadow's eyes back to Mystique and found himself smiling as he agreed.

"She's stunning," he admitted. "In many ways."

"This has happened very quickly for you," Darcio hurriedly continued when Reule scowled at him. "You aren't the sort of man who doesn't know his own mind, so I'm not questioning that. Your feelings aren't to be doubted. The entire Pack is convinced of that as of this afternoon." Darcio cleared his throat as he hinted at activity which would have been more private had he not been Packleader. "It isn't so easy to be as certain of her feelings, though," he remarked. "There's a turmoil of emotion within her. It overloads *my* senses. Then again, I'm not as strong an empath as the rest of the Pack."

"She isn't any easier for me to fathom, I promise you," Reule said patiently. "She feels things from the past and the present all together. Even she isn't aware of where one leaves off and the other begins. She had an attack of anxiety earlier and she couldn't even breathe. Even now I'm not certain if it was my asking her to be Prima that panicked her, or some remembered fear from the past."

"Perhaps a combination of both. It was selfish of you to place the burden of becoming Prima on her so soon."

Reule chuckled and cast his friend a sideways glance. "So I told her. But she accepted with enthusiasm. And despite her intermittent confusion, Mystique has proven herself to be a woman of conviction."

"So I see. She's already taken to Liandra. But then, Liandra is cut of the same cloth as her brother. Warm, friendly, firm when she needs to be. It amazes me how certain of people Mystique can be with no empathy or telepathy to guide her."

"She has excellent instincts," Reule noted. "Mostly when it comes to the motivations and intents of others. Perhaps it's a 'pathic ability we aren't aware of. Perhaps not. Few people seem to take her by surprise."

"Unfortunately, I think much of that is life experience. I suspect she saw the black side of what people can and will do to further their own agendas."

"Yes. Too much black side, if you ask me."

Darcio watched carefully as his Prime's gaze shifted to the sullen face of his heir.

"What has he done?"

"The unforgivable. And yet, she insists I forgive him for Amando's sake. Not for her own, but for Amando's and Rye's own sakes." Reule shook his head. "Her ways are not my ways, but how can I ignore when she begs me so well?"

"Hmm. How easily we hardened warriors can fall beneath the kiss and caress of a singular woman," Darcio mused.

"That's almost as bad as smitten," Reule warned with a laugh.

"You know, I'd have thought this afternoon would've

put you in a more contented frame of mind," Darcio complained good-naturedly.

"Speak to me in the morning. I plan to be far more contented by then."

Mystique's head lifted up when the Prime Shadow's laughter bolted down the length of the table. She looked at Reule with amusement and he gave her a broad wink. Since she could just imagine what the companions were discussing, she blushed red hot and lowered her eyes.

"Beasts," Liandra declared, snorting at the masculine display. "It's beyond time there was a woman among them. One who can temper their wicked manners. That Darcio alone has a wild streak as wide as the flatlands."

"Darcio?" Mystique was incredulous, making Lia laugh.

"Well, perhaps more so in his youth. And with Reule right beside him. Though our Prime was relentlessly serious and responsible when it came to building a home for us, he countered it with quite an untamed aspect. But I shouldn't be telling tales. He was much younger then." Liandra reached to squeeze her hand. "He needs something besides his Pack in his life. And he has found it." Lia sniggered through her nose. "There are a host of disappointed noblewomen here today."

Liandra lifted her chin in the direction of several groups of women who were milling beyond the tables having whispered discussions behind their fans. Mystique had been aware of their attention, but she'd dismissed it as unimportant.

"I can't be concerned with their judgment," she said with a convincing shrug. "I'm only concerned that I behave in a manner to make Reule proud."

"Oh, he is proud. And more. You may not feel it, but

I do." She leaned in with an eager sparkle in her fern eyes. "He's completely enthralled by you. He barely looks away. How can you stand it? I'd be checking my teeth for bits of food if someone looked at me like that."

"Lia," she scolded with a giggle. "You're incorrigible."

"Come, let's see if it's started to snow yet." Lia stood and reached for Mystique's hand, drawing her up as well. "You can tell me all the details about Reule I've only gossiped about."

Mystique adored Liandra's impudent character instantly. She reminded her of Amando, but she also shined beyond her brother's personality with her outright audacity and mischief. But her love of breadcakes, a habit she swore was bad for her waistline, she completely blamed on Amando.

Now Mystique obediently followed as Liandra led them on a winding path through the crowded banquet hall. They were just passing when one of the groups of women clustered nearby moved directly into their path. A buxom redhead with a slim waist and round hips stepped forward. She had beautiful blue eyes and her dark lashes had been dusted with gold, making them glitter whenever she blinked. Her wealth was obvious, if a bit overstated, in her adornments.

"Liandra, dearest, so sorry for your loss," she said in a voice like refined silk. Her bearing, right down to the sympathetic touch of a fan against Lia's wrist, was all perfection and grace. "Do introduce us to your friend."

Liandra visibly hesitated, worry ghosting through her frond-colored eyes. Manners seemed to win out and she smiled tentatively. "Mystique, this is Lady Jocelyn. Lady Geneva"—she indicated a proud-looking brunette with a pinched nose—"and this is Lady Theodora." The final lady was also brunette, but she was clearly much older than the other, her thick hair shot through with gray and silvery white.

"A pleasure," she responded graciously.

"Is it?" Jocelyn queried with a direct blink of her blue eyes. "Not many outlanders care for the Sánge. I've been dying with curiosity all night, wondering what could possibly make you different. But I'm at a loss. Why, I haven't even a clue what species you hail from."

"I find the Sánge to be a fascinating culture," Mystique said carefully, avoiding the rest of the questions left open by Jocelyn's speculations.

"But then, you should. I hear you were left for dead in the wilderness, with no hope of home or hearth. I suppose mucking around with us is better than the beasts beyond these walls."

"She's done more than muck," Geneva piped in, "if she's wrapped a male of Prime Reule's appetites around her pretty fingers."

"More like she wrapped her fingers around him." Jocelyn snickered, hiding the graceless laugh behind her fan but keeping her eyes on her target.

"Jocelyn!" Liandra snapped, her hold on Mystique's hand squeezing tighter.

"Oh, please, Liandra. From rags to riches inside a week? Powerless to Prima? One doesn't have to think too hard about what she's done to secure her comfort."

"Beware, upstart girl." Theodora spoke up, her warning ominous in its aged tone. "Becoming Prima doesn't guarantee you the love of the Sánge people. There are those who won't abide an outlander bride for our Prime."

"Whether they can abide it or not, it will happen," Mystique promised her, the steel in her voice sending a chill through the women. "You have warned me, now I will warn you. Speak softly in the future, ladies, if you think to burn me with words. Fire flashes back on her who strikes the match."

"You have nothing to frighten us with," Jocelyn whispered venomously. "You aren't 'pathic as we are. An assassin could be behind you this very instant and you'd be powerless to read his intentions. One so weak as you are won't survive long if you continue to reach above yourself."

"Mystique, don't listen to this bitchiness," Lia said, tugging on her hand. "They're just jealous. Jocelyn thought she was woman enough to become Prima and she's just shocked to find out what everyone else already knew." Liandra drew Mystique closer. "Reule would rather wed a goat than someone like her."

"Apparently so," Jocelyn sneered, looking at Mystique.

The slap seemed to come out of nowhere. The contact was so brutal that Jocelyn crumpled to her knees, cradling the bright red mark on her cheek as she looked up in total shock. Mystique bit her lip to suppress the burst of laughter the expression triggered. Liandra stood over her victim, her bosom heaving with her fury, her gloved hands curled into fists. When Theodora stepped forward, the young blonde snarled out a low, aggressive growl.

"How dare you!" she spat furiously. "How dare you treat your future Prima so disrespectfully! And during my brother's light and dark mourning! You insult me, my family, and your Prime! You will be lucky if a good slap is all you suffer for your insolence!"

"Lia," Mystique said softly, laying soothing hands on the petite woman's shoulders. "I'm certain Jocelyn has just learned the error of her ways. It's best we leave her to contemplate her actions."

"She'd better," Liandra muttered angrily.

Mystique led her out of the hall, ignoring the fact that a great deal of attention had become focused on the altercation. Once they were well away and exiting the keep onto a balcony, Liandra had calmed down enough to at least uncurl her fists. The cold, dark air around them stole their breath and they could smell the imminent snow. Lia paced the long balcony along its stone balustrade, back and forth, her breath clouding wildly around her, her hot cheeks a bright red that set off her sparking eyes.

"Lia, calm down," Mystique scolded gently. "I didn't expect everyone would be pleased with a stranger suddenly finding so powerful a niche in their society."

"You cannot let them treat you like that. She's right. Any appearance of weakness and they'll be on you like Jakals. You aren't like us and they know it. They know that whenever you're without Reule, they're free to think and feel against you without fear of reprisal. That means they can plot against you too."

"Not with Chayne close by," Mystique reassured her. She stopped her new friend's pacing with a hand and pointed through the glass of a nearby window. Chayne was leaning against a wall watching them, amusement dancing in his tan eyes.

Lia flushed even darker when she realized the Prima Shadow had likely been right behind them all along. "Oh. I forgot."

"But I thank you for championing me," Mystique said softly, leaning in to press a kiss to her companion's temple. "It meant a great deal to me."

"Well . . . I . . . you've been so kind to me. You've made a difficult day something better. It's almost as though Amando brought us together. Which was how he spent his life. As Prime Envoy, he kept peaceful trade flowing between us and those who can't stand us. It was a great talent."

"Well, you struck no treaties today." Mystique chuckled.

"No. But I was quite satisfied with what I did strike." She giggled. "I'm not generally the violent type, but damn, that woman makes me seethe."

"I'm afraid you may have made an enemy today."

"Two. Theodora is Jocelyn's mother. No doubt you noticed the familial snobbishness. Theodora groomed Jocelyn with aspirations of being Prima Mother. In a way, I feel sorry for Jocelyn. I don't think she knows how to think of herself as anything but future Prima. She will waste her life striving for the impossible. I'm afraid I'm not going to be the target of her contempt. You are the threat, Mystique. You destroy all she's been raised to believe for decades. It could make her quite mad."

"Well, she's underestimating me if she thinks I have no strengths or power to protect me. Firstly, Reule will never let harm come to me. He has sworn it to me, and I believe him with all of my heart. And now, apparently, I have you as well." Mystique squeezed her. "Look. You were right! The snow has begun."

Both women looked up at the floating white flakes. Liandra laughed as she shivered hard. "The first time I ever saw snow was when I was ten years old. We had traveled through tropics and deserts, rainforests and then woods. So many years. All of my life, in fact, up until that first fall when we came to the Jeth Valley. We had no experience with snow, had never truly known how cold it could possibly get. We had barely been here long enough to make shelters, never mind appropriate ones for something we weren't expecting. So many of our people died of exposure and sickness. Mostly the elderly who hadn't already died in the last decade of journeying. I was just a child, but I remember that cold and that snow. Most Sánge despise it. But some of us younger ones, we look on the first snow as a tribute to survival and new beginnings. I know Amando did. And so do I."

"I can see how you would," Mystique said, feeling deep admiration for what the Sánge had survived. Liandra turned to look at her very directly, a winsome smile on her lips as they trembled with chill.

"Reule saved our lives, gave us hope. Drove us to survive. He was only twenty-two years old. His parents had died when he was sixteen, making him a boy king. Luckily, he always had Darcio protecting him. Amando . . . Amando caught his attention three years after we arrived at Jeth."

"How?"

She laughed. "That's a story I need to be in a warmer place for."

"I'm sorry. I don't feel the cold so much. Let's go inside."

They walked inside and Mystique reached out to touch Chayne's shoulder in acknowledgment as they passed him and he fell into step behind them.

"Amando hated fighting," his sister reminisced. "Any sort. He would have chastised me fiercely for that slap."

"True enough," Chayne agreed from behind them. "He was always making peace."

"When I was a teenager, we worked the fields as an entity, the entire village, all those of working age and strength. It was a lot of people doing grueling tasks in rough country and unpredictable weather. We were grateful for all we had, but it wasn't an easy life. Tempers sometimes came up short. Reule was famous for having a short fuse back then. He was a little wild. A lot angry. His parents' murder had taken its toll. I suppose Darcio just couldn't defuse his temper that day and he got in a roaring fistfight with Rye."

"Rye?"

Chayne laughed at that. "Rye and Reule couldn't possibly count the fistfights they have had. Their personalities conflicted more than you might think. Rye is lighthearted and Reule is too serious sometimes. Unfortunately, Rye knew this too well and liked to goad Reule. Still does, though not so much now that Reule doesn't rise to the bait as easily. I remember this fight. You're talking about when Amando sat on Rye's chest to hold him down and . . ."

"I was getting to that!" Liandra scolded him. "Don't ruin the story."

"Sorry," he said with an unrepentant chuckle.

The story was full of humor, good memories from both Lia and Chayne, and the magical ability one man had to soothe souls with logical words of calm. This had been Amando's third 'pathic power. The power to soothe tempers with just the good-natured sound of his voice. Reule had instantly liked the jovial young man, and they'd become fast friends. He'd won over the others just as quickly, and when Reule had begun to add friends to his Pack according to their skills and the needs of the tribe, it had been Amando who had filled the role of Envoy, traveling far and wide with Reule to set up trade routes in what would normally be hostile territory.

"I credit Amando with the success of Jeth almost as much as I do Reule," Chayne said, making Lia's eyes mist over with pride. "There were times when it was only his skills that kept us working together, or kept us safe from harm."

"Mystique."

The group stopped short as Rye stepped out in front of them. Mystique caught her breath, an instinctive hand going to her throat as she looked up into the Prime Blade's serious blue eyes.

"I wish to speak with you in private, if you would be so kind," he said politely. But something about the way he held himself seemed too rigid, too threatening to her. She shook her head in refusal.

"I'm busy at the moment," she said stiffly. She felt Chayne step up closer to her, but sensed his confusion over their behavior. She dreaded the idea of causing conflicts within the Pack when its members were already torn up over Amando. With a sigh she touched Chayne in reassurance. "Very well. We will speak. Chayne, Lia, excuse us a moment."

Rye moved aside, holding out a hand to indicate the way to a small room off the corridor. She stopped short inside the door and watched nervously as he closed it. She reminded herself that two 'pathic persons remained right outside and she had nothing to fear.

"Yes, Rye?" she prompted, meeting his cold blue gaze. She could easily sense that the easygoing man she had first known had yet to return.

"I take it you ran crying to Reule about our little encounter?" he speculated. "Is that why he's so hostile toward me?"

"He's hostile because he wishes to be. I don't control his emotions," she retorted.

"Oh, but I think you do. A man will bend easily to the wishes of a woman who makes him feel the way our Prime felt when he was fucking you this afternoon. My, my, quite the display of affection."

"How dare you!" she gasped, her cheeks staining red

with anger and mortification. She hadn't realized the Pack would experience her lovemaking with Reule! Or she hadn't wanted to. Her breasts stung with a chill, as though she'd been stripped naked in front of this dreadful man.

"Listen carefully, my lady," Rye said, contempt lacing his warning on the "my lady." "You aren't Prima yet, so you have no command over me. And I will never allow that to happen. I will never have you deciding life and death for me again."

"You ungrateful bastard," she hissed through her teeth. "You curse me for saving your life, and then use that life to threaten me? Is this how you show your love to Reule?"

"Don't dare speak of my love for my Prime! You sully it with your very breath! I've known him all my life! Reule, Darcio, and I were born together, raised together, and became men in hardship together. You, with your overnight passions, can never know what it is to carve a niche of loyalty so deep in your heart as I have."

"You call this being loyal?" she said, aghast. "He embraces me, cherishes me, raises me up above all other women he has ever known, and you trap me here to insult me and swear vengeance on me? To deny your fealty? This is how you pay him your respects?"

"I will show my respect by prying those wicked claws of yours out of him before you ever become Prima. I'll be doing Reule a favor!" Rye's hand darted out before she could react, and he grabbed her by the arm. He drew her up close, his mouth against her ear until she felt the rush of his heated breath. "I'm Prime Blade for a reason, unfortunate girl. I lead armies in a harmony of movement and strategy unlike anything you've ever conceived of. If you think I cannot rid myself of one troublesome outlander woman, then you're mistaken."

Mystique's heart was pounding and she grabbed at his fingers, trying to pry them off her arm where they were squeezing so hard it was agonizing. She realized how frail she was in comparison to that big, powerful hand. That he could snap her bone if he desired it. She looked desperately at the door, wondering why Chayne didn't come and stop this.

"Oh, I'm more powerful than Chayne," he answered her thoughts. "I can block both of our minds from him . . . from anyone. I could wring your neck and no one would know until you were dead on the floor. Unfortunately, I was seen entering the room with you. It isn't my goal to alienate my Prime in the process of ridding myself of you. As it is, I'll have to face his temper come morning because of you."

"Rye, please," she begged him, her eyes smarting with tears of pain. "Explain this rage to me. I saved you, but not Amando, and that makes me evil? I don't understand your logic. Why have you made me a target? Why is this all my fault?"

"Because we never, *never* lost Pack until you showed up! Suddenly you're here and Amando is dead! A single drop of water in a pond causes ripples for great distances. You were the drop, and Amando drowned shortly after." He shook her hard, making her neck crack. "Who are you? What are you? None of us knows. Who's next? You think I'll sit back and let you sleep beside my king? That I'll allow evil to lie next to him?"

"You think I'll hurt Reule? That I'll kill him?" She was so horrified by the idea that she gagged. "By the Lady, you've gone completely mad! Why would I kill a man who's making me his queen? Giving me a glorious home? Loving me like I have never known love in all of my life?"

"Protecting you, as promised."

The statement was followed by a blindsiding punch from a huge fist that landed squarely on Rye's left cheek. Rye went flying, his gripping hand wrenching Mystique's arm hard before finally releasing her. The heir hit the ground with a jarring crash and Mystique felt a familiar muscular arm catch her around the waist, keeping her from toppling over onto Rye. That arm drew her back into a beloved body of warmth and strength, and her heart ached with relief as she leaned back into Reule, clutching his biceps. He nuzzled her ear gently.

"Are you all right, baby?" he demanded softly.

"Yes. Yes," she breathed, turning her face to his until her nose rubbed his cheek and she could draw in the familiar masculine scent of him.

"I'll believe that when I see your arm later," he said grimly. He turned hard eyes onto Rye, who was trying to orient himself enough to sit up.

"Reule—"

"Don't defend him, Mystique," he snapped harshly.

"Reule, he's sick. Not physically, but in his mind. I could feel it when he held me. It's like a poison in him that he cannot control. He needs healing and care, not rage and retribution."

"Damn me, *kébé*," he said, turning to kiss her forehead fiercely. "I cannot let this go unpunished!"

"Reule, I'm not asking you for that. Only listen." She turned herself toward him. "I think I can heal this just as I healed Chayne. I think . . . it may have been a combination of the voltage he took and the shock of losing Amando. This isn't the Rye you know. Not the Rye I was coming to know. He's suspicious and paranoid.

Filled with grief that blinds him to truth. I know it doesn't seem like it, but it's just as much a wound as what Chayne suffered, only it isn't visible through anything but his behavior. Please. Can't we place him somewhere safe where I can convince him to allow me to heal him?"

"I don't want you anywhere near him," Reule snapped just as the door opened to admit Chayne and Liandra.

Liandra ran at Mystique and she turned from Reule to hug her newest friend. Mystique had felt relief and safety with Reule, but Liandra's ready warmth made her want to cry like a child. She resisted the impulse, gathering her dignity as others looked curiously into the room from the hall.

"Chayne, the door, please."

Chayne obeyed promptly and they were closed into a measure of privacy once more. Reule reached out for Mystique, his hand falling on her waist and drawing her back to his side. Liandra shot her a quick look of amusement over Reule's possessiveness.

"Rye, you've greatly insulted me. Twice now you've laid abusive hands on a woman under my care and protection. There's a price for that and you will pay it," he gritted out ominously. "By the Lord, Rye, this is beneath you! You must be mad, because the man I've known for nearly a century would never do such a thing."

"Reule, you're a fool," Rye said, spitting blood onto the floor as he gingerly touched his face. "She's leading you around by your cock and you don't even know it."

Liandra's gasp was just barely drowned out by Reule's roar of fury as he pushed Mystique back and grabbed for Rye. He hauled the Prime Blade up by his formal jacket, yanking him to his feet, then shoving him into the nearest wall. Rye fought back this time, clutching

Reule in return and using a mighty heave of strength to reverse their positions against the wall, their wrestling bodies crashing into a small table and sending a vase shattering onto the floor.

Mystique couldn't bear it. She couldn't bear to see two friends battling each other, nor the possibility of someone getting hurt. She could tell with a glance at Chayne's worried features the situation was flaring out of control. Acting on her well-trusted instincts, she stripped her red kid gloves off and shoved them at Liandra, who took them readily without fully understanding why. It didn't matter. Mystique was focused only on Rye.

"Damn you, Reule, can't you see? She's been here only a week and already she's destroying your Pack! Why can't you see? Why would you pick an outlander whore over your Pack if she weren't somehow influencing you?"

"By the Lord, Rye, I'll kill you if you don't shut up!" Reule promised viciously.

Mystique approached them, watching the straining muscles and power balance very carefully. She saw Reule look at her just as she reached for Rye. She held out stretched palms and fingers and waited for only a heartbeat as Reule switched the force of his fight from trying to shove Rye off to trapping him against himself and keeping him from moving. Mystique's hands folded around Rye's face, her palms against his ears, her fingers fitting firmly over his cheeks. The physical balances of his mind sprawled out before her, showing her the way within seconds.

Reule caught Rye's weight as the surprised heir succumbed, his eyes rolling back just before they closed. Chayne was there in an instant and the three of them guided the giant down to the floor.

"By the Lady, I swear I've never seen him like that," Chayne whispered. "He was like a zealot. Hating." He looked up in wonder at Mystique's guarded eyes. "I didn't know you could do that."

"No one does. I'd like it kept that way," Reule said shortly. He wiped the back of his hand across his damp forehead and looked at Liandra. "Is that clear?"

"You needn't worry about Liandra," Mystique said sharply.

Reule found her tone surprising and amusing. It pleased him whenever she defended his people. Even when they didn't deserve it, as he felt Rye did not.

"So, my sweet lady, what would you have us do with your patient?"

"Is there a strong door with a lock somewhere?"

"Your wish is my command. Which is to be expected, seeing as how you've been leading me around by my—"

"Reule!" Mystique cut in with a horrified laugh. Liandra snickered. "Seriously. This isn't like healing damaged tissue. What's wrong with Rye is only partially physical. I believe his mind isn't something I can heal without his help or permission. I can't explain why it's different, but my instincts tell me it is."

"I'm learning to trust your instincts," Reule remarked. "And so should you. You ought to have known better than to come here alone with Rye."

"I didn't think he would hurt me," she argued softly.

"*Kébé,* he practically strangled you last time!"

"By the Lady," Chayne hissed. "That's why you were so angry at him. That's why you wouldn't make him Shadow!"

"And I should have told you, Chayne, but I was trying to temper my response and minimize his humiliation so he wouldn't hold it against Mystique. I wasn't thinking about his power, that he'd use it against you like this. I wasn't thinking at all." Reule's self-disgust was obvious. "I thank the Lord and Lady my shortsightedness didn't get you killed, *kébé*."

Reule rose to his full height and reached to draw her close. He inspected her carefully, what he could see of her, and gently ran fingers over her bruising arm. "If I hadn't felt his rage . . . I'm the only 'pathic being in this city more powerful than Rye. The only one he cannot block out."

"Hush now," she soothed in a dulcet whisper, her fingers touching his lips tenderly. "All is well. You've kept your promise. And I never once feared that you wouldn't."

It was an impressive realization for them both. It made a smile twitch beneath her fingertips. He kissed them before removing them, then drew her up tight along the length of his body.

"How long will this last?" he asked, glancing down at Rye. "I'd rather not drag him out in front of his peers like this."

"I really don't know. Can't you reinforce it somehow?"

"No. He needs to be conscious before I can make a suggestion of my own. Chayne. Find Saber and tell him to send three strong guards here. We'll go into the hall and make the announcement everyone has been waiting for. It will hold everyone's attention and allow the guards to move him discreetly."

"Announcement?" she asked.

He chuckled. "Yes. The one about making you my bride."

"Oh! I . . ." She flushed. "I forgot."

"An auspicious beginning," Liandra said, giggling. "Amando would have loved this. Well, not the fighting part or seeing Rye acting like a loon, but . . . well, the funny parts." She circled a hand as if to wrap up her meaning in an obvious ball.

"We get the point," Chayne said dryly.

"Come, Mystique," Liandra said, ignoring Chayne's sarcasm and Reule's scowl in order to pull her out of his hold and drag her off. "I simply must have a good seat so I can watch Jocelyn have an apoplexy. I'll bet she turns purple."

Chapter 13

The weak snowfall was on its way to becoming a full-fledged storm by the time the banquet drew to a close. Those who lived at far points of the city or beyond the walls were invited to stay at the keep. Liandra and Justas had been invited to remain for the entire seven days of light and dark, and they'd accepted even before the snow. So Reule didn't have to search hard or far in order to find Mystique as the hour grew late.

"Why aren't you married, then, if you want a family of your own so much?" he heard her familiar low voice asking as he neared the door to Liandra's chambers.

"I haven't found a man worthy of accepting." Reule could almost hear her shrug the subject aside. "What of you? Do you suppose that you've always wished for a husband and children? I think of what you've told me and imagine you as a healer much too busy to think of making a family. Or perhaps your independent ways made you undesirable. That happens in some cultures, I hear."

"I don't know what I've wished for before. Only what I wish for now," she responded softly, the warm emotion in her tone shooting right through his heart.

"Aren't you afraid?" Lia asked in a whisper. "Of the

responsibility? Of . . .. of committing to a single man for
the rest of your days? You've known Reule only a week,
and you've no past to use for comparison. Aren't you
curious?"

Reule felt a quick and stony stab of jealousy limned
in fury. The jealousy was at the idea of Mystique
making opportunities to compare him to other men, and
the anger was directed at Liandra for speaking the intolerable suggestion aloud.

"Lia," Mystique scolded in a light laugh. "It isn't
about physical relations. That doesn't matter. Trust me
on this."

It *doesn't matter*? Reule frowned irritably. Granted,
he'd been a little wild and a tiny bit selfish in his haste
with her earlier, but it still *mattered*!

"I knew Reule was my destiny the very instant he
first touched me," she confided vehemently. "I was
barely conscious, but I remember feeling him coming
for me. Everything I had within me was focused on his
coming. Then he was there, and I touched him, and I
just knew. It was like coming home to the perfect place,
Liandra. When you come into contact with someone
who makes you feel like that, then you'll know it too.
No fear. No curiosity. You'll just know it in your soul."

"What . . ." Liandra cleared her throat, hesitated. "Do
you suppose one could feel this way with only a look?"

"Well, I suppose so. I . . . Liandra! There is someone!
Someone you've seen, right?"

"No. Of course not. I've merely had a ridiculous
crush on the fool for years. If it was destiny, you'd think
the idiot would have figured it out by now." Liandra
snorted derisively. "I gave up on that nonsense a long
time ago."

"Clearly not, or he wouldn't have been the first to

jump into your head," Mystique teased mercilessly. "Tell me who it is!"

"I never would! Not to you! You aren't even a telepath and he could snatch it out of your stray thoughts one day like that!" Lia snapped. "I'd be mortified and humiliated. Since there are no other Sánge for quite a large distance, relocating is out of the question. Therefore, I'll keep it to myself, thank you."

"He could just as easily take it from your mind," Mystique countered.

"No, because I'm the stronger telepath. Thank the Lady. I'm even stronger than Amando was telepathically, which kept him from knowing. A good thing too, because I know he'd have let it slip one day, or tried to play matchmaker."

"Are you hinting that this man you have a crush on is Pack?" Mystique crowed. "He is, isn't he?" She laughed riotously as Liandra furiously tried to shush her. Reule grinned as he leaned against the wall, continuing to eavesdrop. His *kébé* and her uncanny sense for reading people had uncovered Lia's secret.

"Stop! Please!" Lia begged. "He wouldn't . . . couldn't notice me even if I fell in his lap, Mystique. His position would make taking a mate all but impossible without resigning, and he will never resign. He would die for Reule. It's all he knows, and all he'll ever know. I'm resigned to that. So please don't tease."

Darcio. She could only mean Darcio. Stunned, Reule thought about the development and realized that Liandra was correct on many counts. Darcio wasn't likely to take note of a girl of her station. Especially not the sister of a Packmate. She was a noblewoman meant for a serious-minded relationship and commitment. Darcio was, and always had been, fully committed to his position as

Shadow. It was a job that never ended and had no set hours of on and off time. It would be unfair for Shadow to wed a woman and then pay her no attention. Spend no time with her. And resignation was out of the question. Darcio would never consider it.

Poor girl. It was exactly as she said, a foolish sort of dream that it would be best for her to overcome.

"Sweet Lia," Mystique said, her tone now all kindness and sympathetic understanding. "You cannot speak to me of the impossible. I'm quite certain that becoming the queen of Jeth was very impossible to the girl I once was."

Reule took the responding silence to that remark as his cue to step into the room and make his presence known. When he did, he found his *kébé* stroking her fingers through Lia's fair hair in consolation, the girl's head resting on her shoulder. It was like watching a mother soothe her daughter, and the richness of the emotion it stirred inside him froze him in his tracks. He could suddenly imagine her doing the very same thing for their daughter one day. Coming to her mother with a broken heart or confessions of a young girl's crush. Only the hair slipping between her fingers would be black, like his, and her eyes would sparkle like diamonds.

The image in his mind made his heart thud in a hard, pounding rhythm. He wanted her then. Right then. Needed her in a way he'd never needed another being in his entire lifetime.

"*Kébé*," he croaked, his voice harsh with lurching emotion. She looked at him quickly and her eyes widened, first with pleasure, then with obvious understanding. He struggled not to emanate emotion, wanting to maintain a measure of privacy for his feelings. Liandra sat up and smiled warmly in greeting.

"Well, then," she said briskly, shooing Mystique off her bed. "I've kept you so long that my Prime has come looking for you. I myself am exhausted." She affected a wide and obvious yawn. "Have a fair night, Mystique. My Prime." She stood up and herded Mystique directly toward him. He wanted to grab Amando's sister and kiss her in gratitude. Instead, he snatched up Mystique's arm and swung her out into the hall.

"Good dreams," he wished the other woman just before hustling his intended down to the other end of the long hall. He'd housed Lia in Amando's rooms, on the same floor of the keep as the rest of the Pack. That meant he was in his bedroom moments later, the door slamming heavily shut behind him as his willing captive turned in a swirl of skirts to face him.

"Reule," she whispered as he faced her, his face no doubt as savage as his need.

"Take off your clothes," he commanded her hotly.

She drew in a deep breath, but though she didn't protest, she didn't move to obey either. He watched her very steadily, slowly beginning to walk a tight circle around her. He liked watching her. Watching her breathe. Hard. The confines of her corset was doing outstanding things to her pretty breasts so that every deep breath sent her swelling over her neckline. His crest dutifully circling the edge of that neckline made him smile. His expression made her gasp, and he wondered what he looked like just then to make her react in such a way. Probably like a man intending to leave his mark on her in all sorts of ways, which was exactly what he was.

"Let me explain it like this," he offered, his tone low and purposeful. "By the time I marry you, I want my child growing inside you. I cannot produce this desired outcome while you're fully clothed. Although . . ." He tilted his dark head and seemed to contemplate it for a moment. "Well, that's not entirely true, but I'd much prefer you fully nude as opposed to . . ." Reule felt his entire body stiffen with heat and need as a host of lascivious options began to flood his mind. "By the Lady, Mystique, *take off your clothes*."

This time she was the one to tilt her head, her crystal eyes narrowing into sensuous little slits as her lips tipped upward at their corners. She reached up with a single finger and teased at the bow her laces were tied into just beneath her cleavage, her hips swaying in a way that made her skirts swish in a soft pendular motion.

"I've heard much about what you want," she mused, "but is there no consideration for what I want?"

He grinned at the little tease. "I plan to consider your wants quite thoroughly," he told her. He laughed when that had her cheeks turning pink with heat. He reached to remove his jacket, shrugging it off his shoulders and tossing it aside. He began to pull at the ties cuffing his shirt around his wrists, purposely bracing his legs into a wider stance so that his muscles flexed beneath his snug trouser fabric. He knew she liked to look at him but was especially drawn to the strength of his legs. An avid horseman, he had that aplenty.

"Those are very interesting promises," she noted, her voice breathy with arousal. She wrapped a lace around her finger and tugged, unwinding the bow easily. She touched the flats of her palms over the velvet covering her bosom. She ran her hands down her bodice, slowly, the stroke loosening her laces and hardening Reule's body. The entire dress was attached to her body by the six-inch gather of those front ties, so once they'd loosened significantly, the entire gown merely slid off her body.

This left her in her corset and an underskirt of black

linen. She reached behind herself and untied the skirt, which also fell to the floor. Reule watched with a breath-locked greed as she stepped over the pile of fabric, wearing only the corset and stockings tied with garters. She walked toward him and he caught the flash of dark red curls tempting him from between pale thighs.

He reached for his vest, but her hands covered his and she moved until the tips of her breasts just barely touched his clothing. She took over disrobing him, sliding his vest back off his shoulders, her hands slipping over them and then down his arms. She reached next for his waist, slipping fingers and palms over the rigid muscles of his sides, belly, and lower back, as though she were scouting ahead of herself before she gripped the fabric of his shirt and began to drag the tails free of his pants.

"Turn!" he commanded, grabbing her wrists before she could touch his bare skin beneath the loosened shirt. He held her arms up above her head in a single hand and spun her around sharply so her back was to him. The submissive lines of her body in this exposed position were so alluring that he was a little overzealous when he slid his free hand down her raised arms, over her chest, and on until he was beneath the restrictions of the corset and cupping her breast. His fervor sent her stumbling back into his body, her shoulders snug to his chest and her bottom even snugger against his erection. She pivoted her hips, just an inch or two, and it rubbed her provocatively against him.

Reule groaned savagely, his mouth suddenly against her neck, the slide of fangs warm and deadly sharp against her pulse. She was gasping for breath now. Obligingly, he freed the laces of her confining corset. Once it had fallen away, he knelt behind her to peel off her stockings. He grabbed her by her hips once she was fully nude and spun her back around while remaining on his knees. Her fingers slid into his hair as he nuzzled her belly. The scent of her arousal washed over him.

"I can smell how much you want me," he rumbled roughly. "Stand with your feet farther apart, sweetheart. I'm going to kiss you."

"Reule . . ." Her fingers curled anxiously in his hair, mirroring the tension evident in the way she said his name.

He ignored her apprehension, sliding his hand up along her inner thigh until she naturally made way for him, allowing the familiar stroke of his fingers against saturated sprigs of red.

"More," he urged her hoarsely, his hot breath spilling over her intimately. He squeezed her thigh and she abruptly stepped out, obeying him and trusting him as he knew she'd trust no one else. The warm, moist scent of womanly musk was matched instantly to taste as he kissed her. Then he slid his hands tightly around the backs of her thighs and drew her fully onto his mouth, flooding himself with the erotic essence of her. She cried out, obviously surprised by the sensations or by his enthusiasm. Very possibly both. When he slid his tongue over her, she threw back her head and groaned with exultation. Her clitoris was flushed and swollen and he stroked and tickled against it until he felt her shaking, squirming, and all but ripping his hair out to clutch him tighter to her. Her leg lifted off the floor, a knee hooking onto his shoulder. It just about drove him insane, watching her give herself over so fiercely to the seeking of pleasure.

Reule taunted her until she was begging him and he was supporting almost all of her weight while she trembled. He continued to feast on her, only he suddenly added the timely thrust of two fingers into her. His tongue swirled around her clit, then he sucked her greedily.

Mystique screamed. It was his name, punctuating long gasps and shuddering groans as her body clutched tight around his buried fingers. She collapsed completely and he had to catch her and ease her quaking body to the floor. He covered her with his body as he stripped his shirt away. He was kissing her an instant later, hearing her react with a little sound of eager appreciation as she tasted herself on his lips. She was so damn sensual, feeling everything so keenly and with such enjoyment, she had the ability to unravel all of his control and obliterate his good intentions. He needed to be inside her again, remembering what it felt like to be in her body's embrace. He tore at his remaining clothes as she framed his hips with spread thighs. His aching cock was freed an instant later and then her prisoner once again in a single deep thrust.

Mystique was too hot and wet for sanity, so he shouted out like a madman when her body clutched him in its heavenly trap of silk and sweetness. "By the Lord, baby, there are no words," he gasped, feeling her legs wrap around him eagerly.

"You don't have to speak," she panted. "Just love me, and don't stop."

"Such terrible demands you make of me," he teased her on rapid breaths as he looked down into her passionate eyes.

"I'm afraid I'm quite the nag," she retorted with a giggle. The laugh tightened her inner muscles, causing a vibration, and he groaned with pleasure.

"This is madness," he swore. "There cannot be this much delight on the mortal plane."

He punctuated the observation with a soul-searching

kiss. After a long minute of tangling tongues together, he decided it was time to move. His first thrust made her whimper and he felt the reaction from the tips of his toes to the very seat of his groin. He hilted himself harder into her, earning a squeak of delight. Before long, he was driving hard, fast, and deep as he could, abusing her body to the utmost, but all she did was cry her enjoyment and dig her fingers into his buttocks to urge him on. She came like a wild thing, bucking beneath him, thrusting her breasts against his lips until he had no choice but to suck and sear her with even more stimulation. His body screamed for release, begged to be allowed to join her, but he was a man possessed of a promise. So instead, he regained his wild rhythm and forced her oversensitive body into a fiercer, further point of pleasure.

Mystique built toward that point as he sank so deep that she was overflowing with him. Something about the pitch of his thrusts was too perfect and she shook in a sort of fear of what was coming. Her own body was beyond her, and he'd wanted it that way. She clung to him by her fingernails, reality swirling around her in keen feedback.

"Reule!" she sobbed, tears squeezing out of the corners of her eyes and spilling down into her ears.

"Oh, Lord, *kébé*," he groaned ferociously. "Tell me. Now! Tell me where!"

She didn't think she understood, but then she comprehended all too eagerly. The first raging ripples of orgasm penetrated in time to his pistoning body, and again, it was with a sharp arch of her back that she presented her breast to him. There wasn't even time to see it happening. One second there was nothing, then the next the blistering ecstasy of his bite surrounding her right nipple. She felt herself exploding hotly into his mouth, almost as though she were spilling herself inside him while she orgasmed, just as he did an instant later inside her. He lurched against her so hard it was almost as though he were seizing. He released her breast in order to roar with pleasure, his head thrown back, fangs gleaming.

The first thing she felt when she began to come back to awareness was the warm, wet trickle of liquid running up her chest. Reule was braced on both elbows above her, his arms quivering, his chest heaving for breath. He was dripping sweat onto her, the salty fluid mingling with her own, but what she felt was thicker. Heavier.

Blood. Her blood, rolling in two rivulets down her breast and over her collarbone. She suspected the underside of her breast had a similar sensation, except Reule was pressed against her so she couldn't feel it. She waited while he struggled for recovery, watching herself bleed with an odd sort of fascination. She wasn't afraid or horrified, most likely because of her medical expertise. The rapture of his bite was too incredible for her to ever find fault with it. It all just seemed so natural. No different from hardening, swelling, touching, or licking.

"Oh, damn, baby, I'm sorry," he murmured suddenly, drawing her full attention as he shifted his weight. She watched with a flutter of excitement as he bent his dark head and touched his tongue to one of the gleaming red lines and slowly licked along the path with a raspy efficiency. His lips closed over the small pool against her collarbone and a powerful aftershock of delight slithered through her. Since he was still inside her, he felt the reaction. She felt him smile against her skin. He reached the tip of his tongue to the second rivulet. She felt him growing hard inside her, more so with every inch he cleaned away.

"I think you're insatiable," she accused drowsily, her voice husky from gratification.

"Mmm, perhaps. But only with you," he noted, his lapping tongue next traveling to the underside of her breast. "What you do to me, *kébé*, is indescribable. I wish it were within the realm of words, so I could explain how you make me feel. But I like that I cannot give it speech. It keeps it sacred somehow."

His words, for all he said they weren't adequate, turned her inside out. Her body began to tremble with emotion and she tried to sweep the intensity of it away before he became aware of her feelings. Something made her fear her emotional response, made her feel weak for it. She didn't want to spoil the moment with a haunting of ghosts from a past she was growing to despise, so she focused on the man nuzzling and licking her. She sighed with instant relief and contentment. This she could give him. The pleasure of her body. The eagerness and desire of a lover who wanted him beyond reason. She channeled all of those more frightening emotions toward that end.

"Where would you choose?" she asked him as she shifted provocatively beneath him, squeezing inner muscles around him in temptation.

"Choose?" he asked roughly, his concentration all askew once more. He closed her last neglected wound with a few thoughtful licks.

"Your bite, Reule. Where would you choose?"

"Anywhere," he groaned as hot blood pulsed into his flesh inside her, swelling him into thick steel. "You are ambrosia, *kébé*, no matter where."

"Tell me where you'd like to bite me, Reule," she

invited him persistently with a sultry arching of her body, displaying her curves and his options.

"Here," he growled dangerously, lowering his mouth to her throat until he was sucking her pounding pulse. Then he shifted and took her left nipple deep in his mouth. "I liked this so very much as well." He reached to wet the tip of his finger, stroking it over the curve of her hip. "But here would be so sweet. And then . . ." He insinuated his hand between their bodies and his fingers stroked over her sensitive nub. "What would you say if I chose here?"

"I don't . . ." She caught her breath. "How? I don't see how you could."

"Ahh . . . well, it would require the artful use of this magical mouth of yours. You would drink as I would drink, *kébé*."

The image flared into her imagination and she gasped with surprised fascination. "Oh! I'd like that! Please, let's do that."

Reule groaned with heartfelt fever over her enthusiasm. "*Kébé*, you'll be the death of me."

"I can think of worse ways to die." She giggled.

Chapter 14

Mystique opened her eyes to the overcast light of late day and released a tiny groan. She wanted to move, but her body rebelled. Every muscle ached, and she was decidedly sore in very personal places. She'd been counting on her naturopathic abilities to preempt this sort of misery, but she supposed that she ought to have given a little more commitment to sleep in order for her body to find time to heal itself. As it was, she'd spent the entirety of the snowstorm in bed with Reule. Two days and three nights.

She glanced at the window and squinted against the glare of light, attempting to judge the weather. She didn't see the blinding swirl of snow today, so she took that as a good sign. Or a disappointment. She groaned at herself. She was becoming a slave to her sexual appetites. To Reule's sexual appetites. He couldn't seem to get enough of her, and she couldn't seem to get enough of being wanted in such insatiable ways.

But she wouldn't mind a tiny little break, she thought. She reached up and pushed back her hair, slowly turning her head to look at Reule. He was sound asleep on his back, an arm thrown over his eyes, his naked body sprawled in display along his side of the bed, only a sheet draped over his thigh for a cover. That and the length of her body were the only things keeping him warm in a terribly chilled room. The cold compelled her to move, reaching for the warm blankets that covered her and transferring them onto him. He didn't even twitch in response and she stifled a giggle. He was more exhausted than she was. She'd apparently healed herself more than she'd realized.

She slid out of the enormous platform bed, shivering wildly as she reached for Reule's robe and wrapped herself in the fluffy warmth of the knitted fabric. She'd fallen in love with the robe and had declared her intention of stealing it. So she made good on her promise and, after a quick peek out of his bedroom into the hall, she escaped across the hall into her own room.

She closed the door firmly, leaning back against it with a sigh, as though she'd just escaped from prison. She giggled at the notion. If that were prison, she'd dedicate herself to a life of crime.

"That good, hmm?"

Mystique gasped, her hand flying to her throat. She laid eyes on the grinning blonde and exhaled a relieved sigh. "Lia! You scared me!"

"I felt you wake at last, read your intention to escape your jailor, and thought I'd meet you here," she explained, gesturing to the seat she'd taken in the small sitting room. "You know, I think Amando is the only one who could appreciate the type of mourning you and Reule are engaging in," she noted with a chuckle. "Although it is traditional to wait until after the wedding before indulging in . . . um . . ." She snickered. "Well, I'm a virgin, so I wouldn't have a clue what you're indulging in. I do in theory, but there has to be a difference between theory and practical application, because frankly, I can't imagine locking myself away for nearly three days doing what was described to me."

"You could always read a couple 'pathically while they're making love," Mystique suggested with a grin.

"Now that would be rude and . . . kinky." She chuckled. "Why, are you volunteering?"

"You may be a powerful telepath, but not powerful enough. Reule would catch you at it and he'd likely have a stroke."

"Stroke. Thrust. Wiggle. I'm not picky."

"Liandra!" Mystique gasped with laughter. "You're incorrigible!"

"No. I'm bored. Please, please tear yourself away from your carnal obsessions and spend time with me before I go stark raving mad."

"And where is Justas?"

"Justas! Doing manly things, I'm certain. He idolizes Reule's Pack. Every time we're invited here, he throws himself in with whatever they're doing." She lowered her voice. "Darcio and Chayne are just down the hall playing Iron Rubicon to championship levels. Poor fellows. They're so bored, yet required to remain nearby. They *were* having physical contests. I so enjoyed the wrestling and endurance displays." Liandra sighed, an avaricious look entering her eyes. "They strip down to their breeches and challenge one another until they're both gleaming with sweat. But Chayne's recent illness limited them, so they switched to challenges of the mind." Lia exhaled noisily with disappointment.

"And you're allowed to sit and watch this? I thought a lady was to be chaperoned around men."

"I'm not allowed to be alone with a single man. Multiples are acceptable." She twitched a smile. "The idea being that the honor of two men is stronger than that of one. Anyway, Justas is younger than I am, and I'm head of the household now. The idea of a chaperone doesn't even occur to him, so I find myself with a new sort of independence. I can see why you like it."

"Believe me, with Para around, I'm not that independent."

"Yes, but you'll notice Para no longer squeaks at you about propriety. Instead, she's floating around the keep looking like a proud mama cat whose daughter has licked up all the best cream."

"Lia!" Mystique broke into giggles as she headed into her wardrobe, Lia at her heels. Mystique opened the closet and found that the wardrobe was packed with new clothes. She had no idea how Para managed it. Even Lia exclaimed with delight at the vast array of colors and fabrics. Since it was winter, everything was made of heavy materials like velvet, wool, cashmere, and furs. Liandra lifted out an overdress made of a pale gray animal fur. It was light and warm and just about the softest thing she'd ever felt.

"Oh my," Lia breathed. "Para didn't make this. Only a master furrier could create something so perfectly wrought. You can't even feel the seams! Mystique, Reule must have ordered this days ago. It is extraordinary."

"Surely not Reule himself." She dismissed the idea, reaching to join her friend in stroking the fur's softness.

"Reule himself," Lia insisted. "No attendant could demand the time and effort required to complete a gown so quickly, exactly to your specifications. Only the direct order of the Prime himself could have brought this about."

"Oh." Mystique turned away abruptly, hiding her face as a tide of confusing emotion rode over her, causing her heart to race wildly.

"What is it? What's wrong?" Lia asked with concern, draping the dress over a nearby chair. She reached out a comforting hand. "Did I say something to upset you?"

"No."

"Now, yes, I did, or you wouldn't be upset. Please tell me," Lia insisted softly, ducking around Mystique so their gazes met.

"I . . . I don't know. I'm just suddenly so afraid. I keep getting these rushes of fear over the stupidest little things. Remarks or dresses . . ." She glanced at the offending garment before resting a hand nervously against her throat. "And Rye. Rye's behavior drives ice into my soul. Yet I feel driven to understand it. I have to figure it out. Figure how to cure it. It is life and death to Rye that I do, because Reule won't tolerate a traitor, no matter how long they've been friends. But more importantly, it feels like it is life and death *to me*."

"Of course you do! Rye threatened your life, Mystique."

"No! No, it's not that! It's s-something else. Damn me and my cursed memory!" she spat suddenly. "I know this is my history rearing up and I wish it would just show itself already!"

"Hush now," Lia soothed, hugging her tightly. "Be careful what you wish for. It sounds as though this history of yours was no healthy place to be. I'd rather you never found it if that's the case."

"You sound like Reule," she said softly.

"I'll take it as a compliment that you compare me to my Prime." Lia stepped back and straightened her posture into a no-nonsense bearing. "Now, let's get you to a bath. You reek of lust and Lady knows what else."

"Lia!"

* * *

"Reule."

Reule jerked awake sharply, sitting up and catching the hand on his shoulder by the wrist. There was a moment of disorientation and then he realized the owner of the wrist he was twisting was Darcio. He released him instantly and rubbed at his bleary eyes. "What are you doing here, Shadow?" he asked grumpily. Then he jerked his attention to the bed beside him.

Empty.

"She left hours ago," Darcio informed him dryly. "I wouldn't invade your privacy or sleep unless it were urgent, you know that."

That got Reule's full attention. "What's wrong?"

"A patrol has returned with news of an outlander caravan headed toward the city."

"A caravan?" Reule threw his legs over the side of the bed, drawing an agitated hand through his hair. "Darcio, there's almost three feet of snow on the ground. Who in hell would travel now?"

"That's part of the issue. Saber's men report they've never seen the like of them before. The caravan is on runners, with horses to pull. A lot of furs for warmth. Outriders. But no goods that can be seen. Saber doesn't think they're out looking for trade. There's more of a military look to them. But it's not an army," Darcio assured quickly at Reule's sharp look. "Just a contingent of men. It's damn strange. Like a hunting party."

"Well, let's hope they aren't hunting Sánge. I'm in too good a mood and I'd like to stay that way." Reule got up and began to gather clothing, jerking the items on as he frowned and concentrated on Darcio's report. "Maybe that's all they are. A hunting party off course after the storm. Perhaps from a tribe deep in the woods we haven't seen before."

"Right now, I'm just happy they aren't Jakals. I've seen enough of those bastards for a lifetime."

"Is Chayne with Mystique? Where is she?"

"She and Liandra are entertaining themselves in the infirmary. They're mixing a store of rather noxious potions. Liandra doesn't seem the sort to be a medical whiz, so I'm at a loss as to how Mystique is actually keeping her amused."

Reule paused in shrugging on his vest to look at his Shadow speculatively, remembering the innocent words of admiration Liandra had spoken to his mate. "I wouldn't be so quick to make snap judgments about Liandra," Reule remarked simply. "I believe there are surprising depths to Amando's sister."

"Liandra," Darcio grunted, "has far too much fascination for things that are inappropriate for a woman of her station."

"You mean she's willful and independent, rather than a painted doll like so many of the other women we know?"

"Yes. I mean, no." Darcio's features twisted with confusion and he glared at Reule. "What is it you're implying?" he asked his Packleader with uncertainty.

"I made no implication. Merely an observation." Reule dragged on his boots and grabbed a heavy cloak. "You're the one who cannot decide if it's better for Liandra to be a woman of spirit or a statuette."

"Frankly"—Darcio raised his voice as they moved hurriedly out into the hallway—"I couldn't care less either way! Why are we even discussing this?"

"Good question. You're the one who brought up the issue of Lia's talents, or lack thereof."

"This is a ridiculous topic," Darcio groused as they paused at his room so he could dress for the outdoors as well.

"So let's change it. Did Saber give you any numbers?"

"Large. No threat to us, of course. But the Sánge outside the walls would never be able to stand. Saber is already doubling the guard and gathering contingents just in case. You know Saber has a 'pathic sense for trouble, and he says he's not getting any real warnings, but he also feels that could change if the situation isn't handled delicately."

"To hell. I wish . . ." Reule stopped himself.

Darcio didn't. "You wish Amando was here."

"He had that way of communicating," Reule said in needless explanation.

"I know," Shadow agreed softly.

Darcio followed his Prime's long, purposeful strides in silence until they were almost at the exit to the keep. "Do you think it's wise for Mystique and Liandra to spend time together?"

"Shadow, I've no intention of choosing my wife's companions for her. And what the hell is wrong with Liandra?"

Reule watched Shadow scowl darkly, and he was fascinated by the reaction. The emotions radiating from Darcio were just as intriguing, in spite of his struggle to keep them under wraps. Something about Liandra had gotten under the Prime Shadow's unflappable skin. They stood in the slush of cleared-away snow in the courtyard, waiting for the stable hands to bring their horses.

"There's something about that girl that just . . . disturbs me," Darcio said quickly, as though the confession disturbed him more.

"Is this just a general disturbance or is there something specific? A 'pathic problem perhaps? Or is her behavior inappropriate with you?" Perhaps the young woman had changed her mind and made her feelings known after all. Reule thought it unlikely, but his companion almost seemed to be reacting as if she had.

"I'm not a girl in need of chaperoning," Darcio snapped irritably at the suggestion that he couldn't handle something of that nature on his own.

"I never said you were," Reule said, suppressing a grin as Darcio worked himself up.

"All I know is that I have a feeling this girl is going to wreak havoc in our lives if she starts hanging around here. Mark my warning, Reule. Saber may be the one who can sense danger, but I can sense trouble, and she's it in spades."

Perhaps even more than Darcio realized, Reule thought with amusement. He wondered why this was coming up now. Liandra had always been a fixture at the keep whenever Amando was home from his sojourns, so why did Darcio have a problem with her now? What had changed?

Amando was dead.

Just like that, the iron curtain had dropped away. As long as Amando had been Pack, honor made it unthinkable for any Packmate to consider Liandra as anything but the kid sister of a man who was like a brother to them. Now that safeguard no longer existed. Liandra had never been served up to Darcio before as a potential satisfaction for his appetites. Reule suspected she'd inadvertently captured his attention, and his knee-jerk response was this defensiveness. Considering Shadow's obligations and his views on relationships, nothing would come of the situation. But in the meanwhile, it'd be entertaining to watch Shadow jump through a few mental hoops. His old friend had a sanctimonious pride in his imperturbability, and it would be amusing to see him thrown off balance.

"I'll keep your warning in mind," Reule managed with a straight face as Fit was led toward him, "but until you have a specific example of her discordant influence, Liandra is welcome in my home."

Reule ended the discussion by swinging up on Fit and heading toward the deep snow blanketing the city below.

Liandra drew back from the cold glass of the window-pane and shivered. Mystique was checking on a young man who'd been caught in the storm and was brought in half frozen an hour earlier.

"They left. I'm telling you, Mystique, something's wrong. Not even Pack willingly goes riding out in this kind of weather. I can't read Reule, but Darcio was extremely tense."

"Darcio is always tense," she remarked dryly as she drew up close to Liandra, looking out of the window briefly for herself. She watched the men as they urged the horses through the portcullis. But it was when the portcullis itself was lowered behind them, even though it was the middle of the day, that she bit her lip with a twinge of worry. "What would worry Reule enough that he would order the gate to the keep closed? We're at the end of a miles-long city."

"It's habit for him to use every precaution," Liandra reassured her as she laid hands on her shoulders. "Reule remembers too well the dangers we constantly faced when we first established ourselves here."

"I suppose." But Mystique's belly was suddenly a knot of nerves and fear. Chills raced across the backs of her shoulders until she shivered.

"Come away. The windows make for pretty views, but they are drafty."

Mystique allowed Lia's hands to guide her until she was turned completely around. She stopped dead still, however, when her eyes met Chayne's. The tension running the length of the Prima Shadow's frame was palpable, a sign of the seriousness of the situation. His presence had never been intrusive, and he truly had become like a shadow to her, there but hardly noticed. It didn't escape Mystique that he now stood closer to her than he ever had before.

"Chayne?"

"An unknown group approaches Jeth," he told her readily. He tilted his head, listening internally to the voice of the Pack. "Reule is just being cautious at the moment. No overt threats have been made. It's an unidentified caravan, large enough to cause trouble to the outlying farms if that's what they wish to do."

"I see. Thank you, Shadow."

Mystique took a breath to calm her edgy nerves. Reule would handle the situation. If it developed into circumstances requiring her skills as healer, she was prepared. For now, she would stay where she was.

Now all she had to do was try not to worry about Reule.

Reule stood on the great Jeth wall at the midpoint, watching the caravan approach the gate with steady purpose. It was clear that Jeth had been the travelers' goal all along, at least as far as destination was concerned. Much to the dismay of his xenophobic guards, Reule had pulled all soldiers back behind the walls. He didn't want to flex his muscle in front of these strangers if it wasn't necessary. That was no way to encourage others to change their opinions about the Sánge.

However, the outer portcullis remained closed tight. Friendly, not foolish.

It was Saber who called down to the leader of the caravan in salute, Reule remaining silent and allowing him to do his job. He stood in stony preparation for any eventuality.

"Hallo!"

The cry went out and the caravan of men responded by drawing to a halt. Reule narrowed his eyes on the group as Saber spoke with the lead rider. There were a good eight sleds on runners, three of which were single-man cutters meant for speed and distance. The outriders numbered a good thirty. And they were all men. The lack of females hinted that this was no casual party.

These people hadn't been caught unawares in a storm. They were even better prepared for it than his people would have been. Everyone wore thick furs. Lap robes covered the drivers and passengers alike. Even the horses were thickly built, a breed strong enough to draw sleds through miles of deep snow, their coats made of long, heavy hair for warmth.

Reule kept in careful contact with Saber as he spoke with the lead rider.

"Greetings and welcome to Jeth," Saber said evenly from his safe station about five feet above the head of the man on horseback.

"I greet you as well," the rider returned. "My party wishes to break our travel in your city."

"First we would know who you are and where you're from, my friend," Saber said evenly. "We get few visitors in this wild place."

"I can imagine," the rider agreed. "We are Yesu. We come from a province in the deep north."

"There's nothing but savage mountains to the north," Saber noted.

"Aye. As I said," the rider agreed. "The Yesu are a mountain tribe."

That actually took Reule by surprise. He'd never heard of a civilization in the mountains behind his city. They were impassable. The fact that these people had approached from the mouth of the valley in spite of coming from the northern range was proof enough of that. They must be from a farther, more accessible point.

"We didn't know there were mountain tribes, and we've lived in this valley for over sixty years," Saber informed the stranger readily.

The leader of the Yesu laughed, the sound echoing merrily against the walls of the valley. "The Yesu rarely leave their mountain home," he agreed. "But we have heard of your people and this growing city. We're pleased your tribe has survived in this rough country. It speaks well of your breed."

Saber's response was a knee-jerk reaction. "You do know this is a Sánge city, do you not? Not many people seek out Sánge company so willingly."

"The world is too wide and diverse to let customs come between cultures. My people, you will find, are more tolerant than most. We wish you no harm."

Reule knew the man was speaking the truth. So did Saber.

"Might I know whom I address?" Reule called down from the midwall.

"Lothas, Second Command to our great lord Derrik, High King of all the Yesu tribes in these mountains. And yourself?"

"Prime Reule, leader of the city and province of Jeth."

The man touched his open palm to his heart and made a slow, respectful bow of his head. "Greetings and deepest respects from his greatest majesty, High King Derrik, Prime Reule. I'm bid to earn welcome on behalf of our people."

"And welcome you shall be, Second Command Lothas. Is this your only purpose in coming to Jeth? To strike up relations with the Sánge? I have to admit, it's an unusual occurrence." Reule searched, but could find no hostility toward the Sánge in this man's mind. He did discover, however, a group of minds among them that would bear close watching. There was something innately chilling in some of the psyches he touched. But it was a small and select portion of the group. The rest were neutral, intelligent, and as open in mind as they were announcing themselves to be.

"We don't blame you for your caution, Prime Reule. We know of your reception among other tribes. We are, as I said, far more tolerant than most. I'm certain there will be things about the Yesu you will find not to your taste, but we hope you will be just as accepting."

"You will find us so in spite of our caution, but you didn't answer my query."

Lothas laughed again with his ringing mirth. It actually made a smile play over Reule's lips. There was an infectious quality to the man. "True enough! No, my lord, the purpose of our travels, unfortunately, isn't so pleasant as I believe meeting your people will be. We've come down from the mountains in search of a foul murderess, and we've tracked her to your province. We come to beg your assistance or any information you might have."

And in an instant, Reule knew.

They were looking for Mystique.

Chapter 15

The bottom had dropped out of his world and the entire Pack went sharply rigid with the whiplash of his emotional fury. Reule felt Darcio's hand circling his upper arm, squeezing hard to focus him on the task at hand. His voice was hard as he forced himself to speak.

"We'll speak of this in the comfort of my keep. Enter Jeth and be welcome."

Reule turned away and moved with speed as he laid commands into the minds of his Pack.

"Bring Lothas and the higher-ranking leaders to the keep as guests. House the outriders in two separate locations in the city. Opposite ends, preferably. Dividing their ranks will keep them harmless. Offer a guard for Lothas if he wishes it, out of respect. Chayne, take Mystique to my rooms. Keep her there at all cost. If you allow her to gainsay you, I'll have your head. Is that understood?"

"It's quite clear, My Prime," he agreed firmly.

"Saber, I want heavy patrols around the city, especially where the armed men are staying. Don't make it too obvious, but make certain they feel our presence. No one is to show even the remotest hint of hostility,

Defender. Make certain that's clear. Unless the Yesu threaten to harm someone's life, don't move against them. Warning, firmness, informing them of our laws—all of that is acceptable, but not violence or posturing."

"Understood, My Prime," the Prime Defender said grimly.

Reule jerked on his riding gloves as he approached Fit. Again, Darcio reached out and stayed him with a hand against his arm.

"Easy, Reule. You could be mistaken."

Reule narrowed his hazel eyes on his Shadow with a sharp turn of his head. "Do you think I'm mistaken?"

Shadow didn't respond, and that was response enough, he knew. He felt the tension in his Prime, like a whipcord of lightning that burned fierce and fast. And there was fear. An enormous amount of fear unlike anything Darcio had ever known Reule to feel before. He hadn't even known Reule could be so afraid. Darcio was the weakest empath among them, but even he could feel Reule's growing storm of pain like a fist closing around his heart.

"Reule," he said softly, "you're the leader of a powerful city that will stand behind you no matter what you decide. Don't ever forget that. Don't ever doubt it. This Sánge tribe would sacrifice itself if you commanded it. They know their lives would mean nothing without you, and they'd be willing to prove it with their last breaths." Darcio reached out to pat Fit's flank, as though they were speaking of simple things instead of life, death, and fate.

"Good," Reule said with bite. He looked hard at his friend. "I love her, Darcio. No man, *no army*, will ever take her from me."

"Well, you might just be realizing that," Darcio said with a snort, "but your Pack figured it out days ago."

With that remark, Shadow turned and threw himself up into his own saddle. Reule looked at him, amusement shattering his fearful tension. He reached for Fit and swung up onto his back. He patted the horse's withers. "Come, old friend. Let's go protect our lady."

Fit shook his head and whinnied in agreement.

"Chayne, this is ridiculous! Why won't you tell me what's going on?" Mystique demanded explosively as she paced the breadth of Reule's private sitting room.

"Reule will be here any second," he assured her firmly.

Mystique glared at him. He stood like a sentinel—a *jailor*—with arms crossed over his chest and the legs *she* had healed braced firmly apart.

"Aw, come on, Mystique," he groaned, "that isn't fair."

He was right. It wasn't fair. He was only protecting her and doing what Reule had asked him to do. She walked over to Chayne and touched an affectionate palm to his jaw. "I'm sorry, Chayne. Forgive me."

"Mystique . . ." The tough man flushed under her affection like a young boy kissed by his mother in front of all his friends. She giggled and kissed his cheek anyway, knowing he was pleased regardless of what he'd show to her or others.

"And you get the apology even though it isn't fair for you to read my mind when I can't do the same in return," she said pointedly. "I thought there were manners about that."

"Yeah, well, the rules change when there's . . . um . . ." He hesitated, then sighed. "When there's potential danger."

"I see." She ignored the gist of his words and focused on the etiquette. "So you're saying that when the Pack is on alert, reading the minds around you becomes acceptable?"

"Automatic, really. Not all at once, of course, because that would overload us, but it's more efficient to do away with speech. Did you know the Sánge had no spoken language for centuries?"

"No," she said, honestly fascinated now.

"We're all telepaths. There was no need. Then, as the other races began to cross our paths—"

The intriguing Sánge history lesson ended when the door flew open and Reule strode into the room.

"Shadows."

It was a sharp command and both Chayne and Darcio hastened to vacate the room, closing the door behind them. Mystique looked at him, her brows drawing down into a wrinkled line of worry. Reule's heart turned over as she looked into his eyes with nervousness shimmering through her emotional aura. All he could think of in that moment was how beautiful she was. The curve of her soft cheek where it arched beneath her eye, the endless glittering facets of those gemlike irises, and the pale perfection of skin he now knew was soft and flawless along every inch of her body. A body he now knew better than his own. Its scent. Its varied flavors. Its devastatingly precious warmth.

Reule threw aside his cloak and gloves and crossed the floor to her in three huge strides. He swept her up against him, capturing her mouth. She reached up instantly, unquestioningly, and grasped him by the back of his neck, opening her mouth for him. His hands tightened on her desperately as he filled himself with her taste and drew her warmth into himself. He felt as though he'd crossed the world, rather than the city, to reach her. It was as though their days of lovemaking had happened in another lifetime, rather than having ended a few short hours ago.

When he'd had his momentary fill of her mouth, he buried his face against her neck and drew deep breaths full of her sweet scent. "Mystique," he exhaled, her name shuddering out of him, his eyes closed against the sudden burn within them.

"Reule, please," she begged softly, her hands stroking through his hair, "you're frightening me."

It was the last thing he'd wanted to do. He'd wanted to reassure her, tell her that she need never fear anyone again, just as he'd promised her. But it would have been a lie. There was someone for her to fear.

Herself.

Whatever had happened, Mystique had blocked it out with a vengeance. Knowing her now, knowing her heart and her need to rescue the lives of others, there was one act that could so destroy her psyche that she'd repress it with everything she was.

Taking the life of another.

Oh, she had the courage to do it if she were pushed to the sticking point, of that he had no doubt. But doing a thing and accepting it were two different issues. Now realization and acceptance were imminent, and he didn't want to tell her. He'd sensed that it'd be better if she never remembered, and he'd been right. To drive her to murder, the circumstances would have to have been . . . unimaginable. It shredded his heart to think of it.

"Remember one thing," he whispered roughly against her neck. "I should have said it before, but I'm a man, and that makes me two parts fool and one part genius. My brilliant part loves you with all of his heart, Mystique. The fool parts as well, only they never know the right time to admit it." He pulled away to look into her stunned eyes, blinking back emotion. "Do you hear me? I love you as you are now, as you were before, and as whatever you become in the future. You have my heart and always have. Since the moment I first felt your sadness and knew that someone who could hurt so deeply had to also be capable of equal amounts of joy, love, and passion. And I was right. I was so right."

He caught her startled mouth again in a slow, tender kiss. He waited until he felt her melt bonelessly against his body, then closed his eyes and turned himself over to the emotion rushing through him. By the time he finally lifted from her swollen lips, she was hardly holding up any of her own weight, and her slumberous eyes glittered.

"Reule," she said with breathy wonder. She reached up to cradle his face in her small hands, her bemused smile so sweet it hurt. "Tell me what happened. Don't bear your trials without me. I will be your wife and—"

"You *are* my wife. In every sense that matters." He grasped her waist tightly, squeezing for emphasis. "Remember that, Mystique. You are my wife. My queen. And all will treat you as such or they will answer to me."

Mystique felt the sudden rush of icy dread in every vein of her body. Her breath came quick and her eyes rounded with fear as she began to understand.

"Who?" she whispered. "Who has come for me?"

Reule wanted to curse himself and all of his fate for doing this to her, but he couldn't when it was fate that had brought her to him. He decided to be as direct as always. "They call themselves the Yesu. They have your coloring of skin and seem, for the most part, a fair and pleasant people. A mountain tribal clan. I've never heard of them before, but I read them as honest and well-intentioned."

"Then why are you so upset?"

"They've come in search of a criminal they tracked to this wilderness." He took a breath to steel himself. "A murderess."

Mystique blinked up at him and he grasped her mind. He heard no thoughts, only felt the stunning impact of his words.

And then she laughed. A single sharp burst of humorless laughter. She wrenched herself free of his hold, stumbling back. She turned and clung to a chair for support. Her dazed eyes searched the room, as if to find the answers she'd been seeking all this time. She laughed again, but this time he heard the hysteria creeping into it.

"Mystique, an accusation doesn't make a truth," he reminded her gently. He stepped toward her, but she jerked and raised a defensive palm to keep him at bay. The wall it flung up between them stung, but he wrestled the emotion aside. Her need must take precedence here. "Baby, listen to me. I haven't even spoken to them yet. They're being settled in the city. The leaders will be brought to Jeth Keep."

"What if—"

"No!" He barked it out so hard that she jumped. "Do you hear me, *kébé*? You're safe here. You'll meet your accusers on my arm, as my Prima, and you'll damn well act the part! I don't care who they say or think they are, *you're my wife.* You'll be treated as such or there will be an answer for it. I won't hide you and I won't act ashamed, and by the Lord, neither will you!"

She blinked at him, finally realizing what he'd been trying to say to her this entire time. It didn't matter. None of it. She could have slaughtered a dozen men, and it didn't matter to him. He loved her, and that was all he needed to know.

Mystique threw a hand up to her mouth to stifle a

hard sob. In the next instant he was there, gathering her up against the steady strength of his body. "Stop," he commanded her gently. "You wouldn't be capable of slaughtering a dozen men, *kébé*. For starters, despite your spit and fire, you're far too tiny to pull that off."

She laughed weakly and dropped her head against his chest, clutching at his vest. "You make jokes now?"

"When better? I can't bear it when you cry, love. I'd rather make you laugh."

Mystique didn't know which one she wanted to do more. She was holding in giggles and sobs and was too overwhelmed to keep either to herself. He chuckled softly as she gave in to both, grasping him as though she were afraid he'd disappear. He cradled her close as he let her sort through her vacillating emotions. He wasn't expecting her to suddenly leap for his mouth. They bumped roughly. She was teary-eyed and sniffling, but she was committed to the kiss. So he let her pull him down into the bliss of her soft lips and seeking tongue.

He didn't necessarily like that there was fear behind her need, but he understood it. Nevertheless, he didn't want her thinking she'd earn his support through the value of her body. He swept her up in his arms and found them a seat, keeping her mouth the entire time. He eased her away after a few minutes, ignoring her protestations. He wanted her, he always wanted her, but not this way.

"Listen to me, *kébé*," he said firmly, boring his gaze into hers, "you've nothing to be afraid of. No one is going to abandon you or betray you. As much as I love to love you, in a little while we'll be greeting the first outlander guests to come peacefully to this keep. It's an important moment for this Sánge tribe. But it means nothing if they think to threaten you. Do you understand? I don't need to love your body to remind myself that I'm loyal to you above all others, Mystique."

"But over your tribe?"

"You are part of my tribe now, baby. Don't you understand that yet? You are Sánge now. A Sánge queen. A Sánge tribe protects its every last member with all they are. Needless to say, the Prime, Prima, and Pack get twice that effort."

"Twice 'all they are'?" She tried to resist, but she had to laugh. "Is that even possible?"

"Hopefully we won't have to find out. I plan on settling this as peacefully as possible. Now, I want to dress you good and proper. You'll be holding your head very high when you face your accusers, my love. Para is waiting in your room. Liandra as well. You will look the Prima."

"And not the *kébé*?"

"You'll be all that and more. For me. Forever. But this is about making an impressive, united appearance in the midst of a power struggle. I won't have them thinking I'm ashamed of you, or you of yourself."

"I'm not ashamed," she said, her chin lifting stubbornly. "And whatever happened, I was the one who ended up lying half dead in the wilderness." She spoke strongly, only the twisting of her fingers giving away her nervousness. He caught them in his hands.

"*Kébé*, it's very likely that they're 'pathic. Guard your emotions and thoughts. You're good at keeping others out when you put your mind to it."

"I know I can."

He grasped her chin and tilted her up for his kiss. "I'll come back to get you after I speak with the Pack. There will be a banquet tonight, so save your best dress for that, but second best for this greeting. Understood?"

"Yes."

* * *

"I say the black with the city seals," Para argued as she continued to braid and loop Mystique's hair into an intricate coif. They'd agreed no jewels, since it was still daylight and it would be unlikely the lady of the keep ran about fully bedecked. Instead, a simple wire of gold would crown her when they were done, dangling tiny rubies and charms against her forehead. She'd been told it had been Reule's mother's favorite. That meant everything to her as her reckoning approached. She wished she could have known the previous Prima.

"No. She wore that already." Liandra dismissed it with a wave. "Tonight she will wear the fur gown. It's perfect. Pale and gray. An angelic softness. She'll be a fairy queen."

"Yes," Mystique agreed. "You're right. I could wear the black with the seals to greet."

"No. No black," Liandra argued sharply. "It has a shadowy, sinister feel to it. Again, we'll do light colors. This one!"

She pulled it out and Para gasped, part scandalized and part delighted.

"During mourning?" she cried.

"Oh, to hell with that," Lia scoffed. "He was my brother and I say wear the damn dress and knock their boots off."

Lothas was comfortably ensconced, with the four other ranking men of the hunting party, in a large and beautiful parlor that displayed an eye for balance, taste, and a great deal of wealth. Quality was present without being garishly flaunted, and Lothas liked that. There were no attempts at pretension, nor did he feel as though this were part of an effort to impress. They'd been treated with a careful measure of respect, an understandable wariness considering how most people treated the Sánge, but also an enthusiastic curiosity.

The five men remained standing as a matter of respect, waiting for their host and hostess, the Prime and Prima of Jeth Province, to arrive before taking their ease. Lothas hadn't heard that the Prime had taken a bride until a few minutes ago, and he knew he must remember to find a suitable gift of respect to honor the event if he thought to make an ally of Jeth's Prime.

Lothas glanced at his companions, his gaze resting on Knar. Since he was the impetus behind this manhunt, the man ought to be pleased with the distinct progress they'd made since the snows had fallen. The blizzard had been uncannily propitious. Since the Yesu only traveled on the ice and snow of their homeland, they only came to the lowlands for trade and other purposes when it snowed. The storm had allowed them to pick up the trail of the criminal Knar sought. However, Lothas saw little appreciation in the surly Middle King. They were lucky to break their journey in comfort and welcome while combining the interlude with information gathering.

Besides, High King Derrik had been considering the opportunity of opening trade agreements with the Sánge for some time now. Though the Yesu were a severely reclusive society, there was no denying the value of the grains and crops that the Sánge bravely cultivated in this wild place. The Sánge were also well defended and situated in this valley, their Prime clearly a very clever man who had planned his city very carefully for the sake of security. In the event someone should threaten the Yesu, allies like the Sánge could be a strong front of protection and warning.

Their reception so far had been a friendly one. He'd heard that this tribe was neutral in both trade and behavior. The only people they had steady hostility toward were the Jakals. But the gypsy empaths were vicious little rodents, and if not for the depths of the icy mountains protecting them, the Yesu might have trouble with them as well.

Lothas heard the turn of the door latch, and he stepped forward to greet his host. The double doors were pushed open by a dignified male attendant who quickly stepped aside. This movement revealed a large, impressive male Sánge with dense black hair hanging in a shaggy halo down to his shoulders. His deeply tanned complexion was startling to the mountain clan males, but it made Lothas smile. The windblown cold and the sun reflecting off ice and snow gave the Yesu males ruddy faces, but otherwise they were pale. It was a difference to be admired.

Lothas had seen but a glimpse of this male at the wall. Now the dignity of his dress and the bold assuredness of his stance broadcast his security in his power. A formidable, respectable man, Lothas thought with approval.

Then the Sánge Prime held out his hand to his left, just beyond Lothas's line of sight, and the golden-gloved hand of a woman settled gently into it. The woman he drew to his side drew a collective gasp from all five Yesu. That she wasn't Sánge was instantly obvious from her porcelain-perfect skin. Lothas was the most traveled of all of his people, his position taking him far and wide on behalf of King Derrik, and though he found them to be unique and even exotic, he rarely found women beyond his own species to be beautiful. He sup-

posed this woman was the exception, because she
could easily have been Yesu with her familiar coloring.

She was small and delicate, a tad too thin perhaps for
his tastes. However, she was still quite dazzling in a
high-waisted gown that seemed to be made of pure
gold. It gleamed and sparkled as its skirts swished
around her hips and ankles, a graceful, short train of
gold lace trailing behind her. He appreciated her intri-
cately dressed hair, its deep red color unique. She wore
a simple circlet of gold wire in her hair, possibly a mark
of her station. The Prima of Jeth. She looked every inch
the queen she was, and there was a moment when Prime
and Prima's gazes met, a long heartbeat of obvious
bonding and devotion snapping between them, and then
they moved forward into the parlor.

"Pretentious, murdering *slut*!"

The exclamation shattered the moment into millions
of terrible pieces, and even as Lothas turned in fury to
address Knar's horrifying outburst, he noticed in his peripheral vision that Prime Reule drew his bride close to
his side in protection, almost as though he'd expected
this unruly behavior. Lothas reached out in just enough
time to slam a hand open-palmed into the chest of the
wildly advancing Middle King, halting him in his tracks
as he tried, of all things, to lunge for the Prima. Even if
Lothas hadn't stopped him, Knar never would have
made it. Out of nowhere, two sturdy-looking Sánge, one
light-haired and one dark, stood between their leaders
and the contingent of guests.

"Lothas, you fool! Don't you see? That's her! Posing
as a queen, for the love of the gods! You murderess
bitch! You'll pay for what you've done!"

"Knar! Shut up!"

Lothas's bellow right in Knar's face had the Middle King drawing back sharply at last. "How dare you speak to me in such a way! You're here at Derrik's command and for my benefit. This is your duty! You were sent to bring my son's murderer to justice, and there she stands!"

Knar swung a meaty finger up to point in the Prima's direction. It drew Lothas's attention to the royal couple just in time to see the threatening storm of fury building in the Prime's narrowed eyes. Feeling the situation rapidly declining out of all control, Lothas turned furiously on Knar.

"I think it would be wise for you to recall that we're guests in this keep. That our men are separated in the city. That we're here strictly by the good graces of the man who stands holding the woman you're insulting! Look in their eyes, Knar," he said through gritted teeth, "and tell me how long you think we'll live if you keep up this tactic."

Knar did as instructed and swallowed visibly in apprehension as he took in the united front of the Sánge warriors, who had increased by two once again. One was the guard from the gate, a hard, callused man with eyes dark enough to be pure ebony; the other a sleek, streamlined fellow who had the glint of a killer in his eyes and hid deceptive power in a lanky frame. Lothas shoved Knar back hard, letting the other bewildered men catch him and keep him on his feet. The warrior was barely shy of committing an act of treason and beating the Middle King idiot to a pulp. He couldn't care less if the man fell on his ass.

Lothas quickly turned to his hosts and their contingent of protectors, holding his hands palms out well above his waist and the dagger situated there. "It seems, Prime Reule, that we have either a misunderstanding or a terrible coincidence. I'm not inclined to solve the issue with violence, and pray you're not either."

"You, I believe," Reule noted, his voice barely outside of a growl as he contained his anger impressively well. Had their roles been reversed, Lothas didn't think he'd be so fair to a group entering his home and calling his wife a whore and killer. "This one, however"— Reule pointed back to Knar as rudely as he'd pointed to the Prima—"I'd sooner serve up to the asylum for midmeal than trust."

Lothas frowned. He'd heard the Sánge were literally a bloodthirsty species, but hearing these words from the ruler himself gave him a chill. "I can see how you'd feel that way. Knar has acted rashly, with insult and lack of finesse, but in all fairness I must ask the Prima if she is indeed the woman we search for. She has the coloring of my people and it seems odd . . ."

"What is her name?"

The men fell silent as the lone woman in the room finally spoke up. She held herself with proud posture and sophistication, chin level to the floor, head high and confident, and she spoke with a soft, modulated tone.

And with the accent of the Yesu.

She was addressing her accuser, stepping a little farther forward before her mate stopped her with a hard hand clamped on her waist. She was a brave little thing, but it was wise for the Prime to restrain her protectively, although he was fairly certain Knar would do nothing to harm her when they were so obviously surrounded by her allies.

"What's the name of this girl you seek?" she demanded again.

Knar looked as if he wanted to lunge at her, at the

very least spit in her face, rather than respond to her request.

"Sylva," he hissed at last, "and you well know it!"

"Sylva," she whispered, her hand reaching down to her waist where her husband's hand lay. She clutched his fingers tellingly. She was afraid, but Lothas couldn't tell whether her fear came from guilt or the accusation itself.

"Gentlemen," the Prime of Jeth said, stepping in front of his wife in an aggressive stance. "I've arranged for a banquet to welcome you. I believe this is a matter best discussed over bread and wine. With civility and decorum," Reule stressed harshly. It was clear he would tolerate no more slander against his mate. Especially not at his table as he hosted them.

"You're a fair and generous man, Prime Reule," Lothas said graciously, inclining his head. "I'm certain this is a matter easily cleared up with intelligent conversation and deduction."

"Very good. My attendant Drago will see you to your rooms on the topmost floor of the keep. You'll understand if I restrict you to that floor until we've had a chance to settle this matter at dinner." It wasn't a question, merely a notification. Again, Lothas didn't blame him. The Prime gestured to the dignified man who had admitted them earlier. "Drago, see their every comfort is attended. Come, my beloved," Prime Reule said in a significantly softened tone as he lifted her hand to his lips in affection. The kiss was warm, lasting a heartbeat longer than necessary, and it was so intimate that the Second Commander knew without a doubt this was no act. The woman was the Prime's in every sense of the word. That cherished kiss told it all, both carnal and heartbound, and Lothas knew he was going to have a fight on his hands.

Unfortunately, he suspected Reule was going to be more reasonable than Knar would ever be, so it wasn't the Sánge Prime he was worried about.

Chapter 16

Mystique remained completely composed until she had reached the landing. Then, abruptly, she began to tremble and shake until her knees gave out beneath her. Reule swept her up against himself in a rush of resplendent gold fabric. Her arms wound around his neck, her face hiding against his throat as the Shadows looked on with worry and a protective anger. They said nothing, knowing Reule would care for his woman with all haste and capability, but he felt their banked hostility toward those who had upset her. He was proud of her. She'd earned their loyalty on her own merit, rather than his say-so.

Reule turned from them and carried Mystique into his bedroom, laying her on his bed and quickly climbing in behind her so he could draw her into the warm, safe armor of his body. He withdrew the length of golden wire from her hair, tossing the circlet aside somewhere. He rapidly undid what had no doubt been Para's best work on her hair to date, but now that they were alone he preferred her hair loose and long and spread wide for his pleasure. She smelled clean and warm, all the uniqueness of herself, but deeply blended with his own scent. She bathed in his bath, slept in his bed, reveled in his body. Of course she would reflect him. And he was fiercely glad of it. She was his, and no one would or could change that.

When he'd undressed her hair to his satisfaction, he stroked gentle knuckles down her temple and cheek, pausing to brush a thumb over her petal-soft lips. She turned her gaze to his, looking up at him as he hovered on an elbow above her.

"Sylva," she said. "It seems so simple a name for so complex a life."

"To that end, I prefer Mystique. You're as much a mystery as ever. You remember nothing of these people? Only Knar seems to recognize you."

"Knar was the only one who knew the woman they're looking for. He's a Middle King. The Yesu have one High King, but many lesser Middle Kings who all answer to the court of the High King. The Middle Kings lead individual tribes in the mountains. And King Derrik rules those Middle Kings in turn."

"I wonder how they live," he mused, making no commotion over the information she was recalling. She'd known a lot about the Sánge as well. Apparently the Yesu had had detailed information on Jeth for some time. This was likely to be where she'd earned some of her knowledge.

"There are villages and communities buried in ice and snow, and wonderful caves tiered against mountains like nature-made buildings. Places like the Crystal City, the home of the High King, are vast and beautiful. A tall, vertical metropolis in stone honeycombs; ice slides and wooden ladders access the different tiers, and the higher you go, the more of the mountain range you see. I've only been there once. We stayed on the uppermost tiers and it was like looking toward the end of the world. That high up, all you see are caps and clouds."

"It sounds like you were young," he said in a soft, neutral tone, giving nothing away of the reality that she was without a doubt Yesu. He didn't think she realized what she was revealing, and he didn't want to disturb the chain of memories. But he wanted to try to direct the conversation at least a little.

"I was twelve. Since I'd been born in Sapra, a very small village, I felt like I had entered the Edge of the World. We moved into the Atham tribe after that. That's the tribe Knar is Middle King of now. Not so big as Crystal City, but not so small either."

Reule monitored her emotions as she spoke. Whenever she said "we," there was affection and love, but it churned up that sorrow within her as well. If he asked for elaboration, it might trigger emotions that would get in the way of her steady remembering. Knar fell into the same category. When she said his name, the disdain and fear she felt had little to do with what had transpired in the parlor.

"So you've lived there ever since?"

"Yes. The Yesu don't switch tribes often, but my mother married a man from Atham. After they died, I had too many people who depended on me, so I didn't move away even when—"

She broke off, and like a steel gate, everything slammed shut inside her. He wouldn't let her off so easily, though. He cupped her chin and cheek in his hand and looked down hard into her eyes. "Even when trouble began?"

"I . . . I don't . . ."

"You do, you just don't want to," he corrected her firmly. "*Kébé*, it's important that you remember this.

These details can make all the difference in what will happen tonight."

"Why? Will you protect me more if I'm not a murderess and less if I am?"

She was being nasty and hurtful on purpose, pushing him away as she went from receptive, warm, and soft to hard, stubborn, and afraid.

"Rather the opposite, I'd think," he said just as harshly. "I'll need to protect you more if you're guilty of that crime than if you aren't. Tell me what you remember, *kébé*. Your parents died? How?" She looked at him with surprise, expecting him to cut to the meat of the issue rather than peripheral memories. He gave her a small smile and stroked his thumb over her forehead. "Tell me," he encouraged her.

"My father—natural father—I don't know. I don't think I knew him. Or I just don't remember. But I remember Mama and my stepfather. Strangely, Rye reminds me of my stepfather. Rye before, I mean. Easy, charming, and an incorrigible flirt. A merchant. Very successful. I . . . I think Knar and he were friendly. I remember . . ." She shuddered and burrowed against him, her small hands actively clasping him around his back. It broke their eye contact, and he let it happen for the moment. She might better manage her memories if she pretended to speak only to herself, eyes closed as tight as they now were. "Things are confusing. I start talking about one thing and then my mind is flashing onto something else, and I don't know . . . I don't know where it all belongs."

It was the flashes that held her trauma, he knew. He felt them, read them, seeing them in his mind like a chaotic indulgence in hallucinogens. The flashes sometimes ran backward, like when Darcio sorted through a body memory. She strained to push him out, but she was too emotionally overwrought. She stopped speaking, somehow knowing the minute he slipped into her mind and read directly from her. There was much of it in Yesu, a language he didn't have a hope of understanding. That seemed to be mostly from her youth. The Common language, or the "trade" language, one more easily exchanged between tribes, came as she grew older. It had been the same with his own experience. They'd learned the Common language during their journey to the wilderness.

The Yesu, he realized, were a far vaster civilization than he'd comprehended. His idea of the area bounded by the mountains behind them was sorely mistaken. Most of her memories surrounded a gracious woman with a noble bearing and a way of seeming constantly amused by her surroundings. She smiled and teased as she corrected and guided and disciplined. This had been the woman who had taught Mystique tolerance and the sweet, elegant facets of her personality. Her shrewd stepfather, whom she saw as her only father and had loved devotedly, had been similar to Rye in ways she hadn't come to know yet. A scrapper, a survivor, and one who negotiated with everyone on all subjects except his right to live his life.

This was the man who had taught her patience, charm, and her diplomatic ways of defusing anger and violence before the rift became irreparable. He'd taught her, to her mother's dismay, that wearing breeches and learning to hunt, ride, and survive would serve her just as much as good manners and ladylike elegance. He was the reason she couldn't bear the idea of Reule laying a hand on Rye. There was a flash of jealousy in Reule as he recognized the connection Rye would forever share with her because he was so much like her father.

"He was a good man. They are both good men," she murmured against the cloth of his shirt. "When he realized I was different, Kisto could have been horrified and might have shunned me and my mother both, but instead, he embraced me."

"You were his daughter, and he loved you," Reule whispered soothingly.

"Most Yesu have the Intuition. But a very few of us are born special. Some tribes fear and reject these types, others tolerate, and still others accept them wholeheartedly. Atham tolerated me. Because I could heal. It was in their best interest to do so, and I had Kisto's reputation and nobility to protect me." Her laugh was bitter. "While he was alive. When he died, everything was calm at first, no better no worse, and then one day . . . it all changed."

The day, or rather the incident, screamed at him in snatches of violent, thrashing imagery. Since he saw it from her perspective, the event was wrought with emotion and fear, pain and the crush of betrayal.

A small home, two rooms deep, full of Mystique's beauty and touches, hung end to end with dried herbs and things he knew through her but had never seen before. The surroundings were familiar. She was safe and content. She tended familiar faces, curing and healing, some just needing loneliness eased and a few kind words. Some urgently begging her to help find lost children, pets, and others by pressing things into her small hands for her to use telemetrically.

But one day home became hell.

A man, young and bull strong catching her alone and

making advances that her usual humor and diplomacy couldn't dissuade. Reule closed his eyes as she began to tremble against him with the memory.

"Sylva, you're so pretty . . ."

"I'm busy," she said, slapping his hand away from her hair. The hand returned and touched the back of her neck. "Do you need healing or not?"

"Oh, yes. I have an ache for you to cure."

He grabbed her hand and shoved it against his bulging crotch. She jerked back with all her might, and his hold released so she came free and spilled back onto the floor while male laughter echoed around her. She glared with icy fury at Harrell and his two attendants as she hastily picked herself up.

"Never touch me again!" she spat to the wealthy, spoiled whelp. "I don't care who your father is, I'll cut your balls off and use the tiny little things for doll's eyes!"

Harrell went purple with fury when his men stifled snickers at the insult. "Why, you little bitch whore!"

He lunged for her and she, being the lighter and smarter, dodged him easily and shoved him ass over teakettle onto the floor. She stood over him, hands on her hips, grinning.

"Come now, Harrell. Let me cure your toothache and then you can be on your way. Stop behaving like an ass. We grew up together! I know all your tricks! Now give over and let me go back to work."

But they weren't children anymore. He'd grown into a boorish man used to getting his way in everything. She saw that the minute his small slate *eyes narrowed on her and his teeth bared. He lurched off the floor, grabbed her, and shoved her into his men. Apparently the maneuver was well rehearsed. Her Intuition told her, as they caught her under an arm each, that they'd done this to women Harrell had wanted before. They wouldn't lose their jobs so long as they went along, and they often were given the leftovers as a bonus.*

She hadn't taken the instinctive warnings seriously enough and now she was trapped, held up taut and tight as Harrell came up swinging. The brutal impact of a fist the size of half her head sent her braid whipping and blood spraying. Her brain shifted, her perception fogged, and bright painful lights burned bright behind her lids.

As she reeled between levels of consciousness, thick fists closed around the front of her dress and tore the fabric apart. Her breasts spilled free, baring her to leers and laughter, goading and crude appreciation. It all blended badly in her spinning brain. A brutal, sickly wet mouth clamped onto one of her exposed nipples, and a rough hand squeezed her with bruising force on the opposite side.

Reule jerked himself free of the memory with a ragged gasp, his arms locking around her in an iron embrace. He'd been right. She never should have remembered this. She would have been better to live free of it forever. She was panting in short, panicky spurts and he knew that the memory went on without him. He couldn't bear to watch what was coming, to be inside her mind as she was raped and violated, but neither could he let her remember it alone. He couldn't spare

her, so he'd learn what it meant to be a woman in a
moment like that. What it meant to be the woman he
loved in a moment like that. He swallowed back all of
his emotions, his rage most of all, and reopened himself
to being in her mind, in her memory, in her moment.

*Finally her mind righted itself to impress upon
her the real danger she was in, that she'd already
lost a part of herself she'd never be able to regain.
Her body stung with bruises, welts, and the bite of
dirty nails into her delicate skin. She was wet on
both breasts from saliva and she'd been bitten
more than once. At the moment, her assailant was
fondling her bottom and simultaneously trying to
rip away the rest of her dress. She was grateful
that she had, as was her habit, worn breeches
under her skirts. Besides the added warmth, she
enjoyed the option of dropping her skirts to get
them out of her way when she worked on busy,
strenuous days.*

*She waited, bearing the assault on her body
with gritted teeth and closed eyes, until Harrell
succeeded and sent her entire dress into a puddle
on the floor around her legs. He stepped back to
see his handiwork, his surprise at her unexpected
trousers barely registering before she dropped all
of her weight onto the hands supporting her. They
instantly tightened to hold her up and her feet flew
up from the floor. She struck hard and fast, once in
Harrell's crotch, and then again in his face as he
doubled over in pain and shock. Then she pushed
off from his bulky body, sending the surprised
attendants sprawling into a table full of glass and
ceramic flasks and tubs. They let go, spilling her to*

*the floor as they landed in the minefield of shards
they were creating.*

*She scrambled to her feet and bolted for the
door. Instead of running into the ice and snow,
into the humiliation of the crowded town, she
grabbed the jacket she wore for short trips between houses and swung into it. She tied it tight
and then grabbed at the waist of it for the double-
fanged dagger she carried to protect herself from
unexpected trouble when she traveled. Never had
she thought that trouble would show up in her
own home.*

*She wrapped her fist around the center hilt,
right between the fanged blades, and readied herself for a fight. Harrell was as furious as anyone
she'd ever seen in her life. He'd always had a
temper and a nasty mean streak, but she'd never
realized how truly evil he was until now. He
charged her, a towering wall of muscle and wrath
that dwarfed her petite frame and strength. Regardless, there was no hesitation as her blade
caught Harrell up under his bottom ribs . . . only
the purest sorrow she'd ever felt.*

"Ah, damn, baby," Reule said roughly, pulling her up
to his lips and snapping the flow of the memory to a halt
just as she recalled the surprising ease with which sharp
metal slid through boneless belly, allowing Harrell's
momentum and his own weight to send her nearly elbow
deep into his gut.

Mystique took his kiss with greed and desperation.
Feeling his affection in that moment, after knowing what
she'd done, was like water at the end of a desert. His culture, his role in life, made the taking of a life in defense

of himself and his people a practiced experience. Justified and principled in its fashion. It hadn't been like that for her. She'd spent her life saving and healing others. It had been a psychic tragedy to be forced into that position. It should never have happened.

"But he was a prince. The son of the Middle King, Knar, and he was used to having his way," she said with soft, hitching words against his lips. "I was in shock and couldn't move from the scene of my crime. An act of high treason. They dragged me into the square, stripped me, whipped me, and hung me by my ankles for two days, exposed to the populace and the elements. On the third night, someone, I don't know who, cut me down, threw something on me, and flung me over the back of a horse. They led me beyond the village and sent the horse running. All I remember of him was what he said just before he slapped the horse forward: 'Only fools kill a child of the gods.' I guess he thought killing me would anger our gods."

"Damn right it would have," he said fiercely as he rolled her beneath his weight and kissed her deep enough to burn fast fire over her face and throat. He did it to drag her back hard into the present. He did it to remind her that she was his now, under his body and under his protection. Reule forced her to recall every nuance of all she'd achieved and earned, how that past was as good as a world away, and how deeply she was loved.

She'd survived insurmountable odds. Passing out of the mountain range untracked, reaching the wilderness, losing her horse in a moment of exhaustion and crawling into a cold shelter where she had, no doubt, intended to die. How she'd done it, Reule would never know. He didn't think she'd ever truly know either.

And it no longer mattered. She'd clarified what was important. The difficulty would be in helping her cope with the trauma of the memories. It was no wonder at all that she'd repressed so much.

"Now what do we do?" she asked him softly, her wide diamond eyes haunted once more with the weight of sorrow. "Knar ordered me beaten, humiliated, and exposed, but I was also . . ." She swallowed hard. "To entertain the guards for a week before I'd lose my head."

"Lord damn me to hell," Reule swore, his long, dark lashes closing against the imagery those words stirred up with violent vividness. How close he'd come to never knowing her! Never loving her! Somewhere, he realized, there was a Yesu man to whom he owed his entire future. A man who had stood against a blood-thirsty town and an irrational king, risking death to set an innocent free. To send Reule a gift precious beyond all mortal measure. "What will we do now?" he repeated hoarsely. "Now, my foundling love, you will close your eyes."

She drew her brows down in perplexity, making him smile gently as he rubbed the wrinkled knot away into smoothness with affectionate fingers.

"Close your eyes, *kébé*," he said again, his purity of tenderness washing over her. She obeyed him, allowing him the liberty of touching his fingers to her eyelids and lashes. "You now have to reconcile the life of Sylva, the spirited Yesu healer, with Mystique, the apothecary and love of my heart. In the end, the combination of these women will become my Prima. My beloved wife. My soul mate for all eternity. Find her, sweetheart." He lowered his lips to hers, unable to keep from kissing her. The craving grew more powerful with every second, so he indulged, drawing on her deep, passionate mouth until she was breathless and flushed. He drew back, his taste buds tingling with the dazzling flavor of her. "Find her and give her to me."

It was as though she'd been waiting forever for his permission to do just that. Her hands sank into his hair with deep enthusiasm as she dragged him back down to her lips.

"Roll," she whispered before seizing his mouth. Amused, he obeyed the command instantly, rolling over the bed until she was sprawled over his body and he lay beneath her, open to a spectrum of possible demands. She wasted no time. "I want to make love to you," she whispered against his mouth. "I want to find who I am while you are thrusting inside my body."

Reule groaned soulfully as her words sent fire whipping through him, making him urgently hard. Hell, he was always half aroused around her anyway, so it wasn't so big a leap. Her body sang a constant song to his, but hearing her speak so blatantly was like an aria of the erotic.

Mystique got onto her knees, straddling his hips as she drew her skirts out from between them. He felt the thin rasp of silken undergarments as she notched her hot sex directly to his and rubbed herself against him through the layers of fabric. She reached for his hands and drew them along golden cloth and warm skin, over her breasts, corseted waist, and hips. Here he latched on to her, gripping her as she rocked and rubbed teasingly against him, making his body rage with need.

"Damn, woman, you're asking for a fast, mean tumble," he gritted out through his teeth. "There's no lovemaking to that."

"Oh, but there is," she insisted in an insidiously sexual taunt. She slid her hands over his chest through the fine fabric of his shirt, the lack of skin-to-skin contact maddening to him. "If this is fast, then the issue of what woman I am is resolved fast, and what more loving a thing could you possibly do for me than to push me past all this uncertainty and confusion?" Her hands drew low down his belly, all the way to the laces of his breeches. She lifted her bottom and slid both hands between their bodies, fingers running sure and wicked over the pulsating steel of his erection. Again, the fabric separating them was pure torture. Reule twitched and groaned under her assault, his hips rising into her palms. She made a delighted, hungry sound and shaped him harder to her hand.

"I'm open to negotiations," he confessed on labored breaths. "Damn me, how do you get me to this place so fast?"

She leaned forward, licking his lips in sexy little increments as she answered him. "Oh, because I want you so very obviously and I'm not shy about it. Because you know just thinking about you has me wet and ready. Because your cock loves the hot, tight haven I provide for it."

She honestly was pushing it to the extreme, and she damn well wasn't pulling any punches, Reule thought furiously as his blood rushed and pounded in his ears. His fangs exploded in his mouth, demanding attention and appeasement. His chest felt too small for his racing heart.

It wasn't his right, their unspoken agreement giving her all the power, but in a very real sense, it was *all* about her power. Her power to drive him out of his rational mind. He barely knew how he managed it, but he'd dumped her over, freed his aching body from the confines of his clothing, and torn through thin silk to expose her in a matter of several insane heartbeats.

She thwarted him at the last minute, making a final

stand as she rolled over and presented him her bottom while she rose up on her hands and knees. He'd not taken her like this as yet, so the choice was perfectly in theme with her shock treatment. He knew even as he tossed up her skirts that this was lunacy. She was burning emotion with wildness and sex, her heart raving for dominance and the feeling of being in complete control. She was more than willing to sear through his self-command to get it.

And a more willing sacrifice she would never find.

He didn't even test her readiness, something he normally would not neglect. He took her at her word and her scent and that was all. He seized himself in hand, gripped one of her teasing hips, and drove into her so hard and fast that her knees came right up off the mattress. Her angled hips sent him straight to the depths where her cervix lay and he felt the sweet connection right to his toes. Apparently she did too, because she went reflexively tense from head to heel as she cried out her pleasure. She tossed back that mane of bloodred hair and shuddered. It drove Reule to the brink of sanity to be so inundated.

The next few minutes were a blind blur of deep, slow penetrations that tightened his testicles with pleasure and made her writhe back against him with every pivot of his hips. He felt her body quivering around him lightly, and then he reached around her thigh and slid skilled fingers through damp curls. The combination of touch and thrust fell instantly into a strange staccato rhythm that worked in perfect concert to steal her reason. She came hard and fast, strangling his aching shaft in unbearably beautiful pulsations, her low, keening cry humming against all of his senses wildly.

And that was when she took her control back.

He reached to draw her toward his craving fangs, but she reached around and stopped him with a hand on his chest. She was panting hard for breath, looking back at him through a wild fall of red, and she gave him a positively evil smile. Or so it seemed to him when she said, "Not yet."

And then the little minx pulled away from him and tumbled herself right off the bed, leaving him there on his knees, aching and stunned as he watched her try to find balance on wobbly legs.

She had apparently decided to get undressed, he realized with a sort of horrified humor. He fell back onto the bed with a pained groan as she stripped with an impressive alacrity. When she crawled over him less than a minute later, he'd just barely eased away from the agonizing pressure in his body that came with an unfulfilled need to culminate. His shirt was stuck to his body in a wash of sweat, the rest of his clothing little better off. To his immense relief, she decided to strip him next. He was all-out chuckling in seconds as her little body crawled industriously over his, pulling here, tugging there. Parts of her were waved under his nose, some of them damned provocative as she turned this way and that to get access to boots, ties, and better angles. By the time he was naked, Reule thought it was impractical for a man to survive such torturous arousal. One more touch, one more flirtation, and he would explode . . . blood or no blood.

And so, of course, she wrapped her hand and her mouth around him as though she were a starving waif and he a feast. She kept every inch of her body below his waist, all out of his reach save her head and her hair, both of which he gripped with numbing blindness. Her mouth was hot, wet nirvana, dipping in time to the jerking impulses he had to thrust his hips. The ecstasy of it drove through him in hard shards until she had him shouting out curses he hadn't used since he was a boy. Anything to keep from begging her, which was apparently what she wanted to drive him to. Just when he was ready to become violent and drag her into submission by her hair, she released him and sat back on her heels so she could run hot, slow crystalline eyes over his hard, hurting body. She leaned forward just slightly and blew on his wet cock until he growled rather savagely in warning.

"What is it, baby?" she said with a low, sexy laugh meant only to add to his torture.

"Get your teasing little ass up here," he snarled at her fiercely, "or I'm coming after you."

She was kneeling between his knees, so it would be easy for him to capture her. But he wanted—no, he *needed* her to come to him. Needed her to finish exorcising whatever demons were driving her to do this. If it meant swallowing back some aggressive male pride and urges, than so be it. He loved her. It was as simple as that.

"What would you do if you had to come get me?"

Damn. He could tell by the tone of her voice that the idea of pushing him to that point was exciting to her. Was that what she wanted? To drive him to near or actual violence? No. Not after what she had been through, surely. Or . . . maybe because of what she had been through? Was she playing with fire just to see what it would take to get herself burned?

"I'm warning you, *kébé* . . ."

"Oh?"

She sat between his ankles, leaned back on her hands even farther out of reach, then slowly placed one foot outside of his left thigh and one foot outside of his right.

Reule only needed to rise up slightly on his elbows before a glance down his body led him to the sight of gorgeous pink petals of feminine flesh. She was so wet and ready that he could see it. Hell, he could practically feel it, that's how badly need throbbed through his body. And all she did was watch him with blatant curiosity.

"I have half a mind to put my mouth on you and make you come until you pass out," he swore vehemently. "But I can't."

No. He couldn't. He'd been tortured to the edge of orgasm a minimum of three times, and his body was screaming for release. So he reached down and grabbed her ankle, making sure she wasn't going anywhere he didn't want her to this time. He looked at the delicious sight of her a moment longer and she obliged him by lying back completely and arching her back and hips up from the bed. By the Lord, this bite was going to be his choice, he swore to himself. It was going to turn her inside out. He wouldn't let go until she had screamed herself numb.

He lurched forward, awkward and raw as he dragged her ankle up to his shoulder. Her brows lifted and her smile widened as he did the same with the other for the opposite shoulder. Her legs flexed, her thighs spreading to welcome him, the sight was too pretty to bear. He watched himself slide against her, watched the swollen head of his enflamed cock notch into that wet, snug entrance to her body. He forced control on himself and entered her by slow, excruciating inches. He even watched as her tight little channel swallowed him up, every single bursting increment.

And then the beautiful little bitch threw back her head, offered up the pounding pulse of her throat, and showed him exactly who was in control. The need was on him like a storm and his breath rasped violently as he fought to focus. But it was hopeless. She was determined to have her way, even if she had to cut herself to get it. He was too primed, the deep-seated throbbing of his body an agonizing thrill.

In an instant, long white teeth were sliding deep into the line of her throat until her breath stuttered and gasped with instantaneous pleasure. Because his lips were against her throat, he felt her cry vibrate against them as her body burst all around him. First with the convulsions ripping through her that struggled to squeeze the essence out of him, and then the explosion of hot, salty-sweet blood entering his mouth.

Mystique's entire body was locked in orgasm, the astounding bliss of it crackling through her like an electrical conduction. She doubted she would ever get used to the instant crushing impact of pleasure she felt when those sexy teeth drove into her, milking her as her body in spasm was presently trying to do to him. She felt Reule swallow against her and knew such a sense of amazing satisfaction that she was breathless. But she knew she had asked to witness Reule at his most volatile by manipulating him so. Then she felt him lurch deeply forward into her, grinding himself down so deep toward her womb, she felt the rise of a counter wave of release from a completely different place within herself.

And then Reule sank his teeth into her a second time, deep into the line of her shoulder, and she shattered. She made no sound, her vocal cords frozen in spasm just like everything else, as she crested over and over. By the time he bit into her breast she was barely conscious enough to feel the sudden searing heat pulsing from his body and into hers. At last, he found release in deep, satisfying rushes that made him cry out from low in

his throat and chest. It seemed to grip him in endless
minutes of pleasure, her sense of time distorted as nu-
clear orgasm devastated her consciousness. When Reule
finally unlocked the bite of his jaw, Mystique had succumbed to a dead faint.

Chapter 17

"I love you, Reule," she said at last.

They were the first words to slip out of her in all the time he'd spent gently trying to rouse her. He'd been too rough, too brutish. Again. And she woke speaking the words of his most perfect absolution.

He looked down into her face, stunned, as her lashes fluttered up and her eyes sparkled like silver prisms. Her expression was one of satiation and, amazingly, love. For him. In all of his lifetime, he'd done much to earn love and devotion from a great many people. He was used to accepting love with pleasure and grace. But it wasn't until that very instant that he knew what it felt like to actually need the love of another, and fear he wasn't entirely worthy of it.

She was too remarkable, too passionate, and too perfect. Even her fears, flaws, and stubborn little irritations wrapped his heart up into a neat little package and served it back up to him. Now she lay in a stupor of pleasure, covered in the indelicate markings of his claim on her, and she told him she loved him.

"Why?"

She smiled at that, her eyes closing briefly as she

struggled with humor, the light of it dancing in her pupils as she stroked her hand up the path of muscles along his arm.

"Because if I don't you'll toss me to the Yesu." She sighed.

"That isn't funny," he snapped, rising on an elbow to loom ominously over her. "Don't even joke about it."

"Well then, don't ask me that ridiculous question the next time I tell you I love you," she scolded back with equal warning. "I don't give trust nor love easily, and I don't like having them questioned when I do."

"It was a legitimate question," he complained. "You held yourself in reserve until now, and I wanted to know what had changed."

That surprised her and he watched her startled expression with a smug satisfaction. She was far too knowing for her own good. "Reserve?" she asked a little nervously.

"I'm an empath, baby. I don't need a declaration to feel your love. Though don't think I don't find declarations enjoyable."

She snorted out a soft laugh. "So you already knew I was in love with you?"

"Well, I was reasonably certain." He chuckled.

"Well, I wasn't," she complained. "Not without knowing who I was. It was like offering you only half of myself, and I knew that wasn't how I loved. Not the proper way." She softened as she reached to stroke her fingers over the beginning bristles of his whiskers. "And that is what has changed. I know all of myself now. You can't give something you don't have. Now that I have all of me, I'm giving me to you."

"Mmm, no. Just your heart. Give me just your heart.

The rest is yours, *kébé*. I won't take away any of your independence or your rights like your people so callously did."

"Just my heart?" She lifted a brow.

"Well, and the occasional loan of this delectable body," he amended with a chuckle, bending to lick one of the wounds he'd made once again. "And your loyalty." He thought about it a moment. "Fidelity. Fidelity too."

"I don't know . . . this list is getting awfully long," she complained. She burst into giggles when he nipped her earlobe in punishment. "Why don't we simply say that we will give one another exactly what we get from each other for as long as we live."

"That sounds suspiciously like a marriage vow." He grinned. "I think I will have the minister add that to our ceremony."

"And when will that be? I don't mind letting the Yesu assume I'm Prima, but I won't parade myself like a fake before your people. It would be an insult. It's no way to earn their trust."

"I know. That's why only the Pack and Amando's family will be at this meal with the Yesu."

"Oh! You just reminded me of something," she exclaimed, pushing herself over until he was on his back and she'd crawled atop him. She looked down into his eyes. "I wish to make Liandra Prima Counselor."

"Your first Pack," Reule said with pleasure. "I hadn't even considered you'd find someone so soon. She's an excellent choice for so prestigious a role. Amando's little sister."

"She's a very powerful telepath, someone I'm well advised to have constantly at my side in this 'pathic society. It will keep everyone honest."

"Ah. I see you've been making friends with the darker side of my court," he said with a frown.

"Nothing I cannot handle for myself. Especially with Liandra by my side. She is a fighter, that one."

"Rather like her mistress," Reule mused with a chuckle.

"Perhaps. But she's also very wise and has proved herself invaluable and indispensable in the mere hours I have spent with her. My Intuition screams for her with every fiber of my being."

"Hmm. Not to mention it'd place her well within reach of Darcio."

Mystique gasped, her eyes widening.

"*Darcio?*"

"Not to fear. Her secret is safe with me."

"I know that." She tsked irritably, slapping his shoulder. "But why do you say Darcio? She didn't tell me . . . and how did you . . . ? Never mind," she said hastily when he cocked an amused brow at the ridiculous question forthcoming. "What of Darcio?" she asked, suddenly eager for information.

"Completely oblivious," Reule chuckled. "Darcio lives to serve me and the Pack. He doesn't know how to live for himself. Well, to be fair," he amended, "Darcio loves me and the Pack, so in that way he is serving himself. It pleases him enormously to be here. But I don't think he's ever considered sectioning off a part of his life that has nothing to do with us. Perhaps, though, it's time my Pack learned to cultivate themselves more richly outside of Pack duty and loyalty."

"They'll learn by your example," she said fondly, stroking a finger over his lips before dipping her head to kiss him. She pulled back an inch, cocking her head. "Does Darcio even notice her a little?"

"I shouldn't say, since you cannot always protect

your thoughts. You do have impressively selective mental defenses, however. Have I mentioned that?"

"It takes a singular sort of focus, and I'm better at being open and giving than I am at shutting off and out. You're dodging the question," she noted.

"I am. Let us allow them to work it out for themselves, shall we? We will make Liandra Pack after you're made Prima and Pack yourself. The rest will unfold as it will. Now, however, I think I need to send you off to Para. I've made a disaster of your pretty efforts to make me proud."

"You were pleased," she said with satisfaction.

"I'm always pleased," he assured her. "With you."

"I don't give an icy damn, Knar! If you do anything to overtly threaten that woman again I'll cut your throat and keep your kingdom for my future children to play with. Do you understand?" Lothas said with a low and ominous sort of roar. "Or better yet, I'll let the Sánge Prima do it. If she is who you say she is, then that will mean she will have single-handedly bested a royal family, and *she* will have your kingdom for her future children to play with!"

"You've been charged by Derrik himself to bring that whore down!" Knar blustered furiously. "And I refuse to sit at table dining with my son's killer!"

"Yes, you will," Lothas gritted out. "The Yesu are a mighty tribe, but we're spread far and wide and cannot afford to make an enemy as powerfully determined and notorious for their vengeance as the Sánge. You look me in the eye and tell me you don't think Prime Reule wouldn't slaughter an entire world full of Yesu to protect what is very obviously his." Lothas took a deep, steadying breath. "Now you will sit at this table and be civil and you'll let me do my job. As you said, Derrik has charged me with putting an end to this matter, and I'll find a way to do that. A way that won't get us all slaughtered in our sleep."

Lothas was finishing his lecture just as Reule and Mystique were announced by Drago once again. The bodyguards and other attendants filed in behind the couple who were, Lothas had to admit, looking even more grand than before. The Prima was dressed in an off-the-shoulder gown made of a beautiful silver-white fur, the craftsmanship worthy of her queenly bearing. She wore a silver pendant around her throat set with a ruby, an etching of the city crest lying on its front facet. She was gloved again, but this time with simple white silk to midforearm. Her husband was dressed completely in state, an honor to his guests that wasn't unappreciated by most of them, the resplendent red and black a striking counterpoint to the simple pale prettiness of his mate. Another young couple entered shortly after, and the small group settled in their seats after a round of greetings and introductions.

The underlying tension could have been cut with the dagger at the Prime's waist. Still, everyone remained either polite or quiet through the first course of the meal, a hot, hearty soup the mountain clansmen enjoyed greatly. Knar, of course, stubbornly refused to eat a morsel. He did remain quiet, however, though he shot evil glares of hatred at Mystique. Not the wisest thing to do at a table full of empaths who honored her as a friend. But the Sánge tolerated his rudeness as long as he remained firmly in his seat.

Lothas turned his attention to the Prima when she

delicately cleared her throat just as they were beginning
their main dishes.

"Commander Lothas, did His Majesty happen to
mention to you that his pig-mannered son attempted to
rape me before I killed him defending myself?"

She took the entire table by surprise, causing a ruckus
of shocked coughs and chokes as food was sucked down
the wrong pipes. Even her husband turned his head to
cough, but Lothas had a suspicion it was more about
covering an inappropriate chuckle than anything else.
Knar was apoplectic. So much so he was turning purple
and couldn't regain wit enough to even roar.

Mystique gave him a kindly, patient sort of smile and
Lothas found himself resisting the urge to laugh himself. She had some serious backbone. She was nothing
like what he'd expected. He'd thought to catch up to a
corpse or a vicious little animal woman and cold-
blooded killer bent on survival at all costs.

He was partly right. She was bent on her own survival. She had to be to survive the journey out of the
mountains alone after three days of torture, not to mention running unarmed and unarmored over the deadly
wilderness. And she had a vicious streak in her, otherwise she couldn't taunt the father of her victim so cav-
alierly. But in the grand scheme of things, it was a small
streak. Otherwise she was wholesome and bright,
charming and clever, and shrewdly confident. She held
home court advantage, of course, but she hadn't made
these allies with tricks and lies. They were 'pathic and
principled, and they would never harbor a fugitive without feeling justification in the truth of a matter.

And if what she had said was the truth, then there
was indeed justification.

"Liar! Lying bitch!"

Knar lost all control, the entire table crashing with the impact as he threw himself over it in a bid for the Prima's delicate little neck. Out of nowhere a streak of golden hair flew to meet the tackle and the drawn blade Knar had managed to sneak into the room. Food, drink, and pewter tableware went flying as everyone lurched back and away from the violence and mess. When the spray of wine and food settled, Darcio had the upper hand over the screaming giant. He had one hand clenched around Knar's throat, the other wrapped around the hilt of a knife that was run clean through Knar's left shoulder, pinning him down to the wooden table. Darcio was driving a knee into one thigh and grinding a second knee into the man's groin. Knar was convulsing in pain, unable to move and unable to stop squealing in agony so long as the Prime Shadow held him in purposeful perpetual pain.

Calmly, as though he weren't struggling with a man nearly twice his bulk, Shadow lifted his gaze to Reule's. "My Prime?"

Standing order for any Shadow was that anyone who threatened harm to the Prime or Prima of a Sánge tribe was subject to instant death at the hand of the Prime Shadow protecting that royal. Darcio, by all rights, shouldn't even be bothering with asking Reule for permission he already had. But this was a special circumstance. Reule glanced at Mystique, who was safely drawn back from the melee behind the solid protection of Chayne's body. The Shadows had worked in perfect concert, and Reule was quite proud of the display.

Reule made no nod to Shadow. Instead, he lifted a single brow of query and looked toward Second Commander Lothas. "You have your answers," he said dismissively. "She admits to being the woman you seek, and she admits to the crime of murdering a prince," he said, sending a pointed look toward Knar. "Among your people, is an attempt to murder or rape ignored and forgiven just because the criminal is royalty? Should my Shadow have stepped aside and allowed this Middle King to violate my wife by virtue of his birthright?"

The unspoken point was clear. Reule could let Knar go, let him do his worst in the name of retribution. But that didn't mean there wouldn't be wide, resounding repercussions for that pardon based on royalty. The Yesu would have a war. Reule would kill Knar anyway for hurting his beloved bride, and people would suffer for years in repercussion.

The point was, the Yesu needed to decide how much honor they were willing to trade away for the sake of a small, rage-filled man who had raised a selfish, immoral boy. A son who had cost a girl her conscience, memory, and past life.

Everyone stood in the room waiting, watching Lothas as his eyes moved over Knar and then returned to Reule. Then he looked at Mystique and frowned.

"So was that the way of it?" he asked.

"Harrell and two attendants caught me alone, ripped my clothes away, and brutalized my body. I fought back. Too well, apparently," she added with sharp regret. "Without a trial I was accused and convicted and tortured. I escaped before he could throw me to his army as promised." She swallowed hard, but didn't look away even though several of the other men in the room lowered their eyes in shame of their sex. "Reule found me within a couple of weeks, I think. I'm not clear on how long it was exactly. He found me, fed me . . . gave me a home and a name and began to love me. The rest is as you see it." She spread out a hand to indicate them all. "I have no witnesses to offer you, except my . . ." She smiled a secretive little smile. "My husband has lived the memory with me. If you wish to bring forth a Yesu telepath . . ."

"No. That is unnecessary. I think you have survived enough humiliation for a single lifetime. Prime Reule, you may dispose of him as you see fit," Lothas said with finality.

Knar squawked out a protest as Darcio eagerly awaited Reule's choice. Reule reached out to pick up Mystique's hand, kissed its back as he drew her to the warmth of his body.

"Come, let's go to the Pack's dining hall and see if we can't repair our supper." He encompassed the room with his eyes at the invitation. Then, finally, he looked to Darcio. "Join us afterward," he invited him softly.

Reule led the others out of the guest hall, and Drago shut the doors on Knar and Darcio.

One Month Later . . .

"So, how was he today?"

"Better," Mystique said with a smile. "Rye is a complex man. Something I didn't give him enough credit for in the beginning, I believe. His charm blinds women to his depths. His way of keeping them, and others, at a proper distance."

"Reule has been spending a lot of time with him," Liandra pointed out as she emptied a freshly made salve into its proper jar. She had proven herself to have a knack for concocting medicines, and she liked passing her time doing it with her Prima as they chatted and discussed the happenings around Jeth.

"I know. It was a very hard thing for Reule to understand how Rye's love and loyalty for him could be corrupted into a reason for hurting me. I think they have both learned a great deal about themselves and about each other. Rye will never love me the way he does Reule, and I don't expect it. We have come to like each other again now that Rye has begun to deal with his guilt over Amando's death. My husband worries still, but . . ."

"But he always worries. At least where you are concerned."

"Rye won't hurt me," she insisted. "He's well beyond that. In fact, he's ashamed of his behavior. He's too hard on himself. He feels bad when he still feels anger toward me, but it's natural for it to linger during healing. It was the irrationality and the impulse-control problems that made him dangerous to me, and most of that was cured with my naturopathy."

"It must be hard for him, not being able to trust himself and knowing Reule doesn't trust him."

"It is. But it will all return with time and patience. I have faith in him. Reule does as well. Soon Rye will find it in himself. Mercy, what are you making? It smells vile."

"It's burn salve," Liandra said with surprise. "And it smells like sweet beggar's root. I love that smell." Lia sniffed the jar deeply.

"Ugh. I hope you paid attention to your ratios. It seems off to me."

"You're off," Lia tsked with disgruntled pique. "My salve is fine."

"Ladies."

Lia and Mystique looked up at the door to see Reule lounging against the frame. His big shoulders blocked out the light from the infirmary, his figure limned in sunshine. Mystique was in his arms instantly, and he was deep in her mouth an instant after that. He drew in her flavor with deep satisfaction until he had no choice but to let her go or drag her somewhere private. Come to think of it, he mused, he was growing rather fond of the dark alcove under the first-level stairs.

Mystique wrenched herself away, shoving playfully at his chest even though it was rather like a pesky fly trying to move an elephant. "Stop that," she scolded as she drew her fingers over her kiss-dampened lips and flushed prettily. Since she had gone through the Pack ceremony, connecting herself to all of the men as their Prima, she had become much, much more sensitive to their presence and awareness. Her Intuition had almost become premonition, just about as good as reading minds. Even Reule couldn't hide from her uncanny ability to know his intentions. Like wanting to visit certain alcoves . . .

He chuckled. He liked to think up wild things sometimes just to fluster her. The trick was, he had to be serious about each and every one of those wild ideas, because he never knew when she would get that speculative look of invitation in her eyes.

But he surely enjoyed finding out.

"Lothas arrived safe and sound. He says Derrik is only a day behind him. That blizzard two days ago was perfectly timed. And you know, I never thought I would say that?" He chuckled when Lia did, nodding her head vigorously to boot.

"I think with winter able to bring new friends to visit with new treaties and trade, and also keeping the Jakals driven into caves and shelters and the deserts, you might come to appreciate the season," Mystique mused as she cuddled back up to her husband.

"It'd be a miracle, but it may have its merits after all," Reule said with a disbelieving shake of his head. "As for you, Liandra," he said, shifting to a serious intonation, "you become Pack come the end of the month. Are you prepared?"

"As prepared as one woman possibly can be." She plopped down her salve and leaned eagerly forward. "Did you know that Delano is teaching me to defend myself? Mystique gave me some of her boy's clothes and it's so liberating I could sing! Darcio caught me riding astride the other day and nearly popped a blood vessel. One would think he'd be used to it, since his Prima does it often enough, but no . . . he starts sputtering and growling at me like I committed a crime."

"And what did you say to him?" Mystique asked archly.

Lia flushed. "Something that I shouldn't repeat, never mind having said it in the first place. Needless to say," she continued loudly over their snickers, "he won't be bothering me again."

"I wouldn't bet on it," Reule muttered.

Mystique elbowed him in the ribs and smiled broadly at Lia.

"Makes me wonder what he thinks of me. Ah, well. You just do whatever you feel like doing," Mystique said sagely. "Prime Shadow has no right to say anything to you about your behavior."

"That was the nicer way of telling him what I said." Lia giggled. "Well, I'd better get dressed for dinner. I've had to triple my wardrobe since I moved into the keep permanently. Now we are actually entertaining the head of another state. It's so exciting. I've a dress picked out for Derrik's arrival . . . I wonder what he looks like. All the Yesu men are so big! I know you say the women are big too, though you couldn't tell to look at you, but honestly, how big does a girl have to be to not feel small around those guys? They're giants!"

Liandra was pretty much talking to herself at this point as she hustled past the Prime couple and into the outer hallway. Mystique was used to this habit Lia had of chattering to no one in particular, but she still found it amusing. She looked up over her shoulder at her husband.

"I adore her." She sighed happily.

"You said that yesterday about Chayne. And the day before about Delano."

"And every day about you, I hope," she rejoined.

"Without fail," he agreed. "*Kébé*, I've something I need to tell you."

"Oh?" Mystique turned to face him, wrapping her arms around his waist as she tipped up her chin. "What is it?"

"Well . . ." He cleared his throat and she could tell he was actually nervous. The idea bemused her. She drew back to get a better look at his rugged face.

"Did you do something wrong? Though I can't imagine . . ."

"You're pregnant," he said in a rush. "I know you don't know yet, but all males can tell if a woman is pregnant. It's . . . it's a Sánge trait. We can smell the . . . the change. We can tell if a woman is sterile, or fertile or . . ."

"Pregnant."

"Pregnant," he agreed with a grim sort of exhalation. "I've been awfully high-handed about this whole . . . thing . . . and I never actually asked if . . ."

Mystique giggled, her hand flying up to suppress the sound an instant too late, which earned her a black scowl from him.

"Reule," she chided. "Are you trying to find out if

I'm happy about becoming a mother, even though there's nothing I can do about it now?"

He opened his mouth, but no words came out as his brain tried to untangle the nerve-wracking possibilities. "Yes," he confessed at last. "And you think I'm an idiot, don't you?"

"No. I'd never think that," she scolded him. "Silly, yes. Idiot? Never. Yes, my love, I'm delighted to know that I'm going to be a mother. The first Sánge/Yesu baby and the new heir to your throne. Why wouldn't I be proud? I love you. Para will be tickled pink. Rye will need some reassurance. And . . . *oh, by the Lady*, you mean they all know already?" She gasped. "All of the men know already? How long have you known? How long have all of you known? Just when do you begin to 'smell' a pregnancy?" she demanded.

"Um, about seven days after."

"Seven days?" He nodded and, by the expression on his face, she had a feeling she was about to kill him. "Reule, just how pregnant am I?"

"Well . . . do you remember that afternoon when we first met the Yesu and you got seriously—"

"A month!" she squeaked. "You've known for an entire month and you didn't tell me?"

"Well, technically it's three weeks and three day—"
"Reule!"

"Baby, its Sánge tradition. We wait until the first month goes by just in case there's a problem, so expectations aren't . . ."

"Oh, so, if I miscarried you'd be the only one to know? The only one to feel the loss? The only one to mourn? You selfish bastard!"

She shoved him, hard, this time making him move by using her power to weaken his muscles for an instant.

He stumbled back, cursing as he caught himself up against the wall. It was a dirty trick, but, damn, he admired her for it. Still, he had her by the wrist before she could flee and jerked her back, pinning her against the door frame.

"It's tradition, and it's not selfish. It's caring and sensitive. Do you have any idea how many women shed a conception in the first twenty-one days in this society? How often it happens to a fertile woman in her lifetime? In a lifetime of four centuries, average, that would lead up to more devastation than you can possibly realize. So no, I wouldn't feel loss. I wouldn't mourn. Just a little sad that it wasn't meant to be. But don't stand there and condemn me for sparing you that sadness. That is the essence of the love I feel for you, Mystique. I will spare you pain whenever I can. I promised you that, remember?"

"Yes," she said, softening as a wave of sheepishness flowed over her. "I'm sorry." She cuddled up to him now, her hands stroking over his back. "I'm focusing on the wrong thing, aren't I?"

"That's a fair statement." He chuckled. "But I hear irrationality is a trait of pregnancy."

"Hey. Don't push your luck," she growled at him sternly.

"Very well," he said, lowering his head until his lips were touching her cheek, rubbing gently to and fro. "What shall I push, then?"

"You're a very naughty man." She giggled. "We have guests coming to dinner and I need to get dressed."

"Yes. Which will require you to get undressed first." Mystique felt his fingers tugging at the laces between her breasts. "I've been known to be quite helpful in that regard."

She drew in a deep breath, lifted her gaze to his, and looked at him with nothing short of complete and adoring affection.

"Have I mentioned lately," she breathed, "how very, very happy I am?"

If you loved DRINK OF ME,
read more of Jacquelyn Frank's unique blend of
fantasy and romance in
NOCTURNAL.

Amara couldn't even count the places she ached in. As usual.

She opened her eyes and for those two instants between waking and awareness, she hoped for the miracle of opening them to her gloriously dismal little room in the county workhouse. She never would have thought she would long for the days when she had worked hard labor just to have a dim little windowless cell to live in. The small gray mattress on the canvas and coiled struts had been big enough for only one person, and the cell itself had only been long enough to tightly fit the bed, and wide enough to fit a nightstand and a small dresser besides. The lights and digital readout clock alarm had been automatically shut off at sleep hour and had awakened her with a blare an hour before she was to report for her shift. It had been a tedious, cramped way to live, but it was better than the alternative of starving or being raped at night in the streets by local gangs because you had no safe roof over your head.

It was better than *this*.

She opened her eyes to the bright glare of overhead lights and shock-white walls. It gave her an instant headache, all that brilliant brightness, and she groaned as she tried to blink her stinging eyes into adjustment.

As always, within seconds of her first opening her eyes, the door opened and Raul stepped into the room.

"Good morning," he greeted her with his usual efficiency and lack of sincerity as he went about his morning routine, which consisted of taking several tubes of blood from the permanent port imbedded in her arm. He checked other vital statistics pertaining to her body just as he always did, and she lay there stiffly acquiescent.

It wasn't as though Amara had much of a choice.

Not anymore.

"How do you feel, Amara?"

"Sore. Tired. Bitchy." She affected a sweet smile that was glaringly false. "And I have a headache."

Raul made his usual "hmm" of comprehension. He never pretended to give a damn, and it was obvious that he didn't. There was no use being nice to her, she supposed. From what she knew, she was one of many, many lab rats and it wouldn't pay to get too attached.

Especially when the so-called Phoenix Project had a rumored mortality rate of 90 percent.

"So tell me, Raul," she said conversationally, scooting herself up in bed and trying to avoid the tangle of leads they stuck in her hair, against her scalp, every night. Most of the women had shorn off their hair, keeping it peach fuzz short or completely bald, the stickiness of the glue from the leads just making it easier to deal with, but Amara refused. They'd taken enough away; she wasn't going to let them have her long, platinum blonde hair too. Besides, what else did she have to do all day? She could afford the time it took to wash and work free the adhesive. So what if her hair was thinner than it had been from being pulled out in the process? It was still long and it was still hers. "What's on the agenda for today? Drug testing? Narcos? I admit, I dig the narcos so long as they don't give me hallucinations. Those last ones were a bitch. Or are we gene splicing? Maybe . . . ooo, don't tell me! Radiation therapy? No? C'mon, not even a teensy clue?"

"Do you have your period?" Raul asked, ever-efficient and bored, even in the face of the questions they both knew he would never answer.

"Nope. I might be PMSing though. Bitchy, remember?"

"And all of your implants are comfortable?"

He meant had any broken through her skin. She was very delicate skinned, and her body liked to push out their implants at various intervals, spitting them out in defiance as if to say *"take that, fuckers!"*

Amara loved her body.

Knowing Raul would check for himself despite his courtesy of asking, she showed him both forearms and calves where she had been implanted with tracking and disciplinary devices. They promised to keep her confined to the grounds or kill her if she dared try to escape. They could inject a reservoir of tranquilizers on command if she got rowdy. They could give her a bitchin' case of heaving nausea for punishment if she copped an attitude and didn't comply with the medical personnel and their constant testing and assessments.

Luckily, they didn't count being a smart-ass as having an attitude. Otherwise, she'd have been puking for the entire three months she'd been there.

"Big day today."

Raul turned and left after that rare parting remark and she gaped after him.

Big day today? What the hell did that mean? A cold feeling of dread infused her every cell as she wrapped her arms around herself against the chill and hurried into the small cubicle shower off her room. It was the only amenity this place had over the workhouse. A private bathroom. But that was probably because it made it easier to control other bodily samples and monitoring of private behavior. She had figured out there were cameras in her room and bath pretty quickly. She might have to put on a show every time she went to the damn toilet, but at least she'd caught on before they'd caught her masturbating or something. Perverted jerks. What in hell did science need to know about that required them to watch a woman pee?

Big day today.

Ninety percent mortality rate.

She doubted it was going to be a good day.

Then again, it never was.

Books by Bestselling Author
Fern Michaels

__**The Jury**	0-8217-7878-1	$6.99US/$9.99CAN
__**Sweet Revenge**	0-8217-7879-X	$6.99US/$9.99CAN
__**Lethal Justice**	0-8217-7880-3	$6.99US/$9.99CAN
__**Free Fall**	0-8217-7881-1	$6.99US/$9.99CAN
__**Fool Me Once**	0-8217-8071-9	$7.99US/$10.99CAN
__**Vegas Rich**	0-8217-8112-X	$7.99US/$10.99CAN
__**Hide and Seek**	1-4201-0184-6	$6.99US/$9.99CAN
__**Hokus Pokus**	1-4201-0185-4	$6.99US/$9.99CAN
__**Fast Track**	1-4201-0186-2	$6.99US/$9.99CAN
__**Collateral Damage**	1-4201-0187-0	$6.99US/$9.99CAN
__**Final Justice**	1-4201-0188-9	$6.99US/$9.99CAN
__**Up Close and Personal**	0-8217-7956-7	$7.99US/$9.99CAN
__**Under the Radar**	1-4201-0683-X	$6.99US/$9.99CAN
__**Razor Sharp**	1-4201-0684-8	$7.99US/$10.99CAN
__**Yesterday**	1-4201-1494-8	$5.99US/$6.99CAN
__**Vanishing Act**	1-4201-0685-6	$7.99US/$10.99CAN
__**Sara's Song**	1-4201-1493-X	$5.99US/$6.99CAN
__**Deadly Deals**	1-4201-0686-4	$7.99US/$10.99CAN
__**Game Over**	1-4201-0687-2	$7.99US/$10.99CAN
__**Sins of Omission**	1-4201-1153-1	$7.99US/$10.99CAN
__**Sins of the Flesh**	1-4201-1154-X	$7.99US/$10.99CAN
__**Cross Roads**	1-4201-1192-2	$7.99US/$10.99CAN

Available Wherever Books Are Sold!
Check out our website at **www.kensingtonbooks.com**